D0852896

THE SKINS
OF DEAD MEN

DEAN ING

THE SKINS OF DEAD MEN

A TOM DOHERTY ASSOCIATES BOOK   New York

THE SKINS OF DEAD MEN

Copyright © 1998 by Dean Ing

A Forge Book
Published by Tom Doherty Associates, Inc.
175 Fifth Avenue
New York, NY 10010

Forge® is a registered trademark of Tom Doherty Associates, Inc.

Designed by Helene Wald Berinsky

Library of Congress Cataloging-in-Publication Data

Ing, Dean.
    The skins of dead men / Dean Ing.
        p.   cm.
    ISBN 0-312-86530-9 (acid-free paper)
    I. Title.
  PS3559.N37S58   1998
  813'.54—dc21   98-19408
                                                              CIP

First Edition: November 1998

Printed in the United States of America

0 9 8 7 6 5 4 3 2 1

For Sophia, in hopes of a closer acquaintance. . . .

ACKNOWLEDGMENTS

Where I got it right, it was often with the patient advice of people like Tom Ewald in Ashland, Carmon Phillips in Ruidoso, Rob Heaney in whichever Cessna he's flying, and the Civil Air Patrol's MSgt. George Miller, who explained how it all works in New Mexico. Belated thanks, also, to David Carson, who really does know where the bodies are buried. Where I got it wrong, I alone am responsible for several detail deviations from fact in the interests of the story.

And to local Anglos, it has always been pronounced "Ree-ah-do-so. . . ."

THE SKINS
OF DEAD MEN

CHAPTER □ 1

So what was T.C. supposed to do, armed with a tire iron and confronted by the two guys hauling a terrified seven-year-old off like a sack of meal? Once she got a glimpse of the boy, the rest was pure adrenaline, and pure T.C.

The tool she wielded had begun as a short spring leaf from a '37 Chevy, making it nearly twice the age of Teresa Contreras, aka T.C. But some enterprising Mexican had liberated it from a nearby Puerto Vallarta junkyard for a tire tool. When it had been worn down and buggered up enough, it had been sold again as an *obtenero*—a getter, with a wrap of electrical tape for a better grip. What it got was abalone, at least the few said to be subsisting along the rocky shoreline south of town, if you were subtle enough and quick enough to get that old piece of spring steel under the critter to flip him over before he clamped down on his rock. That's what T.C. had bought the *obtenero* for and why she was noodling along the rocky bottom that afternoon just off the Yelapa Road in maybe six feet of salt water with only swim fins and a leaky mask. Even if she'd been able to afford scuba gear on a schoolteacher's vacation, she wouldn't have known how to use it.

If T.C. had carried a little more subcutaneous fat and a little less soccer-jock muscle, she'd have been floating visibly at the water's surface that afternoon, so there might've been one less murder around Puerto Vallarta. Or there might have been one more:

hers, because those scumbags weren't particular how they treated women when they wanted something that much. They wanted the boy. They damned near got him on the first try.

Her part in the whole thing was an accident. Unseen, she'd come up among the rocks to hyperventilate a few breaths, pausing to admire *Los Arcos,* those offshore stone outcrops that dominate Puerto Vallarta's bay like a fleet of Spanish galleons, and she vaguely heard what sounded like a male-female argument in English on the shallow side of her rocks, not really listening because she'd had enough of those futile dialogues on her own. Then she'd let the half yard of steel in her hand help pull her down again, kicking lazily along in her search for the elusive abalone. Then, to her left, she saw legs scissoring near the rocks ten feet away, one pair long and bare, the other pair trousered, with running shoes. The sand was roiling, but it seemed to her that the bare legs looked female, and another set of trousers flailed a few yards away, and T.C. couldn't ignore the fourth set of feet—in deck shoes and lashing the surface—because they were so small.

She launched herself into the shallows and brought her legs up under her, found uneven footing, stood up suddenly in four feet of water. To the men struggling with their victims, T.C. must've seemed a small sea monster. She did nothing in the next few moments to dispel that idea.

The woman, a long-haired blonde in shorts and halter, was bent backward under her attacker's bulk, yelling her head off, eyes squeezed tight and clawing at the head of the burr-headed guy who pinned her against cruel stone. Another time there might've been other tourists nearby, seeking some of the lush jungly ambience near the shore, but the woman's screams weren't bringing any aid. T.C. brought up the *obtenero,* caught the tall man across an elbow with a wild swing, heard him curse for the first time. He was staring over his shoulder, and T.C. looked where he was looking.

She saw the second man, Latino coloring like her own and wearing one of those short-sleeved shirts of every possible color, thigh-deep in water with both hairy arms wrapped around a child wearing a blue and green "I heart Seattle" T-shirt and jeans, one outsized hand clapped over the boy's mouth. When T.C. took a clumsy, duckfooted step forward, the little dark man managed to climb from the water with his squirming burden. That's when the kid bit him, so hard his captor wrenched the boy's head getting free, and for one horrific instant T.C. wondered if she'd popped up into a domestic dispute. Bad news, whether in Puerto Vallarta or home in south Tucson. But the next instant, for T.C., was worse.

She saw features that reminded her of someone: the sturdy limbs, liquid brown eyes and long lashes, small nose, and a wide, expressive mouth that was snapping like a turtle's every time one of those big hairy hands got close enough. One of T.C.'s friends had a phrase for what happened to her then—he called it testosterone poisoning.

She didn't yell or curse. Her dark amber eyes squinted nearly closed, teeth bared in a snarl, and she brought the curved steel *obtenero* whistling around like a swung lariat as the dark man's shoes slipped on wet kelp-slick stone, and he had to let the boy splash down to keep from falling back into T.C.'s swing. She caught the man against the back of his ankle, and the tendon felled him, Achilles redux. As he croaked something she didn't hear and wouldn't have reacted to if he'd just identified himself as the pope of Rome, his head came down to her level. She almost took it off with another swing that connected at the side of his temple and raked down to leave an ear hanging at an odd angle. If he'd done anything but slide down with his forehead against stone and his chin in the water, her next blow might have killed him.

As T.C. whirled, her swim fins tripping her badly, the burr-head with the gimpy elbow flung the struggling blonde against stone by her hair one-handed, and her head struck the rock with a melon-like *thwop*. The little kid didn't see that, flinging himself into the water an arm's length from T.C., who grabbed him beneath the chin with her free hand, rolled onto her back, and hauled his freight into deeper water, strong kicks with swim fins propelling them, and with his good arm Mr. Burr-head drew a small automatic pistol, aiming it directly at T.C. with a snarled, "Ah, shit, shit!"

She traded stares with him as he cursed again, realizing that the boy she held against her midriff would probably take the shots intended for her. She dipped a shoulder then, the kid letting himself be twisted so that less of him was vulnerable with T.C. as his shield, her own right side actually tingling with her anticipation of impacts.

For whatever reason, Burr-head didn't fire, maybe because T.C. was fifty feet from shore by now in broad daylight, bobbing with the water's surge and widening the gap every second. Her ex had once told her that most pistols weren't accurate farther than he could throw a saddle, and Beau would know about such stuff. Burr-head shoved the pistol out of sight, did a fast survey of the area— still no tourists around, or even one of the locals, but his concern gave T.C. the idea she should've had earlier.

"Help, rape! *Ayudame*," she shouted. Now Burr-head was stumbling down to grasp his fallen comrade, favoring one elbow, grasping at a flaccid arm with his good hand. Either the dark man was made of Styrofoam or Burr-head was in buff shape, because he finally hoisted the smaller guy higher one-handed by the back of his belt.

T.C. didn't realize how much energy she'd spent until she began to feel dizzy, fifty yards out. "Kid," she huffed, "can you swim?"

"A little," he said, but feeling her release him, he turned to her, dog-paddling furiously, those big eyes showing their whites. "No! Too far," and he tried to climb onto her.

But T.C. dealt with kids his size on a daily basis, both in the classroom and as a sports coach. "Relax," she ordered, spinning him easily, grabbing him under the chin again. Now she moved more slowly, blowing like a porpoise, knowing that neither of them would reach the shore if she didn't get those black spots out of her vision. The boy was trying not to cry, his shudders resonating against her body, and T.C. tried to slip her hand from the cord loop that secured the *obtenero* to her wrist. Finally she gave it up, getting some use from the flat steel as an extension of her hand, some cool recess of her brain telling her she was gradually getting a second wind. And the *obtenero* was her only weapon.

From the treeline a few hundred yards distant, three men picked their way down to the sand, approaching at an oblique angle. It was probable that from their angle they couldn't see the long-legged blonde sprawled on that boulder but, as Burr-head slapped the face of his companion who was now up on one knee, clearly he had seen the other men, and the situation was not to his liking. The two scumbags had already begun a staggering run up toward the Yelapa Road before T.C. got her personal tug-and-barge arrangement turned around, her swim fins paddling them slowly toward those rocks.

It turned out that the good guys were locals from one of the vacation villas nearby, who had indeed seen the woman sprawled on the rocks and who angrily scanned the treeline as a car engine started up somewhere out of sight. T.C. caught a glimpse of a dark sedan racing off toward town as she and the boy scrambled toward the silent woman sprawled on the rocks, the boy bawling, "Mom, Mom!"

One of the Mexicans kept murmuring, "Okay, *chica*, no problem," as he smoothed the woman's blood-smeared blonde hair, perhaps a prayer of hope or merely a guess because the woman was still breathing. Yet she wasn't responding to the tears and entreaties of the little boy who gripped her as he sobbed, despite the fact that her eyes were open. When T.C. saw that one blue eye had dilated, she pulled the boy away and hugged him, rapid-firing her request in Spanish that they get *la rubia*, the blonde woman, *a un hospital muy rapido, por favor.*

The Mexicans carried the victim to a Toyota pickup held together by patches of rust, so T.C. sat in the pickup's bed and cradled the woman's head, the boy now dry-eyed and trembling. He watched his mother's face as they jounced onto Camino Doscientos, Mexican Highway 200, and from there, with horn blasting, past the interminable line of new high-rise hotels along Mismaloya Beach into the center of P.V. During that long drive, not once did the blonde show any sign of life, discounting the stream of her urine that trickled through holes in the vehicle's metal bed. T.C. managed only two positive things: She shed the *obtenero* from her wrist, and she finally got the boy talking, trying to take his mind off the condition of his enviably gorgeous mother.

His name was Al Townsend, he was nearly eight, and his mother's name was Gail. He didn't have a dad, not exactly, and the two of them were staying at some big hotel on the other end of town, he didn't know its name but it was way, way out near a lot of boats, and he would know it when he saw it. And if Mom was looking at him, why didn't she say something?

T.C. did not want to tell him what she really thought, but she wasn't the sort of teacher who spun handy fantasies for kids. "When people are hurt, Al, sometimes they can't move for a while. You've got to be brave for her until she can talk again. Okay?"

He nodded at that, the sturdy little shoulders shaking with the effort not to cry, peering earnestly into his mother's lovely pallid face from which, now, all traces of frown lines were missing, as from the face of a marble nymph.

Gail Townsend was really some *chiquita,* T.C. admitted to herself: statuesque, long-limbed, full-breasted, the kind of *Baywatch* blonde you saw in TV commercials fawning over a De Beers necklace or murmuring "Nice pants" to some great-looking dumbshit on a Harley. Some dumbshit like Beau Rainey, who had ogled the long-stem all-American blondes even while married to brunette little Teresa Contreras Rainey. Probably liked them better than T.C.'s model, the short Latin bombshell type with sinew in her curves. But T.C. had cut him out of the remuda, and as Beau used to say, "What you rope, you ride."

An echoing fender bender behind them caused T.C. to glance backward. A blue Ford sedan had tried to bluff a Puerto Vallarta cabbie, which was like bluffing a Miura bull. Through the windshield of the blue sedan, T.C. thought she recognized the general features of the driver but said nothing to the boy beside her. *That's what you get, trying to cowboy with a stove-up elbow,* she thought. Neither of those vehicles behind them was going anywhere for a while, and neither was anyone else northbound behind them on Avenida Mexico. "Al, do you know those two bad guys who hurt your mom?"

The boy blinked, frowned as if over a test question. Then a shake of the head. "Don't remember them," he said. *Cautious answer, not the usual absolutes you get from kids.*

"Why were they trying to take you and your mom away?"

Now a hooded glance. The boy swallowed and looked away. Then he gave her an elaborate shrug and turned his gaze to his mother again. T.C. tried once more. No, said the boy, he didn't know anybody else in Mexico.

Wonder of wonders, Emiliano Zapata Hospital had an emergency room and knew how to use it, not that it mattered in the long run. T.C. would have preferred to leave little Al Townsend in the waiting room, but she hadn't forgotten those guys in the blue Ford who just might've been trying to follow them through town. She kept the boy's hand in hers, the air-conditioning reminding her that she was barefoot in a one-piece swimsuit, and T.C. spoke Spanish with the motherly staff member while the blonde was wheeled behind a curtain in one of several alcoves.

There was really very little that T.C. could tell *mamacita* about Gail Townsend beyond the fact that she was *Norteamericana* and mother of the boy, and that she sounded plenty healthy just before her head bounced off those rocks. Asked if she had actually witnessed the attacker fling Gail against the rocks, T.C. did some quick reconsidering. Whatever she said, it wouldn't lessen the injury, and a yes might mean that T.C. would be stuck in Puerto Vallarta awhile. Well, said T.C., she was turned away at the crucial moment, but that's what she thought must have happened.

When *mamacita* asked her own name, T.C. gave it without thinking but denied she had a local address yet. Then the young sawbones started giving orders from behind the curtain, orders that put goose bumps on T.C.'s arms, and *mamacita* pulled the two of them farther away and donated a long, sympathetic look because she knew T.C. understood the doctor's Spanish.

When the orders from behind the curtain became more despairing, the older woman excused herself. Seconds later, as T.C. was asking Al whom they should call in case his mom was hurt, her gaze was arrested by a now-familiar blond burr haircut, the man evidently alone and turned away from T.C., speaking bad Spanish to a young staff member.

T.C. quick-marched her small charge down the hall and into another curtained alcove. The guy might not have seen them, though he wasn't favoring that elbow; he might be coming to apologize, but T.C. doubted it; and his buddy with the torn ear, the one who probably needed a few stitches, wasn't in sight. She lifted Al onto the gurney in their alcove, pushing aside a neat stack of paper garments, and stood so that she could see the waiting room one-eyed.

This was not the time to be buddy-buddy, so she stood near the boy, the only way she could tower over him. Hating herself for that, she took his chin gently, turned it up so that he had to see how stern was the look in her eyes. "Albert Townsend," she said firmly. When you used a kid's full name, it generally meant serious business. The name was a guess, and not a good one.

"Talal," he corrected.

She swallowed, thinking about implications. "Talal. I asked you why those men were trying to take you away, and you wouldn't tell me. I want to be your friend, but you have to tell me. Now," she insisted and risked a glance down the hall. *Mamacita* was out again, hurrying toward the exit, probably trying to find T.C. Burr-head moved casually in the same direction, but a uniformed policeman entered the waiting room, and T.C.'s heart capered with joy.

"They want to steal me for my dad," Al said, very softly. "Mom doesn't want them to." The cop saw Burr-head. And smiled. They began to talk, easily, fraternally.

Blessing whoever had put those paper clothes on the gurney, she began to shake them out, the cap first. Without taking her eyes from the cop: "You're sure that wasn't your dad back on the beach?"

A blink, and a frightened negative headshake.

"Where is your dad?" It seemed likely, for one brief instant, that she'd be taking little Talal Townsend to his dad anyhow because, thirty feet away, Gail Townsend was flatlining.

"Mahabad," the boy said, with an accent that sounded authentic to T.C., but how the hell would she know? "It's in Iran," he added helpfully.

And damned if T.C. intended to take him *there*.

CHAPTER □ 2

Covered in her stolen paper garments from cap to slippers, with Al completely hidden under the gurney's top sheet and the pillow placed so that he seemed two feet longer, T.C. pushed the gurney through swinging doors into the hospital's inner corridor, afraid to look back. Perhaps they simply weren't noticed by harried staff members. After a couple of wrong turns she saw an exit sign, snatched up the kid, and fled outside with him. It was only a short walk to the beach, hand in hand, and with her paper duds stuffed under a shrub she was once again anonymous. A middle-aged couple strolled past with friendly smiles near the palm-shadowed verge of the beach.

When the boy pulled his hand from hers, she knew he wasn't going to be the accommodating type. "We can't leave Mom," he said, his back against a palm trunk, gazing toward the hospital.

"She's where they can take care of her," said T.C., wishing she could tie up again with the pickup guys, knowing she needed to get back to her own rented room a half mile from where this whole sorry screwup began. The boy's expression was a road map of doubts, and she tried again. "That big blond burr-headed guy who hurt your mom, did you see him there in the hospital? He was right there, Al."

A headshake, fear added to doubt. "My mom says never go with anybody you don't know. I don't even know your name."

True, and reasonable, but she wasn't certain the kid should have her name yet. "Your mom's right. Is there anybody here that you know better than you know me?" She fixed him with her best stern schoolmarmish gaze. "I'm not having much fun either, young man, and we need time to think. We ought to get a little farther away from the people looking for you. And they're already watching the hospital."

Now, for the first time, he gave signs of thinking ahead. "Call my grampa. I know the number," he said, starting to walk toward the sand.

He stayed a few paces from her, near enough to talk, distant enough to run. Smart kid, though she had yet to meet a half-pint she couldn't catch. Yeah, but did she want to fight him? The kid was a biter. "Okay, okay! My name is Ms. Rainey; my friends call me T.C. I teach school in Arizona, and as soon as we get to a phone we can call your—is it your grandfather?"

The boy nodded and smiled at some old memory. "Mom's dad. We got a phone in the rooms," he supplied. "Over there." He pointed across the bay toward the curve of the north shore where white high-rises with orange tile roofs gleamed in the sun, a bus ride away. But if those men had been following the boy, they probably knew that too.

"Maybe; or we could do it from my place. First, take off that T-shirt. Let's try a little French laundry."

As he complied, she explained that turning a shirt inside out could do more than hide a stain. It could also make you look a little different. She helped him tug the shirt on, rolled the legs of his jeans as high as she could. The shirt was now more green than blue, and up close it said, "elttaeS traeh I," but now the kid was better disguised than she was.

"Got some money and stuff," he muttered and handed her a sodden mass from the right front pocket of his jeans. Some of it was Mexican, mostly the new little two-color *peso* coins. But some of it was U.S. bills, and a scrap of notepaper with "Las Palmas, rm 516" printed in blue ballpoint. When T.C. looked up, he smiled again. "In case I got lost," he said. So Gail Townsend wasn't a total idiot. *Hadn't been,* T.C.'s perverse imp reminded her. And the kid didn't need to know that, not just yet.

With no pockets, she bade him keep the money and asked if she could borrow a few dollars, and he said, "Sure." "I need shoes and stuff," she explained, because kids needed some sense of purpose in strange surroundings, and when he took her hand again she felt a lump of gratitude rise in her throat.

As neat as P.V. is along the tourist beaches, that's how neat it isn't in the bustling center of town. Discarded foam cups and paper filled the gutters, and T.C. would have stepped on broken glass a dozen times if she hadn't been careful. She remembered a big *mercado* where prices were decent on Avila Camacho, a half mile away. En route, she watched for a bus, and for a blue Ford.

A curbside *tienda* put the market out of her mind. A cheap wraparound skirt, cotton blouse, and blue deck tennies set Al back eleven dollars and change. "Jeez, you have little bitty feet," he marveled as she tied the laces.

"You'll go far," she said, winking, and he laughed and absolutely broke her heart. It wasn't quite Littlebo's laugh, but it would do.

They caught a southbound city bus ten minutes later, the usual grunting, swaying behemoth crammed with locals, cheap as Chiclets and a better thrill ride than most. Al pressed himself close to her, uneasy with such proletarian travel, wary of all these swarthy folk jabbering in an unknown tongue. Obviously, Gail Townsend hadn't been the sort to immerse herself in the real Mexico. Nowhere in traffic did T.C. spy the bad guys, but if they were friendly with local cops they might have other vehicles.

During their ride she thought of the Federales. Yes, but anyone capable of co-opting the local cops might also have a story good enough for the Mexican feds. For that matter, Al might not know the whole story. It might be that Gail Townsend was officially the bad guy in a custody fight. *Ponymuffins,* she decided, *that flattop bastard killed a young woman in broad daylight and aimed a gun at her little boy.* Until someone held her down and forced another view on her, T.C. would keep her own opinion as to who wore the black hats. It had been a long time since she wished Beau Rainey was near to hand, but she could've used him now, even though he exhausted his command of Spanish with *vamoose* and *lariat.*

The bus was almost empty at the turnaround south of town, where the street became a two-lane highway through rank jungle. T.C. tugged the boy down the rear steps, chiding him in comical, rapid Spanish meant for the driver's ears. She didn't have the local accent but maybe, if questioned later, he would not recall a yanqui woman and child.

When the bus had disappeared ahead of a vast turd of blue exhaust, Al said, "I have to go."

"To pee? My place isn't far," she said.

"If I can't see it from here, yes it is," he insisted and moved out of sight among lush big-leaf foliage. She heard a car approach, melted into the greenery, saw a taxi whiz past.

Suddenly, in the aching stillness, her whole day seemed a bad dream, now evaporated into sun-dappled silence. For a moment she willed it to be so: no violent confrontation, no tragedy in the emergency room, no nightmarish collusion between murderers and cops.

And no resurrection of Littlebo, who would've been just about Al's age now. With that awareness flooding her, she had an instant's fear that young Al Townsend would never emerge from that wall of greenery, that this time she'd had the chance to help and somehow failed, and she gasped with relief to see him trotting into view, zipping up. She hadn't failed yet.

She led him on a ten-minute walk to the driveway she'd missed the first time she'd driven her rental Nissan there. She pointed out the little black sedan she'd rented, a luxury she now regretted, parked with others where she'd left it. T.C.'s room was one of several in the villa that, like many others, seemed crocheted by vines to the cliffside above Bahía de Banderas south of town. She told Al to hang back and watch where she went and to follow after counting to five hundred by fives. "My door says 'Conchas Chinas' on it, the rooms are all named for local beaches," she told him. "Can you spell China?"

"I'll be in third grade," he said, dismissing the question.

Not if you flunk vacation, she replied silently. "I'll leave the door open so you don't have to knock," she said aloud and strode past a wrought-iron entry gate to the tiled central gallery that became a balcony overlooking the rock-strewn shallows. The vista was lovely, almost affordable, and she was about to give up her last two days of it for a kid who, a few hours ago, she hadn't known existed.

Tourist places like this trained their staffs to go about their work quietly, invisibly, and she knew better than to assume that Al would not be seen. The first thing she did when Al slid into the room was to lead him to the writing desk and indicate the telephone. If this kid liked his independence so much, let him think about consequences.

"Al, if you know how to phone your grandpa, you have a choice to make. If you're sure he can come and get you right away, today or tomorrow, maybe you should call him." He picked up the receiver, a modern Touch-Tone. She held up a hand, and he hesitated. "But think for a minute. The men who hurt your mom seem to be friends with the police. I don't know why. Maybe they listen in on phones here. If they do, you could be telling the bad guys where we are. And that's the thing they don't know yet." Another guess. The hospital had her name.

"I bet my mom will call home when she wakes up," he said, still holding the receiver.

A one-beat pause; kids could read volumes from your least change of expression. "She might not be able to, Al. Don't count on it. And by the way, if you don't speak Spanish, maybe I should start the call." She took her shoulder bag from the closet, rummaged inside, pulled out her Day-Timer with its ballpoint pen. "Better write the number down for me."

He did it, writing the name in careful cursive that made her sorry she'd said she was a teacher. If Ray Townsend was Gail's father, she'd taken her maiden name back—or had never married. The kid even knew the area code, 206, but an international call was a little more complicated.

She was looking at what he'd written when the phone rang, and both of them jumped like rabbits. T.C. grinned at the boy as she reached for the receiver, then paused. "Who do I know here?" she asked aloud.

"It might be Mom," the boy pleaded.

"She doesn't know where I'm staying, Al." The ringing continued.

In a flicker of motion, Al Townsend made the decision for her, snatching up the receiver. "Ms. Rainey's room," he said as she stared at him in dismay. "For you," he said and thrust the receiver at her. Instead of swatting him, she sighed and took the phone.

"Digame," she said and paused. Then, in Spanish: "Yes, I did, it's outside now. No, it's a black Nissan. *Lo siento,* I don't recall the license number, but how many black Nissans do you have? Perfectly all right. Yes, I have it for two more days. *De nada,"* she finished and replaced the receiver very carefully.

"It wasn't about Mom?" Hope fought for a place in the child's gaze.

"I'm not sure. It was the car rental people—so they said." *How many black Nissans? Well, try asking how many Teresa Raineys have rooms in P.V., or rent cars. And the agency has my address.* She stood up briskly. "I think maybe it was about you, but they don't want me to know that." Then, blurting it, "Al, you're not safe here." With that, she darted again to her closet.

The boy stood up as if ready to bolt. She told him to take the cash from her Day-Timer's pocket and disappear into the jungle near that little black Nissan, and if people came for her he must hide, then call his grandfather somehow.

"I'm sorry," he said, pausing in the doorway.

"Get out of here," she said, studying the slinky black number she'd brought just in case she met someone. Well, she'd met someone, all right, too *chingada* many someones, and had assaulted two of them. She left the dress and the matching heels, and most of her other vacation finery, and her big soft-side luggage and toiletries, too. Let 'em think she'd be back. What working woman in her right mind would abandon such things? *None, which tells me I'm nutty as a piñata,* she told herself, zipping her overnight bag and taking a last look around.

She walked to the villa's side exit, fumbled the car key out, and unlocked the door, calling Al softly as she slid behind the wheel, but he didn't show until she started the engine. Then he simply appeared as if by some parlor trick. He piled in without delay, seeming to enjoy this part of his adventure, and ducked down from sight only when she insisted, heading back into town.

The road twisted too much for fast driving, and T.C. feared that every car they passed would turn back to give chase. Several driveways beckoned, but she found the short street leading down to Amapas, a narrow road running just above the bay and roughly parallel to the highway. Then, turning around with the Nissan nosed half into roadside foliage, she turned off the ignition. She could barely see the parking area outside her villa, a half mile south along the low cliff.

"What are we doing? We going for Mom?"

"Not right now, Al. We're just going to hang out for a few minutes, see if we're fugitives, or if I'm crazy. I'm not sure we'll find out this way, either."

"Miz, uh, T.C., do you know my mom or something?"

Her look was one of disbelief. "I never saw either of you before. Any of you," she added with a sweep of her hand that took in the scumbags as well. "Why?"

"That's what I was gonna ask. Why? If you didn't know us, I mean."

"Long story," she said brusquely.

"I'm ready," he said.

She couldn't help a giggle then, the most un-T.C. thing about her, which tended to escape when some ploy of hers fell flat on its butt. She sighed. This particular trip down memory lane was one she seldom ever took aloud, but for little Al Townsend somehow she didn't mind. It even promised relief in some way she had not yet come to terms with.

"Once I had a little boy," she began, and told him all he needed to know: that the boy's name was Austin Rainey, and he wanted to be a rodeo cowboy like his dad. That he was dark like his mom, with eyes like Al's and strong little limbs like Al's too, and when he was four, he was allowed to see his first rodeo with his mom, T.C., and his dad, Beau Rainey, Beau the bull rider, a lean, quiet dropout—oh, all right: flunkout—from the University of Arizona, who also did some team roping and such. And they watched from the stands, and after Beau came home covered in glory and muffin dust, with only six stitches and a nice piece of the purse, Littlebo, which was Austin's nickname, knew what he wanted to be and seemed to know, too, why his dad talked so funny. All the other cowboys, and every buckle bunny who hung onto them too, talked the same way. And some dipped snuff.

At this, Al stuck his tongue out a mile, and so did T.C., nodding and smiling, before she went on: And because his mom had so much work as a teacher and as a soccer coach after school, Littlebo had no one to care for him while his dad cowboyed, but some of his friends had ladies, or hemi-demi-semiladies anyhow—Al wasn't quite sophisticated enough for that one—and Beau Rainey swore that Littlebo would be took care of jes' fine. And T.C. bought it, wondering aloud which of her Beaus was the younger, and waved them off one Thursday morning in Tucson with blown kisses.

And never saw Littlebo alive again. There was this town, King-man, Arizona (said T.C.), with a scheduled rodeo, and Beau was towing the horse trailer up Route 93 in that pin-striped Dodge pickup they couldn't afford, a regular cowboy Cadillac, after sun-down through endless god-awful desolation where people drove like they wanted to be certain there was no tomorrow.

So for some, there wasn't. From all accounts, Beau Rainey was driving close to seventy, respectable for him, when some idiot in a Firebird blasted by at over a hundred without room to pass, making Beau cut the wheel, correct, correct again as the trailer with its terrified pony began to skid, and the trailer hitch held and took the Dodge sideways off the highway in a slide that covered a hundred yards, ending without even a rollover.

The Dodge was a good, tough vehicle with a safe gas tank, but Beau kept a pair of plastic jerry cans secured on the trailer, and they were full when the slide began, but when the trailer walloped the pickup it compressed the passenger's side of the bodywork while it let the driver's door fly open. The Dodge was still upright, but the trailer's impact squashed a jerry can like a grape, with a spray of gasoline that became a fireball. Beau Rainey, who always ignored safety belts was, as they used to say, thrown clear. Clear into a chunk of sandstone that broke his back and put him into a coma for days. He would walk again, but he would ride no more bulls.

Littlebo, secured by his seat belt, apparently never lost consciousness in the cab. He was screaming, too small to open the jammed door and too panicky to think of rolling down the window or to leap from the other door, which was already open. Or maybe Littlebo was thinking of the flames that danced about the cab, with more liquids beginning to ignite.

The motorist following, who saw the whole thing, was a big, strapping guy named Ross Downing, whose long slide stopped him on the other side of the highway. He sprinted fifty yards to the pickup and did not realize the driver lay unconscious, near enough to the blistering heat to sustain second-degree burns. The screams of the dying pony sounded like a man. Then Downing saw the tiny human trapped like an animal sacrifice in that pinstriped cage and, according to the next motorist on the scene, hurled himself into the flames.

Downing managed to burn his hand into useless meat, then ran around the pickup with his big coat flying like a cape, his hair aflame, and literally dived through the open door into the cab. By now Littlebo was breathing fire, and Downing would have died had he not held his breath for the ten seconds or so it took for him to wrestle the boy from that seat belt.

Downing got out of the Dodge and smothered Littlebo's flaming clothes by enveloping him in his big woolen coat. Not until he felt a passerby flailing at him with another coat did Downing realize that he was blazing like a candle.

Well, it was a wonderful try, a heroic try, and it came within an inch of killing Ross Downing. But it didn't save Littlebo, four-year-old Austin Rainey, whose lungs had shriveled in that highway furnace and who never made it to the hospital.

T.C. had blamed Beau at first, certain that in his happy-go-lucky, what-the-hell way he had contributed to the accident. If they'd caught the damned fool in the Firebird, T.C. might've had someone else to focus her rage against. But they hadn't, and only when she visited the horribly burned Ross Downing weeks later did she hear from what was left of Downing's lips that Beau Rainey had been driving like a sober citizen and had done what any other good driver might have done. T.C. cried, not for herself this time but for all the poison she had spewed at her husband since the wreck, and for how he must've felt about it when his protests went unheard. She went to Beau, still in a hospital bed where he hadn't been able to escape her, and said what needed saying.

Too late. It was just like the dumb, stubborn, determined Beau Rainey to start the divorce proceedings flat on his back, and that's exactly what he'd already done, and she didn't try to—

T.C. broke off her account, slid down in the seat with her hand atop Al's head as a police car, then a plain sedan, then another police car roared by on the highway fifty yards from the Nissan's nose. No sirens, but they were using all the road.

T.C. swapped looks with the boy. "Well, let's see if they hope we're waiting for the sunset," she said gaily and started the engine, waiting until she saw three cars dart into the parking area she'd so recently vacated, turning around again so she could take Amapas into town and the tunnel near upscale Gringo Gulch.

"We gotta get my stuff from Las Palmas," said Al, as they were going through the tunnel. "Power Rangers and stuff."

"You think they aren't waiting for you there? No, we're heading for the air terminal," she said.

"Won't they be waiting there, too?"

"Probably," she said, winked, and placed a finger on the tip of his nose. "But they don't know how many cards we can play."

CHAPTER 3

T.C.'s hole card was that unlike most tourists, she knew about the *collectivos*, Mexico's lowest class of bus travel, strictly speaking not real buses at all. *Collectivos* careen along the secondary roads of Mexico as vintage Volkswagen microbuses, so jammed with impoverished Mexicans that sometimes you can't see light through the windows. T.C. also knew she needed to cash a few traveler's checks at the airport, lousy exchange rate or not, with the Nissan parked near the airport rental lot.

She left Al where he could seem to be watching the planes take off while keeping her in sight, while she cashed some fifty-dollar traveler's checks. She spent two minutes studying the *Atlas de Carreteras* in her bag. Whatever direction they took, she didn't want it to be on a road where a low-clearance Ford could beat a VW.

She wandered over to a woman sweeping up litter and asked about a *collectivo*. The last trip of the day, she learned, should have already left the *aeropuerto* for Aguamilpa, a village many kilometers inland. But *¿quien sabe?* Look for a yellow vehicle.

T.C. gave Al the high sign and went outside, wondering where they would go next, and there turning around in plain sight not far from a big upscale terminal bus was a thrashed lemon yellow brick of a VW microbus. It might have been thirty years old, carrying a dozen swaying heads attached to people who couldn't all sit down because the middle seat had been removed long ago to make room for extra bodies. She yelled, running for a hundred yards, easily outdistancing the astonished Al, and the *collectivo*'s driver finally stopped for them.

As they approached, T.C. warned the boy to say nothing in the vehicle, no matter who spoke, unless he could say it in Spanish. They got a few glances and a nod or two, but these were taciturn folk who could not afford cars or shanties nearer town and seemed incurious about those who could.

They sat hugging their knees on the floor, enveloped in the odor of Latin poverty: sour sweat, badly tanned leather, and tortilla musk. It compelled T.C. to review images of her California childhood, the period when she rode herd on two younger brothers while both parents labored in the fields. Memories of a hard life, now recalled with warmth and longing, and she smiled with her eyes closed.

Al spent a lot of time inspecting the grumbling old bus, noting the cheap thin pipe secured by screws to the inside of its roof, burnished by a generation of toil-hardened hands; the tattered sandals of standees; the two youths who lay on the high back shelf obscuring any view through the rear window. By the time they reached San Juan de Abajo, the driver had his lights on and only a half dozen riders were left. T.C. took a seat then, pulled Al onto her lap though he was really too big for that, and watched their progress higher into the jumble of green on steep slopes, following the path of a stream that burbled along the valley to their right. The road was, of course, an abomination. Good!

Aguamilpa was the end of the line. Really and truly the end, T.C. learned after they trudged across the dusty dirt road to a *tienda* lit by lanterns redolent of kerosene. After buying shuck-wrapped tamales and bottles of cool apple-flavored Manzanita soda pop, she asked the wrinkled shopkeeper how they might get farther east. The old girl didn't know; she had never gone far in that direction. Sierra Zapotan, she added, pointing with her chin, as if the phrase explained everything.

There was an inn, however, a staunch, whitewashed mission-style structure that might once have been some landowner's little palace. The manager, a fellow in his forties with pomade-slicked hair, a guayabera shirt and ill-fitting dentures, showed no surprise at the woman who registered as Señora Marisol de Massey y Ocampo with her child, which meant she mustn't try to use a credit card. The lodging wasn't any better than T.C. expected for the price: no hot water, and you took a roll of toilet paper with you to the unisex toilet.

But the manager did have an antique dial phone, as T.C. learned after Al was snoring softly on the bed with mosquito net carefully arranged around him, when it finally occurred to T.C. to go and ask the man, armed with her Day-Timer and cash. Señor Pomade spent an eternity figuring out that it would cost her five dollars for each three minutes, expensive as the room itself, and T.C. nearly changed her mind when he insisted on initiating the call. For that, he needed the number. She showed it to him, hoping the jangle of her nerves didn't show, and he handed her the receiver before he crossed the room to watch his black-and-white TV.

She counted three rings before a mature male voice announced that this was Townsend and Townsend, wait for the beep, please leave a message, they'd call back. "Oh, damn," said T.C., because she didn't want to tell Gail Townsend's fate to a machine. And for all she knew it'd be ruinous to identify herself. She had no idea how sophisticated Mexican police might be. "My name is Marisol," she began just in case the manager were listening, "calling from Mexico. Gail Townsend has had an accident. Actually, not an—"

"This is Elaine," said a matronly contralto, one of those cautious people who screen their calls. "Gail's had an accident?"

"I'm afraid so. Could I speak to Ray Townsend please?"

"My husband will be out tonight until, I don't know when. Please tell me what's happened to Gail." Her tone didn't suggest *please;* it said, *I knew this would happen.*

"Mrs. Townsend, Talal is all right, but two men tried to take him by force and Gail fought them, and I'm afraid—you should call Emiliano Zapata Hospital in Puerto Vallarta. I don't think the news will be good."

"Al? Oh my God, that awful man . . . is Al at the . . . what was the name of the hospital?"

T.C. repeated it. "It's the main hospital in P.V.," she said gently.

"Is Al there with you?"

"Not there, but yes, with me. He's fine, but he doesn't know what . . . I haven't told him—"

Now the voice of Elaine Townsend hardened. "Put him on, if you please."

T.C. hesitated. "Well, he's asleep right now. He's had a long day, Mrs. Townsend, but I promise—"

"At eight o'clock in the evening? You can't get him settled down before nine." Definitely suspicious now.

"It's an hour later here, and—"

"You called him Talal, didn't you?" A sound of revulsion, almost a growl, from Seattle. "I know who you are, you're one of Zagro's people. I don't know what you expected to gain by this, whoever you are, but—but my husband is having this call traced and, and Gail isn't even in Mexico and why can't you just leave things as they are?" The woman's voice caught in a sob, panicky, trying to maintain composure but failing at it.

Into the woman's labored breathing, T.C. could only say, "I hope your daughter will be all right, Mrs. Townsend. And I'll get Al back to the States. Trust me."

"Trust you," Elaine Townsend echoed, scorn dripping from the phrase.

A furious reply begged for utterance but T.C. quashed it. She hadn't made this call to have a blistering argument with a frightened mother who was probably going to feel a lot worse after calling the hospital. *And you know damned well she will, and then maybe she'll believe I'm on her side. Nobody is tracing this call at her end, the poor thing is alone in her house, she's scared and she's bluffing, and she knows something about her daughter that I'd love to know.* T.C. replaced the receiver without another word and took several settling breaths. It was still possible that Gail Townsend had made it, might even now be sitting up, busting the chops of some guy from the consulate, demanding they find her son.

In which case T.C. herself was, in fact, the kidnapper. The idea was absurd enough to be funny if it wasn't so horrifying—a great line of thought to pursue if she was trying to regain her calm, think it all out, play the percentages.

In all likelihood, Gail Townsend hadn't made it. The boy's father would be the next of kin. What had the grandmother said, Zadro? Zagro, that was it. Sounded Middle East to T.C., but was he Al's father? The goddamned Iranian ambassador? Maybe that didn't matter so much right now. What mattered was their getting across the mountains, wearing tennis shoes, for Christ's sake, without being waylaid for their footgear like those guys in *Treasure of the Sierra Madre*. From what she'd seen on the way in, this was no place to be hiking around with a seven-year-old without anything faintly resembling a weapon, not even an *obtenero*. Maybe she could go to the *tienda* and worry out loud about snakes, get a club or something.

Feeling a bit more gathered now, she moved across the room with a manufactured smile. Señor Pomade might be more helpful on the subject of eastward travel if she waited until a commercial.

□   □   □

The calls of distant roosters woke them the next morning, and following T.C.'s example Al splashed cold water on his face without getting any in his mouth before they left their room. She hadn't expected breakfast to be part of the deal, but it was, papaya and lime, sugary flat bread, and coffee that Starbucks would kill for. The manager had told her the paths were safe, and often traveled, from Aguamilpa to Zapotan or San Sebastián. But her map said Sierra Zapotan was a piss ripper, and the town itself was fifteen miles distant near a surfaced road. San Sebastián was twenty miles to the southeast.

She hoped to stay on the rough stuff as far as possible for a while, within reason, and took Al to the little *tienda* a hundred yards away. The little old lady was there, looking as if she hung by her knees from the roof beam at night, as if she'd been there longer than dirt and would be there after it all blew away, and she shrugged off T.C.'s mention of snakes. Oh, yes, they were all over, she agreed, but the *viboras* would not bother those who did not bother them. But if one were concerned, or hungry, one merely used the machete.

This was more like it, thought T.C. The little shop sported a dozen machetes, all new though not terribly sharp, some with a blade as long as her forearm. Her purchase cost all of four dollars, six counting the fresh tamales and soda pop that went into her overnight bag. T.C. let Al carry the knife in his belt, the boy immediately taking on a swagger like a buccaneer, which brought a shared tender glance to both women.

T.C. found the local outfitter, as the manager had promised, near his corral where the dirt road simply ended in a sign that said FIN DEL CAMINO, redundant as a no swimming sign on a sand dune. Maybe it would also be the end of the road for any pursuit, she thought.

Cowboys, she decided, must be the same everywhere. The guy was rail-thin and roughly her age, with hands like alligator hide and lace-up boots, and he treated her as though she were a queen. But when he gave her a price for travel by saddle horse to San Sebastián, she knew it was serious haggle time.

Though she had some of the lingo, most of that was in English T.C. had absorbed from Beau, and she wasn't any great shakes on a horse. They'd have to have a guide—for one thing, simply to bring the saddle mounts back—which made it pricey. Then the horses. But hold on, said T.C., remembering something she didn't know firsthand, trusting that if she quoted Beau she wouldn't sound like an idiot: They didn't need two horses on mountain paths; they needed one good mule with a high-cantled saddle. A mule was surer of foot in broken country, and with the right saddle she and the *hijo* could ride together, being no heavier than a man. She silently hoped she'd got it all right.

At this the outfitter sucked a tooth, hands thrust into hip pockets, and squinted at her with new respect. Finally he nodded, with a smile that was really something to see, ugly as roadkill and just as genuine. *Veinte dolares* for the mule and guide, in advance.

A half hour later, she climbed into the saddle of a big mule with a mane the same color as her own, wondering what kind of rinse it used for that luster, insisting that Al clamber up by himself, which he did by stepping on her stirruped foot, swinging up behind, and clinging like an abalone to that saddle cantle. They were led by the outfitter's son, a boy of ten or so, who seemed neither pleased nor displeased with the prospect and who rode a little mare with a saddle sized for him.

Through all of this Al Townsend remained subdued, not even trying to interest the Mexican boy, who became a regular little wrangler in his roll-brim straw hat. For a time their path paralleled the creek that the road had followed, T.C. leaning far back against Al on the downward sections. They glimpsed many patches of corn, growing in places steep enough that the roots must need pitons for a grip, with now and then a visible roof thatch or a pen of interlaced saplings, and once the unmistakable stink of pigs near a clearing. The jungle of Jalisco wasn't uninhabited, just damned near impenetrable.

When the sun was high overhead, T.C. asked their guide to stop, and they found a flat spot for lunch where she could look back on the valley they'd left. If anyone followed them, he was doing it off the trail—*lotsa luck, waddie*—and T.C. began to feel a bit less stressed. She shared tamales with Al and the Mexican boy, whose name was Javier and who had brought no food, or anything else beyond an old machete and a cotton blanket. When she realized she had nothing to open her soda pop with, young Javier simply took his machete and, with a practiced flick, removed the cap.

Al didn't eat much, and Javier kept glancing up at the sun. The lad claimed they were halfway there, *más o menos*, with a waggle of one hand, and he did not try to hurry them, but T.C. could tell he was wishing they were in the saddle again.

When they remounted after relieving themselves off the trail, she made the mistake of asking Al how he felt. "I want my mom," he said, more sullen than anxious as they followed Javier's mare higher, now enclosed by lush greenery that suffused the sunlight.

The character of the jungle began to change in the higher elevations, from broadleaf trees to a sprinkle of long-needle pine and *madrona*.

If she told Al she'd talked with Elaine Townsend, he would wonder why he hadn't been present. She didn't want to say, "Because you're an impulsive little scamp and you might try to make our decisions and I don't need that." Instead she said, "Al, your mom was seriously hurt, and I'm trying to do what she'd do if she could: get us back to the States."

"You have a cell phone?"

At this innocent yuppie request, she chuckled. "No, and if I did I'd be afraid to call the hospital. We saw what happened after I took one little phone call, thanks to you. I don't think anybody knows where we are anymore."

"I sure don't," said Al.

"But you do know things that I need to know if I'm going to help, Al. That means you need to tell me. I wouldn't ask if I didn't need to know."

After a moment he said, "Uh-hunh." Another long silence, then, "I'm not s'posed to tell about my dad, and stuff."

He sure liked that word *stuff.* "Well, let's see if we can discuss it without him, okay?"

"Drop it on me," he said, and she grinned, delighted. Judging from his speech patterns, Gail Townsend must've been one jazzy cupcake.

"Is this the first time people have tried to take you away?"

"I don't think so. Mom had to move twice; my grampa said that was why."

"Where did you move from?"

"Iran. It's a place near Europe."

"You lived in Iran?"

"When I was little. I don't remember it much. Some." Trying to be accurate, doing his best. "I wore funny clothes. So did Mom."

"Who was trying to take you then?"

A longer pause. "My dad, I think. Jeez, look at that bird," he broke off, as a large-beaked creature in psychedelic hues flickered among the trees.

"Al, did you change your name when you came back from Iran?"

"Uh-hunh. To Townsend."

"From what?"

"Zagro," he said, a "bingo" of sorts. "It's a Kurd name."

She looked around. Kids in her charge watched their language. "What did you say, young man?"

"Kurd," he repeated.

She laughed outright. "I thought you said—never mind." *Ooh, boy, I'm scooting through a jungle with a kid for a guide, and another kid who belongs to some of the most tenacious, hard-core Muslims on earth. And that's about all I know about them. Except that they'll kill you as casually as bopping a fish on the head. But that burr-head was no Iranian if I'm any judge.* "Al, why was your mom in Iran to start with?"

"She lived there with my grandparents a long time ago. I think Grampa had a job there. Then they all came home."

"With you?"

"That was before," he said irritably.

"But you lived there," she persisted.

"My mom married and then went back there," he explained.

"To live with your dad," T.C. supplied. Finally a guess that worked.

"Sure, but after a while she didn't like it, I guess. We came home while I was little, just her and me."

"And your dad didn't want you to," she prompted.

"I guess not. But I think they were friends for a long time, after. Gramma told Mom she shouldn't keep writing for money, so I guess she was."

"Zagro, huh? Kurdish." She recalled the second man, the one whose ear she had whacked down to half-mast while he held Al. The man was dark, Latin-looking, but maybe Iranian? "You're sure it wasn't your dad holding on to you in the water?"

"Nah. I remember him, kind of. Great big guy, real strong, had a beard and stuff. Used to scare me."

"But you haven't seen him since Iran?"

"No. But I don't want to go back with him. He was scary. Gramma says he'd do anything now to get me back. I don't want to talk about him."

"Okay, Al, I understand. Uh, one more thing, though: Were your mom and dad divorced?"

"I'm not s'posed to—"

"I need to know. It makes a difference," she said, "to police."

"Yeah, when I was still little, okay? Cut me some slack, T.C." At this, young Javier twisted in his saddle, studied them impassively, turned back to the trail. If Al's words hadn't meant anything, their tone had said volumes. You didn't speak to your mother that way in Javier's society. If your dad didn't beat the frijoles out of you, the priest would.

Jesus, what a little hotshot! She still couldn't tell whether Al was just bright and determined, or as spoiled as last month's tuna salad. He had reacted to his mother's injury as anyone might and risen above it better than most. But spoiled kids could do that, too, with an unerring focus on themselves. Time would tell. *And so what? Quit assessing him, judging him, you're not filling out a Social Development Report on the poor little bugger, Ms. Rainey. You're not his teacher. Or his mother,* she added silently.

In midafternoon they met a larger path, scarred stones on the trail suggesting frequent use by horses, the trail following another brook still higher. They got occasional glimpses far down the valley behind them and, as the afternoon waned, thin tendrils of smoke marking a village that lay below the tree-defined outline of a ridge miles away. Judging from her map it could have been San Juan de Abajo. In any case they'd put a hell of a piece of real estate between themselves and Puerto Vallarta. It just might be clear sailing now. . . .

They struck a dirt road late that afternoon, their shadows preceding them, and almost immediately were overtaken by a *collectivo.* Her map said it was headed for Federal Highway 15, and she let it go. A half hour later, with San Sebastián in sight, she saw another yellow microbus coming the other way. She told Javier her intentions and tipped him a handful of Mexican coins as he folded the mule's stirrups over its saddle and tied them together, and they made the transfer right there on the road. The little wrangler kicked his mare into a trot beside the old microbus for a moment, waving his hat merrily as if taking leave of old friends, as if he had said more than fifty words to them during their ride, before the mule put an end to that nonsense, and then T.C. settled back with Al in the almost deserted vehicle, and Al was asleep within seconds.

She knew they didn't look enough like locals, certainly couldn't imitate the local accent. The driver said his destination was Ameca, and they didn't pick up a dozen passengers through Mascota and Mixtlan. En route, with Al jostled into waking again, she plied him with questions about Seattle, alert for insights, avoiding controversy. He went to public school and lived in Bryn Mawr not far from where his mom worked at Boeing. It was the same company his grampa worked for, or had, and the parents of half the kids in school worked there too. When he said Boeing, Al made it sound like Valhalla, like it made you somehow special, worthy. She had never thought of a major U.S. city as a company town, but perhaps Seattle was exactly that.

When T.C. remarked that they had probably flown to Mexico on a Boeing plane, Al nodded. His mom had said it was a "stretch," as if that was something special too. Maybe it was; it sounded as if Al knew more about it than she did. He probably absorbed such things by osmosis, the way she had learned about rodeos and cowboying in general when her own interests ran to books and kids and organized sports. Beau had argued that rodeos were organized, but she'd known better than that the first time she saw one. Let a Brahma bull out of a chute with some dumb twister like Beau on his back, and the next ten seconds or so were about as organized as an earthquake in a lunatic asylum, and nowhere near as healthy.

No, Al didn't have a girl, but he liked to chase them. They played G. I. Joe after school sometimes, waiting for parents, or traded sports cards. He thought the Sonics were way cool and the

Seahawks too if they'd ever get a quarterback, and oh, yeah, the Mariners were okay, but he didn't think he'd go out for Little League until they had something for you to do besides stand around waiting for the ball. "Mostly baseball is waiting," he observed, a deadly dismissal from a kid as full of beans as Al was. And T.C. agreed and mentioned soccer where, she exaggerated, anytime you're not moving for three seconds they carry you off the field. Like basketball, he said. Yeah, like that, she said, and they slapped hands softly, grinning together.

Their fellow passengers sat and watched these goings-on with solemn, unblinking interest the way behavioral scientists might watch a newly discovered species, and it reminded T.C. that they were a long way from fading into the social woodwork of Mexico. Hell, she hadn't even coached the boy in it. And it was time she did, she realized, as cathedral spires poked up into the skyline dusk of central Mexico.

She gave an *"hola"* to the driver when they reached the outskirts of Ameca, a little city perhaps half the size of P.V., and Al had the good sense not to ask questions as they climbed out and stretched their legs.

She took his hand, and they turned toward an intersecting dirt road, walking slowly through the dust until the *collectivo* was out of sight. Then they turned and retraced their steps, T.C. kneeling to pick up a handful of fine dust, which she rubbed on her arms and into her skirt. "Do like I'm doing," she said.

"I will not," he said with absolute finality, as if she'd asked him to wear a dress in a Fourth of July parade.

"You wanta look like other people, Al, or would you rather stand there with a sign saying, 'Look at me, look at me'? If people notice you, we just might not get back home, either of us." In the dusk she could see the comical way he glanced around self-consciously when there wasn't a soul in sight and not a *casita* within fifty yards. She helped him get his smudges, explaining that poor Mexicans could not all stay clean all the time, especially at the end of the day after doing richer people's scutwork, and even his jeans said he hadn't done a lot of work that day, maybe not even recently. His machete was too new, too clean, but they could rub some scratches into the blade, maybe nick it on a rock.

It was near dark as they reached the middle of town, passing doorways lit by the flicker of television or made charming by the languid strains of an amateur's guitar. Instead of eating their last tamales, they stopped in one of the little short-order places two steps off the sidewalk. While they ate hot meals of rice, beans, and mutton—Al wasn't charmed by the taste—T.C. struck up a dialogue with the young cook, who was also the manager and the only waiter of this six-seat restaurant.

She was assured that the man's sister operated an inn with rooms, very clean, no fleas, in the same structure where they were dining. The guest entrance was around the corner, he added, and the lady should mention him for a better price. This was no surprise to T.C., who knew that while the price would probably not be better, the waiter would get his kickback. Many extended Mexican families ran a bewildering variety of services to make ends meet and carefully apportioned the various incomes.

The building itself took up half a block with its walls crowding the sidewalk, a fort of limestone with bars of wrought iron over windows that were more like embrasures. It abruptly occurred to T.C., turning at the street corner with Al in tow, that those windows had, in fact, once been embrasures when besieged landowners had to defend themselves with muskets against the original rightful owners. Ameca had been there a long, long time, and that building had been a real little *palacio*. Things change. Now the people who owned it had to work for their keep.

The handle in the door rang a bell somewhere, and presently they were invited in by a heavyset woman in her forties with a lovely shawl and a beatific smile for dutifully silent Al. Once that street door was closed again, T.C. felt almost at home; wealthy friends in old south Tucson lived in much the same ambience.

They stood in an alcove at the edge of a softly lit atrium, with its own little jungle prospering under an open sky. Rich odors of food vied with perfumed blossoms as T.C. dickered gently for a price. It would have been an insult, she felt, to demand a look at the room, but the woman led them up a stone staircase, showing them into a room with windows facing both street and atrium. Airy, with a tall ceiling and ancient carven furniture, it was a piece of history. Al Townsend was fresh out of vinegar, notwithstanding his grandmother's claim—but after all, it was his bedtime anyway.

The old-time Mexican custom, borrowed from the Spaniards, was to stay up late, perhaps have a final small meal. T.C. wandered downstairs, chose one of several wicker chairs in the atrium, and kneaded her feet luxuriantly. It was not long before the beshawled woman returned in company of an old fellow whom she introduced as *el patron,* her father, El Señor Gilberto Moreno de la Vega.

T.C. had not given herself a name yet and was ashamed to lie to this slender, erect gentleman of seventy or so. She gave her proper name, and he took her hand in the old way and did not sit down beside her in his own atrium until T.C. asked him to.

Yes, her journey had been tiring but enjoyable. The *hijito,* normally so full of energy, was already asleep, as was proper. Oh, yes, the room was entirely satisfactory, charming in fact, she said, accepting a wonderful little goblet of genuine Oporto, too sweet for her and probably dearer than single malt scotch. Señor Gilberto studied his wine, velvety black in the dim light, and observed that few *Norteamericanos* came to them in this way.

What way? Well, covered with the dust of back roads, traveling with only a single small and expensive piece of luggage.

It was that obvious that she was from the States?

To the practiced eye, he shrugged, and waited.

And then, thinking with each phrase *this is a big mistake,* she told him.

CHAPTER 4

It wasn't that she panicked, exactly. It wasn't physical exhaustion either, for a *macha* like T.C. who swam, worked out and ran laps, and refereed two dozen little hellions at a time. It had to be the old boy's grand family manner, she decided, that made her unburden herself.

Señor Gilberto didn't remind her of her father, but of the men her father had revered and trusted, men raised on noblesse oblige, who welcomed responsibility and hard decisions—*All right, then, playing God, somebody has to do it,* she thought. She didn't tell him everything, but too much for real caution: The boy had been entrusted to her by hard circumstance to bring him to his mother's people in *Los Estados Unidos.* But the boy's father employed powerful men hoping to intercept her.

"I don't think they want to hurt him," she said in answer to a question by Gilberto, "but they would destroy me in a second." *Like shoot me and watch me drown,* she added to herself.

Was *la señora* perhaps fleeing from men in the drug trade? She said she didn't think so, but they had influence with police.

"Men of influence with police, in these times, may be in that trade," said Gilberto. "They are the sort who do violence to women without a moment's thought. It is the curse of our time which, if you will forgive me, a million buyers in the North have brought on us all."

She nodded and mulled that one over. The connection was possible, she said. She had no way of knowing and didn't want to know. She wanted only to get her small charge safely across the border.

And then? "Then return him to his mother's family. They know I have him but little more. I should probably telephone them again," she admitted.

For a time the old fellow hmmmed to himself, sipping, thinking. Then, "We have a telephone. Do the evil men know the boy's family?"

"I regret that they do. They must."

"Then you must not contact the family by telephone."

"But I already have," she said, and his brow went up.

"Then they may well know what was said," he replied.

"If they do not know where we are," she began.

He put up a hand. "I am not familiar with details of their machines, but I read newspapers. I watch the television. And I know that if they have influence they may listen at that location—where?"

"Washington," she said, instead of Seattle.

For the first time he laughed, a gentle, sad whisper of a laugh. "Washington, and men of influence. Ah, God."

She hadn't thought of that, such a simple thing: They didn't have to pick up her calls from Mexico; they could do it from Seattle. But Christ, she had no experience with this shit, skulking around dodging cops *and* robbers. She supposed aloud that he was correct, that she'd made a mistake. She didn't have to repeat it, though, and they spoke of what might be mistakes and what might be wise decisions.

When she caught herself stifling a yawn, old Gilberto caught it too and studied an ornate pocket watch. "Of course if you were stopped by such people, you would have to deny that you had received any help getting to *el Norte,*" he murmured. "I think God would smile on a falsehood of that sort. You—forgive me—you are Catholic?"

She had to admit she wasn't.

He said it was regrettable because at times there were certain options open to Catholics, means of crossing great distances in relative safety. But other options might be available to her and the boy.

"I wish I knew what they are," she said.

"I think it is best if you did not know too much, for the welfare of all concerned. We have agreed that travel by the usual commercial means would probably not be wise. The *cartelistas* have their ways, the military have theirs. And honest workingmen have ways as well, and they can be helpful to those in need. Would you be interested in travel that is slow but safe?"

"I hope it will not be much slower than a mule," she smiled.

"Quicker than that," he agreed. "Very well. I believe produce trucks pass these very streets before dawn en route to Guadalajara. I also believe that they might offer vacant seats to people who are afoot at such a time. Beyond this, I cannot say."

She felt a prickling of her skin at the way he said "believe," as if his belief was absolute. And he hadn't said he didn't know more than that, only that he couldn't say. So what more could you ask of an old fellow who has his family to think of? "I believe," she said, stressing the word ever so slightly, "I would pay dearly for such a thing."

"Pah. This is not a commercial exchange, señora," he said with a wave of his hand. Then he released a sly little smile, almost that of a lover. "But if that is what you believe . . ."

"Such is my belief," she murmured, with the kind of flirty, sidelong glance her mother used to give her father, the kind she'd never thought she would use. If she'd had a lacy little fan, she would've simpered at him from behind it. The twinkle in the old boy's eye said she had pleased him. "What must I do now, señor?"

"Sleep. You will be awakened in time." He did not stand but stirred as if expecting to.

"I cannot tell you how much this means to us, señor." She arose slowly so that he did not need to move fast. "The only thing I wonder is, why you would take such an interest in our troubles on such short notice?"

And now he seemed to become ten years older, but maybe it was just a trick of the shadows. "Who knows? Perhaps I have sins to expiate. Or perhaps you remind me of someone," he said, his gaze distant.

Dear God, his reason for jumping in was no different from mine, she thought, climbing the stairs. The old fellow was pouring himself another glass of Portuguese wine, in no hurry, as if he had everything scoped out. She hoped he wasn't kidding himself.

□   □   □

The woman woke her very early, and she rousted Al from the pallet she'd made for him. There was no time for breakfast, but the woman pressed a warm newsprint-wrapped package, pungent with odors of food, into her hand before T.C. and the sleepy child stepped outside into the cool of a predawn morning. The wait was perhaps fifteen minutes, though it seemed an eternity, but when she first saw the misaligned headlights approach down the narrow cobblestoned street she knew it would be their ride. It was a big stake bed truck with brakes squalling even before she raised her hand, the driver a taciturn mustachioed gent in a denim jacket who let the passenger door swing open, blipping his throttle, letting it speak for him. He only grunted when she thanked him. A moment later they were rumbling toward the outskirts, and two moments later Al Townsend was asleep again, his head cradled in the crook of her arm despite harsh so-called music from a portable radio with a speaker that was, if not damaged, then surely demented.

Nearing the rooftops of Guadalajara, they drove into a flush of bronzed dawn, the driver silencing his radio to speak for the first time. He sounded well educated for a farmer and, though he never referred to *el patron* in any intimate way, T.C. thought they might be kin. They would soon reach the central market, he said, and from there the bus station was a short walk.

She said she must travel north toward Monterrey and asked his advice, unfolding her map booklet for him as Al began to stir. After a few moments the driver chuckled and groomed the near

side of that floral mustache. He often whiled away slack times playing cards, he said, with a fellow who trucked his produce down
from Manalisco and would begin his return journey before noon.
He was certain that *el patron*'s influence extended that far. Would
la señora accept that alternative?

She studied the map and agreed. The Manalisco road was another of those that seemed to get worse in a hurry, then worse
still. But it promised to take them toward Aguascalientes, a giant
step in the right direction.

When they reached the center of Guadalajara, a mix of the
traditional and modern and probably as populous as San Diego,
the huge central market was already in full swing with restaurant
and grocery buyers arguing prices at warp speed. Their driver
never actually said that he had left his helper at home to leave
room for her, but T.C. read between his lines. He seemed non-
plussed, even uneasy, when T.C. and Al pitched in to help drag
crates of vegetables to the tailgate, but it pleased him, and when
at last they had time for conversation, T.C. asked how much she
should pay for the ride.

Though he was not insulted by the offer, he declined it. "I
have sons of my own. But it might be welcome to your next
driver," he said gently. It was his only hint that he knew their
travels might be risky.

They breakfasted on sweet rolls and strong coffee in foam cups
from a pushcart, and T.C. told herself caffeine was okay for the
boy if she made it half canned milk. Al drank the potent Mexican
coffee as if enjoying forbidden fruit, maintaining his silence, eyes
alert to the unfamiliar city around him. The sun was high when
their driver excused himself, returning shortly with a jaunty step.
T.C. made a silent wager that when he fiddled with that mustache,
he was pleased with himself.

"My friend Agustin assures me that you will be welcome. He too
has children," he said. And so it was that T.C. and Al left Guadalajara in the forenoon of their third day without ever visiting the
Orozco murals, the *catedral,* or any of that great city's other at-
tractions. They did take time for midday bowls of *birria,* a dizzying
concoction of steamed lamb with mild chilies, cumin, and oregano.

When Al, his mouth full of *birria*, asked what the word meant, she told him it translated as "a mess," and he managed to mumble "cool" without missing a morsel.

"Thought you'd like that part," she grinned. "They should've named you Calvin."

"Who's he?"

Oh, Lord, he missed the greatest comic strip in history, she sighed. "Kid in the funnies. Before your time. His buddy was a tiger named Hobbes."

"Hobbes," he mused. "Tiger. Girl tiger?"

" 'Fraid not."

"That's what they should call you anyway," he said, half serious, as she answered the beckoning of Agustin.

Agustin's truck used old sheet metal signs for its aft side panels and moved within an invisible cloud of pig scent as they left the city behind. Agustin was, to put it mildly, inclined to conversation, with a belly that jounced to the tune of each pothole and a soccer shirt that suggested common ground to T.C. It soon became clear that beyond accommodating a grandee of Ameca, Agustin had no interest in his part of their trip. He did not know, and did not care, why his passengers had chosen this kind of transport across Mexico. People occasionally did, for varied reasons, and they furnished companionship as well as Pemex gas, and that was sufficient for him.

And Agustin was a family man, which did not prevent him from making a guarded pass after speaking to Al in Spanish and assuring himself that Al couldn't understand him.

"If you truly want passengers who will pay your fuel bill," she said offhandedly, "you will not pursue this any further." And he turned to other matters without a pause.

They took on fuel at Ixtlahuacán and T.C. paid, and before they had driven up out of the Rio Verde Valley the road became the usual bad Mexican joke. After the next town it abruptly became little more than groupings of ruts. Once you chose a set, you were committed as far as the next crossing.

Agustin's farm stretched along a hillside beyond the far side of Manalisco, and before they reached it they made a new agreement:

For five dollars, he would put them up with his family and find them another ride *al Norte*.

T.C. had never spent a night on a Mexican farm but thought it might be a good idea for Al to play with Agustin's kids. She paid the man then and there, smiling at Al's delight when he saw two barefoot little boys running to meet *Papá*.

Agustin told his boys to take good care of the gringo child and to stay away from the old boar, then escorted T.C. to the long, ramshackle adobe ranch house. Outside, the place was a scatter of farm machinery, tractor, delapidated pickup, assorted fowl, and trash.

Inside it was different: Señora Rosa evidently had firm ideas about housekeeping. The plump little woman stood unblinking while Agustin introduced their overnight guest, with no sign of acceptance or rejection. When he had left them, however, she took both of T.C.'s hands in hers. "I hope you will forgive our poor accommodations," she said, and T.C. said she wished her own apartment were as neatly kept, and after that they were friends.

T.C. unwrapped her food package in the kitchen, part of which was open to the sky, and Rosa accepted the roast chicken as part of their evening meal—fried cornmeal, green tomatoes, and beans, Rosa apologizing because squash wasn't yet in season. The way Rosa used lard, it was no wonder she and her husband wore so much of it at their waists, but T.C. had the wisdom to keep silent on the point.

With their pleasant magpie chatter, the two women passed the remaining afternoon, Rosa snagging a three-year-old girl at one point for an introduction before the waif scooted outside again, chewing on a tortilla. Until dinnertime, T.C. saw no sign of the boys. *Gotta quit being such a worrywart*, she told herself. In a place so isolated, what could happen?

She found out after Rosa clanged the living hell out of an old harrow disk to signal dinnertime. Agustin's oldest boy could have pushed Al into the stock pond—and had. Al could bloody the kid's nose for it—and did. They could both stop Agustin's younger

son from crying over this donnybrook, and become better friends
for it, and sneak down to the pens where the old boar deepened
his wallow, and step shin-deep into yuchh, and find a half dozen
hen eggs in places where the boys knew to look, and Al, clumsy
in his new role, could break one, and he did. The trio showed up
looking like the wrath of God Almighty and smelling worse, but
with eggs to put aside for breakfast. T.C. was aghast; Rosa simply
pointed them toward a series of wooden water troughs outside and
went on setting the table.

Agustin's hired help evidently lived elsewhere. The family
butchered their own meat, made slabs of caustic soap, grew their
own fences of spiny, broadleaf maguey. Their clothes were store-
bought, however, and T.C. noticed that Rosa let their vegetables
soak in a dilute vinegar and water mix before preparing them for
a meal. Dysentery, then, was an avoidable problem even here.

T.C. translated for Al at the table and found that he had
learned a few words of *la raza* during that glorious afternoon; she
warned him against using some of them at the table. Agustin excused himself afterward, driving away in his pickup to arrange the
next leg of her trip. With no telephone and no TV, the women
moved outside to handmade chairs beneath the roof thatch. Rosa
made it clear to her sons that no further filthification would be
tolerated. Anyone returning dirty would do without *pan dulce*
later. There were those, T.C. reflected, who would object to brib-
ery with sweetcakes, yet Rosa's tribe left and returned on their best
behavior.

Agustin returned late, having canvassed several neighbors, saying that she had a choice. He could drive them to a better road
before dawn where they could catch an early *combi*—much the
same as a *collectivo*—or they could stay another night and accom-
pany a rancher's wife who was driving all the way to Zacatecas.

She consulted her map and chose the latter, offering another
five dollars for the extra day, which she knew had probably been
Agustin's strategy.

She and Al slept on pallets that night, waking often to the rustle
of corn shucks in their mattresses, falling back asleep quickly. The

next day was full of chores for T.C., and some were left for Al with his new friends, Agustin having left for a neighboring farm at dawn to help out. It seemed that the farmers hired one another from day to day, preferring to call it hired help instead of casual communism.

When they left Agustin's farm, the morning was fresh and cool, with Rosa driving the pickup—herding it, rather. The boys all cavorted in the back while the tiny girl sat between the two women, watching T.C.'s every move as if she had a report to write on this strange creature. And throughout the short ride, T.C. wondered, *Are those slimeballs still after us? Where are they looking, and how thoroughly?*

The ranch looked much like those in Arizona, with well-kept outbuildings and telephone lines stretching to the big house. A carryall and a newish pickup were visible near the house. The rancher's wife, a tanned, attractive rawboned woman in jeans and suede blouse, emerged with a smile and a wave. Rosa did not leave her pickup, perhaps feeling uneasy amid these rich surroundings. She left after sharing hugs with both T.C. and Al, who called, "Bye, *cabrones,*" to the other boys, earning him a gasp of dismay from T.C.

The tall woman laughed. "Agustin said you spoke English," she said in Spanish and put out a gentle hand to ruffle Al's unruly hair.

"Yes, but Al is becoming bilingual all too quickly," T.C. replied in English. The woman immediately switched to the northern tongue, introducing herself as Ana Flores as she ushered them into a house redolent of polish and old leather with a maid and a grand piano in the parlor. Ana's husband raised fine horses as well as beef, but with her children grown and gone she valued her weekly shopping trips. "I do not need to buy anything; it is recreation," she confided as a servant girl poured coffee for the three of them. "You must have a story to recount. Perhaps you will favor me with it on the journey," she added, the English phrases flavored strongly by her native language.

Within a half hour after they settled into her big Ford pickup, the road improved enough for conversation without shouting. T.C. learned that Ana Flores had taken a degree in Mexico City before fleeing its horrendous smog nearly thirty years previous. And Ana listened carefully to T.C.'s bare-bones account of their travel problem. Though T.C. didn't dwell on the deadly aspects of the pursuit, she did say in Spanish that she had left the lad's mother near death in a hospital and that she feared that Al might come unglued if he knew it. Whenever they switched to Spanish, Al always studied their faces for hints.

"So it must be your intent to cross the border as illegals," Ana said at one point.

"I haven't decided. I'm not even sure we need to, but I don't dare call his grandparents again in case their line is monitored."

Ana nodded, drumming her fingers on the steering wheel, a smile playing in the small wrinkles around her mouth. Finally; "Teresa, I had thought of going to Aguascalientes instead of Zacatecas. I have friends in both places. But I have a sister in San Tiburcio, much farther north, and I have developed a sudden desire to visit her. Would that help?"

T.C. looked at her map; San Tiburcio was halfway to the border. She stammered her gratitude, explaining to Al that by day's end they would be much nearer to their goal. Ana took a cheerful interest in her part, admitting that it was the most exciting thing to cross her life since her dalliance with a military man years before. Then they spoke a lot of Spanish and chuckled together until Al begged them to quit.

The roads continued to improve during the day, Al moving to the rear of the pickup at his own request after a rest stop, the gusts blowing his hair like grass. Apparently Al Townsend seldom enjoyed such déclassé adventures as bouncing in a pickup bed. The phrase "poor little rich boy" crossed T.C.'s mind more than once.

It was Ana Flores's idea to make a call to Seattle, after T.C. mentioned the need. "I will do it after I return home, tomorrow or the next day," she said, her eyes dancing.

"I appreciate it, but I don't think you should. You must remember that whoever's listening may make you sorry," said T.C.

"*Por qué*, for what? I happened upon a woman with a handsome boy and gave them a ride east to Guanajuato. They said their goal was Mexico City. The woman had no money and begged me to call for her, simply to say that the boy was healthy and in good spirits. Ah . . . and that he would be returning north by air! As a good samaritan, I could do no less." Her gestures were expansive, her smile infectious.

"You have a wonderful criminal mind," T.C. said in frank admiration. "Why would you do this?"

"I like you. I do not like governments. Besides, it is good for women to have a few secrets," said Ana with a comic flutter of her lashes that removed twenty years from her. "Now you, why would you want to take the risk of that telephone call?"

"The grandparents must know by now that their daughter is injured, or worse," said T.C. "They may already be in Mexico, and they must be terrified over the fate of the boy. They will need reassurance, and they will certainly have some way to find out if I call Seattle again." She paused to think of it; shook her head. "Can you imagine how they must be feeling right now, with no idea how the boy is doing?"

"You take responsibility very seriously," Ana said.

"I think it must be my hobby," T.C. replied in mock despair, and both of them laughed. After a moment: "You know, I keep thinking how different it would be if this were happening in the States."

"Everywhere, men are men," Ana said.

"But it's different, the way people are helping us here. I feel like I can confide in you and you're actually interested. People in the States would just get me out of their hair as fast as possible."

"Perhaps," said Ana after a moment's reflection, "in the north they have not all been disappointed enough by those they elect to serve them."

"We're getting there," T.C. said darkly and copied the Townsend telephone number from her Day-Timer on a scrap of paper.

□　　□　　□

In San Tiburcio, the younger sister of Ana Flores struggled to maintain middle-class status and obeyed Ana as if she were the mother. She traded clothing with T.C. that afternoon and found that a pair of her old *huaraches* fitted Al's feet nicely. Al did not want to give up his T-shirt but relented when they found him an embroidered denim jacket that was just enough too large to look authentic. T.C. skirted a lie by assuring him it was unisex and then had to explain it. Boys were boys, he retorted, and girls were girls.

"Hold on to that thought, Calvin," T.C. told him.

There seemed to be a well-developed travel grapevine among the lower-middle-class folk of San Tiburcio. The church had a bulletin board; the *mercado,* another; and each plaza had one or more. T.C. used the telephone of Ana's sister to inquire into three possibilities of northbound transit and chose the couple traveling by 1993 Chevrolet to Nueva Rosita, three or four hundred miles to the north on a major highway. She almost froze that night, sleeping on a pallet on the porch, because the altitude of San Tiburcio was roughly that of Denver, and with her lung capacity she had not suffered much from the thin air.

Ana drove them to the plaza after a light breakfast, where they spotted the gray Chevrolet sedan and then did their warm leave-takings. The Chevy was the typical article of Mexico, with three of its four corners showing damage because Mexican insurance took a lackadaisical view of fender benders and many Mexican drivers have always had a similar view of survival on public roads.

The driver was not an uncommon sort, either. He was roughly T.C.'s age, slender and smug, with a fair command of English and a pert, pregnant young wife whose English was so scant she evidently did not know when, halfway through the trip, hubby made a blatant proposition to T.C. in English.

It was the fresh-faced innocence of the little wife that kicked over T.C.'s testosterone bucket, though she normally had some tolerance for the machismo of Latin men. Anglos seemed to think that machismo equated with manliness, or perhaps aggressiveness, while Teresa Contreras had known better than that all her life.

She knew that machismo is a concept drilling straight into the soul of sexual politics. The Latin macho believes he is a superior bedroom athlete who must be allowed to try for every woman he fancies—but who will cut the liver and lights out of any man who tries for *his* own woman.

They were bypassing the town of Saltillo at the time, and the walk might not be difficult. In English, T.C. said, "I am interested only in the bedding of clever men. The boy speaks English, you moron. Shall I translate that for your wife?"

He laughed as if it were of no importance. "The lady has spirit," he said to his wife in Spanish.

"The lady has friends, and a long memory," she replied, also in Spanish. After that, his conversation tended toward comments about elections, weather, and other pressing matters as they descended from Mexico's highlands into the humid valley of the North.

The husband's revenge was to deposit T.C. and Al on the Plaza of Sabinas in late afternoon, a few miles short of Nueva Rosita, guessing correctly that she would not know the difference until too late.

She had finally abraded away her last friendly connections, it seemed, less than a hundred miles from the border. They had tacos and carbonated drinks on the town square, Al trying out his few new words on local boys who were interested only in selling him Chiclets. From a woman vendor, T.C. learned that she had an extra option in the railroad. A second-class bus seemed less likely to be watched, however. With no better alternative, they waited until dusk for the bus to Piedras Negras.

"When can we call Mom?" Al asked as T.C. studied her map.

"When we cross the border," said T.C., using her finger to trace a thin red line that followed the river's blue line. "See, the road runs along the river from Piedras Negras to Acuña, and we can take a good look at it from the bus tomorrow."

But Al was not interested in maps. "Does the bus cross the border?"

"Some do; this one probably doesn't." Unlike more traditional

Latinas, T.C. had no close kin in Mexico and in the past ten years or so had crossed the border only in flight, surrendering her passport on demand. As to crossing on wheels these days, she had no idea what rigmarole might be involved.

"Won't we be okay when we get there, T.C.?"

"Once we get past the Mexican side, I'm sure we will," she replied with confidence. "But we may have to get off a bus at some little village and swim. I just don't know, Al."

Their vehicle had probably been a Texas school bus twenty years before but would never pass a stateside vehicle inspection again. No one showed any interest in them and, when they reached Piedras Negras, the city's nightlife was in full chat. They paid too much for a room with twin beds, T.C. wishing they had walked farther from the neon, the music, and the laughter that lapped like a tide against the buildings near the city's center. She imagined that it would keep her awake, and that those sleepless hours would give her time to decide on a strategy. Two more bad guesses.

CHAPTER □ 5

Piedras Negras is separated from Eagle Pass, Texas, by a famous watercourse that is occasionally in flood, sometimes a creek, but never as imposing as its legends. T.C. and Al stood near the Rio Grande in midmorning like idle tourists and watched traffic cross the bridge into the United States until she realized that no idle tourist would show so much interest in such plebeian goings-on. Then she took Al's hand and hurried away with him.

"Hey, where are we going?"

"I don't know," T.C. admitted. "Wherever she's going." She nodded toward a fortyish woman dressed in skirt, blouse, and sensible shoes, carrying two empty net bags as she walked purposefully from the bridge and down a side street into Piedras Negras. That woman had come from Eagle Pass, and she had spoken only a casual phrase to the Mexican border guard as she passed. Net bags were the standard equipment in Mexico for shopping.

They walked several blocks before the woman led them to a *supermercado*, more faithful to a Safeway than to a traditional Mexican market. Grocery items and pharmaceuticals were often cheaper in Mexico, though the rule was not dependable. T.C. was watching a daily tactic by stateside households. But which items to buy as everyday bargains?

Inside the market, T.C. paused at a magazine rack, watching the activity around her. Al selected a comic book, opened it before he realized it was in Spanish and looked up in dismay. "Jeez, I can't read this," he said in disgust.

"*Pobrecito,*" said T.C., only half listening.

Al said, "I know that one." Her glance was her question and he answered it with, "It means 'poor you, and I don't care.' " His own glance was an accusation.

"Depends on how you say it, Al," she smiled at him. "Right now, I care about all these ladies shopping. Look, pretend I'm the boss and take my bag so I can concentrate, okay?"

He grumbled, but he did it. She drifted along the aisles, selecting a bag of chips and a package of conical brown sugar candies as camouflage and as bribes for Al. No sugar for him anytime soon, though. If a kid like Al got a sugar rush he might head for that river like Evel Knievel.

She saw the lady in sensible shoes again and took careful note of the items going into those net bags. She then switched her attention to a rather pretty young thing, also with a net bag and in a dress that was almost certainly a one-piece servant's uniform. T.C. picked a new net bag from a display rack. The Kraft paper bags of the North were freebies you didn't expect in most Mexican markets, and net bags were the natural alternative.

The time was about nine A.M., and a slow second-class bus to Acuña would put them far upriver by noon, across from Del Rio. But she would have the same problem there unless she opted to cross the river somewhere between the towns in broad daylight with Al—and if caught on the Mexican side, she was in for trouble. Illegal crossings were currently international news items, and Mexican authorities were understandably touchy. She decided she wouldn't mind so much being stopped by U.S. officials; she could prove her citizenship if she had to. The thing she most wanted to avoid was showing her identity on the Mexican side.

But she needed a story that would pass casual inspection, and she didn't have one consistent with a shopping foray. An Eagle Pass telephone book would help a lot. Hold on—border or no border, people phone home from the store, she thought, and sure enough, the *mercado* was upscale enough that it had an Eagle Pass directory, maps and all. She perused it while Al fidgeted.

Now what? Choose a common name? According to that directory, the Martinez tribe in Eagle Pass was huge; maybe she should claim one as her sister. And one phone call would blow her out of the water. Okay, forget that approach. If she had to give a phone number, it should be the number of somebody who didn't answer.

Who wouldn't be home? She stood in a fugue for long moments and then, for no conscious reason, recalled the toothless old woman in that *tienda* at the end of a Mexican dirt road. Poor old girl, she probably spent sixteen hours a day on the job. Quickly, T.C. searched the yellow pages for grocers. There were plenty of them, most with corporate names, but a Tom's, and a Dad's, too, and a Rosen's, on Garrison. There was exactly one Rosen, Norman, in the white pages, with an address on State Loop 431. The phone book's map showed that Garrison was an arterial that ran out in the direction of the loop road, too. Should she call and try some kind of scam with the Rosens?

Ridiculous, she told herself. Too much complication was as bad as too little. She wrote the salient details down in her Day-Timer because that was how she memorized things best and went back to her shopper surveillance.

Meats, dairy products, and fresh vegetables didn't seem to be popular items for international household trade. Maybe the locals knew those things would be confiscated. She selected lightweight boxes of cereal and, because the pretty maid had made the same choice, two cans of menudo. "Gimme that machete, Al," she said, spying its handle in the bag she carried. He did so, and she placed it on a shelf before moving on.

"Hey, that was mine!" His tone suggested that a small insurrection might be brewing.

"Stuff a sock in it, Al. I don't think folks in Eagle Pass use machetes a whole lot," she replied. "I'll get you another one sometime." The candy, chips, menudo, and cereal filled the bag halfway, and she chose a pack of incredibly cheap scrub brushes on impulse. They were tight little bundles of wire-wrapped broomstraw, so they weighed next to nothing, and they lent a kind of homey atmosphere to her selections, clearly visible through the net.

Retracing their steps back through town she counted five women trudging in the same direction, all laden with Mexican goods. She studied the boy's clothes. Those huaraches of his might pass muster, but then again . . . She bought him a pair of chintzy leather sandals and then sat down on a park bench to help him put them on. She took everything out of her net bag, scuffed the bag underfoot to soil it, and transferred her Day-Timer from her hand luggage to the soiled bag while refilling it. All her other things, the huaraches, too, went into her expensive bag, which she left under the park bench. It would be gone in five minutes, she knew.

"Ew, yuck, gross, girl shoes," Al snorted when he had the sandals on.

"No they aren't," T.C. lied. "They just don't look so much like you mugged a drunk for 'em. And if anybody asks, you love them. You hear me, kid? The only reason I bought them was, you threatened to throw a fit if I didn't, and then somewhere you lost your Nikes, and Auntie is pretty pissed about that. See, I'm your Aunt Teresa and I'm visiting from Arizona, and Gail Rosen, that's your mom, sent me shopping from Eagle Pass and you had to come along. Okay?" He looked down at the sandals again, with all the enthusiasm of a drenched pussycat. T.C. would not be deflected: "I said, okay?"

"Rosen? I don't get it."

"They're in the phone book and they run a deli, and now you know as much as I do. And the Rosens are just across the river, Al."

A gleam kindled in his eyes. "We're gonna crash the border right here, aren't we?"

"We're going to try to bluff it out. If we crash, Al honey, neither one of us is going to like it."

The bridge was in sight now, and Al's hand tightened on hers. "You want me to create an excursion?"

"Diversion," she corrected. "And no, thank you very much,

I've had about all of both that I need for a while." But it was clear that the kid was pumping himself up for this, not scared, just excited. She didn't want him pumped, but when you got a lemon, you made lemonade. Despite his swarthy coloring, Al's speech would tag him as born in the U.S.A. "Hey, what's the funniest thing that's happened to you recently?"

"Not much. Missed a lump of pig crap another kid fell in."

"No," she said patiently, "in school." They turned onto the approach to the bridge.

"Huh." Silence for a moment. Then, "Well, just before vacation there's this kid Hersch who was passing notes, and—"

"Don't tell me until we're, uh, until I ask you to. Then tell me. Tell me everything you can remember about it. Just ignore people, pretend the guys in uniform aren't there unless they stop us."

They were very near now. A middle-aged woman passed an armed, uniformed Mexican with a nod and smile to continue on her way. A young man in chinos and expensive shoes stopped on demand, showing his wallet, the mumbled exchange lost in traffic noises. Then he shuffled on, probably hung over.

T.C. slowed, wondering whether she should simply pass by. "Now," she said to Al.

"Now what," he said, fifty feet from the Mexican border guard.

"Hersch? Passing notes?" She didn't scream it, but she wanted to.

"Oh, yeah. Well, Hersch's this duh-h-h with a crush on Mara," he said, stoking his fires.

And now they were ten paces away, now five, and T.C. said, "You're not all gooshy about Mara, are you, Al?"

And while he was hotly denying it, they passed abreast of the guard, who glanced at her her bag, her legs, her face, the boy, and her legs again, with no objection to any of it, and murmured, *"Buenas días, señora,"* and she wished him a good morning in regular old Tucson English, and that was that. Never in her life had she been so glad that her parents, good modern Methodists, had brought her up to speak unaccented English.

It was on the U.S. side that she almost lost it, determined now to enter Texas without showing her ID. Something about the pair of them caused the tanned, pleasant-faced guard to look twice. He asked about fresh fruits. "Nope. Just what was on my shopping list," she said, with a smile that might have been too tentative.

"The boy yours, ma'am?"

"My sister's," she said.

"So Hersch wants me to pass his notes on," Al suddenly said, as if someone had pushed a button on him somewhere. "And Ms. Burford catches me and . . ." he went on.

"And who is your sister, ma'am?" Al, meanwhile, was droning on like an Energizer bunny.

"Gail. The Rosens, out on the loop road. Please shut up, Al."

"The folks with the deli?" Oh, yes, she had to pick a delicatessen, thought T.C., who nodded. "Kosher salami sandwiches," the guard continued. "The one on Main?"

Al wasn't shutting up, but thank God she had done her homework. "I think Garrison, but what do I know, I'm visiting from Tucson."

"So Ms. Burford says why don't I just read the note out loud," Al plowed on, resolute as a military parade.

"You should've driven over, all that stuff," the guard said, scanning the net bag.

"Not me, my insurance is no good in Mexico," she said.

"Menudo is, what, pork innards? And why would a family that buys kosher wholesale have to shop in Piedras Negras, ma'am?"

Oh shit, shitshitshit, the most unkosher meal in the solar system, she thought. She stared at him for two beats. "Why would folks who sell kosher in Eagle Pass want to buy their pork menudo across the river? I believe you've just answered your own question," she said evenly. "But if you won't tell, I won't tell."

The man threw back his head and roared, and when in desperation she fished her passport from her Day-Timer, he waved them through without looking at it. "Oh, by God, but that's rich," he was saying as T.C. passed through. "From now on I got the Rosens right where I want 'em."

"I didn't think my story was that funny," Al said as T.C. fought to keep from trotting into Eagle Pass.

"You were a scream," she assured him.

He shrugged. "Beats me."

"Now there's an idea," she muttered, and when he looked up to get his cue from her expression she winked, and then he could laugh too.

□   □   □

The first thing she did was call Seattle. The answering machine had a new message in a gruff male voice: "Due to a death in the family we can't come to the phone right now, but please leave a message. We would especially like to hear from Al, in person."

The Townsends, she figured, were probably in Puerto Vallarta. Well, now that Al was in the States, she didn't intend to worry about Mexican cops and robbers even if someone was listening in Seattle. "Mr. Townsend, this is Teresa Rainey in Eagle Pass, Texas. Al is, well, let him tell you himself," and she handed the phone to the boy.

"Hi, Grampa, it's me. Grampa?"

"It's their answering machine, Al," she explained belatedly.

"Ah, shoot. Hey, tell Mom we crashed the border again today, like when I was little, T.C. and me. It was neat, wait'll you hear how we got away from some bad guys. Is Mom okay now? I'll call again when—durn." He handed the receiver back. "That thing always beeps me off before I'm done."

"Maybe," she said, replacing the receiver in its cradle, "that's because you're never done."

She could have rented a car to San Antonio, but it was fewer than two hundred miles and T.C. had no assurance that she would ever be reimbursed for this quixotic adventure, an adventure that, she was certain, now lay behind them.

They took a Greyhound, switched to an airport shuttle in San Antonio's humid midafternoon, and sat in the air-conditioned terminal scarfing pizza when their flight was called around half-past four. T.C. had sighed heavily when she passed her Visa card over at the American Airlines ticket counter. This was one expense she would ask the Townsends to cover.

"You'll like Tucson," she told the boy as they moved along the corridor to the plane. "It's not as muggy as Texas."

"Cool."

"Not exactly, but—oh, right. And we'll get there a lot faster than we've been going," she joshed him.

"Whadjoo expect from a Boeing," he said archly.

They were passing a flight attendant, who smiled at Al. "Actually, it's a Super Eighty," she told him. "McDonnell-Douglas made it."

"Oh, boy," he gloomed, with a serious headshake in T. C's direction. "You sure it'll get us there?"

Behind them a matron asked, "What did he say?"

And now the attendant's smile froze in place. "Would you take a seat, please," she purred.

Al let himself be tugged along. "Just don't tell my grampa," he said. Boeing people, it seemed, were a clannish bunch.

They were only a few minutes late out of San Antonio and made it up in Dallas. By sundown they were unlocking her little white 1980 Datsun station wagon in the Tucson International parking lot, greeted by a furnacelike blast from inside.

"Ow, ow," said Al, shifting on the hot seat. "Smells like our gym in here."

"I should've taken those damn sweatpants out of the back," T.C. apologized. "But hey, when you're a jock, you smell like a jock."

"Huh. Try telling that to my mom."

She drove to the Nogales Highway intersection, newly subdued by little Al's reminder: He still did not know about his mother. Should she tell him? She felt guilty with her knowledge, but it would help no one to tell him now. When he did find out, wouldn't it be best if he had a family support system in place?

What would I want for Littlebo? she asked herself. *I'd want family close by when he was told, is what.* Mollified, she turned on Twenty-second and told Al about the permanent rodeo grounds nearby.

"Real cowboys?"

"Uh-huh. Sometimes called vaqueros around here. And sometimes they practice getting stove up, so maybe, if we have time, we could watch.'' She also advised him to watch for the old Spanish influence in south Tucson. ''When you get back to Seattle you won't see much of the mission-style homes.''

''You mean like the missions for those homeless guys on the wharf in Seattle?''

She explained that it was just the opposite. ''Guy named Lovegrove turned the barrio into a rainbow some years ago, and this you've got to see, Al. There are those who haven't forgiven him yet, but I think it's cool. I bet they don't have anything like it in Seattle.''

Having given in to her ethnic pride, she detoured past stucco homes vibrant with extraordinary hues of peach, blue, and pink. Some of south Tucson's rambling, tile-roofed homes hinted at the land grant days, and the owners were anything but poor.

He gazed at a whitewashed place, carefully fenced and thick of wall, that they were passing. It would fetch two million if the owners ever felt an irrational desire to sell. ''Jeez. You live in one of these?''

''Oh, no, Al, I'm not from one of the quote, good, unquote families here. In fact, I'm originally from California. We're coming to my part of south Tucson. The old town had its rich and its poor. Guess which part a schoolteacher lives in.''

''*Pobrecito,*'' he said. It tickled her so much she didn't correct him.

Her apartment was part of a fourplex, once a fine old home of a single story, its courtyard now a bit seedy. T.C. locked the Datsun and took her bag of Mexican goods along, using a key to get them past the wrought-iron gate. Al looked around him with a curiosity no longer aloof. He had seen a lot worse poverty than this in the past few days.

She unlocked the front door and ushered the boy inside, snapping on the living room light, setting the air conditioner immediately to flush some of the mustiness from her two-bedroom place.

''Where's the phone?''

"On my desk in the dining alcove—but wait," she added abruptly. She knew he'd want to call Seattle, and the last thing she wanted was for him to learn about his mother's fate from a heartless answering machine. "The house rules are that I'll make the call. But before that, we use the bathroom, and I've got dibs on it first."

As she waited outside the bathroom hearing the last tinny notes of his tinkle, she thought again about old Señor Gilberto's warning. If anyone was monitoring the Townsend phone, they'd heard her say she'd been in Texas earlier in the day. She would have to warn Al against saying where they were now, just in case. She and Al would sit tight in Tucson and wait until she could speak directly to the Townsends. If her call were traced to her apartment—well, a law-abiding citizen could raise hell over things like that.

It could take days before she got in direct contact with the Townsends. In the meantime, perhaps she should mull over the idea of a call to inform the FBI of her suspicions. She breathed a sigh of relief, confident that here in the States, she could trust her government.

CHAPTER □ 6

Some hours earlier, while hurrying by shuttle toward the air terminal, T.C. and Al had wondered aloud about an imposing structure in the heart of San Antonio. It was, said the man across the aisle, the Tower of the Americas. Virtually at the foot of that tower on East Durango Boulevard sits a small array of San Antonio's federal buildings, and in many of the rooms the lights frequently burn late.

Now, in one of the rooms often unoccupied because the U.S. government is generous with office space for friendly governments, the lights were on. It was large enough that the voices of four men echoed as they sat at the desks they had pushed together. Their vending machine coffee was cold by now, employed only to hold down corners of a map that was partly obscured by telephones, laptops, and notepads. Two other desks were covered with their traveling bags, two-suiters and soft-sided sports bags the size and shape of conga drums.

Some of that luggage held business suits and toilet articles. And some of it would have blown the circuits of air terminal baggage sensors. Their early-model Learjet permitted them more than express transport; its diplomatic status let them travel without the restrictions of commercial air travel. Arrangements of this sort, even after the Cold War thaw, remained far more common than the working public was allowed to suspect.

The tallest of the four men, a rangy, narrow-hipped fellow who smoked unfiltered Camels in rooms too stifling for a cigar, operated under the name of Thomas Perrin. He put down the phone he had answered, ran a hand over his blond crewcut, and made his smile broader than necessary. "That was Tucson on the scrambler and, gentlemen, we're in business."

Anatol Kerman, the first man to react, had arrived in the western hemisphere only that morning. A graceful, handsome specimen of medium height, alert as a terrier, Kerman spoke very serviceable English and was known to be acting for the Man. For the duration of this operation, Perrin would use the expression the Man, as he usually did. His little group of facilitators, handpicked by Perrin, had worked with him before. They did not need to hear the name Ravan Zagro, so Perrin did not say it.

In their own minds these men were not mercenaries, though the pay was outstanding. Among their shared conceits was the notion that their work somehow transcended petty national disputes. Tom Perrin did not expect ever to meet the Man in person, unless Perrin found himself in Turkey. He didn't mind; Zagro had earned a reputation, the kind of reputation that made you nice to his emissaries. Perrin had not seen Kerman smile until now as the Kurd said, "You have the boy?"

"We have him spotted," Perrin replied and made a production of reaching out a strong forefinger. He placed it on the map at Tucson. "Goddamn if they didn't make it, all the way to the Rainey woman's place this evening." The others had been briefed on Teresa Contreras Rainey. He fell silent, staring out at the lights of San Antonio. Then, "I wonder if she did it all with cash. We'll probably know tomorrow."

Kerman kept his hands under control, but one knee bobbed with nervous energy. He said, "You had him spotted in Puerto Vallarta, Mr. Perrin, and the results were not pleasing to my cousin. How soon shall we fly to Tucson?"

"Let's not fire up the Lear just yet," said a sandy-haired man, Dexter McLeod, whose faint accent had once been clearly Scot and who had two major assets in Perrin's book. For a man of modest size McLeod had great physical strength, and his obedience to Tom Perrin was beyond question. "Now that we're in the States, Mr. Kerman, we must be a wee bit more careful."

" 'Specially with witnesses to the P.V. thing," said the fourth man, the only one whose hair was graying. Cody Beale had once set sail for a career with the Federal Bureau of Investigation, only to founder on the shoals of law school. An ex-cop now, Beale was large and blocky with a ruddy complexion, and he had an absolute genius for shmoozing with police.

"You have said that the Townsends will fly back tomorrow," Kerman said, "with the body. Surely that will mean more complication if the boy is returned to them. They will be on guard."

Perrin's temporary assets, in addition to the Tucson fellow, included a man in Puerto Vallarta and another in the Seattle area, monitoring telephone taps on the elder Townsends. An outgrowth of industrial espionage, this sort of civilian spying was becoming as pervasive as the common cold. "We'll operate on that assumption," said Perrin. "So we've got to separate the Rainey woman from, uh, Al—"

"Talal," said Kerman. "He is Kurdish."

"Right. Separate them before the Townsends show."

Beale put in, "And without any more rough stuff, which we gather is why you're over here." His inflection said, *How can you have it both ways?*

Kerman sighed and made a sleight-of-hand gesture. "I was sent because my cousin received word of the first attempt."

"I didn't try to shade my report," Perrin shrugged, the half lie coming easily. "We screwed up; *I* screwed up. Cost me a sore elbow and a bonus to a Mex plainclothes cop who played too rough," he added ruefully, rubbing the elbow as if to reassure himself about it. Half to himself, and not without a certain good humor, he murmured, "Who'd believe this effing little Latin porpoise could pop up and catch us flat-footed like that? I thought for a minute we'd been set up. Took me two days to realize it was sheer coincidence. 'Cause coincidence is magic," he said, with a wink toward McLeod.

"And we don't believe in magic," McLeod duly replied, a familiar response to an old dictum.

"Please understand," said Kerman, "that I am concerned only with the safety of the child, Talal. Somewhat less with his extended family." Now his voice dropped virtually to a croon, "And not in the slightest with any other creature. Such is my mission. I was given no alternative. I must return with the child unharmed." Kerman's smile was that of an athletic Buddha.

"Well, hell," said Beale, "if that's all, why don't we just go and get him?"

Perrin gazed thoughtfully at the map. "We will. But Dex is right, we don't want to risk a run-in with the Tucson police, and the only asset we've got in place is a temp, the private cop surveilling the woman's apartment. I'm calling him off as soon as we get located. And don't even suggest it," he said, with a cold grin toward Beale. "If we had a few days, we might develop somebody on the local force, like in Puerto Vallarta. You've already said you don't know anybody local in Tucson we could use NQA." No Questions Asked, their lingo for the kind of lawman who would moonlight as a temporary employee for the right price; in blunter terms, a mercenary of the moment.

The big shoulders lifted and fell. Beale's connections were far-flung, but not in Tucson.

Kerman: "I am not naive in these matters. A single federal agent could simplify—"

"We're about as close as you're going to get to the feds, Mr. Kerman," said the big blond, "that is, if we're smart." His wry grin flicked on and off again. "I see it's necessary to clarify something while we're all together, but just a moment." Perrin picked up a phone, dialed a long series of digits, went through two password rigmaroles. Then he said simply, "Kerman party, priority bravo, immediate flight into Tucson, accommodations for four. . . . Then wake him, we want to be there ten minutes ago." He listened for a moment, then said, "That's confirmed," and replaced the receiver.

What he had to say now was not for his assets, who knew exactly how things stood. It was to remind Kerman where *he* stood. Perrin's view of this antsy little Kurd was simple: a pain in the ass that Perrin had brought on himself by that one-in-a-million screwup in Mexico, and a pain that his superiors said must now be endured, cheerfully if possible, forcefully if necessary.

Perrin looked at each man in turn, then at his wrist. "We can be wheels up in an hour, and I don't want any doubt about who's running the operation. Mr. Kerman, you are an active observer, not in the chain of command. Theoretically, if I suggest some action from you, you're free to refuse it, but you won't give orders. And with due respect, I'm not trying to insult you when I say you aren't a head of state, and this isn't a priority alpha."

"I understand," said Kerman, who now glanced at his own elaborate timepiece. "But this woman, it seems to me, would be far more, ah, tractable? Tractable," he repeated, "facing some agent of government."

"Our organization isn't a government in the accepted sense, as you must know," Perrin reminded him bluntly. "Much as it would like to be. We can request information through channels, much as Interpol and the World Health people can do, and you can be damned glad because without it we still wouldn't even know those prints belonged to a fucking Tucson grammar-school twat, let alone have a dossier workup on her. But on a priority bravo, we don't have direct access to federal agents."

"So fuhgettaboutit," Beale put in, marking him as midwestern.

"That'll do, Cody." Kerman had made no overt gesture toward the big man, but Tom Perrin had seen his pupils contract. Perrin stood up. The others did as well, stuffing their equipment into big sports bags atop clothing. "Besides, Mr. Kerman has a valid point. We don't need our Ms. Rainey to see me again; we need her to see what she *wants* to see: the mighty umbrella of her federal government unfolding over her and the boy."

McLeod chuckled. When Perrin cranked up his bullshit generator, his sarcasm could be almost British.

"I suppose I shall understand that one day," Kerman said tightly.

Perrin knew better than to throw a friendly arm over the Kurd's shoulder. A warm grin worked much better, so he used it. "I'm saying we should do it your way."

"Without federal agents?"

"Yes and no." Perrin opened the office door with a final glance around. "And since we don't have one, we'll simply have to create one." He nodded toward Cody Beale.

CHAPTER 7

Alight sleeper since childhood, T.C. came fully awake with the first ring of her bedside phone. Before the second ring, she grabbed the receiver, hoping that her small charge in the spare bedroom would not be wakened. After four rings her answering machine would have assumed command. And by that time Al would have been swinging from the drapes near his half-open window, especially if he heard that stupid answering message she'd thought up.

It had taken her two series of anonymous obscene calls to accustom herself to giving away nothing in her response. "Yes," she said, with a glance at the glowing numerals near the phone. She might reasonably have said, "Who the hell thinks it's civilized to be calling me at four-thirty in the morning?"

As clearly as if he were in the next room: "Oh, Lord, T.C., I thought you were in Mexico." The voice of Ross Downing sounded genuinely contrite.

"Yeah?" She propped herself up, closing her eyes, a faint smile now exercising her cheeks as she warmed to the familiar soft growl of his baritone. Of the few men who might call her, Ross was the only one who could rob her of irritation regardless of the hour, although—or because?—theirs had never become a sexual relationship. "Then why—no. You guess what I was about to say."

This was a game T.C. enjoyed more than Ross did. She never

tired of the way his mind worked, almost like ESP. His reply was a plaintive, "Do I have to?"

"Hey, Crispy, you called me," she chuckled. That nickname had been his own idea. She thought it was awful.

"Mmm, okay, why did I call if I thought you weren't there, and the answer is, I knew you were."

A cold pang pierced her, for reasons she could not identify. But they were safe in the States again, and she relaxed. "Now, that is downright spooky, 'mano." Her nickname for him this time, short for *hermano,* brother.

"Now don't go mystical on me, T.C. I meant that I expected to get your voice on the machine."

"Ah. And what were you gonna tell it that couldn't wait for a sane hour? Wait, I'm getting a vibe. It's because the call is cheap now," she guessed.

"True," he said, a little too quickly. "You must be wearing a pyramid on your head." Ever the rationalist, he would make fun of her interest in the inexplicable.

And suddenly she knew, intuition and awful memory combining. Instead of blurting out her conclusion, she kept it light. "So go on, pretend it's my machine."

"Right. Well, Ms. Mean Machine, I couldn't sleep, and my rehab team could get testy if I wake someone up just to ask her if she's an insomniac too. But I happen to know this answering machine in Tucson that's got to be feeling pretty lonesome, despite how she makes fierce faces at me over the phone, and I thought I'd just call and say 'howdy,' or maybe just listen to the message. I don't really have anything to say."

"Yeah you do," she replied and waited. And waited. "You've had another autograft," she said at last.

"Allograft, but that's picking nits. Indeed I have." After she'd visited him several times, she had become familiar with some of the jargon. A skin graft shaved from an untraumatized part of your own body and spread over a burn area was a self-graft, an autograft. An allograft was from some other person. A xenograft was the third kind, usually pigskin, and it didn't last as long. "I give you an A-minus on it, teacher. Number seventeen; if anybody tells you that's a prime number, you can redefine prime as not one of the better cuts." He paused. "Prime cut? Skin graft? Oh, well." He fell silent.

"I got it, Ross. Maybe your funnybone's just more warped than mine."

"Maybe I just wanted to wise off to a machine that wasn't going to talk back."

"No wonder," she said, hoping it didn't sound like pity, though, of course, it had to be.

"No wonder what?" he said, and she realized he didn't want so much to talk as he wanted to listen. She owed him that, and a lot more. It wasn't Ross's fault his sacrifice had been for nothing.

She tried to oblige. "No wonder you called. Don't give me that shit about not being able to sleep. That's what medicines are for. You can sleep, all right, but you'd rather be awake than dreaming." This time it wasn't a guess.

The sigh from his end was profound. "A lot rather. Sometimes it's not too bad, more like opening a mystery in the middle and living three pages of it. Interesting."

"But this wasn't one of those times," she prompted.

He laughed, his little falsetto bark that always reminded her of the aging, macho movie actor that, in fact, Ross's old photos resembled a bit. "You nailed it," he said. "Just one very bad page. Makes no sense now, but when you're in it, boy, does it ever have credibility."

"You wanta talk about it?"

"Not a lot. All I really wanted was a good laugh. That machine of yours will usually do it." Now he imitated her, a low-pitched growl she had practiced for her taped message: "We're feeding the attack dogs and cleaning the Uzi, but you *will* leave a message if you know what's good for you." Then he added, "How was that?"

"Verbatim," she admitted. "By the way, what's so special about that Uzi thing?"

"You don't know? Wonderful. A little assault rifle, they say. I gather a guy named Uzi Galil invented it. I expect any Israeli would know more about it than I do."

"I could've used one in P.V.," she said abruptly. "Tell you about it sometime. Right now I'm going back to sleep."

"I have this image," he said dreamily, "of your machine snarling that rough stuff in your room with a four-poster and chintz, all in pink with a regiment of teddy bears piled over everything."

He had never seen her place, probably never would, though he had a standing invitation. It touched her to think he imagined her bedroom as a little girl's. "Well, you missed it a mile. And I thought you were psychic," T.C. chided. *Sometimes I really do think so,* she added silently.

"Lose a few, lose a few," he misquoted. "Almost light here, so I'll be getting up."

"You're at the Ferguson place," she said, realizing he probably wasn't at one of the clinics.

"The cabin," he corrected. "Nice and quiet up here. Ruidoso lives up to its name in the summertime."

The bungalow of Ross's crusty old friend, Orville Ferguson, lay on the outskirts of Ruidoso, New Mexico. It was a resort town bisected by a trout stream whose burble and plash had given rise to the name Ruidoso. She said good-bye to Ross Downing and snuggled under her single summer sheet, knowing full well what he hadn't wanted to say. She had visited Ruidoso, and it wasn't a noisy town, even with the stream. But the bungalow was near other houses, and sleeping on the couch at his cabin she had heard Ross Downing wake himself from some of those dreams of his. She knew why Ross seldom stayed in town. Anybody hearing him in the throes of a nightmare would have to think seriously about calling police—and about wearing earplugs. It had driven her from the cabin so that, on subsequent visits, she slept at the bungalow miles from her friend.

□   □   □

Al woke her two hours later. Puttering around the kitchenette in sweatsuit and athletic socks, she found that the milk in her refrigerator had gone sour. She defrosted orange juice and stirred margarine into bowls of hot cereal, which Al scarfed up only when she added honey, before she tried another call to Seattle. Again she made the call, heard the same message, and suggested the Townsends call her at the number she gave. Then she told Al, "Say something. Anything but 'help!,' " she joked.

He talked fast this time: He and T.C. wanted Mom to call right away, and mush wasn't so bad if you put honey in it. Then he handed her the receiver. "Roadrunner beeped me again," he said with seven-year-old cynicism. Then, with that bewildering change of pace her students had prepared her for, "We gonna shop for my machete?"

"I don't think the local supermarket carries 'em, but we'll look while we're getting some things. Milk, for one. Flavored yogurt if you like it."

"Some more of that sugar candy?"

She knew he had ferreted out all the cones of brown sugar she'd bought in Piedras Negras. "And rot your teeth? Your gramma would skin me."

"Mom won't let her," he said with confidence as she tied the laces of her Nikes, relishing their comfort. *Poor little guy, let him be cheerful as long as he can.* Very soon, the boy would be swept back to grief in Seattle, and her brief stint as surrogate mother would be ended. She decided to help him enjoy his innocence as well as she could as she zipped her essentials into the little Velcro wallet that wrapped around her ankle beneath the elastic of her sweatpants and did not interfere with her jogging.

As they walked through the courtyard, the early summer day was shaping up as usual: low humidity under a hard blue sky, already warming at eight o'clock in the morning. She adjusted one of her old baseball caps for Al and wore the gray Stetson Beau had bought her when they were dating. It was only a few blocks to the market, so she was only half crazy, running in her sweats in Tucson's June. "Al, you up to a little run?"

"In these?" He still wore those sandals, and he still didn't like them. They weren't exactly running shoes, she admitted to herself.

"Okay, but I need to work out a little, so we won't take the car. You just walk along and I'll run circles around you."

After a block of this he grew embarrassed that a girl, especially a girl old enough to be his mother, was jogging around him while he walked. He pulled off the sandals, thrust them into his hip pockets, and set off barefoot after her. She wasn't prepared for that. Even in Seattle, it seemed, kids developed horn on the soles of their feet by June. And Al's wind was as good as hers. She judged that he had the makings of a good little soccer forward.

The school where she taught wasn't really on the way, but she detoured to show it off. No showcase, it was already collecting graffiti of the sixth-grade variety after a recent sandblasting. The playground had a jungle gym and the kind of obstacle course she termed a "break-your-neck" arrangement, and she found that Al could cross the horizontal ladder hand over hand better than she could.

Puffing, grinning, they leaned against the bars of the jungle gym and were glad they wore hats. Then, squinting toward the perimeter cyclone fence, "Damn, they still haven't fixed the hookey gate," she mused.

"What kinda gate?"

"Boy, have you been deprived," she kidded and explained as they strolled to the high fencing that bordered an alley. "It's not really a gate. Some delinquent bent the bottom out." She pointed to a place where a big dog or a determined child might squirm beneath. "If you're seen going under the hookey gate you get a note to your folks. Well," she went on, readjusting her Stetson, "right down the alley a few blocks is the store. Bet I beatcha," she said and led him off, setting a hot pace toward the end of the fencing fifty yards distant.

She didn't look back until she failed to hear him pounding along, and after she glanced back she was laughing too hard to sprint. Al had spun around, squirted through the hookey gate, and now stood in the alley, leaning one hand on the fence with perfect nonchalance.

"I'll get you for this, Calvin," she shouted, but now he was off ahead of her, his high-pitched laughter a goad and a soaring uplift for T.C. She didn't catch him for two blocks, and they walked, hand in hand, the rest of the way. She had to stop giggling because in some mysterious way it threatened to become tears. She had always rejected the idea of trying to adopt, or to get herself pregnant again, without a husband. Yet during the past few days, the notion had flickered past her awareness several times like a rotating beacon, illuminating her loneliness for an instant, flashing away again.

They bought more groceries than she intended, naturally, and at the video store on the same block he talked her out of the three quarters in her ankle wallet to play a gory video game called Single Combat. Each of them carried a big sack to her apartment, sweating, swapping riddles, discussing the things they might do in Tucson. It was a real downer, he said darkly, that she had no joystick on her computer for video games, and she agreed though secretly pleased. No kid of hers was going to grow pale indoors in summery Tucson.

Approaching the courtyard she noticed the unmarked blue Chevy panel van parked directly behind her little Datsun, decided against putting a note under the wiper. The impolite nitwit was probably delivering something. She did not notice the gray Ford sedan parked on the street, engine running. In a region where car interiors became broilers, engines were sometimes left running to serve air conditioners until their radiators boiled.

In the courtyard, two men in business suits sat bareheaded on the lawn furniture, in the inadequate shade of a pepper tree. The two stood up as T.C. fitted her key into her door.

"Morning, ma'am," the larger one called. She nodded politely, let Al in, and shut the door. Perhaps they were visiting another tenant. It did not yet occur to her that one apartment was vacant and the other two tenants had day jobs.

She was emptying sacks in the kitchenette when the knock came, discreet hard little raps from big knuckles. Al had already turned the TV on and would have responded but, "I'll get it," she said, and did.

It was the pair in sober suits and ties, a mismatch, one a compact sort with curly reddish hair, the other very large and graying, with "cop" written all over him. As the big man stood waiting to be asked in, he showed her a wallet with an expensive shield, not just flashing it but with practiced ease. She thought the shield might have said "deputy chief" but later could not be sure. He thrust it back inside his jacket and gave her a big smile. "Agent Fox with INS, ma'am, and this is Agent Rankin. And you'd be Mrs. Teresa Rainey?"

"INS?" She felt successive waves of fear and elation and realized that she was being a lousy host, and anyway she'd offered her perfectly valid passport to that border guard who hadn't even looked at it. "Come in. You'll get sunstroke out there without a hat."

"Immigration and Naturalization," he explained, stepping through, the silent Rankin following with a nod.

"Oh, I know what it is; everybody in the barrio knows," she smiled. "But I don't even know any illegals, let alone hire them. Please, have a seat. Orange juice? Or I could make coffee."

A negative headshake, the smile determinedly in place as Fox glanced at the boy watching television. "That's not on our docket, Mrs. Rainey. Time is limited, so I'll get right to it. I guess you knew you'd been followed through Mexico." When her face changed, he put up a slab of a hand, waved it side to side. "Well, not your fault, but you were. What the subject didn't know was, he was followed, too. Now we need you to ID the subject from his mug shots, maybe pick him out of a lineup later. This fella's looking at some pretty serious charges."

"But how did you know—never mind," she sighed. "If you had contacted me down there, my life would've been a lot simpler."

"We couldn't, but I'm not at liberty to explain that, ma'am."

Well, that was the kind of stonewalling you expected from cops, she thought. "I'm not certain I'd recognize a man I didn't know was following me," she explained with a shrug.

"Would you recognize the one who killed the woman," Fox began, then halted at T.C.'s furious grimace and the side-to-side jitter of her headshake. Her mouth miming "no," she darted her eyes toward Al across the room, then back to the big agent. "Uh, hurt the woman, I mean. You know what I mean."

"I think so. Big blond guy, as tall as you? I saw him a second time at the hospital."

"I'll be damned," blurted the sandy-haired agent who had seemed to be watching the TV, or perhaps just watching Al watch it.

"Same man," said Fox. "He gets around, we'll give him that."

T.C. felt the shiver come, rubbed her arms through the sleeves of her sweatsuit. "My God, I don't see how he could do that—follow us, I mean."

"We think he lost you for a while. Picked you up again in Guanajuato, and he nearly had you in Mexico City."

"But we didn't"—she froze and picked up her cadence with—"know he was even on the train." And now the goose flesh grew into armies that marched down her spine like migrating tarantulas.

"Well, he was, and so were we, so you weren't really in danger. We wouldn't let that happen." He smiled, the very picture of a man she should depend on. "You needn't worry about it now. We just need you to come downtown, look at some pictures."

Guanajuato, huh? And a train ride, and both of those details were lies he'd bought into. So the rancher's wife, Ana Flores, had made that call she'd promised. And the Townsends' phone was tapped, all right. And Ana's little misdirection scam had worked better than she could possibly imagine.

"Sure, I'll be glad to, Mr. Fox. Just tell me where, and I'll be down today. Right after lunch, in fact." Like hell. She'd be on her way to somewhere else. Seattle, maybe.

"I'm sorry, ma'am. We need immediate identification. I hope you'll understand; we can take you there and bring you right back."

"But the boy," she began.

"Bring him along," Fox gestured expansively. "Or, well, it's not standard procedure, but Rankin here could baby-sit the kid for an hour. We'd have you back right away, before lunch." His words had turned cozening, seductive. "We have a lot of flexibility in cases like this."

I just bet you do, hijo de puta, T.C. thought, now virtually certain this big lump wasn't INS. But if she asked for another look at his ID, things could get sticky in a hurry. With a thunderclap revelation she realized she didn't give a good goddamn if he *was* a real official of this or any other government, he wasn't getting his big paws on Al Townsend while she was in the picture. But he didn't intend to wait, that was obvious. And did she want her apartment trashed while she fought and screamed and kicked and bit and maybe got stuffed into her own closet?

She built him the kind of smile she used for guys preparing to write her tickets. "Well, when you put it like that, sure, why not?"

She stood, hoping her knees wouldn't give way, then said, "Oh, let me give the boy his medicine before we go. Believe me, we don't want him to miss a dose. It'll just take a minute. Could be serious otherwise," she added and turned toward Al, who was no longer watching the tube but regarding her with granite calm, his eyes gleaming. "Al, did I leave that stuff in the bathroom?"

"I dunno," he said, not committing himself, and stood up. "Whatever you say, Hobbes."

Her laugh was a tension breaker but unfeigned, the two men smiling through their uncertainty, and she wondered if the kid had any earthly idea what was about to go down.

Because the structure had once been a sprawling home, her bathroom was an add-on, its one small window over her tub facing the alley. She closed the door, knowing that big bozo could see her do it, because she didn't want to alert him by shutting the door to her bedroom. She turned on the water in the sink, stood in the bathtub, and opened the window intending to boost Al out. "Those are bad guys," she whispered fiercely, and he responded with a brisk nod. She kissed his forehead. "Get out of here."

But when Al's head and shoulders were outside, he suddenly wriggled back. "The guy that hit Mom is in the alley," he said, his expression no longer optimistic. "Him and another guy. Dunno if he saw me." And there went the last possibility that Mr. Fox was somehow genuine.

"Take it all, Al," she said louder than necessary. "I know it tastes bad." Softly to the boy, "Push the lock button." While he reached for the doorknob she stepped down on the floor and dropped to her knees, reaching into the false cabinet beneath her sink, which held only plumbing and a spare roll of toilet paper.

Beau had tried to unclog the drain once and she knew the gypsum wallboard hid a narrow passage for plumbing and conduits, the kind of renovation that was cheap though it robbed interior room from a once spacious home. An adult would get stuck in there, but it ran the length of the structure at a right angle to the alley. Beau had said the passage ended at a little door near the external apartment meters, and she had taken his word for it. Enough light came from somewhere down the passage to reveal pipes.

The wallboard split with a dull, drumlike sound when she slugged it, coming out in three pieces, and she waved the boy toward the cabinet.

From just outside the door, one booming rap. "No more games, lady," said the man who called himself Fox. "We know about the alley window," and she suspected he must have some kind of communication with others outside.

She was squatting. "Go as fast as you can," she said to Al as he started into the hole.

"Go where," he begged.

"Anywhere!" Her mind whirled, then steadied. Yes, almost anywhere was better than in the hands of these people. Her morning foray for groceries gave her a focus. More loudly than she intended, she said, "Go to the Single Combat place. If I don't show up, go to the police."

"I think they're going out a window," said the big man, whether to his companion or a radio, she couldn't tell.

"There's spiders," he quavered, looking back, his voice very soft. The bathroom doorknob rattled. Hard.

Jesucristo, probably black widows at that, she thought, wondering how such places were swept. She grabbed a big hand towel, thrust it to him. "Here, use this," she said, with a light slap on his rump.

The bathroom resounded with the splintering crash of a foot against the door. T.C. drew a breath and screamed as hard as she could, a real falling-off-a-cliff earsplitter.

"Go ahead, yell your fuckin' head off. Nobody else is home," said Fox, almost jovial. Oh, yes, they would've checked.

Al's feet disappeared. She could hear the faint swish of his jeans as he moved. She crammed the broken wallboard into the cabinet and closed its door quietly, using the floor mat to cover a few telltale fragments.

Another crash against the door, with attendant splintering noises, and as she scanned her shallow medicine cabinet she wondered how a cheap little door had survived two such savage assaults.

She took the other towel from the rack, emptying her pint of rubbing alcohol into the balled half of it, and screamed again.

Between the explosive sounds they were making, she could hear diminishing noises of Al's progress, and to cover it she began to scream nonstop.

With both of the men attacking her door now, the central door panel began to cave in. She stood in the bathtub and, when the big man's face appeared red and slit-eyed, she shouted out the window.

"Run, honey, run! That's right . . . ." Maybe they'd think he had dropped into the alley.

And then the door failed completely, and as the smaller man fought through its failed panel she towel-whipped him, the alcohol-drenched terry cloth catching him across the neck and face once, twice, before he could get a hand up to ward her off, but now as the little one yelled with eyes closed as he wiped furiously at his face the big man bulled his way in too, and she had her little throwaway Bic shaver in the other hand, flailing away at them both, screaming, slicing with the razor, kicking the smaller man who was down on one knee in the wreckage of the door, letting go of the towel when Fox grabbed it, going for his face with the razor and her sensibly trimmed nails, and as he cursed and tried to backhand her, she ducked under it and then she saw little Rankin's fist shoot up to meet her.

Not even a sensation of pain, or of falling. Blank.

CHAPTER □ 8

"Few hours at best before the shit hits the fan," were the first words T.C. made out. "We can bring some pressure on the local force, but if the Townsends are quick enough, our clout may not be enough." Then, like an idiot, she turned her head and saw that she lay on her side in deep shadow on the floor of a vehicle that had no side windows and did not seem to be moving. The same glance proved that the speaker was that same son of a whore who'd smashed Gail Townsend's head in. Sitting beside him on the bench seat of a van was a smaller man she'd never seen before, handsome and Latin looking. She quickly shut her eyes.

Then, "Tape," said the blond, and an instant later a ripping sound, and then he tore a piece of tape from her temple, taking some hair with it, and more of the sticky stuff went across her eyes and, because her luxuriant, shoulder-length hair came to her temples, he wound it completely around her head. Only then did she realize that she couldn't speak either because they'd already taped her mouth, and her hands and feet were secured, probably with the same stuff. She could flex her body and breathe. Period. Her face rubbed against some rough fabric like heavy canvas.

"I assume that is necessary," from the seat. Accented but not Latino.

"She saw you. Saw me too, but she could already identify me.

She's playing possum, Mr. K.'' A light kick against her shin, and she jerked. "Aren't you, Teresa?''

Why even try to tell him to go diddle a duck when her mouth was taped? She hurt in lots of places, especially at her jaw hinges—and now her shin, with a pain that grew worse until it throbbed.

The blond raised his voice over the strident drone of a passing engine, from its sound, a small aircraft. She wondered if an Arizona Highway Patrol plane was circling, as Mr. Blond demanded, "Who taped the eyes?''

A familiar basso from behind her, near the front seat: "I did. Mouth, wrists, ankles. The usual. Shoulda taped her nose, too, before I got her into the duffel bag. One of these cuts the little heller gave me is still bleeding." It was the voice of the man who had called himself Fox when he flashed that badge.

"You dipshit, the tape over her eyes came loose, and I'm afraid little Ms. Rainey got a good look just now.''

"That changes things," from a fourth voice, also familiar. Hankins? No, the name had been Rankin.

"We'll talk about that later, since she's listening. Aren't you, Teresa?'' Another kick on the other shin. Pain that glowed and spread like an ember in straw. If not for those sweatpants, it would have been worse.

She managed to nod her head as another plane went over, this time a jet, very near. She wondered where they were, and where Al Townsend was. And she wondered most of all when the agony in her shins would begin to taper off.

"Pity to bruise swimmer's legs like those, but we do what we must," said the blond with good cheer. Abruptly, salsa music flooded the van, and someone was kneeling very near her face, and something cruel was biting into her throat. Mr. Blond, very softly: "If anyone gets interested in us, he dies, Teresa, but first you do. You'll just bleed out without a sound. Any doubts in your mind about that?''

She shook her head carefully, not wanting to get her throat cut by accident. Somewhere outside, the laughter of two young men as they passed and, ". . . shoot a few landings before lunch with everything blue and cavu," fading away before the pressure was removed from her throat. Before lunch? Then she hadn't been out more than an hour. And now she had an idea where they might be: in the vicinity of Tucson International south of town, maybe behind a hangar, or inside one. But the bastards had thought they were vulnerable when those men walked past.

The salsa music winked from existence. The slight vibration she felt had to be the van's engine, running to keep the air conditioner on. Movements beside her suggested that Mr. Blond was settling himself beside her, getting nice and comfy. "Teresa," he said, "we know all about you, and about the boy, Talal. We know how he got out of that damned bathroom, and I can vouch that he's a pretty decent little broken-field runner." His chuckle suggested a harmless joke on himself. "And we heard you tell him about single combat. There's been too much combat already, wouldn't you agree? We're really his friends, but he doesn't know it. Nothing bad will happen to him, so you don't have to worry about that either. Now, we'll find him, that's an absolute. Make no mistake."

T.C.'s spirit climbed on a thermal current of hope, rising above her pain. *Who're you trying to convince, asshole? My kid's three touchdowns up on you.* But she nodded and hummed, "Mm-hmm."

"And we know you sent him off somewhere, but we don't know where. You're going to tell us. You may not know it yet, but you are. Because if you don't, you're going to get a lot of this."

And he held her by the hair with one hand, pressing her nostrils closed with the other. For a moment she just accepted it, waiting for whatever pain he would inflict. But then she couldn't exhale, her ears popping with the effort, couldn't inhale, either, which was worse, but now he was astride her legs, and he must have known the panic that would overtake her, something worse than mere pain, a sense of catastrophic doom not in moments but *now,* this instant. For the next moments nothing existed for her but her hopeless struggle in the wild imperative to breathe. A darkness began to descend in her mind, her thrashing less vigorous.

Then she was free to breathe, pulling precious air in through her nose, breast rising and falling fast. "And that was only a taste," the man said, cool, dispassionate. "You may think you can get used to it, but you can't. People just aren't made that way, Teresa. And if you don't give us what we want we can keep this up until your heart bursts. And we will."

And he pinched her nostrils again.

This time she passed out, but not before she knew a terrible weakness throughout her body, a starvation of her tissues that was more frightening than any localized pain.

He was shaking her as she came to, and he had peeled the tape partly away from her mouth. "Try to scream and I'll put you under really bad, this time," he warned as she inhaled great gasps, her eyes still taped. "Sometimes it causes brain cells to die." But she could feel that tape slipping upward like a tight hatband near the back of her head. "In fact, I'm going to do it again anyway. Unless you tell me, right now, where you sent that boy."

She kept gasping, chiefly just because he was permitting it, and every second of breathing was a godsend. But she realized they were time-limited, and they didn't like being around other people, and whatever they didn't want was something she should provoke.

"Please, not again," she sobbed.

"What did you mean about single combat?"

Virtually babbling: "It's a game. He plays it."

"At the schoolyard," he guessed quickly.

How did he know about the schoolyard? Easy to agree, but there hadn't been many people there, only a couple of children on the swings. She knew a better lie. "No, a video game."

"So where does he play it?"

"He saw it before. Wanted to play it. I promised—if he would run with me this morning—I'd let him."

The cruel fingers slid to her nostrils again. "You're stalling for time, Teresa." And he pinched her nostrils again but released them as quickly, almost playfully. "That's a no-no. Where is the game he plays?"

She paused as long as she dared. "Greyhound," she said, moaning it.

"Oh, shit," said the big man from in front.

Blond: "The Greyhound station? Where's that?"

"Downtown." As his big, smothering hand moved across her face, she added rapidly, "I don't remember the street! Somewhere near Broadway."

"Check the map," he said, and she heard the rustle of crisp, heavy paper in the background.

"Right, right." Fox's voice, and then after twenty more seconds of glorious breathing, she heard him say, "Here it is, uhh, Mesilla and Church. Mile and a half from her place. Ten minutes from here, fifteen at most. We take Campbell to Broadway, no sweat."

After an eternity of five seconds, musing as if to himself: "Bus stations have video games. It's about the right distance for a run. Okay, gentlemen, make it happen." More softly, then: "Teresa, if we don't find the boy there, you won't get another chance, and it's not a fun way to die. You sure you don't want to change your story?"

"He may have gone to the police by now," she said. "I can't—" But then the tape went over her mouth again, and her captor was talking to the others as the van thrummed away. From the traffic sounds nearby she decided they'd been parked outside the airport, because they didn't have to pay a toll. She hated crybabies, but she sobbed softly, feeling the van's side panel against her shoe soles, drawing herself into a ball as small as possible.

Mr. Blond reminded Fox not to risk a speeding ticket and told him that he should double-park just long enough to let two of them out, then circle the block. A brief discussion proved they feared another breakaway run by Al the moment he saw any of them, but the foreigner said he thought not. "I shall go with you. He should recognize me, and then all will be well."

"He knows you?"

"I am almost certain that he will."

"You sure you want him to get back in the van, under the circumstances?"

After a long moment: "It is the simplest way. Talal and I shall sit in front, and there is extra room behind this seat for that, that bag.''

Behind the backseat? Room for what? Then an icy tendril of certainty caressed T.C.'s body. Room for her in a duffel bag, the same way they must've taken her from the apartment. Because she would be in no condition to complain about it. Ever. That meant it had to happen, the knife or suffocation or whatever, while the van was circling.

When Rankin was called from his front seat some minutes later, she knew that the job of murdering her would fall to him. He might even enjoy that, after the way she'd whaled away on him with an alcohol-saturated towel. Blond told him to help arrange a blanket, which felt like one of those cargo pads from U-Haul. It went over her, and then Rankin sat down where he was told, the small of his back snugged against her head and neck. He still smelled faintly of rubbing alcohol, and that gave her a stab of fierce pleasure.

''Just a couple of blocks now,'' said Fox as the van turned a corner.

Blond said, ''We'll just hop out and slide the side door shut again, but you'll be sitting there.''

Rankin, anxious to please: ''Doing what?''

''I have to explain everything, McLeod? Hiding that little bundle of Mexican joy. I don't care, picking your nose. Making faces. It's only going to be for, what, four seconds? Five?''

''Got it,'' said the man whose name was not really Rankin but McLeod, reaching a hand back to pat T.C.'s rump, then to run his hand stealthily along her flank, feeling up between her buttocks. It was then that she saw the sliver of light past the blanket flap, McLeod's motion tugging the tape farther over her head and slightly away from her left eye. She had never thought she'd ever be glad that the Contreras women all had oily skin and sweat glands that would defeat duct tape. She could even see the tanned, corded forearm of another man wearing what looked like a pilot's wristwatch.

Then something else went on between the men with subtle

movements of clothing and grunts, including a "hmm?" and an affirmative "uh-huh." Finally, from Blond, "Then I'll get in back here with Mr. K and the boy up front."

"It'll work," said McLeod. They were figuring out the details of hiding her dead body from Al, as if it were an event she could not affect in any way, and the arrogance of it sent a scalding wave of hatred through her.

From Fox, or whatever his real name was: "Here we go," as the van slowed.

With the inertia of the stop, T.C. rubbed her head sideways, the blanket pulling away a vital inch while the tape sagged farther, perhaps caught on the blanket now, and she saw the big blond's hands at the side door, the tanned foreigner at his back.

"Come on, Kerman," urged the blond, both of them hopping out as the door slid aside and the blaze of Tucson's noon flooded the van's interior. Their backs were turned for that instant, and her feet were planted firmly against the side panel, and when she discharged every scintilla of that stored energy through both legs, it sent Rankin-McLeod sprawling sidelong, her bound feet flipping her heels over head, her legs following through, and she tumbled against the edge of the open door hard enough to hurt, kicking furiously, both legs pistoning again and again as she fell writhing into the middle of the street while men cursed aloud.

The damned tape still obscured one eye, but the other one told her she was about to be collected by a moving Chrysler, but the driver's panic braking prevented it with a foot to spare. Blond was skidding on his knees toward her but rolled away to avoid being struck, and some passerby was shouting in astonished Spanish, and then a horn was honking insistently, sounds all around of brakes squealing and tires squalling, Blond darting a fast look back toward the van, making a snap decision that snapped a second too late because, while he was reaching into his jacket, she forced her heels to thrust her past the Chrysler's nose and he'd either have to shoot her through the metal or dart around the car while she continued to flop and roll. A woman screamed in the near distance. Somehow, in the urgency of the moment, T.C.

didn't care whether she got run over. People had been known to live through that.

Out of the chaos of noise, distinct cues to her immediate future, as though she'd been attuned to their frequencies: an engine howling somewhere near, shouted commands hoarse with fury, a vehicle door slamming, a howl of tires under torture. A raggedy young guy dropped down beside her, unwinding tape from her wrists, his face registering stark disbelief as she came to a sitting position. "My God, lady, what'd they do to you?"

She removed the rest of the tape, then passed both hands down her face, wiping away the tears and the perspiration of her captivity, and gave him the palest ghost of a smile. "Domestic dispute." Her own shaky laugh: "Foreign, too, come to think of it."

"Huh? Maybe you better lie down," he said, as an older man knelt beside her, asking if she was hurt.

She said she wouldn't know until they helped her up, and while leaning against the Chrysler's nose she exchanged a weak grin with the guy at its wheel who, obeying the honks from behind him, slowly drove off shaking his head. With a man at each elbow, she moved to the sidewalk, traffic resuming now as if nothing had happened, and she was immediately surrounded by people asking questions, tuning up to argue about what they'd seen, one woman shouting, "Anybody called the police?"

"I've got to go pee," she said suddenly. More or less true, but what she really needed was to get away. Blond's people were clearly willing to take chances in public. If those guys thought Al was in the bus station they'd probably be back, the massive Fox showing his badge around for credibility, and she wanted no part of that. Something nagged at her memory, something about bringing pressure on the local force. Blond hadn't said that for her benefit, either. If that meant the police, she wouldn't risk finding out.

She thanked all and sundry, nodding and smiling for them, brushing herself off, fluffing her hair as she strode with increasing confidence into the bus station. People streamed in behind her, but almost all were men, and of course they didn't try to follow her into the bathroom.

She tried to urinate but found she was too wired to succeed. She washed her face, with a brief hopeless attempt to do something with her hair using only her fingers, reminding herself that McLeod, who probably hadn't been seen at all, could be slithering into the station at any moment.

With that thought prodding her, she hurried back into the larger room, walking quickly, and veered toward a line of waiting passengers. She went through a side door, ignoring the hubbub, to the area where buses waited. Then she was running through the broad arena, her shins protesting with sharp throbs at each step, fleeing the shouts, the confusion, the thousand questions the police would want answered. She might have to visit the cop shop later, but only if Al Townsend wasn't where she'd told him to go.

CHAPTER □ 9

er taxi driver thought she was pulling a scam but the auto-matic teller machine was practically on the way, and what the hell . . . As the bills extruded from the ATM like impudent tongues, she thought, unconcious of irony, *Kids are really expensive these days.* She hadn't entertained such notions in years. It was, in some way, a comforting thought.

Outside the supermarket she paid the driver without waiting for change and secured the ankle wallet around her wrist under the sweatsuit's sleeve. As soon as the taxi disappeared, she trotted across to the video store and called too much attention to herself when she darted inside calling, "Calvin!"

He stood at the shoulder of an older boy, enjoying spurious on-screen violence while hiding from the real thing, but she didn't see him until he wheeled away and piped, "Hobbes, over here," looking at her, then past her to scan the entrance. The kid had the instincts of a fugitive, she decided.

She knelt to hug him, ignoring the curious stares of a half dozen kids with quarters to waste. Then, "I've been looking all over for you, Cal. You better come along if you want lunch."

"I'm sorry," he said, making a show of it, taking her hand as she led him outside.

Though this neighborhood was her turf, she felt naked on the street now, expecting to be apprehended at any second. They needed a place where she could sit and think in a friendly environment, and her apartment was no longer one of those places. Her car would be off-limits too.

Al settled her internal question with, "How 'bout that lunch?"

She chose one of two nearby cafés she frequented, greeting the waitress by name, pulling Al to a booth near the rear exit. She ordered chorizo and eggs; Al wanted the Bigburger.

She reached across the table and pulled a sticker burr from his hair, then moistened her paper napkin in her water glass and proceeded to plow a few furrows through the dust on his face. "How do kids get so dirty so fast?" she murmured affectionately.

"Jumping through jungle gyms," he replied, holding his chin up to assist her, "and going through hookey gates."

"You went to the school?"

"Big burr-head musta heard me kick the end out of that tunnel in your house," he said. "I got a long head start, but he gained on me so I went to your school."

"Al, honey, there was nobody there to help you."

"Ha. Where *is* there?"

"Right here," she said, patting his hand, grinning.

He grinned back. "I was afraid they'd get you."

Why tell him the horrific details? "They nearly did. So, you got to the schoolyard," she prompted. "And?"

"Durn guy tried to tackle me, but I dodged. Jungle gym bars are pretty wide for me, so I ducked inside. I yelled a lot, but nobody came, so he's trying to reach in and I'm ooching back so he gets his head and arm inside and I bite his finger and he bangs his head on the bars and he's cussing and while he's caught in there I take off and roll under the hookey gate and then I get into somebody's backyard and hide behind a trash barrel. You know you guys have real big red ants in Arizona?"

She ruffled his hair and said yes, she knew, trying to get past the lump of gratitude in her throat because her kid was such a quick learner and, when he had to be, mean as a rodeo bronc.

While washing down her pungent sausage-spiced eggs with iced tea, she thought about hidey-holes. Seattle was Al's own turf, but it was a long way off, and her means were limited. She thought long and hard about using one of the Latino contacts who moved illegal immigrants around one step ahead of the *migras,* immigration cops. She kept coming back to the fact that whoever these murdering sons of bitches might be, they were already in Tucson, with too much information on her and possibly some clout with the authorities.

She left Al in the booth and used the café phone to call Gonsalvo Amado, who taught fifth grade and had asked her out a few times. She had a vague notion of getting a ride to Phoenix or Willcox, where she could catch a bus. Gonsalvo's answering machine said he would reply when he returned home from his summer job, and she gave up on Gonsalvo. She didn't intend to be in Tucson that long.

If only she could get to her Datsun! But she trembled at the thought of approaching it when her enemies might be awaiting that very thing. She was ready to steal a car, if she had any idea how you hot-wired the damned things. Gonsalvo's younger brother Carmen would know. According to Gonsalvo, the young man and his *'chuco* buddies would hot-wire a gila monster if they thought there was a joyride in it. For that matter, she could lend him her key—and hope he didn't disappear permanently with her car. But hell, even if he did, she'd be no worse off.

She found the right Amado on the third try. Carmen and his pals were working on a junker, he said. He was wary of her until she said she was Gonsalvo's friend at school and was offering twenty bucks for a few minutes' work.

She bribed Al to sit in place using a piece of pie because he mistrusted the sound of "flan" and spent some time regretting her tactic with Gonsalvo's brother. It was one thing for college-age youths to risk getting shot for their hell-raising ways and quite another to risk it in an innocent chore. She would just have to warn Carmen of the dangers.

Carmen Amado strolled into that café with a virtual parody of a fashion model's strut, as if someone were reeling him in by his jockstrap. Slender, slumber-eyed, almost pretty, he affected the typical sleeked haircut she hated on sight. When she waved, his glance said he wished she had worn something he could rest his eyes on. Though totally ignored, Al scrunched down in one corner of the booth, mightily awed by this paragon of dangerous youth whose every move said, *no chingas conmigo,* don't fuck with me. She knew the thought was unworthy, but in that moment of first acquaintance she cared a bit less whether he caught his butt in a crack.

His words were warm and soft and slangy with big-city *chilango* Spanish currently popular on the street. She made it clear moments after he sat down that she respected his elder brother Gonsalvo, which reined his libido in because who could know whether she might one day be part of Carmen's extended family?

And then she uttered the magic word, *peligroso.* It might be dangerous to take her white 1980 Datsun 510 because evil men had threatened her to obtain the *hijo* who, she assured Carmen, was not theirs to obtain. The men might or might not have the police on their side, but again, they were dangerous men with weapons. Carmen would have to make certain that he was not followed before leaving her car, its key atop the left front tire, in the parking lot of the supermarket three blocks distant. It was important that he do these things discreetly. If followed, he must return the Datsun to her apartment. She could tell him no more than this. Was it enough?

"One question only," he said. "Is your car capable of racing?"

"It is well maintained but not very powerful," she shrugged. "Its tires and brakes are good."

"The five-ten had the Z-twenty engine. Stronger than you think; overhead cam, *un roqueta de arroz,* a rice rocket," he said with a knowing nod. T.C. suspected he knew the specs of everything on wheels. The whole concept charmed young Amado, and by now she could not have dissuaded him with a regimental combat team. He would use only his friend in the Mustang, he said, to drive him to the address she gave. He would need thirty minutes, no more. Also, he would accept no money. It would be enough, he said with a smile to charm a boa constrictor, if she put in a good word for him with Gonsalvo.

She continued to play the hapless female for Carmen until he swashbuckled out to a waiting Mustang and disappeared with her car key into the sun-drenched streets of Tucson. She used one of the checks in her wallet to pay for the meal, getting an extra twenty in change because she was a frequent customer. It was now a quarter of two.

□   □   □

Carmen Amado was better than his word. She was watching from inside the supermarket when her Datsun pulled into the parking lot. She waited, her breast thumping when she saw another vehicle draw alongside hers, but it was the same black Mustang Carmen had ridden in before.

After a moment's slow scan of the area, he knelt by her front tire, kissed his fingertips, transferred the benison to her hood, and ducked into the Mustang's front passenger seat without opening the door, like a NASCAR driver. As she watched the Mustang roar away, T.C. wondered what Carmen would have done if she'd asked him to do something flamboyant.

There were arguments for waiting and watching some more. There were better arguments for getting the hell out of Dodge right now. She carried her few groceries to the car, retrieved her key, and drove around the block alone before pulling up to the automated doors of the supermarket for Al. The boy came out as though fired from a howitzer. She took Aviation Highway before she saw the black Mustang behind her, and when she took the cutoff toward Interstate 10 she pulled onto the shoulder because, if anyone else were following, she figured she'd have a couple of fearless machos to liven things up.

She figured wrong. Carmen Amado waved as he passed, and there she sat, inert and vulnerable, as the Mustang disappeared. Several cars passed before she got underway again, thinking, *You've got the brains of a gerbil, pocho, but I'm glad you were on my side.*

She struck the interstate around three in the afternoon, too focused on her rearview to notice how thoroughly Al was checking out her grocery bag. Her concentration finally snapped when he said, "Whu wuh guhnn," around a faceful of Fritos.

"You're lucky I speak Fritese, pard. Put those away, they're for supper. And to answer your question, we're going to New Mexico."

He swallowed before his reply, "Why are you mad?"

"I'm not mad, punkin, I'm just thinking."

"Don't say punkin, okay? Mom calls me punkin."

"Oh. And you don't like it?"

"Like it fine. You're not Mom," he explained, looking away so that she would not see him lick at the tear sliding toward his upper lip. When he glanced at her again, he patted her arm and said what, in the mind of a seven-year-old, should have made her feel better. "Don't cry, T.C., you were somebody's mom."

For the next ten miles, they said nothing as T.C. mastered her emotions with deep-breathing exercises. It was the thought of Ross Downing that finally redirected her from tears, Ross, and the boy's problematical reaction to him when they came face to face.

"Al, we're going to see a very dear friend of mine," she said, as the sunbaked mass of Apache Peak slid past on their right. "I wouldn't do this if we had any other choice."

"Why? Isn't he nice?"

"Depends on what you mean by nice. He's the kind of guy who will risk his life for a stranger. He did, in fact; he tried to save my little boy's life. He nearly burned to death trying, and . . . and he hasn't entirely recovered. But if you mean will he read you stories and swap a lot of riddles with you, no, I don't think so. He's not that kind of nice. He's dependable-nice, quiet and generous-nice." She gave him a long, meaningful glance, then turned off toward the town of Benson. "I want you to keep that in mind when you meet him."

"Are we there yet?"

"Not by a bunch, Al." She kept studying her rearview as she rolled along Fourth Street into town, turned on Central, and watched the following traffic for perhaps a minute.

"You're afraid those guys are still after us," Al said.

"Damn—durn right I am," she countered, with a mock frown. "Now you made me cuss."

"Did not."

"Did too."

He said nothing aloud, but she saw his lips form "did not" again, and they shared a laugh, and then she turned back and followed the signs to I-10. "Looks like we shook 'em this time," she said.

"You mean for good?"

"I think so. It's possible they might find someone I know in Tucson, get Ross's name. And that's as far as they'll get."

Always capable of one more question than anyone had answers, Al wondered why the bad guys would get no farther. She replied that Ross Downing had been an accountant in El Paso before his accident, and no one, not even Ross Downing, knew she was on the way to see him, and even if they did, there was no way he would be traced to a cabin outside a little town in New Mexico. She also had to tell him that New Mexico was a state almost like any other, where most people spoke English.

Presently, on the bypass near Willcox: "Are we in New Mexico yet?"

"Another hour," she said, sighing.

"It's not like this, is it?" His gaze at the sere landscape of southern Arizona was as bleak as the mountains themselves.

"A lot of it is," she admitted. "Not where we're going, though. They've got streams with trout and a mountain where people ski in the winter. A microclimate, sort of. You'll like it." And then she had to explain what a microclimate was.

He still didn't like what he saw when they crossed the state border and said as much, and when they stopped for gasoline and mandatory kidney-tapping in Lordsburg, T.C. found herself short of temper. She crossly stuffed her Visa card back into her wallet and said, "Zip your lip and get in the car. It's suppertime, Al. I'll let you stuff your face if you'll just quit bitching and drink some milk."

They watched a long freight train slither past beside the interstate as she accelerated eastward, the Datsun's shadow now preceding them. Al maintained a dutiful silence for a time, munching, swigging, a scatter of crumbs in his lap. Then, in an artless ploy to make friendly conversation, "You gonna marry this Ross guy?"

"He's just a good friend, Al. I don't think he's the marrying kind." It was the same answer she'd given herself early in the relationship with Ross. "And by the way, you should call him Mr. Downing."

"Oh, *that* kind of guy," said Al. A dismissal of sorts.

"Al, when you used to be big and strong and looked like a movie star and an accident takes that all away, what you've got left is mostly your self-respect. People don't like to look at Ross anymore. In fact, sometimes he wears a special kind of mask over his face when he's around other people."

Al's "Whaa?" came complete with a grimace.

She shrugged. "If they see his face, they give him looks like you just did. They can't help it, Al. I'm trying to tell you that on the outside he's not good-looking."

"Nuh-uh, T.C. You're trying to tell me he's gross looking," said Al with total decisiveness.

"All right, then, he scares some people. But he can't help that, either. Inside, he's a very nice guy. You remember that. And since he doesn't know we're coming, we'll be in deep dookey if his own guest tees him off."

"Meaning me."

"Meaning you," she agreed. "Look past the burn scars if you can."

"Okay. So long as he doesn't go *booga-booga* at me." From the tail of her eye she could see the boy making claws of his hands for comic effect.

She shook her head and grinned. "If he does, it'll serve you right, kid." She became serious after a moment's reflection. "There's a trick to looking at a person like Ross. You know how when you're climbing a tree you're not supposed to look down?

Well, with Ross Downing, don't look at the rest of his face, just look in his eyes. Not at what's around them, but right into his eyes. There's a sweet guy in there, Al. And that's all I want to say about it."

"Promise?"

"I promise to warm your bottom if you try that smartass talk with my friend," she said with asperity. The boy wasn't fooled. He could tell she was fighting a smile.

With its sluggish river and a skyline freckled by gracious tree-tops in the dusk, the little city of Las Cruces gave the boy a few minutes of optimism. He refused to believe that the river they crossed was the same one they'd bridged into Eagle Pass until T.C. insisted he dig the map from under his seat. Why look at a squiggly blue line, he complained, when the real river was right behind him—and not blue, but babypoop brown. Yet he followed the lines under her tutelage, and by dark, T.C. felt a familiar old satisfaction at the lesson they'd shared.

San Agustin Pass stole the last direct rays of the sun. Al found only disappointment as they passed the vast stretch of gypsum dunes, which T.C. said was White Sands National Monument. "My grampa was here once," he said. "Guess who for."

"Boring," T.C. said.

"You mean Boeing," he objected.

"Same difference," she said, with a "gotcha" look.

"I'm gonna tell him you said that," he said, scandalized.

"And I'll tell him you hung one on that Mexican boy," she said, and all the way past Alamogordo they cudgeled their memories, dredging up sins to announce, enjoying the game immensely.

T.C. took Highway 70 out of Tularosa, headlights spearing upward from the ancient valley into brush-covered hills, then mountains where conifers struggled to survive. In these cool heights T.C. turned on the heater, which knocked Al out faster than a padded mallet, and in growing lassitude she nearly missed the familiar turnoff to Ruidoso.

Eleven o'clock at night, she decided, was no time to be driving up a twisty mountain road, let alone barge in on poor Ross Downing without preamble. She turned around on Sudderth Drive and went back to the scatter of motels near the auto dealership. The Villa Inn and the Super Eight looked good, but she had a thing for Holiday Inns. She would worry about the price later.

Let those assholes turn Tucson upside down, there's no way they can trace me here, thought T.C. as she accepted her Visa card back from the Holiday Inn Express night clerk.

CHAPTER □ 10

Ruidoso, New Mexico, had sucker punched T.C. on her first visit to the forested little resort town. The stands of pine and aspen might have given her a hint of warning, but she had decided on a three-mile run her first morning there, before breakfast. She had struck out brightly and made two hundred yards before she staggered like a drunk and fell. Ruidoso might be warmed by the seasonal sun, but it is nearly two thousand feet higher than Denver. T.C. had simply run out of air before she knew it, as many another tourist had.

On this morning she dressed, then roused Al from his own queen-sized bed and told him about her falling down in a public place, what Ross Downing had called her "rummy act," before they went outside. She would still have her early run, but for the first few days it would be fifty running steps, then a hundred walking, and so on.

Al set out with her, undaunted, but they both were panting all too soon. Walking, he managed, "Is this how drunks feel?"

"Something like, umm, how would I know?" she replied, ricocheting from the trap. Why was that important? Well, for T.C. it just was.

"Yeah, right," he said, unconvinced, walking, puffing. Presently, "What if I should forget and . . . keep running?"

"Huh. Ruidoso will remind you. It's real good about that."

Then she thought of his experimenter's nature. "Just remember to try it on nice soft grass. At the cabin the air is thinner than this."

They covered only a mile, skirting the Medical Center, leaning on each other as they abandoned the running segments long before they reached the motel. They drove the short distance to K-Bob's for its advertised country breakfast, though neither of them could finish one. "I thought I was hungry," Al lamented, viewing his uneaten portion.

"Me too. You'll make up for it. Guaranteed," she promised. "Hey, I forgot to call Ross."

"Phone in the room," he said.

"Ditsy like this? I'd forget again. You try and put a move on that bacon, I'll be back in a minute."

"Gahhh," he said, tongue out, but she was already up and away. Some of what she had to say to Ross was not for the boy's ears. In making that call she did something very, very right, but for an entirely different reason than she thought.

□   □   □

Ross Downing was at his cabin dusting off the welcome mat, T.C. told the boy. Ross had given her a list of groceries to bring, she said, and while they were at it Al could use a change of clothes. The J Bar J, specializing in western garb, wasn't far away. T.C. got the boy togged out with an extra pair of jeans and a nifty, pricey little long-sleeved brown shirt, with a silent gulp at the price tags as she offered her Visa card.

Al wondered aloud why she insisted on Wrangler jeans. "You wanta dress like a real cowboy or don't you?" she said. "Levi's are okay, but Wranglers were designed for cowpokes, more room for your butt, high hip pockets. My ex could go on about it for an hour." Al gave that some serious thought and then bowed to the wisdom of rodeo cowboys, once removed.

After turning in her room key and refueling, she took Sudderth into the center of town and, as she'd remembered, the Furr supermarket was up the main connecting street, Mechem Drive. She cursed softly as she saw the homely bulk of a Wal-Mart nearby. If she'd recalled it earlier she might've saved a bundle.

Of course, at Wal-Mart she spent a bundle. Inexpensive shorts, socks, and sneakers for Al, mid-heeled wedgies for her, a tan blouse that set off her Latina coloring, a gossamer neck scarf in brilliant crimson, a denim skirt, and finally jeans of an unfamiliar brand that she hoped wouldn't shrink. "Don't say it, Al," she cautioned as she checked herself in a mirror in the jeans. "Do I wanta be a real cowgirl, or would I rather save a few bucks?"

"Not much room for your butt," he said wryly.

"It makes room," she countered.

"Sure does," he said with false innocence.

She shook a schoolmarmish finger at him. "That's another one for your grampa, kid." One day, she knew, her hourglass would grow more bottom-heavy, but men seemed to appreciate it as long as she kept it tautly conditioned.

Furr's had everything on the list, and took her Visa card, and shortly before noon they scooted up Mechem past the village of Alto. "That road to the right?" T.C. pointed for Al. "Fort Stanton Road. There's a house over there where we might sleep, belongs to a friend of Ross's. Funny old guy, has a gold mine. You may meet him."

"We're leaving Roodoso?"

"Ruidoso. It means noisy. Shoot, we've already left. You see that mountain with the snow on top, west of us? We're going up around it, not as high as the snowline, though. It's where the mine is, and the cabin is on the same road." The road twisted around Bonito Lake before she turned off to a lesser dirt road, following a creek ever higher along the north slopes of the snowcapped massif that was Sierra Blanca.

She stopped before a rutted side road with a locked gate and fiddled with a big bronze combination lock. "I don't think Mr. Downing wants people here," Al called.

"Not most people," she called back, "but this isn't his lock. It belongs to Orville Ferguson, the guy with the mine." She swung the metal gate open, drove through, then stopped to relock the gate. The NO ACCESS sign behind them, she said, was a nice way of saying keep the hell off this private road.

"And tigers can't read, huh, Hobbes?"

She rumpled his hair and grinned. "Thanks for the handy excuse, but I'm an exception. They gave me the combination, didn't they?"

He nodded, sitting up straight, his eyes bird bright, alert to the ravines and ridges that carved nearby slopes into potentially dangerous corrugations. The Datsun seemed out of breath, straining in low gear to navigate what was now little more than a trail.

When they rounded the shoulder of a ravine and the cabin came in view, Al's wide-eyed reaction was a soft, "Wow, coo-wullll," and it occurred to T.C. that when a kid got nearly three syllables out of "cool," he was registering heartfelt approval.

The cabin had been put together of split logs by Ross Downing's grandfather back in the days when there was local timber to waste, and additions over the years had included a porch that ran its full length, half of it fully screened. T.C. knew that the big window at the near corner had been renovated by Ross into a single thermally insulated pane, the first and least obvious of his high-tech innovations. His solar array lay on the sloping roof, gleaming with its prussian blue rectangles, and twenty feet from the foundation another device leaned to face the sun at a steep angle.

This gadget, his active solar heater designed by Orville Ferguson, was Ross Downing's own handiwork and looked it, a huge thin box the size of a barn door with an insulated wooden back and a glass face. Behind the glass lay hundreds of open-faced tubes, open-topped aluminum beer cans painted black to absorb the sun's rays directly. When Ross tapped those solar cells for power to run a small fan, cold air was forced into that big box, circulating around the sun-warmed aluminum cans. Exiting the box in a pipe through an earth-insulated trench and burrowing under the foundation, the warmed air issued into two ducts so that, when everything worked, the end of the big living room away from the fireplace was almost as warm on a chilly morning as the end with the crackling logs.

Ross had intended, he once said, to pour a concrete-lined chamber in the flagstoned basement and fill it with gravel, so that much more heat could be stored as solar-heated air warmed the gravel. That was his intent before the accident, in the days when he took the muscles in his arms for granted, imagined that he had all the time in the world, spent only a month out of every year at the cabin. Now he spent much of the year up here and was only gradually regaining the strength and range of motion in his arm through repeated operations.

Everything in Ross's life that interested him, it seemed, had been before the accident. He had electricity and telephone lines from Ruidoso, but Ross claimed that burning wood and using city power were offenses if you knew a better way. Ross Downing's phrase for it was good citizenship. T.C.'s heart never failed to melt when she saw him puttering with that ruined hand on his heat system, high-tech when it worked, no-tech when it didn't.

After stopping next to Ross's Cherokee, T.C. forced a tiny bleat from the Datsun's horn, knowing that Ross disliked strident honks up here on Sierra Blanca's backside. Then she got out, apportioning grocery bags to herself and Al.

From the screened portion of the porch, a gruff baritone: "I know you're here, T.C.! Monte knew it five minutes ago."

"Hope I didn't scare him," she piped, her voice sounding thin in the high mountain air.

"Everything scares him," came the reply, as the echo of "scares him" chased itself across a rock outcrop in the near distance.

Al, stumbling because his grocery sack topped his field of vision, looked toward T.C. "Somebody else here?"

"Just Montezuma," she said. "He's what they call a coon cat. You'll meet him, too, when he's good and ready."

The muted thumps of a cane paced footsteps across the porch, and the screen door opened as she reached the steps. "Thanks," she said, feeling the effects of altitude from even this small effort. Ross wore jeans, a long-sleeved flannel shirt in light and darker blue checks, and moccasins that did not need to be laced up, all of it hanging loosely from his frame because they had been purchased for a heftier Ross Downing.

"Watch the steps, Al," she said. Encumbered, she couldn't hug Ross, who was wearing his Jobst mask.

She continued into the main room to which the kitchen was only a dedicated corner and helped Al deposit his sack with her two near the sink. She could feel residual heat from the old wood cookstove near the wall and saw Al moving too near it. "Watch out for old smoky, or sooner or later it'll blister you," she said. Hearing the aysymmetry of the footfalls behind her, she turned and gave her host that deferred hug, going on tiptoe to do it.

"Ow, careful," he said, with a faint chuckle.

"New surgery, you said the other night."

"Always," he said, and then he abruptly turned away, and she saw that Al Townsend had backed himself so far behind her that he was crowding the sink.

"Don't, Al," she said softly, giving him a surreptitious bump with her hip. She moved farther into the big room behind Ross, surveying its open beam trusses, the mule deer trophy head that was older than either of them, several sturdy old wooden chairs slung with thick cowhide, and the bright Navajo blankets hung familiarly across the walls. His desk, previously squatting near the big picture window, was nowhere to be seen, though the heavy file cabinet still stood in a corner of the room. Too heavy, she decided, for him to move. As always the place smelled of smoke, sweet and musky, with a twinge of sourness beneath, sweat, probably. "Tell me what they're doing to you," she said, laying a hand on his good right forearm.

He turned to face her with reluctance. "Come to view the ruins, have you," he said. "It's just another patch on my back, up near my shoulder." She had grown accustomed to sensing facial expressions she couldn't see through the brown fabric Jobst mask, a device molded to the patient's face secured by Velcro straps at the back of his head. On his left hand he wore a glove of similar color, the fingertips cut out and slightly ragged, as if he'd been doing manual labor.

She stared through the Jobst eyeholes into those smoky gray eyes of his and did not yield an inch. "Are we going through that crap again? If I'm used to you, seems like you'd get used to me,'' she said, with a sad little smile.

"You're right. My fault. Long time between visits, I'm afraid.'' Then, with a darted glance behind her that fixed on the boy: "You never cease to astonish me.''

"Oh.'' She turned to find Al, one foot awkwardly across the other, leaning near the small kitchen window and studying the view as intently as if he expected a snap quiz on it. "Al Townsend, meet Mr. Downing, your landlord. He won't bite you. Uh, well, I take that back, Ross. Al *will* bite, but he's had his shots so . . .'' she tapered off at the embarrassment in Al's face.

"Aww, T.C.,'' said the boy, his blush visible in sunlight streaming through the window.

"Glad to meet you, Al Townsend,'' said the burned man with a measured nod.

The boy's hand fluttered up like a wounded sparrow. "Hi.'' He came no closer.

"He's from Washington State,'' T.C. said, as though confessing a flaw. "Apparently they don't learn to wave or shake hands there 'til the fifth grade.''

"Do too,'' Al protested, not charmed in the least.

T.C. let her lips form "do not'' and then saw the beginnings of Al's effort to hide a smile. "Hey, I bet that coon cat's around outside somewhere,'' she said.

"But don't chase him,'' Ross put in.

The boy gave them a quick headshake and then, glad to have an excuse, darted out the door with T.C.'s, "And don't go out of sight,'' hanging in the air.

Ross broke a brief silence after he moved back to the grocery sacks, isolating items for refrigerator, shelves, and storage like the bean counter he was. Shortened tendons in his left leg and foot had forced his toes to curl under, and therapy had not entirely repaired the problem, so he lifted the left foot oddly when he walked. "I've been thinking about that call I made the other night. Don't tell me you wanted an Uzi burp gun for the boy,'' he said.

"Matter of fact, yes." Wishing the introductions had gone better, she began to put things away according to his silent gestures in a routine they had practiced before.

"I should think a set of brass knucks would suffice," he said, "but he could be tougher than he looks."

She giggled. "That damn mask, and you're too subtle anyway. When does the Jobst come off, by the way?"

"I already have one of clear plastic, and I don't have to wear it all the time, but I thought, when you said you were bringing a friend this morning, perhaps we should break me to him gently."

She knew how he loathed the heavy thing he now wore. "Sometimes you're too nice for your own good, 'mano. What I think is, Al has been sheltered too much. Until I showed up, I mean."

"No shelter with you, that's a given," he chuckled.

"You think not?" And then she told him some details: Gail Townsend a casual victim in Puerto Vallarta, Al's heritage, fleeing in stages to Tucson, more bad guys preparing to kill her, their escape in the Datsun.

Ross Downing asked only a few questions during her account and had prepared coffee before she got as far as, ". . . took some little detours to make sure nobody was following us and got into Ruidoso last—" as small footsteps pounded across the porch. "Don't let the door," she began, as the door slammed, "slam next time."

Though he did not approach them any nearer, Al's face shone. "Hey, there's some kinda wild animal out there in that woodpile!"

"Wouldn't be surprised," said Ross. "If it's black with white stripes, give it room."

"Naw, that's a skunk. We've got skunks in Washington."

"So she tells me," Ross said evenly.

For the first time, now, Al squinted quickly at the mask of the burned man, then at T.C. "I can't tell when he's teasing," the boy told her.

"Neither can I, half of the time," she admitted. "What does your wild animal look like?"

"Like the fox fur my gramma has. But littler and skinnier, and brown with great big eyes and ears. And its tail has rings like," and now his eyes widened, seeing T.C.'s grin, "a raccoon! Then a coon cat's not a cat?"

"And not a coon either," Ross answered. "I'll bet you can't say cacomixtle."

Al blinked. "You win," he shrugged.

Ross vented his little falsetto bark of amusement. "Well, when you can, I'll introduce you to him, because that's what he is. They range all the way from here to the West Coast, but you don't often see them. Miners found they keep mice away better than a cat, and they're friendly little guys once they know you."

"Can I feed him? What does he eat besides mice?"

"What he won't eat makes a shorter list," Ross said. "You see any red ants here? Roaches? Crumbs and such in the kitchen?" Into Al's headshake, he went on, "That's some of what he eats. Monte will eat just about anything that he can get his thieving little hands on."

"Sort of like a boy I know," T.C. put in.

"I can say Monte," Al said. "I wanta play with him, he's neat."

"Montezuma was a king in Mexico. Cacomixtles originally came from there," Ross explained. "Tell me when you can say cacomixtle, and I'll see what I can do."

And with a bit of coaching, Al managed to say it, and a moment later he had danced out the door with Ross following slowly to steady that peculiar gait. T.C. watched them through the window, gnawing at her underlip. The meeting of her best male friends had begun badly, but furry little Montezuma seemed just the good-will ambassador those two needed.

□　　□　　□

When the menfolk returned indoors, ring-tailed little Montezuma was perched on Ross's right shoulder, the one that didn't undulate so much when Ross walked. T.C. was amused to see that, while Al still tried to avoid looking directly at the head of Ross Downing, he was enraptured with the lithe brown critter that sat within inches of Ross's ear—or rather, half an ear. Al's personal space from Ross had first been about twenty feet; now it was reduced to ten.

She gave a brief prayer of thanks that Ross did not look the way he had before they had flown him from Kingman to San Antonio. She had first seen him doped with morphine in a small-town intensive care unit, alive only through the umbilical grace of plastic tubes, his head blackened with char and so swollen by body fluids that it was literally almost twice its normal width. His left arm had been so grossly swollen that his wristwatch had not been removed immediately because, said a nurse, no one realized it was there under those balloons of skin.

The standard burn prognosis for a healthy person was that age in years plus percentage of burned body surface area equaled likelihood of death. Downing had been thirty-four; forty percent of his body had been burned. And if his odds on living were less than even, his chances for a normal life were zero. A year later, Ross had told T.C. that the accident hadn't changed him, that he'd always been a pessimist with a mordant wit. She hadn't believed the pessimist part then and didn't believe it now, as he flexed his leg and, she could tell despite the Jobst, gave her a lopsided grin.

Al's sensors were evidently as good as the coon cat's. At the same instant that Monte scampered down from his human perch, Al said, "Somethin' smells good."

"Tuna salad," she said, lifting the big bowl high because it had seemed for a moment that Monte had designs on it, and a coon cat could jump like a flea. However, Monte also needed time to reacquaint himself to the presence of this female and kept ducking his head as he sniffed at her with focused wariness.

"Let him see you put some in his bowl," Ross reminded her, "or he'll give us no peace."

She took a Frito and scooped an ounce of the spicy, cilantro-laced stuff into the little ceramic bowl near the sink. That was all the encouragement Monte needed. He whisked by her and thrust his nose into the treasure, ears toward her like tiny radar dishes, the huge, soulful eyes as bright as Al's.

The dining table, a hand-carved project of Ross's father, was of aromatic cedar, easy to scar but newly pungent after each scrubbing. Al seemed to have a new question with each bite of lunch. Was a kack-o-missile really part raccoon and part cat? Could Al get one, too? When could he see the gold mine T.C. told him about? Did Mr. Downing have a gold mine of his own? Why not? And when could Al call his mom to tell her about all this neat stuff?

Ross answered most of the questions, deflected the last one, and warned the boy against wandering out of earshot, cautioning him as well to stay alert for rattlesnakes. Finally he gave Al a handful of unshelled peanuts for tossing. Montezuma would chase them, but bringing them back intact was not a feature of Monte's repertoire.

When Al had lured the animal outside with peanuts, the adults set about washing and drying the few utensils they had used. "The boy really needs to contact his family," Ross said. "They must be half crazy from worry by now. Trouble is, I'm not sure it should be done from here."

"You think they could trace the call?"

A humorless grunt. "They evidently have special resources, showing up repeatedly as they did, taking the chances they took. I'm afraid they could do more than just trace it."

"You mean I shouldn't have come here."

"No, I'm glad you did, and I think you bought some time. What worries me most is the boy's family connections."

"His grandfather is retired, Ross. I don't see—"

"His Kurdish connections," Ross said patiently. "If you read the newspapers, you know the Kurds occupy some pivotal squares on the big game board of foreign policy."

"I don't give a damn what game governments play. It doesn't justify kidnaping Al. Those men may have killed his mother by mistake, but they intended to murder me in cold blood." She shuddered at the memory. "I think they hadn't decided to kill me until I saw that Kurd, Iranian, whatever he was, in their van. I think the big guy called him 'Kerman' once, usually just 'Mr. K.' "

"Describe him. Describe them all, if you can."

She did, and before she had gone into it very far he excused himself, returning from his bedroom with a minicasette recorder and a request for her to start over. Sipping coffee at the table, she gave descriptions of all the men. Kerman, she said, claimed to have seen Al before and spoke excellent English but the big, burr-headed blond American who had flung Gail Townsend onto those rocks was clearly the one giving the orders.

When she had finished, Ross said darkly, "I don't like it. That facilitator team obviously had some accommodation with Mexican police, and from the way they're throwing their weight around I suspect the same may be true here in the States."

"They murdered an American citizen," T.C. snarled.

"Not on U.S. soil," he pointed out.

"That makes it okay?"

"T.C., I'm not condoning it, I'm trying to think like an official. For the UN to work at all, it has to make allowances, from fixing a bushel of parking tickets to special aid for third world representatives."

"Seems to me this is taking allowances just a teeny bit too far," she said in deliberate understatement.

"You want them as allies, you make 'em happy. There's not a two-bit faction on earth that doesn't realize its hotshots are riding around on U.S. streets, dependent on U.S. goodwill, protected by U.S. policy and police."

"So they abuse the privilege."

"With great regularity. You have no idea how many crimes foreign diplomats and their hired hands can commit, even here, without any worse consequences than a reprimand. Or at worst, say, for out-and-out spying, deportation. That's starting to change, but not quickly enough."

"Murder?"

"Well," he said, pausing a moment, "manslaughter, at least. Yes, it's outrageous. And yes, it has happened. What we need to do is find out exactly how much diplomatic immunity this particular group has. And while we're at it, what wheels the boy's grandparents have set in motion."

"How come you know so much about it?"

A sigh and a headshake. "I don't know enough. But back at business school in Stanford, our courses included international law. Then I was a very junior aide in State for a while."

"Which state?"

"State Department. It didn't take me long to get a bad taste in my mouth there. It's a whole other world. God, I needed shots for everything from typhus to plague. I didn't intend to become what junior staffers called an éminence greasy, and all the international humbug in finance was creating a special need in the private sector for accountants who could follow a paper trail."

She sat back, watching him over the rim of her coffee mug. "So that's the kind of accountant you were."

"I shouldn't tell you this, and you absolutely must never repeat it. That's the kind of accountant I became," he nodded. "More firms are involved in that sort of thing than most people realize. After all, in some cases a lot of money is at stake."

"Millions, I suppose."

"Try billions. Remember the Bank of Credit and Commerce scandal a few years back? B.C.C.I. literally owned the biggest bank in our nation's capital—nearly three hundred branches in this country and connections we tried to trace in offshore banks. We were looking at a lot of flight capital. B.C.C.I.'s alone came to thirty billion or so."

"Flight capital? Sounds like an air force."

"No, but they loaned a corporate jet to President Carter after he left office. That's how far they'd burrowed into us. Flight capital means money squirreled away by corrupt rulers, in case they have to run for it. Noriega was one of them, for B.C.C.I."

"You were in on that?"

"No, but it gives you an idea how involved an accountant's work can be and why the perks were so good. You shouldn't be surprised that my health insurance plan was first-rate."

"Why don't we hear about this stuff, Ross?"

"You do, now and then, but some of the best firms don't exactly push for the spotlight. I'm afraid I can't even tell you the name of the firm I worked for. A few are pretty high profile; one I recall in Houston, Intertect, was a good example. They could buy vehicle registration lists from the Drug Enforcement people, chase down hidden assets, make those S and L robber barons quiver." Now he was smiling beneath the Jobst.

"Ross Downing, golden gumshoe," she said to tease him.

"We preferred to call it forensic accounting," he said primly.

She knew he often worked quietly at his desk with a telephone headset, and his computer table had been mounted on casters. "So, do you still do forensic accounting?"

"No." His denial was cool, detached. "But I do a little consulting, now and then. Barely enough to maintain a few contacts." He saw the look she gave him and was not pleased. "Christ, T.C., wipe that accusing look off your face! I'm—I was one of the good guys. And if you're very, very lucky, I might be able to learn just how careful you'll have to be in the future."

"I'm sorry," she said. "I'm grateful, Ross. It's just a little strange to learn all this after a two-year acquaintance."

"If you hadn't run for cover up here with that boy, you wouldn't have learned about it at all," he reminded her.

She nodded, her mind whirling with these fresh complications, pivoting on one point of optimism: Ross Downing might have contacts that could help. After a sip of her cooling coffee: "I take it you're on that Internet thing."

One side of his mouth slanted up. "Isn't everyone?"

"Some of us can't afford it, Ross. Don't forget, schoolteachers aren't big spenders. But I know people who don't make long-distance calls or buy stamps anymore because they write letters on their computers."

"E-mail. Sure."

"Could you write an E-mail letter to the Townsends?"

"I could if I found their coded E-mail address, assuming they have one, and I probably *can* find out. But you told me their phone lines are tapped, and they're not likely to have a line scrambler, let alone a compatible one. And even without a tap, if you think E-mail is protected by law, think again. It usually takes time, but the Freedom of Information Act lets lots of people read the personal E-mail of other people."

"I never heard of such a thing!"

"Neither did some of the people I was investigating. Now you have," he shrugged, impassive.

"That has to be against the law," she protested.

"No it doesn't, T.C."

"Well, unethical at the very least."

His little yelp of amusement made her jump. "Your ethic, certainly. You know what an attorney's operational definition of ethical is?"

"Educate me. Make me swoon with joy," she glummed.

"It's whatever won't get him disbarred. Tell you what: I never had my scrambler protocols removed from my old firm, and that's one way to route an E-mail circuit so that no one else can backtrack it to me. It's possible that I could contact the boy's family that way."

"Then you'll try?"

"Of course I will." He stood up easily, suggesting that some of those muscle grafts of the past year had strengthened him.

He was halfway to his room when T.C. said, "Don't get your crotch in a crack with those facilitators on my account, Ross."

He stopped, turned back toward her. "What made you call them that?"

"Because you did. Facilitator team, you said."

He ran a hand across the back of his head. "I said that, did I? They're right about this fucking medicine, it makes me crazy."

"It must. You don't usually use the same language I do."

"Well, you can just forget that phrase."

"Consider it forgotten. All the same, what does it mean?"

"If that's what they really are, it means they do this for a living, and some of them are too damned good at it. It means they can stonewall a Justice Department probe. And it means if they get their hands on that little boy, the game is over."

He disappeared into his bedroom, closing the door behind him.

CHAPTER 11

Al came dragging in an hour later, cheerful enough but so listless the flesh around his mouth was pale. "Ran outa peanuts. I could use a root beer," he said.

"No, you ran out of gas, young man. What you could use is a nap," T.C. retorted, noting the boy's signs of overexertion. "First your sugar fix, and then you get to watch the insides of your eyelids for an hour. Deal?"

He agreed and asked where the burned guy had gone.

T.C. popped the top of a root beer but held it high. "Let's have a little respect for the man."

"Mr. Downing," Al revised and got the chilled can and swilled at it. "We've really gotta use his phone, T.C."

She explained that Mr. Downing was hard at work on a means to contact the Townsends safely, then led the boy to the second bedroom and the shared bathroom. She saw that Ross had set up an old-fashioned cot of wood and canvas next to the single bed, with linens and blankets neatly folded. From time to time, through the thin bathroom partition, she could hear murmurings from Ross. By the time she had prepared the boy's cot, she found that Al had already fallen asleep on the bed, a momentary victim of high altitude and hijinks with Montezuma. Hands on hips, her smile a beatitude, she regarded the sleeping child in total satisfaction with this moment.

She had always made Littlebo's bed, but Al was old enough to help make his own bed. Why hadn't she let him help? She knew, and she didn't care. Closing the door gently, she returned to see Ross in the kitchen pouring himself another cup of coffee.

His glance toward her was unreadable, of course, but his long sigh said a lot as he lowered himself into a chair. "Okayyy, it turns out that a Raymond Townsend in the Seattle area did have an E-mail address. But he recently dumped AOL, anybody could guess why, and he's evidently between Web servers right now. Just bad luck all around," he said.

T.C. blinked. "Would you like to put that into English? Even pig latin would do."

"Sorry. When you can't always get on the Net and you grow terminally tired of excuses and promises and commercials by your Web server, some of your smarter citizens will start over. Looks like Ray Townsend is pretty smart. I hope so. He'd better be."

"Drop the other shoe."

"Well, once the boy is in Townsend's care, it will take constant alertness on his part. He'll have to avoid all the tricks a UN facilitator team might use to find Al. Perhaps even legal pressure. I mean, the boy's father *is*, after all, his next of kin."

"And it doesn't matter what they did to his mother?"

"Oh, no doubt it would, if you went back to Mexico to testify, and they might refuse to proceed unless Al were there as well, which would be an open invitation to spirit him away. Oh, yes, and let's not forget that your testimony would have to outweigh what they could bring to court—which might include some Mexican police with bribe money, claiming you're a perjurer or even a kidnapper, from what you've said."

He leaned forward, placing fingertips together as if in prayer, his right little finger pathetically untouched and alone. "I'm trying to show you that when you play against people like these, the deck is stacked, T.C." His gaze did not waver from hers. "Likely as not, you'd wind up in a Mexican prison for perjury, and after all you've done to prevent it, your little friend would be on his way to Iran. Or Iraq or Turkey; Kurds are very active and under siege in all three countries."

T.C. buried her face in her hands. "It's so unfair. *Que chingones matandos,* what murdering fuckers," she moaned. Then she placed both hands on the cedar tabletop and looked at them as though wondering what they might do next of their own volition. Her eyes swept up to meet his again. "But whining's not going to get me anywhere," she said evenly.

"Good thinking," he said. She could divine that wry little smile of his even past the Jobst.

"Help me, Ross. What *will* get us what we want?"

He needed a moment to collect his thoughts. "Patience," he said at last. "Think several moves ahead. Don't do anything like making a phone call without considering the potential outcomes. And especially, don't forget and do something really stupid, after evaporating so neatly from Tucson."

"Like?"

"Well,—like forgetting and paying for something in Ruidoso with a credit card." He saw the look of puzzlement, changing swiftly into horror, her mouth a silent O.

He sat up straighter. "Don't tell me," he pleaded. She gave a bobbing little nod, her luxuriant brows brought together in consternation. "Very well," he said then, and repeated it. "Very well, tell me what you bought with credit cards."

"Gas in, uh, Lordsburg I think."

"Gives them a direction. But it's not a big problem," he said quickly, nodding to himself. "Wait, how many credit cards do you have?"

"Only Visa. What's the difference?"

"If you had several, and used them in different cities in quick succession, it could imply that your cards have been stolen. They'd be less likely to rely on the evidence. Anyhow, what else did you use your card for?"

"Motel room last night in Ruidoso," she said.

A pause, as if gathering his confidence. "It's not on a major interstate, but that's still not a dead giveaway."

"Yeah, but breakfast this morning, and a lot of clothes and all those groceries, too, every smidgin of it on my Visa card."

"Damn. Hold on, where did you call me from," he asked, eyes narrowed.

"Pay phone at that K-Bob place with the whopping big breakfasts."

The big shoulders relaxed a trifle. "That, at least, was a smart move."

"That was sheer luck," she admitted. "I had no idea a person could be tracked like this. It didn't cross my mind that well-connected scum could get their tentacles on my personal records so easily. I just never thought about it." With a quiet hissing intensity to avoid waking the boy: "Jesus Christ, I never took Disappearance one-oh-one! How was I to know? I used my card when we flew from San Antonio to Tucson, for that matter. Then they can follow me from anything I buy on a credit card?"

"I suppose I thought everyone was aware of that," he said, head shaking in commiseration, "the same way I assume everyone speaks computerese. But it's not your fault that you didn't." He laid his gloved hand over hers.

She pulled away, lips pressed to a tight line. "Yes it is. If I'm going to compete on a field that changes every day, I have to learn where all the new traps are set. Just like everyone else," she added. "So I guess I've drawn those people here. What I'd better do next is keep going, maybe double back to Seattle."

He sat back and regarded her with stolid calm. "Given enough money, yes. Have you got, oh, a thousand in cash?" He saw her hot glare of negation. "Forgive me. I'm only trying to clarify what you're up against. As it happens, I could lend you some cash. A couple of hundred here, more from the bank, but not today," he went on, checking his wristwatch.

"I can't take money from you. It wasn't part of the deal, and I don't know when I could pay it back."

"I think we could expect the boy's grandparents to make it good," he said gently. "You can't afford to care about that now. What if your alternative was losing this little boy?"

"You know damned well," she said.

"That's more like it. You've given me an idea already, but it'll mean you must leave Al here for a day or so." He saw new hope in her face and continued, "You should continue to leave a paper trail and let it play out in a city with major travel connections. It might be El Paso, but Albuquerque would fit the trail you've already laid down, turning north."

"Like an idiot," she finished for him.

"Like an honest, naive citizen," he amended for her. "If you want to do this, go back to a gas station in town and say you need, oh, something that hints at your need to keep going—new spark plugs might take an hour. Pay with your card, fuel up, then drive to Albuquerque. You could do that tonight, and if you're going to do this, it ought to be as soon as possible, pretending Al is with you. Take a motel room there for you and the boy, who incidentally will be right here all the time. And by the way, keep an eye on your rearview when you're on the road, just in case these people are closer than you think, because if so, they could get lucky."

"Let's say they did," she suggested. "What then?"

He mulled it over for a moment. "Go to the nearest local police, yell your head off, deny everything—and phone me instantly. Sometimes a small-town police chief will dig his heels in against outsiders, even those with the right ID, riding roughshod over a citizen. With me so far?"

"I think so, but Al isn't any problem for me, and I'm sure he'd rather stay with someone he knows. Why shouldn't he ride along with me?"

"If your pursuers got lucky and the boy were with you, you could get very unlucky. If you're alone, I think the worst that would happen might be that they'd follow you. I don't think you want to risk taking him along like that. There's no denying a slight risk to you in all this, though it offsets a different risk of not doing it."

"You wouldn't have a gun handy?"

He looked at her for a long moment. Then, "I was thinking about that. New Mexico and Texas prohibit concealed weapons, and permits aren't as easy to get as in, say, Arizona and Colorado, so you'd have to be sensible. Meaning sneaky. How long since you've fired a handgun?"

"I used to watch Beau shoot something he called a hog leg," she replied.

A mirthless laugh from Ross. "I gather you watched him ride bulls, too. No, I'm sorry, T.C. Without practice you'd be more dangerous to yourself than to someone else. I can drive again, these days, so I would've volunteered to lay your trail, but no one in his right mind would believe my name is Teresa Rainey when I tried to charge something on your card. Plus, people tend to remember me. Something to do with my rare beauty."

She had learned not to reply to these bitter little asides of his. "I hate arguing with you. I never win. All right: a motel room in Albuquerque. Then what?"

"Call Amtrak from your room. Buy two coach tickets to wherever—Seattle would be perfect but Denver will be cheaper— using your credit card and make sure you pick up your tickets at the station."

"Why not airline tickets?"

"Because if you don't get on the plane, the airline will have a record of it. And these people can get those records, and they'd know you're trying to dump them."

"But not Amtrak, huh?"

"I'm not sure how far they could push Amtrak for information, but I do know you can buy two tickets, get on the train, and then immediately get off again from the next car without anyone being the wiser. The record shows you got on. The presumption is that you stayed on."

She sighed, then narrowed her eyes. "How could you know all this so well when I know so little?"

"I've heard the stories," he shrugged. "Okay, after you leave the train, get back in your car and put away that goddamned credit card for the duration and pay for everything after that with cash. Circle back to us by way of Vaughn and Roswell. You could be back here tomorrow night, having given those people a nice set of misdirections to ponder."

THE SKINS OF DEAD MEN

□   □   □

The afternoon was still sunny when T.C. left, though Al's disposition was not. She had woken him to explain that he must not feel abandoned because she had to run a long errand. No, he couldn't go with her. No, not even when he tuned up to cry. No, not even when he *did* cry.

Ross made the parting a little easier when he said that Mr. Ferguson, the owner of the gold mine, should be paying a visit about suppertime. The old fellow might show Al a nugget of pure gold if the request were nicely put. Meanwhile, Ross himself had work to do in his room and somebody needed to feed Montezuma.

Still, T.C. drove into Ruidoso with the memory of tear-stained little cheeks in her rearview mirror. The spark plug replacement took too long, but, she had to admit while driving across the dry desolation of the Jornada del Muerto, the Datsun did seem more perky with these new plugs.

She struck Interstate 25 in early dusk, drove north attentive to her rearview, and took a nice Albuquerque motel room for two off Gibson near the airport. She checked by telephone for a pair of Amtrak tickets to Denver but found the connections absurd. Kansas City was quicker, leaving Albuquerque the next day soon after one P.M. She ordered a late sandwich and a glass of wine from room service and watched the late news in her room, feeling more alone than she had for years. She fell asleep wondering how it was possible that such *viboras,* poisonous snakes, as these facilitators could raise this much hell without winding up in the news.

The next morning she drove to the Amtrak station on First Street, got her tickets, and enjoyed a light breakfast near the station before putting away her Visa card. She found that shopping didn't pass the time as she had hoped, not when she had to keep looking over her shoulder, but at least the train was on time. With no specific reserved seat, she got aboard with one ticket, got off again, used her second ticket to go aboard a second time, and got off a second time feeling very clever.

By the time the Amtrak pulled out for Kansas City, T.C. was hightailing it eastward on Interstate 40. Several times, she drove around in smaller towns watching behind her without result. She refueled, had a very late lunch, and bought fruit from an open-air stand in Vaughn, paying with cash. Her map showed an alternative route that would cut more than an hour from her return trip. Before sundown she was retracing her route back up the state highway that led to Ruidoso, her mood much improved.

When she arrived at the cabin she saw the familiar rusting hulk of a Willys Jeep parked near Ross's Cherokee, which meant that the old miner was visiting. Al was already outside, capering with pleasure at the sight of her. She grabbed him up in a hug, grinning, blinking away her emotions as she released him. "I see you survived without me," she said.

"Sure. Me and Monte are friends now. I saw a rattlesnake up in the rocks. You bring me anything? Mr. Ferguson's got a real gold nugget on his key ring. Did you see any of those bad guys?"

"Whoa, give me a second, Calvin. I've got some bananas in the front seat." The boy carried the bag of fruit for her as T.C. paused to view the Jeep, which she hadn't expect to find still capable of toting a man over rough terrain. Or, in fact, any terrain at all.

The vehicle was more accurately the festering remnant of an original army Jeep, its hood long since cannibalized for some other purpose of Orville Ferguson, if not his father. Old Orv had bought it as legitimate surplus soon after his discharge from the service in 1945, having fought from a Jeep in Sicily with George Patton's Seventh Army.

Exposed to the elements and likely to yap like a Pomeranian under load, the engine was a tiny thing by modern standards, festooned with more wire and tape than Willys parts. Its windshield, she recalled, was now the glass face of a coldframe at the Ferguson place because old Orv valued his annual crop of hot peppers more than he needed a Jeep windshield. After some ancient argument with a pine stump, one of its headlights had been bashed out. The other, seeming no larger than the palm of a man's hand, now hung from a dashboard switch by heavy wiring so that it could be employed like a handheld searchlight. T.C. had no idea whether the light worked. The notion of riding this loose assemblage twice in daylight, let alone darkness, was an implied insult to life and limb.

The seats Willys had provided were missing, too. To ride this contraption, the old man sat on an overturned bucket that was bolted by its baling handle to the floor, so that the driver slid several inches to each side with the vagaries of whatever slope he was fighting at the moment.

T.C. had accepted a ride once, sitting behind the miner, and had watched with increasing alarm as the gear lever kept jumping out of position so that Orv was forced, again and again, to ram it in place with a ratcheting scramble of gear complaints. She had vaulted out only when Orv shouted, ''Dang brakes won't hold,'' and learned moments later that he wasn't shouting a warning. The brakes hadn't held for years. Orv was merely explaining why he needed to keep the thing in gear at all times.

The capper to this unlikely contrivance was that Orville Ferguson could have bought a dozen more, had he wanted to. According to Ross, the old fellow's mine was a lode so rich he did not need the big workings that made most gold mines obvious from afar. His winter home was a prefab bungalow only a dozen precipitous miles downhill on the edge of Ruidoso—a relic of a failed marriage, a cheerless place where T.C. had slept during a previous visit.

A proud graduate of the Texas School of Mines half a century before, Orv had gradually come to repent the sins of his family vocation. If you could spot a mine from a hundred yards, he would say, it was a zit on the nose of God. Orv spoke like that, religious in his way while proudly nonsectarian. He sounded like the Las Cruces boy he was, but his library was well thumbed, and over the years his outlook had become more tinged by the Sierra Club than the Bureau of Land Management. If Orv had a religion, he would say, it was the land.

T.C. found Ross and Orv Ferguson on the screened porch and took a handshake from the grizzled paw of Orv who seemed to have aged not at all. Of medium height, still whip lean and erect, Orv was dressed in khaki shirt and trousers over scuffed black engineer's boots. On the slippery slope beyond seventy years, Orv creased his permanently tan facial wrinkles in a grinful of dentures. "Well, now, how you doin', ma'am?" He didn't wait for a reply. "I hear you took a motel room the other night. Shoot, you know where the key to my place is."

It had been late, she said, and she hadn't wanted to use his place without permission. He countered with an offer of permanent permission, and she thanked him.

Then she answered the expectant look of Ross. "I made the grand tour," she told him. "No problems, but I owe you some cash."

"Good." Neither of them was more specific than that in the presence of the old man.

Orv scratched the broad bald spot inside his frizzed halo of white hair. "I hope you're up for a little three-handed stud."

"You're describing my ex," she quipped, drawing a cackle from Ferguson. "But I'll sit in if Orv will put away his shooting iron."

As always, the old man wore a revolver in a much-scarred belt holster whenever he left his homesite at the mine. Reluctant to shoot anything that didn't bite first, he had been struck twice by rattlers. It was true that most rattlesnakes tried to avoid confrontation, but some, like the desert sidewinder, seemed to seek it. Some wouldn't even give you an honest rattle. So Orv had sighed and accepted this enmity and kept his revolver loaded with special snake loads that fired groups of tiny pellets in the manner of miniature shotgun shells. Like everyone else who had grown up watching television westerns, T.C. had never quite gotten fully comfortable playing poker with a man who packed a six-shooter.

Al fetched a card table as requested, and T.C. brought the wide-mouthed antique San Ildefonso bowl, the burnished black-on-black variety, with its heavy cargo of steel pennies and old pesos. The pesos were Ross's, their total value amounting perhaps to fifty cents because he had put them aside back when the big peso coin was trading at twenty-six hundred to the dollar. The bowl itself might have brought two thousand dollars from a museum.

The pennies were Orv's, saved from a time when he thought they might become a shrewd investment, literally the equivalent of a penny stock. That stock, Orv felt, had never entirely matured. For purposes of their game, a peso was worth ten pennies. It was perfectly clear to them all that, because the battered cards were also Orv's, he was more familiar with their creases. Every Christmas, the old miner would present Ross with a heavy bag of coins, and roughly once a week through much of the year he would win them back, a pocketful at a time.

They played until the westering sun failed to stifle a cool breeze off the heights of Sierra Blanca. Orv broke off a story about a fishing trip with Ross's father when he saw Al shiver as the boy crowded nearer to T.C.'s side. "The tad's freezing where he stands," said the old fellow, gathering up his cards. "If you can thaw him out by morning, herd him up my way and I'll show him how a mine ought to be worked."

T.C. agreed when she saw the boy's avid nod. Ross made a pro forma offer of a casserole dinner, but Orv declined. "One of these evenings I'm gonna have to shoot that ol' Willys horse, and when it happens I don't intend to walk the rest of the way in the dark."

"You're practically walking as it is," Ross said, with a glance toward the attenuated Jeep.

"Not so loud, young fella; it's sensitive to criticism," said Orv, buttoning the flap on his bulging shirt pocket. "Every time it gets near my Range Rover, it dang near throws me." There was no point in asking why he didn't always drive the newer vehicle. Like everything else he did, he did it because he liked it that way.

The others sat on the porch and enjoyed the dependable spectacle of Orville Ferguson's rolling downhill start in the Jeep, which always involved spats of smoke and farts like a stallion's. Orv had a perfectly good battery, he claimed, but why wear it out? With the old fellow hanging onto the wheel as his bucket slid this way and that, they cheered the mount and its rider like rodeo fans and then moved into the warmth of the cabin.

By silent agreement they did not discuss T.C.'s diversionary trip until after the casserole had been made and consumed and Al was dozing before the TV set at the other end of the big room. Though Ross's questions were gentle and without critical comment, T.C. sensed that he hid some frustration at her answers.

And Ross had some news that was potentially good: a way to get direct contact with Ray Townsend—maybe.

CHAPTER □ **12**

Soon after the Lear landed at Albuquerque Municipal, Tom Perrin drove his little group in a dark green Pontiac rental to their adjoining motel suites on Central, not far from the fairgrounds. The suites were not ideal, but with one of a dozen decoy names on his foreign credit cards, Perrin knew they could stay relatively anonymous. "We're steering clear of Uncle Sam's courtesy facilities for now," Perrin told the curious Anatol Kerman, "just in case someone connects us with that little dustup in Tucson."

"Dustup," Beale rumbled softly, in tones that implied, You mean fuckup. Across the big man's cheek, chin, and wrist ran slick, shining tracks of collodion like slender trails of clear nail polish, covering the cuts the woman had given him. Prizefighters had used collodion over their cuts for almost a century, and Cody Beale was never without a supply. He was a man who bled easily but never seemed to care much.

"Dustup, Cody," Perrin repeated, his smile tightening. "Rhymes with shut up." He was already plugging a printer-equipped computer into the suite's telephone line. A facilitator team could call on any of several regional centers: Honolulu, Oakland, Dearborn, Coral Gables, Queens, Bethesda, and the one Perrin was using now, Houston. Chiefly for Kerman's benefit he said, while typing, "Rainey almost certainly still has the boy with her.

She wouldn't have taken off so fast otherwise." Finished for the moment, he watched the computer screen with folded arms.

Kerman had enough experience with Americans to avoid heavily pressuring this one, but he too felt pressured. He phrased his query with care. "Would you share your insights with me?"

"Tucson's her home turf, and she's left it. Her pattern has been to snatch the kid and run like hell toward a place she knows. Let's see," he went on, running a finger down a sheet on his clipboard. "An hour after she pulled that stunt at the Greyhound station, someone took her car. Houston Center is still keeping track of her credit card purchases, and we know that's been a valid trace because when she bought two airline tickets from San Antonio to Tucson, sure enough she showed up in Tucson."

McLeod had been sitting quietly in a chair, still morose after his recent upending by a trussed-up little female. He sported a couple of adhesive strips from that bathroom tussle, too. Now, with something he hoped might be useful, he said, "You don't suppose she sent a friend with her card to throw us off the scent while she went to ground in Tucson?"

"I thought of that," Perrin snapped. "But the card's user would have to be someone who could pass for her, and someone pretty good at faking a trail. That hasn't been her pattern. A few hours after her car disappeared, someone bought fuel in Lordsburg—that's here in New Mexico. Then a motel room in, uh, Ruidoso. For two," he added, with a meaningful glance at the Kurd. "Then two breakfasts, and clothes, and a hell of a lot of groceries, all in Ruidoso. Also some minor car repairs. Then last night, a motel for two here in Albuquerque. That's the most recent report I got. But," he turned to gaze at Beale, "you say they checked out this morning."

"One-night stand," said Beale. "Description fits her, all right, but the clerk never saw the boy. She could have friends here. Lots of Latinos in—"

The computer screen changed, and Perrin held up his hand for silence while he concentrated. Anatol Kerman had little experience in the nuances of credit card surveillance, but he was a very quick learner. It irritated him when the others watching that screen gave little grunts that may have implied much but told him nothing. Finally, Perrin obtained a hard copy of the data and finished his typing routines before sitting back to study the printout.

"My arse," said McLeod. "It's to be Kansas City now?"

"I've got some good contacts there from the old days," Beale said with complacency.

Kerman, having noted the record of the airline tickets: "Then she has abandoned her car."

"Maybe," Perrin said, his tone guarded. Then, "No, by God, I don't think so! Motel for two, right? But a sandwich and a glass of wine, and no one saw the boy."

Beale: "So? They shared a sandwich, and she doesn't like beer."

"No milk. No soda pop, no tea, no dessert. No kid in that room," Perrin said firmly. "And look here—she bought Amtrak tickets and had breakfast. One breakfast, not two. In Ruidoso, it was two. Gentlemen, this little bimbo has developed a sudden case of smarts. Also, no record of her using that credit card after she met the train. I'm betting the boy is not with her anymore."

"Then where is he? And where is her car?" Kerman said.

Perrin sighed. "Wherever he is, that woman knows. What is it with you and cars, Mr. K?"

"The man has a point," said McLeod. "If her car is parked near the Amtrak station, we have one set of possibilities. If not, another set." McLeod met the gaze of the Kurd, and they shared the tiniest of smiles.

Kerman had noticed that though the two big men tended to growl and snap at each other like alpha male wolves, they seemed to share a lot of respect. Whether Dexter McLeod deserved less respect was debatable, but certainly he got less of it. Perhaps the smaller man was unconscious of his faint, friendly overtures to Kerman, a man of similar size. In any case, Kerman could not afford any evidence of special bonding to the least-respected member of this pack.

"You win, Dex. So what are we waiting for?" Perrin asked. "We can check out the parking near the depot. We know her car, we know its plates. But don't be surprised if she's managed to change the goddamned plates. The bitch is getting sharp on us."

"Oh, shit," said Beale. "More footwork. You mean tonight, Tom?"

"It's what they pay us for," said Perrin, standing. He turned to Kerman. "I won't suggest that you help, Mr. K, but if you choose to, it could speed things up."

Kerman nodded equably. "Thank you, Mr. Perrin. I must help all that I can." He shrugged into a jacket of lightweight suede and watched while the other men saw to their equipment, including a check of their little transceivers.

The drive to the center of town took only ten minutes, but in that time Perrin decided to expand their search. It was possible, he said, that the Rainey woman had switched cars. If so, her Datsun could still be parked somewhere near the depot. Avis and National would have required a credit card, but a check of their parking lots was a more certain option. They dropped McLeod off for a careful check of rental parking lots and continued on to the depot parking area.

After an hour, they had exhausted all likely options. McLeod had already radioed his frustration, admitting that his transmissions sounded odd because he was munching a Payday candy bar. "I could use a big filet myself about now," Beale said as he fell sighing into the backseat of their rental.

"I never knew when you couldn't," Perrin replied as he started the car. He glanced toward the little Kurd in the seat beside him. "We'll pick Dex up and find a steak house. Agreed?"

"You got my vote," Beale said. Kerman only nodded.

Perrin: "Why so quiet, Mr. K? Not hungry?"

"Not very," said the Kurd, who had gone for days without food many times in his life.

"Don't feel bad about not finding her car. Most footwork like this just tells us what possibilities to eliminate. On the positive side, now we're more certain that she didn't leave her car here. Which means she's either still in Albuquerque, or she's gone to wherever she left the boy."

"His name is Talal," said Kerman.

"Yes, Talal," Perrin said, reminding himself that, for this starchy little Kurd, the kid was virtual royalty.

"This child is not just any boy," Kerman said, as if he had glimpsed Perrin's thoughts. "Talal is, or will be, a leader of our people. It is ordained by his blood, Mr. Perrin. Your people have a saying that leaders are born, not made—or something of the sort."

"Sometimes the other way around, depending on what point's being made," Perrin replied, adding quickly, "not that I'd take either position."

"Very wise," Kerman said. "We would say that our leaders must be born and then made. I have been sent to assure that the making of young Talal is properly begun. And it cannot be done in the West," he finished with perfect certainty.

Just to keep the conversation going, Perrin said, "Too bad Talal's mother wouldn't go along with that."

"Tragic," said Kerman. "I recall her as a very young woman. Headstrong, difficult. No Kurd in his right mind would have brought her to live in Kurdistan." A brief silence. Then, "Still, her death was acknowledged with regret. Was there no other way to separate her from Talal?"

"I could have done it if I'd known what was going to happen," said Perrin, looking straight ahead, "but that goddamned Mexican thug was used to roughing up men, and he threw the poor broad around like a big Barbie Doll." This was the one detail he had revised in his report. Neither Beale nor McLeod had been present, and the Mexican would never be debriefed. Whatever the kid might say later, well, he was only a kid, whose version could be dismissed as fanciful. It was simple, intelligent self-interest for the historian to change history.

They picked up McLeod, who had run down one extra lead: a local "rent-a-wreck" agency that did, on occasion, take cash in lieu of credit cards. The night manager had taken some cash from McLeod too, before telling him they'd rented nothing for several days to anyone matching the woman's description. "Worth a try, though," Dex McLeod sighed.

Beale said, "Yeah, it's these little shirttail outfits that play by different rules that can throw you off your game."

At this, Kerman turned to regard the big man in the seat behind him. In the intermittent light of the boulevard, his face seemed expressionless, but the eyes, to Beale, seemed to glow. "Game?"

"Just an expression, Mr. K," said Perrin. "They even taught us gaming theory when I was, um, a federal employee." He knew better than to say CIA to a man like Kerman. Perrin had gone private many years ago, and the Kurd might harbor no resentment along that line, but then again . . . "We take this game very, very seriously." He eased from the boulevard toward an eatery advertising beef and seafood. "You play chess?"

Beale and McLeod were already hustling out of the Pontiac as Kerman nodded. "Very serious game," Perrin smiled. "While we're eating, I have to decide which piece little Ms. Teresa Rainey has played. She may have moved her queen halfway across the board to Kansas City. Carrying a little king with it," he added.

"But you do not think that," Kerman prompted.

"No. I think she's riding her queen's knight. One step to the side and two back."

They did not resume the discussion until they had ordered, as the Kurd sipped his iced water. "Perhaps," said Kerman, "she has decided to retreat behind her castle."

"In a way, I hope so," Perrin said, aware that his men were mystified by all this allegory. To Kerman's inquiring gaze he said, "That's usually part of the end game, and the sooner the better."

Then he fell silent, musing over his options. Not until they were halfway through their meal did Perrin speak again. "Cody," he said, "let's see how good your K.C. contacts are."

Beale paused with an onion ring halfway to his mouth. "Good enough," he said.

"Take the Lear there tonight. Spend a day or two and see if you can pick up her trail there."

"Jeez. It's a big town, Tom. Maybe you ought to pull in another couple of cadre."

Perrin did not intend to ask for additions to his team; it wouldn't look good. "Hire some casuals if you know so many cops. This team stays as it is. Keep in touch through Houston Center."

The big man began to wipe big greasy hands on his napkin. "Anybody want the rest of my onion rings? Feel free."

Kerman thought that grease might be pork fat and declined as the others emptied the basket of onion rings. He consulted the multifunction timepiece on his wrist, then sighed. "And where do we go, Mr. Perrin?"

"To bed," Perrin said. "And tomorrow morning we'll take a little drive down to Ruidoso, dress like tourists, do some backtracking. Little town like that, three of us should be able to cover it while Cody's in K.C."

"And if the Rainey woman sees one of us?"

"We'll look like three other people," said Perrin, catching the waiter's eye. "Sorry about this, Cody, you can catch a nap in flight."

Beale gave a wry shrug he didn't really feel. The truth was that he preferred this singleton work. There was always the off chance that he could bring the kid in alone, a solitary triumph. Given any chance at all he intended to put the woman down. Cody Beale had no special animosity toward women in general, but with this little heller, Rainey, he was anxious to settle a score.

CHAPTER 13

T.C. heard the hoarse shout through the wall and was instantly awake, moving quickly across the moonlit room to Al's side. The boy continued to sleep as though drugged. Then from the other bedroom an agonized, "Ahh, Jeez," not one of Ross's common expressions but undeniably his voice. She pulled his spare bathrobe over her, tripping on its excess length as she padded around through the big room to his door.

"Ross?" She knocked a rapid tattoo, hearing more of what she dreaded, the whistling gasps of a man in great pain. She opened the door and saw him on his bed, a dark mass writhing and mumbling, "Oh, fuck, oh, fuck," even more unlike Ross. She snapped on his bedside lamp and knelt beside him, fearful that he might fling an arm back and knock her flat. He'd done that, once, when she'd come to wake him from the throes of another nightmare. She had slept in Orv's bungalow on the edge of town for the rest of that visit. "Ross! It's okay, you're home in bed, Crispy," she said, shaking his shoulder firmly.

"Whuh! Ain't gonna make it," he said, panting, then rolled over, supine, venting a great exhalation.

"Ross. It's T.C., 'mano. You're okay," she said with quiet urgency.

Now he lay still, his exposed shoulder damp with sweat, and for a moment neither of them spoke. Without his Jobst mask the planes of his features were softly mottled, shining in the light, a caricature of a face. She saw that he had lips now, after a fashion; a distinct cosmetic improvement over the last time she'd seen him this way. The lips moved before he opened his eyes. "I'm awake," he said. "Thanks. I suppose I woke Al."

"Thunder wouldn't wake Al," she assured him, "and you weren't very loud."

"I was changing a tire. There was a bang."

"You don't have to go through it again," she cautioned.

"Yes I do." He turned his head to look at her. "I was using professional equipment, and I don't even know how. Bending over, putting air in it, one of those fat muscle-car wheels, I think. Something flew up and hit me here," he placed a hand at the juncture of his neck and shoulder. He withdrew his hand and looked at it, then made a rictus she knew was a smile. "Well, it's not bleeding anymore."

"It never did," she replied, giving his hand the gentlest of squeezes.

"I wonder," he said. "I remember, the instant after the bang, thinking, Stupid, you know better than that. But the funny thing is, I don't. I have no idea what I did wrong."

"Hilarious," she told him. "I always said your sense of humor would get you in trouble."

"Something certainly did," he said, trying to smile back. He obviously felt like talking, perhaps to reassure himself that he was fully outside the dream again, superior to it. "I was working late, alone, in a hurry. My wife was waiting dinner and I'd promised to bring ice cream for the kids. Butter brickle," he said wonderingly. "And I hate butter brickle."

"I thought you liked it," said T.C.

"I do. The other guy didn't. I . . . he wasn't sure he could get to the store because of the flooding." His elaborate shrug pleaded for understanding of what he could not explain. Closing his eyes again, he frowned in concentration. "It's his own car he was working on, expensive custom wheels. Ohio license plate NYM 238, plain as day, and he was changing to big mud tires. Rock music on the radio. And by the way," Ross went on with a note of disdain, "he knew those sexy cast-metal wheels he'd bought so cheaply had been stolen. Boy, some of the people I meet in here." He tapped his forehead.

She nodded agreement, then said, "Does any of this match up with your real experiences, Ross?"

"Never has yet. Oh, sure, in general terms: a guy is failing to balance his checkbook, or making a U-turn on a busy street, things everybody's done. But it's all these little details that make the moments unique. Intellectually, I know I've created it all, even a wild bedroom tussle once that ended with chest pains. But on a gut level, it's disturbing as hell."

She fought a temptation to share an outlandish guess with him, but the tempo of his speech had slowed now, and his yawn made her decision for her. "You read too much," she said.

"Probably. What time is it?"

She glanced at his bedside clock radio. "A little after three. I can nuke some of that cold coffee for you."

He shut his eyes again and, after a moment, shook his head. "The medication has about worn off, so I don't think this will happen again tonight. Best if I just get some sleep."

She eased back from his bed, pulling the terry cloth closer now that she began to feel the mountain chill. Standing above him, she said, "You never mentioned that. Medication bringing it on, I mean."

"Believe it or not, I never made the connection 'til now. I take the stuff to help me sleep sometimes. Nine times out of ten, it does the job with no downside, or none that I can recall."

"And the tenth time it turns you into someone else."

"It sure felt like me," he insisted, "but it doesn't hurt now. I guess you'd have to be there."

"Wherever you were, it's no place I want to be."

"A warehouse, or a big service station. Can you feature me as a mechanic?"

"Oddly enough, I can." She waved as she snapped off his light, backing from the room. "Sleep, 'mano."

She checked on Al again—he hadn't stirred—before climbing into bed, where she lay unmoving, eyes wide, for an interminable five minutes. Then she pulled on heavy socks and the bathrobe and padded into the big room again, pouring cold coffee and waiting, arms folded, in the dim light of the microwave oven as it hummed.

Curled into a chair, feet tucked under her so that she felt snug in her terry cloth cocoon, T.C. gazed from Ross's big picture window at moonlit solitude and nursed her steaming brew. She wondered whether that medication of his was more damaging than it was worth, and whether Ross had told his support team about these nightmares, and, if he hadn't, whether she should do it herself.

He would probably be furious if she did that, but that didn't necessarily mean she shouldn't. The corners of her mouth turned up as she reflected that she really could see him as a mechanic, but one who assembled precision parts on a satellite or something, not a guy with greasy hands fixing tires.

The smile evaporated as she recalled the words in his nightmare, the horrified "oh, fuck, oh, fuck," of some desperate alter ego. And Ross Downing would sooner swallow his tongue than say "ain't." A bizarre explanation had occurred to her as he'd recounted the nightmare, and again it flitted past.

She felt a chill begin at the base of her spine, and she wiggled deeper into the robe. She hadn't meant it as literal truth, but in his nightmare Ross had, in fact, become someone else. Some poor devil who'd hurt himself badly and, in the surrogate memory of Ross Downing, knew it had been his own fault. She drank the rest of the coffee to quell the chill that had built within her and tried to avoid the wild surmises that, she thought grimly, the damned caffeine had provoked. And presently she slept.

□   □   □

The quarreling of jays woke her before direct sunlight struck nearby Carrizo Peak, and T.C. got an hour of quality sacktime in bed. It was the incense of frying bacon that brought her awake this time, and—what was it? French toast! The essence of breakfast had done to Al what thunder could not, and she found her two favorite males setting the table for a gourmand's wake-me-up.

Astonishingly, Ross was still without his Jobst, and Al, far from standoffish, gazed at the burned man with frank interest. "He sneaked up on me while I was cooking," Ross explained. "I think our lad decided anybody who could create smells like this couldn't be all bad."

Al gave him a thumbs-up, and they both laughed, and T.C.'s heart leaped with joy. They even sweetened a cup of coffee for the boy and wolfed down their French toast with slathers of syrup and I Can't Believe It's Not Butter before rising with groans of false remorse.

Al would have saved a strip of bacon for Montezuma, but Ross stuck it in the refrigerator. "I have a rule about that, Al: Never feed anything to something dumber. Pigs are more intelligent than some people I've known, and Monte's really just a squirrel on steroids. Give him those crusts of toast."

Al fixed him with a sly look. "I dunno if I should. How smart is wheat?"

Ross uttered his little falsetto bark of mirth. "This boy will go far," he predicted.

"But can I go as far as the old guy's mine this morning?"

"Mr. Ferguson to you," T.C. reminded him. "What do you think, Ross?"

"I've got some work to do, but Orv asked for it. Drive my Cherokee. Follow the ruts, careful on the scree. You've been there." He tossed his spare key to her.

The Cherokee's high clearance made easy work of the trail, which followed stone outcrops around the ridge, then upward across a meadow choked with rank native grasses, still green from the spring snowmelt. Here and there on the meadow's flank, young pine trees pointed aloft to challenge nearby aspens, the largest reaching thirty feet or so.

"Trees aren't very big," Al noticed.

"That's because they were mostly planted by Orv and Ross's

dad," T.C. told him. "The big trees that used to be here are now part of Ross's cabin, and the old guys finally realized what they'd done and planted new ones. These don't grow very fast."

"Cabin is neat," said Al, holding on as T.C. negotiated a steep rise. "Does everything neat have to be bad somehow?"

"Seems like it sometimes, but Orv Ferguson built his place with that in mind. You'll see." Now the trail leveled out, and presently they nosed downward. T.C. drove very slowly here, the blocky vehicle tilting sideways.

Al thrust his head from the window and whistled. "Boy! Don't turn now," he warned.

"Quit jumping around and don't remind me, Calvin, this isn't the fun part," she said. On her first visit up here, Orv Ferguson had proudly pointed out the pilings he had sunk to avoid further deterioration of this slope beside the trail. The drop-off was knee-high at the pilings and, in time, would inevitably grow deeper. Grass and wildflowers did not entirely hide the loose rock debris that Orv called scree. The slope continued down for a hundred feet before steepening to clifflike proportions, and the tops of mature pines were just visible, reaching up from the ravine below.

After fifty yards of this, the slope flattened again, and the Cherokee rumbled over a small timbered bridge with stone abutments. A clear seasonal brook burbled cheerfully under the bridge, descending in a series of tiny waterfalls into the almost vertical ravine. By fall, it would be bone dry.

"The creek comes from Orv's pond," T.C. said and steered up a final slope before giving a bleat from the horn. Al twisted his head this way and that for a moment before he spotted Orv's Land Rover and, as if abandoned near a jumble of stone, the skeletal Jeep.

Then, as T.C. stopped beside a small grove of aspen, a burst of reflected sunlight caught the slanting glass of Orv Ferguson's aerie, and for the first time Al realized that he was looking at a very special jumble of stone. "Oooh, wow," he said, leaning far out, then snapping his head around as Orville Ferguson stepped from the aspens. "Hey! Where'd you come from?"

"I like to watch people's reactions," the old man replied, eyes twinkling, his smile taking in T.C. as well. "Some folks dance and tell jokes. I just build things."

"Ross phoned you, I see," T.C. said as the old fellow slid into a backseat. "Hope you don't mind."

"Shoot, it was my idea," said Orv, pointing forward, his finger moving in an arc. "Drive around to the Rover, up on the flag-stones."

She did as she was told, rolling to a stop on flagstones that Orv had carefully fitted into a driveway running beside his big slanted windows. His front entrance was a massive double-door arrange-ment wide enough to accommodate the Land Rover. As the boy scampered from the vehicle, he scanned nearby boulders and the earth that cradled them. "But where's the mine?"

"Inside. I live in it," he persisted when Al's gaze became sus-picious. "No fooling."

But Al was not convinced until they had stepped through one of those big doors and moved down a continuation of the flag-stones past the old man's living quarters. Orv had inherited a small but very rich claim that, he said, had been a streambed millions of years ago before the mountain had covered it. And the old stream had borne a fortune in gold down that mountainside. The stream that now meandered down the mountain some distance away, bearing only traces of gold, had once flowed here.

It had been Orv's idea to clear away all external signs of a working mine and to build a home of fieldstone at the entrance to his father's original workings. With modern equipment and electricity provided by a windmill on a nearby promontory, work-ing the claim required only one man working the old streambed, removing sedimentary earth down to the original bedrock. "Have to move a few yards of tailings—the fine dirt after I've dry-washed the gold from it—outside now and then. Couple of trips with the Rover is all that takes. Some of the potholes in the bedrock are practically glory holes, so I don't need to remove much material to make a pretty good living."

Though she had seen the Ferguson workings before, the place

had not lost its fascination for T.C. Here in a windowless cave supported by steel beams, the old fellow explained his jargon to Al. A "drift" was a tunnel, and "flour" was gold in particles as fine as powder. The tunnel, strung with modern lights, curved no more than forty yards into the mountain, with a single ancient ore cart on comically narrow rails. The Bosch electric jackhammer was lovingly maintained, but judging from the rust along the base of those rails, T.C. thought the rails nearest the mouth of the tunnel must have been in place for almost a century.

But Al thought their host had gone too far with his yarn when Orv spoke of dry washing. Al could understand why the miner ran his gold-bearing sedimentary rock through a two-stage crusher that reduced fist-sized rocks to the fineness of talc. He understood the layer of dust that Orv's exhaust fan failed to clear from the stone-lined "mill room." He simply thought the word "dry wash" implied a big adult joke to be played on credulous boys, and he said as much.

The old man patted Al's shoulder and chuckled, "Don't blame you. It's fairly new stuff. See this thing, looks like an outdoor barbecue that's about to fall over on a steel washboard?" The device was half enclosed by a sheet metal hood that funneled down to a flexible pipe the thickness of a man's thigh. "Well, that's where you dump your ore. There's another word for a dry washer: electrostatic concentrator." He moved to a simple panel with a few switches, flicked three in succession, and folded his arms.

Though the boy had evidently begun to lose interest in all this equipment, the sudden activity of the machine made Al laugh aloud. The big tilted box began to vibrate as if to rise from its mount, and the flexible pipe jumped when a distant exhaust fan began to suck dust from the box. Wisps of dust escaped into the room, explaining the patina and the big industrial vacuum squatting nearby.

Orv shut off his rig after a few moments. "And that's how I get my gold," he said.

"Looks like a cartoon thingy," Al replied.

"Does, I reckon. But look here." He swung the dust hood up

and knelt beside the lower half of the metal box, probing a finger into stiff matting.

Tiny gleams of a deep sun-yellow hue met the boy's eyes. "That's it? That's gold? I thought gold was big lumps of metal."

"Not when it's fine as dust. When it's concentrated like this, I take it to a retort and—" But a glance at the boy's face proved that Orv might as well have been speaking Swahili. Orv exchanged a look with T.C.

"I think he'd be happier looking at those nuggets of yours," she suggested, smiling.

Al's interest had already shifted, and his look was expectant. "You have any pets like Monte?"

With a sigh and an amused headshake, the old miner led them back to his living quarters, where sunlight streamed into a roomful of books. Al showed rekindled interest in a few marble-sized gold nuggets, occasional discoveries Orv had made over the years and kept because he could damned well afford to. The heavy jars of gold dust interested Al only because they were so heavy.

As the boy was swigging at a glass of Tang, T.C. said, "One of these days, you'll be impressed by what you saw today."

"Oh, I know it's real neat, a secret gold mine in your house," Al protested.

"Not exactly a secret," Orv Ferguson said. "But it's a dang sight neater than leaving old equipment and tailings piles all over the mountain. It's just the right thing to do," he said, as the telephone rang.

The old fellow lifted the receiver with, "I'm here." He waited a moment. Then, "Oh, I believe the tad's seen about all he cares to, anyhow. Yep, I'll tell 'em." He replaced the instrument and turned to his guests. "Ross says he's got a surprise for the tadpole, if you get back there by one o'clock. He tells me it's noon and so does the sun." Evidently Orv didn't bother much with clocks.

"Surprise?" Al set his glass down. "What is it?"

"Long-distance call, he says."

The boy's eyes began to brim. "Oh, yesss," he whispered.

T.C. gave the old man a look of comic exasperation. "Why'd you tell him if it was supposed to be a surprise?"

Orville Ferguson, who spent ninety percent of his days in the society of no one but himself, opened and shut his mouth silently, blinking. "Why, I suppose it's because I'm just a damn fool, Teresa," he admitted.

Al gravely shook the hand of Orv Ferguson before they left, and soon T.C. was guiding the Cherokee over sloping scree. Now that Ross seemed to have made the contact she'd hoped for, T.C. felt a growing dread. Soon, Al Townsend would be reunited with his family, to become only a fond memory. Again. It had been a great mistake, she thought, to let the boy caper into her heart, a surrogate Littlebo to be lost a second time.

For his part, Al virtually danced in his seat. "Mom is not gonna believe all the stuff we've done," he laughed.

"It might be your grandparents, you know," said T.C.

"Them either," Al said with inexorable good humor. "It's been *way* cool with you, Hobbes."

y noon Perrin was tooling the big Pontiac sedan toward the
town of Lincoln, on a roundabout route some distance north
of Ruidoso. A few miles farther, he pulled off the narrow state
highway at a roadside picnic spot near Lincoln.

Dex McLeod pulled himself erect in the backseat. "Want me
to take it awhile?"

"No, and whoever takes it next, it won't be any of us," said
Perrin. To Kerman's unspoken question he went on, "I said we'd
be three other people, Mr. K. Can't you just see us driving into
that little burg with our faces hanging out and getting spotted
right away by little Miz Rainey?"

"Bollocks up, that's a fact," said McLeod.

"And you want to watch that Brit shit," Perrin said. "In a small
town it stands out. You know, it might be best if you both let me
do most of the talking in Ruidoso. The less said, the less to be
mended. And I probably should practice my generic drawl," he
went on, with a private amusement that Kerman did not fathom.
"Now pass that cosmetics kit up here, Dex. We've got some active
cover to apply."

Perrin and McLeod were already in nondescript short sleeves,
Kerman wearing a plain white T-shirt of McLeod's under a thin,
dark green nylon windbreaker. It was remarkable, thought Kerman, how different Thomas Perrin looked with the simple addi-

tion of a close-fitting hairpiece of dark curls and with his brows darkened. The baseball cap with its own hairpiece magically transformed McLeod into a blond with a ponytail, and Perrin scissored a blond mustache for him from a broad strip that looked like a sheared pelt.

Then Perrin picked among the jars of foundation creams bearing such labels as Revlon, Esteé Lauder, and Max Factor. "Mr. K, I hope you don't mind getting a bad case of paleface. That and a putty nose is about all I can do for you on short notice." He held up a jar of some creamy pinkish concoction. "Some of it used to make you sweat, but this is good stuff, and it shouldn't be too hot up here."

"Putty? I am not familiar," Kerman began. The very sound was ridiculous. He had spent years among Americans without encountering the word.

"You'll see. You've already got a beak on you," Perrin went on, studying the Kurd with an intensity that was disturbing, "but I can fatten it out, fix you up so your own mother wouldn't know you. A little mustache wouldn't hurt, either."

As Perrin fashioned a mustache for him, Kerman felt like a fool. He had shaved off his own beloved, luxurious curly mustache for this mission, and now he was being told to wear a pitiful travesty of it. Worse, he felt that this American oaf was reveling in his embarrassment, teasing him about the proud prow of a nose he shared with many Kurds. *No, not an oaf: this man has been well educated to his work, and his mind is quick*, he reminded himself. He allowed the American to fashion an addition to his own nose from something like clay and to rub pinkish creamy stuff into his face, his ears, his throat, telling himself the greasy stuff was surely *surely* not based on the fat of some forbidden animal. He rubbed more of it into his hands and wrists and finally sat facing Perrin like some transformed puppet.

"You'll do," Perrin said and moved the rearview mirror to face the Kurd.

The eyes of Anatol Kerman grew wide when he saw himself as no longer himself but a pale stranger. "Forgive me for doubting you," he said with a genuine smile. The man that faced him in the mirror had the same hair, eyes, and mouth, but he would have been noticed in any Kurdish village as an outlander, perhaps a Circassian.

Perrin continued to U.S. 70, and on the eastern outskirts of Ruidoso they passed the season's premiere attraction, Ruidoso Downs. "Steady, Tom," said McLeod with a laugh, knowing Perrin's weakness for racing and for betting.

Without slowing, Perrin nodded toward the distant grandstand. "You like horses?"

"My people find them tough, but filling," Kerman said, straightfaced. It was half joke, half reproach. All too often the nationless Kurds, pursued by troops and helicopters, found themselves reduced to butchering their horses. Perrin's expression said that he had missed neither joke nor reproach but had little appreciation for either.

Presently they reached Ruidoso itself, directed by signs to the visitor center. Perrin went in alone, emerging with maps and booklets after a few minutes. Passing copies to his companions, he briefly studied printouts and the visitors' guide. "Okay," he said at last. "I propose to hit the Holiday Inn first. She used her Visa card there."

"Or someone did," McLeod cautioned.

"Exactly." Perrin returned to Highway 70 and turned right as his map directed. One thing about a small tourist town, it helped you locate places to spend money. Just past Sierra Blanca Motors with its Chrysler and GM dealerships he found Holiday Inn Express as advertised. "Get familiar with the literature while I check a reference," he told the others and rearranged the ID in his wallet before leaving them.

The duty clerk, perhaps a student summer hire, exhibited a common youthful reaction to the tall fellow's Florida private investigator's license; he was fascinated enough to ask more questions than he could answer. "We're not supposed to give that out," he said. "You're a ways from home, aren't ya? What'd she do?"

Mindful of the Datsun's license plates, Perrin crafted a likely story. "Ran off to Arizona with her boy. Husband just wants to be sure they're okay," Perrin said, sliding his wallet into a pocket. "She's not dangerous or anything. Look, all I need is to know if they passed through. Descriptions, did they seem healthy, was she drinkin' heavily, that sort of thing." The Perrin smile and drawl were as unthreatening as Ruidoso's summer sky.

"Oh, a juicer, huh? And with a little kid," said the clerk. "What makes people do that?"

"You'll be helpin' the boy," Perrin drawled a little sadly and very, very smoothly. Passing a twenty to this kid would probably confuse his motives. "I've told you more than I oughta."

The youth turned away, consulted a computer screen, looked up again quickly with a grin. "Sure, Rainey, Teresa. I know the one you mean now. Couple of mornings ago. I wasn't on duty when they registered, but in the morning she returned her key and set out jogging with this little boy. Couldn't have been very hungover the way she carried her mail, a real bouncy-belle, but I noticed they were both draggin' butt when they got back to her car. Old Toyota or something, I think it was."

"Tall, short, blonde, brunette?"

A shrug. "Medium size, maybe a bit shorter. Older woman, thirties I'd say, but a nice-looking lady. Dark, sort of gypsyish. The little kid, too. I mean she was really hot," he said again, with an eyebrow jiggle.

Perrin adopted a fatalist's sigh. "Well, I s'pose they've left town by now. I don't guess you've seen them since?"

"I think I'd remember. You see her jogging once, you don't forget so soon. Hey, is this the kind of case you get all the time?"

Perrin issued a friendly denial, thanked the youth, and strolled outside, shoulders slumped as though he had learned nothing useful. As he reached the car he said, "It was Rainey and the—Talal, all right, from the descriptions. They've checked out."

"And maybe into another motel, or a b-and-b," McLeod offered.

"Could be, if she came back. Since we're pretty sure it was

Rainey, we can bypass some of the places they spent money, but I'd like to drop in on the place where she got the work done on her car.''

They found it easily, filling their fuel tank first, Perrin pulling away from the active pumps before he wandered into the maintenance bay. A thickset, balding gent sat at a stool near a table no larger than a lectern, punching numbers into a hand calculator as Perrin approached and, in his best passive mood, waited. After a minute or so he changed strategies, took a twenty from his wallet, laid it silently on the edge of the table.

The man looked up, his smile proving he dipped snuff. ''You know how to get a man's attention,'' he said without apology.

''White female adult,'' Perrin drawled, ''came through Ruidoso two days ago with her boy. Could be on her way back to Florida, or maybe she stayed.'' The runaway alcoholic wife story seemed too useful to discard, and consistency was a virtue. ''It's not important that I talk with her, so long as I know they're both all right. She bought an ol' beater in Arizona. Someone worked on it here.''

''How d'you know that?''

''Florida police are keeping track of her credit cards, or so they say,'' Perrin lied. ''I'm a friend of the family so it's thirdhand to me. I'm just trying to help with a couple of friends for company.''

''She got a name?''

''Tess Rainey, Teresa.'' When his bullshit spigot was fully twisted, Tom Perrin could spin a yarn as broad as a carpet. ''She knows how to get a man's attention, too. Her husband, Chuck, used to say she was the best short stack he'd ever breakfasted on. Five-two or so, looks like a cantina dancer, driving that white Nissan with Arizona plates when she's not too sozzled. Her boy's about seven, same coloring . . .''

''I don't even need to check receipts,'' said the man, looking straight into Perrin's eyes. ''I'm a family man, but there ain't nothing wrong with my eyes. Another of those twenties and you can ask away.''

Perrin nodded and produced the bill, and the man took it.

"I'm my own mechanic, no point trusting my son to do anything more than pump gas if I'm gonna guarantee the work," he said and spat carefully into what had to be the most hideously anointed coffee can in New Mexico. Tom Perrin nodded intently.

"They didn't call it Nissan in eighty; it was a Datsun five-ten, white, good condition. Running okay but she wanted plugs. Number three was down a little in compression but nothing to worry about."

"I can get a 1980 Datsun anytime, cheap," Perrin said, amused in spite of himself. "It's Tessie Rainey and the boy I'm interested in."

"Yeh, you know how it is." The mechanic squinted toward the distant pine groves. "She hung around the station in late afternoon while I changed her plugs. My boy couldn't take his eyes off her. I finished up the job soon as I could so he wouldn't miss a filler neck and piss high-test on himself." Then, as afterthought: "No little boy with her, though."

Perrin's reply was casual. "Could've been asleep in the car."

"Nope. She was alone and anxious to get started. No offense, but she was sure some punkins."

"She is that. I guess you'd remember if you saw her again."

"Does a bear shit in the woods? But we saw her just that once. Then she skedaddled north up the highway."

Perrin's thoughts leapfrogged over possibilities. "Is there a place where people can stash kids safely for a time?"

"Not up the highway, that I know of. Maybe she left her boy at the movie house near Furr's supermarket while she had the work done here. Folks do that sometimes."

"Where is Furr's?"

The man pointed toward the west. "Mile or so, over on Mecham Drive."

Almost certainly, the Rainey woman had hurried away toward Albuquerque without the boy. "Tell you what: If you'll keep an eye out for her, there's another twenty for you in advance. 'Course if she knows ol' Chuck has me lookin' out for her, she won't like it. She has some pretty wild habits when she's on the sauce." And if the twenty were paid now, the mechanic would not be likely to invent a sighting. Perrin peeled off a third bill.

The mechanic clucked his tongue as he accepted the money. "Well, just between me and you, from what you say I pity Mr. Chuck Rainey. But I envy him a little too," he said with a wink. "Here's my card. Give me a call, this ain't that big a town, even in tourist season."

Tom Perrin was humming a tune as he slid into the rental car and drove back into town. "The last purchase Teresa Rainey made before leaving here was at that service station. And Talal was not with her at the time," he said. "We know where she went then. I believe we'll find she returned after sending us to hell and gone on a wild-goose chase, because I feel sure she left Talal here and it wasn't like her to abandon him, Mr. K."

Kerman massaged his temples with fingertips, head down. "I recall that Americans send their children away for days, or weeks, during this season," he said presently.

"Sure, summer camp," Perrin replied. "Must be some of 'em around here. But even if she left him at one, she's had time to pick him up again."

"And be halfway to Seattle with him by now," McLeod put in.

"We should know in another day or so, from the Seattle surveillance. Meanwhile, I feel sure Rainey is right here somewhere, thinking she's given us the slip, so I'm recalling Cody from K.C. If we're going to canvass this town we'll need all our assets."

From the backseat: "You told me to study these folders. They gave me an idea."

"Wonders never cease," Perrin said.

"That little town called Capitan? Place with the Smokey Bear museum; we drove through it on the way here. It's only twenty miles from Ruidoso. If we stay there, we won't be so exposed."

After a quick perusal of his maps, Perrin agreed. An hour later, they had two adjoining rooms at one of Capitan's few inns, and Tom Perrin was in contact with Houston Center. Cody Beale could not be reached by pager or cellular link at the moment, but Ruidoso's airstrip was long enough for a Learjet. Perrin's third asset, they said, could cover the distance from Kansas City in less than two hours. There had been no helpful developments from the Seattle area, though surveillance reported that Ray and Elaine Townsend had returned from Mexico, and the elder Townsend woman was in a physician's care.

Long before sundown, Cody Beale had begun his hour-and-a-half flight to southern New Mexico, a bit surly at being hurled across the country, as he put it, as if he were a golf ball while Tom Perrin wielded the five-iron. During his brief visit to Kansas City, he reported, he had found not the least sign that Teresa Rainey or the boy had reached the Midwest. It did not improve his mood to hear that Perrin now agreed with him.

Beale felt better soon after he deplaned near the lights of Ruidoso. Perrin had obtained a second rental car for his use and let the hungry Beale choose the location for their late dinner. Beale quickly found it on the airport road, a buffet bistro called Bent Tree Jamboree, where he proved exactly why buffet managers despair to see truly big men arrive.

CHAPTER 15

"We knew Townsend was a Boeing man, so I talked with their personnel people," Ross said as they waited in his cabin for the telephone to ring. "He was in ergonomics—we used to call it human engineering—and sure enough, a couple of the old hands in that section of the plant are friends of his. Seems that one of 'em shares a weird hobby with Ray Townsend. You might know what I'm talking about, Al."

"They play battleship. With real battleships," said the boy, as if that were a perfectly normal pastime.

"Twenty-footers. Fighting models, damnedest thing you ever heard of," Ross said to short-circuit T.C.'s bewilderment. "So my informant lives near the Townsends and he knows about the, ah, recent family problem, and I gave him my cutout number and told him to give it to Townsend face-to-face because Ray Townsend's phones aren't secure. That got him exercised. He told me he'd duck out of the plant then and there. I said Townsend should be calling from a pay phone on the hour, but I didn't get an eleven o'clock call. Next window comes up in about," he consulted his wristwatch, "two minutes."

Unconsciously, T.C. draped an arm about Al's shoulder, dreading the revelations to come. Poor Al was in high spirits, all but dancing with impatience. They both jumped as the phone rang a minute early.

"Ross Downing here," said Ross, and waited. Then, "I realize that, Mr. Townsend. Could anyone be listening in on this call from your end? You'll have to be the judge. I assure you it can't be done from here. The fact is, a friend learned the hard way that the same people who want your grandson also have access to your home telephones."

The wait was longer this time, and Ross fidgeted before replying, "You could do that, but it might be better if you told your friend I was exaggerating. I suspect an investigation would do no more than alert these people that you know they have a Seattle presence, and the evidence suggests they are professionals, and they are certainly dangerous. And government is like the camel filling up your tent. Do you really want to be shoved around in whatever games they play?"

He nodded to himself during the reply, then said, "For the time being, I think that's our best tactic. Actually we're not in El Paso. Do you know what a message firewall is? As luck would have it, I've got a landline firewall to my employer. Your call was forwarded to my residence, and from here it's voice encrypted to El Paso. From there to you it's in clear."

A look of mild impatience settled on the keloid scars that were Ross's face as he heard Townsend's suspicious questions. "I can go into that another time, but for the moment let's say my career used to be forensic accounting. A close friend of mine, her full name is Mrs. Teresa Rainey. She brought the boy back from Mexico at some risk to her own life and, by the way, though she probably wouldn't tell you this, at considerable damage to her credit card balance. I understand she spoke to your wife some days ago. Right, they're both here with me. No, I'm afraid he doesn't. Teresa didn't think she should tell him without, um, well, she thought that would be up to you. I have a speakerphone but it's not on. Al's right here, I'll put him on. Oh, should we go outside or stay close by? Of course, you're probably right."

With that, he handed the cordless receiver to Al, who began with a burst of energy. "Grampa, guess what, I know an old guy lives in a gold mine! Sure, I'm fine, T.C. snuck me all the way back

from Portapotty, or whatever they call it, she speaks Mexican and
runs faster'n I do. Oh, T.C. is Teresa, she lives in Tucson, but
there were these real bad guys that knocked Mom down, and they
nearly caught us so we came up here to the mountains. Can I talk
to Mom now?''

The boy's manic enthusiasm began to diminish in stages then,
waning with each exchange as T.C. stood beside him, Ross stepping away to gaze from his window. Apparently on request, Al gave
a highly subjective version of the Puerto Vallarta encounter.
''... Then we got some Mexican guys to take Mom to the hospital,
but the bad guys came after us there too. No, but her eyes were
open. Not anything. T.C. said she was prob'ly hurt too bad to
talk.''

T.C. felt a subtle pressure against her flank as the boy leaned
toward her, literally for support. ''She didn't? Grampa, she *had* to.
Everybody wakes up. Yes, they do, unless they...'' And abruptly
tears were spilling down his cheeks, the little torso shaking as this
seven-year-old tried to make sense of the senseless. ''I don't believe
you! She's mad at me again, isn't she?'' The briefest of pauses
preceded a moaned, ''Nooo, she's not, she can't be!''

He spun to face T.C., who could only stand dry-eyed and absorb the confrontation. All but shouting, in the voice of a younger
child: ''If my mommy was dead you would'a told me, T.C.! She
couldn't be, her eyes were open!'' He saw her sad headshake and
fell toward her, his gasps vibrating against her stomach as he repeated, ''But her eyes were open...''

T.C. took the receiver, hugging Al to her. ''Mr. Townsend? Teresa Rainey. Forgive me for waiting, but I didn't know what else to
do. When you come right down to it, I haven't known what to do for
about a week. I'll tell you this: When we met up with those men
again in Tucson, they had a foreigner named Kerman with them, a
Kurd I think. It's pretty clear that Al's father is behind this.''

A thin piping from Al repeated faintly, ''My mommy's not
dead, she's not either, she's not...''

Ray Townsend's voice was husky and drained, its vitality doubt-
less sapped by the stress of the moment. ''Ms. Rainey, I've thought

of a million possibilities since those calls from Mexico. My wife is in, well, not the best of health; she's under a nurse's care. I've daily wished that I were under sedation, too, until this morning. The past hour is the first time in a week that I've felt as if my own life might still be worth living.''

While holding the receiver, T.C. guided the sobbing child to their bedroom and urged him with gestures to lie down. "Your grandson has talked about you every hour," she embroidered, "and you've raised a real Boeing fan. I'd say he's worth whatever it takes you to get through this." She tiptoed back into the big room, easing the door shut. "Kids are resilient. You'll see."

"That's what's kept me going. I have to tell you, I even tried to figure how you might be helping Ravan, Al's father. It wouldn't wash. In Puerto Vallarta I spoke to hospital staff, and apparently you made Al vanish at exactly the right moment. His father would have moved heaven and earth to take him halfway around the world, though I find it hard to believe that Ravan would have done such a thing to Gail. Their parting was bitter, but before he took Gail and Al back to Kurdsistan he was a devoted father and husband. Devoted by our standards, I mean. Back at home, according to Gail, he gradually reverted to something like the standard Islamic lord of the manor.''

"You knew him, then.''

"I did once. A very big man in the affairs of a stateless people. When he was still in his teens he helped a Boeing contingent escape from Iran during the terror days. Like an idiot, I had taken Elaine and Gail there with me. We owed Ravan Zagro. What I did, God forgive me, was to help him come to the U.S. later as a student. Of course Gail saw him as a hero; maybe he was, damn him.''

"And the rest is history," T.C. furnished.

"Biology, I would say," Townsend grumped.

"For what it's worth, I saw the two men who attacked Gail, and so did Al. Neither of them fit his description of his father.''

"Al saw them? At close quarters?'' Townsend's voice became sharp with inquiry.

"Yes, and a couple of others later. There's a bunch of determined people after Al, but they seem to be led by a big American instead of your Ravan what's his name.''

"Zagro. I guess that's better than no consolation at all," Townsend said.

"Mr. Townsend," she said, "now that—"

"Ray," he said. "Please. I'm a bit confused over your name."

"Just T.C. is fine. But now that I've made you tell Al this terrible thing, maybe I can help him adjust to it. Gail was alive when we left the hospital, but I gathered she was failing. Is there anything more that Al should know?"

A long pause before, "I suppose not. I understand she . . . passed away within an hour. We brought her back here, never mind all the hellish details. The cremation was yesterday. I'm not sure Al will ever forgive me for that.''

"Of course he will," she insisted. "You didn't have any choice, and I'll see that he realizes that. I think the thing to do now is to think about our—your next move."

"Isn't it obvious? Give me a day to get there and I'll—where are you, by the way?''

T.C. glanced at Ross, who had moved near her again. "It's not that easy to give directions, but we're safe in a friend's cabin. Ross Downing. I'd better let you talk to him again. I look forward to seeing you, Ray, though you're going to leave a big hole in my life when Al leaves us.''

"Tell me about it," said Townsend with his first hint of wry good humor, counterbalanced by, "He's all we have left now."

She surrendered the instrument to Ross and hurried to comfort the devastated boy. Al remained inconsolable, eyes puffy, stammering out a fantasy to her. It was apparently drawn from a few experiences when his mother, furious over his boyish misconduct, had banished him to her own parents for a day or so. The fact that the elder Townsends were doting grandparents was beside the point, in Al's mind. Mom believed he had deserted her in Mexico, he said, and intimated that she was now giving him a taste of his own bitter medicine.

T.C. found herself wishing that Gail Townsend were alive and well if only so that T.C. could kick her imperious butt for a goal. She heard Al's hopeful fantasy to the end before telling him that, while still in the emergency room, she had known Gail Townsend would probably not survive. "I didn't know for certain, Al, and it wouldn't have been right to jump to conclusions."

"You should've told me," he said then, converting some of his despair to accusation.

"Maybe I should have," she replied. "We'll never know how many mistakes I made." The tightness in her throat stopped her there.

And Al divined it, regretting his words. "You got us here, Hobbes," he said, giving her hand a pat. His smile, though forced, was full of real affection, and then they shed tears together.

□   □   □

Hours later, enjoying an extravagant sunset with Ross on his screened porch, T.C. let her gaze stray to the boy, who sat some distance away outside flicking peanuts for Montezuma to chase. "I gave Ray Townsend the standard schoolmarm line about resilient kids. God, I hope I was right," she said quietly.

"Seems to be coping. He'll have another day or so to do it here before Townsend can break away from his troubles at home."

"That soon," T.C. sighed, the matchless sunscape forgotten, her eyes now following Al.

"Maybe a bit longer. You knew from the outset, he's someone else's child." The reproach could not have been more gentle.

"Not in here, I guess." She tapped herself between the breasts. "But if that little boy can cope with life turned upside down, so can I. I suppose you gave Ray Townsend directions to us."

"Only as far as Ruidoso; you know how confusing it can get after that. He can call my local number from there and stay in Orv's place in town if he chooses to sleep over. Oh, hell," he finished, shaking his head.

"What now?"

"I forgot to clear that invitation with Orv." He picked up the cordless phone, punched numbers with care. After half a minute he put the instrument down. "I know he's up there, but sometimes the old codger just lets it ring. Could you E-mail him for—no, of course you can't," he said, as though to himself.

Ross stood and slowly walked inside, favoring that damaged foot, as far as his computer desk, where he worked his digital magics and painstakingly typed out a message. Though obviously the master of his computer, Ross typed with deliberation. Those fingers might never regain their full dexterity.

He returned a moment later with a grimace that T.C. welcomed, knowing it for a smile. "He doesn't get much E-mail. That'll get his attention."

"Orv Ferguson has a computer?"

Ross chuckled as he resumed his seat. "Orville Ferguson has three gigs, two hundred megahertz, a twenty-one-inch monitor, and a thirty-four-kay modem—trust me, it means he has more bells and whistles than the *Orient Express*. He's pretty good with it, too. Prints out reams of all the latest mining technology, which reminds me, I've got to get fresh color cartridges for my printer in town tomorrow. Want to go?"

"Maybe." With a sudden impulse she went on, "When you mentioned cartridges, I realized what I'd really like to do. If the noise wouldn't bother anyone, I mean. I'd like to learn how to use a handgun."

"Aren't we past that?"

"Not as long as I'm smaller than most men and look like I might be a woman," she said darkly.

"From anyone else, that could sound like fishing for a compliment. Not from you, never," he assured her. "The first time you told me your name was T.C., I decided it meant 'tough cookie,' " Ross said. "I guess you had to be, looking the way you did—and do." When she'd first visited him in the burn unit, she had dressed as if for a first date, what she privately called her "don't you just wish, cowboy," getup. One look at this poor devil supported puppetlike in a special bed, swathed like a mummy, and she had felt like a *puta barata*, a cheap chippie.

Pushing that old memory aside, she nodded. "And I suppose

changing the subject with that unsolicited so-called compliment is your way of avoiding the handgun thing.''

"Not at all," he said quickly. "In your place I would've got familiar with a purse gun long ago. Say, a thirty-two, something that won't lie like a brick in your handbag or knock you silly when you fire it."

"You have anything like that lying around?"

"Not exactly." Spoken with such deliberation and followed by a thoughtful silence, it seemed clear that Ross was considering a decision. "I believe Orv used to have a little boot gun about your size. I could ask him."

"A what gun?"

"Boot gun, also called an ankle piece. You stash it in your boot top on the inside and just above your ankle. Works better with an ankle holster, or so I've heard. When Orv was carrying a few pounds of gold on him, he used to pack two handguns—a big one showing, smaller one in his boot."

"Why have a big one if a smaller one will do?"

He began to exercise his fingers as he fell comfortably into a lecture mode, explaining why some small-caliber weapons were more accurate, why tiny two-shot Derringers were sold in calibers from twenty-two up to an appalling palm-sized cannon that would numb the hands and wrists of most users, how certain handguns were relatively quiet if they fired slugs at subsonic velocities. He dwelt for some minutes on handgun safety: treating it always as a loaded weapon even if you know otherwise, keeping it out of the wrong hands, plinking at targets that gave no possibility of a deadly ricochet. "But for you, for personal defense, the cardinal safety rule with a handgun," he finished, "is never to draw it in a real confrontation unless you fully intend to fire it then and there. You don't draw it and wave it around; in most cases that's brandishing and it's amateurish. You draw, aim, and squeeze off. Case closed."

T.C. struggled to absorb all this arcane stuff. "I'd think that last thing was obvious. But for my purposes, why use a smaller caliber than I can handle? I mean, why fire it if it won't put somebody flat on his back?"

" 'Cause if it's a heavy caliber and you know it's going to jolt you to your toes, you just might hesitate.''

"And if it's not, I might have to hit someone several times?''

"That's true,'' he conceded, "assuming you have time for it.''

"I think,'' she said, recalling the men flailing past her ruined bathroom door, "I'd rather get used to the cannon.''

"Tough cookie indeed,'' he sighed and stood again, calling to the boy. "Al, we're going to the cellar. Don't worry about the banging sounds, we'll be back upstairs soon.''

A vagrant fear made T.C. add, "But if you see anyone, run inside and call us, okay?'' She turned to Ross. "Okay, so I'm paranoid. But could we hear him? I've never been down there.''

"Hell's fire, it's just an unfinished basement, T.C. Of course we could.'' He led her to the pantry with its rows of stored foods and usable floor space that might have accommodated a small bed. The flooring had always squeaked near an obvious rectangular seam there, but T.C. had assumed it was a simple outsized trapdoor to a crawl space. Then Ross bent stiffly to grasp an old brass handle screwed inboard of that seam, and the entire three-by-six-foot wooden floor came up with a whanging of metal springs.

"Dad built it. Buick trunk countersprings,'' Ross said as a cool upwelling of air met their faces. A few heavy plank steps disappeared into gloom. He reached past a row of canned corn to a wall switch she'd tried once and had assumed it didn't work.

It was good that the basement was suddenly flooded with light because she had to steady Ross in his gradual descent, pulling the door down behind them. "If you come down here alone, you're bonkers,'' she said. "Break your neck, and nobody here to help you.''

"Just takes . . . longer. I'm careful,'' he grunted.

She looked around her, noting the big hot-air conduit that came snaking through from the solar panels outside, the carefully fitted flagstones beneath their feet, the sturdy old shelving made from two-bys back when two inches meant what it said. Ross could have reached up and touched the floor joists.

The shelves were faced with sheets of milky plastic film, behind which she could see vague shapes: footlockers, tools, cartons of books. Ross lifted one of the plastic sheets and secured it by a grommet to a hook screwed into a joist overhead. On the shelf T.C. saw a half dozen aluminum carrying cases, expensive-looking things of the sort photographers used to protect cameras. One of them, she decided, must hold the longest telephoto lens in existence.

Or maybe not. Ross opened one case and extracted two sets of ear protectors, handing one to T.C. "These were Dad's. I'll help you adjust them," he said, sliding another case toward himself, a case much the same size but evidently much heavier. The second case contained cleaning tools and a profusion of ammunition boxes with legends that she only half understood: .45 ACP, 9-mm parabellum, .22 LR, 30 Luger, 5.56 mm. He extracted a dozen ugly little cartridges from the parabellum box and handed them to her, rather too casually, she thought.

"These things are supposed to blow up, aren't they?" She hadn't expected them to be so heavy.

His tone was elaborately patient. "They do if you hit them just right, or drop them into a fire. Were you considering either?"

"Smartass," she muttered.

He chuckled, opening a third case. "Most modern ammo is relatively insensitive, T.C." She could see gray foam rubber in the little case, and from that nest he took a handgun. Neither ugly nor beautiful, it was all black and all business with a soft patina that reminded her of that San Ildefonso bowl upstairs.

Ross turned to her and did something to the tip of the weapon's grip—slid out a small black metal device—and handed it to T.C., then gripped the weapon with one hand and, with modest difficulty, slid a portion of the weapon open. After an instant's scrutiny he let it snap forward. "I gave you the clip, more correctly called the magazine. It holds the bullets, which we call rounds. Then I operated the slide to make certain there's not a round in the pipe. Always do that. *Always.*"

"How many bullets—rounds—will it hold?"

"More than you've got there. This is a nine-millimeter Beretta, model ninety-two. I think it may be too much handgun for a person your size, but then, you're a lot of person for a person your size." He smiled.

She was to learn in the next few minutes that Ross and his father had set up a target range in the basement when Ross was only a boy. He gave her brief instructions in handling the weapon, secured a sheet of typing paper to the box that sat atop a bench at one end of the space, and escorted her to the other end.

"What's in the box," she asked.

"About a foot and a half of plywood scrap layers. It's not the best, but I've had to replace it only once."

He showed her how to insert each round in the magazine, which made her curse when she bent a fingernail. The magazine slid easily into the pistol grip, though operating the slide was a chore. He showed her an approved double-handed grip, knees bent, and assured her that she would need it for accuracy, then told her to aim for the paper and, without closing her eyes, slowly squeeze the trigger.

"Shouldn't there be a bull's-eye or something?"

"If you ever hit the paper, hotshot, I'll draw you a bull's-eye," he said, amused, which redoubled her determination. He adjusted her ear protectors, then his own, and stood behind her left shoulder.

She hardly remembered the pistol bucking in her hand because the god-awful blast drove all else from her mind. Sparkles of dust sifted from the joists. She said, "*Jesumaria,* the noise alone should kill them," and would have turned but he swung her back.

Oddly, she could hear him without difficulty. "You didn't drop it, and I didn't have to catch you. So far, so good. You caught the edge of the right-hand margin. Want to try again?"

In answer, she bent to her task, telling herself it hadn't been as bad an experience as she'd expected. Her second round made a neat little mark on the other side of the paper, and this time she felt the kick more.

He took the weapon then, producing a flow pen from near the

target box, and drew concentric circles on the target. When he gave her the Beretta again he said, "Now the toughie. Drop your protectors down around your neck."

"This thing's loud enough already," she protested.

"You bet it is," he said. "Okay, here's the scene: Some scuffler has been following you on a dark street. You turn to confront him. When you see the knife in his hand two steps away, you grab your purse, fumble out your protectors, get 'em adjusted, pick up the purse you dropped while fumbling because you needed both hands for the adjustments, haul out your trusty Italian equalizer, and blast away. What's wrong with this picture?"

"You really can be an asshole," she said, laughing but doing as he had told her. Then, without giving him time to answer, she swung the Beretta up, somewhat clumsy but shutting everything out of her mind that wasn't on that target, and squeezed off. Twice.

The hammering reports in that confined space were absolutely stunning. She knew she'd blinked while firing, but there it was on the target, a little round mark between two of the wider circles. She swallowed a few times to quell the tiny whistle in her ear. "Where'd my other round go?"

"Give me that thing and I'll show you." Ross took the weapon before they crossed the flagstones and showed her a long scar high on the target box a foot from the target. "Recoil makes the muzzle come up," he said. "That's what you get for wasting ammunition without acquiring your target between rounds. Next time we'll see how long you need between trigger pulls."

"What about right now?" It was pure bravado, and she knew Ross knew it, but bravado doesn't mean you're kidding. He let her try another three rounds, as quickly as she could get the target in her sights again between recoils, and she hit the paper all three times before admitting that she wasn't sure she'd ever hear thunder again. The sweetish odor of powder residue was strong in the confined space.

She had trouble hearing Ross as he put away the paraphernalia, selecting some tools and a bottle that he said he would use later to clean the Beretta, which he had tucked inside his belt at the small of his back.

They came up into the pantry to find Al staring at them. "You guys scared Monte off. Sounded like somebody shooting guns. Smells like it too."

"How would you know how that smells?" Ross asked, not unkindly.

"My grampa took me shooting couple'a times," Al said. It seemed that the boy took it in stride without much curiosity.

In any case, he was distracted by the second call from Ray Townsend shortly after dark. Apparently Elaine Townsend, though gladdened by the news from New Mexico, would be in no condition to travel there. Ray, torn between responsibilities, was pathetically grateful when T.C. went to some pains to convince him on the speakerphone that they were in no hurry to see Al leave.

Then it was Al's turn, and his grandfather deftly steered their talk in cheerful directions. The most confusing part of it, for T.C., was something called the *Yamato*, which seemed to have a bridge, a fanned tail, and nine rifles. Judging from the conversation, Ray's problem seemed to be that, while he had built a transporter to get this strange creation safely to some lake in Washington, he knew that state police and sheriff's deputies took a dim view of the *Yamato* lobbing Christmas ornaments full of lampblack across the lake toward other Boeing squirrels in Iowa and Missouri.

Only when Al was preparing for bed did she learn that the fanned tail was a fantail. The *Yamato*, the *Iowa*, and the *Missouri* were all floating, motorized miniatures of battleships, and Ray Townsend and his friends called each other squirrels. They actually rode inside these tiny leviathans while battling, so they claimed, harmlessly. Washington State authorities espoused somewhat different views although, according to Al, nobody had yet paid any fines.

Returning to Ross, T.C. told him it was beginning to look as if this old retired Boeing squirrel was not going gentle into that good night without first throwing his nuts around a bit.

"He sounds sane enough," Ross replied, "until he gets cranked up on his hobby."

"You'd think it'd be big model airplanes," said T.C.

"That's probably how these guys got into this. Boeing developed pretty slick foils to fly through the water, some years back. It was in all the papers," Ross added quickly, then offered to refill her coffee cup.

T.C. accepted her caffeine fix and then sat quietly watching Ross clean the potent-looking Beretta. More and more, she thought, Ross Downing seemed less and less like your standard model bean counter. But that was not at the top of her mystery list. And if ever she was to satisfy her curiosity about his nightmares, she would need to know how to use this Internet thing. . . .

CHAPTER 16

The following morning, when Ross donned his Jobst mask to visit Ruidoso, T.C. offered to go along. He declined with thanks, though his forbidding appearance to strangers was not the reason he gave. No one, he said, should have to endure a software freak's shopping foray, which might take him down across the flatlands as far as Roswell. "Believe me, with all the UFO cultists in that town, nobody gives my Jobst a second glance. But I'd like to switch vehicles if your air conditioner's working," he said. "Roswell in the summer isn't exactly Paris in the spring."

She waved to him as her trusty Datsun jounced away, wondering what it meant to be a software freak, certain that Orv Ferguson would know and intent on an agenda that she had not mentioned aloud.

The old boy was answering his phone this time, enthusiastic over her curiosity about computers. "I feel like playing today," he told her. "Tell you what: Bring the sprat, and I'll turn him loose at my pond with a fishin' pole. And I'll turn you loose on the Net. High time you learned." She scribbled a note for Ross and was on her way in minutes.

When T.C. parked the Cherokee at Orv's mine, the old fellow was waiting for Al with the most primitive of fishing gear, including a flyswatter to chase grasshoppers. She followed them to the earth-ramped pond, which was no more than waist-deep to a child, and watched Al scamper into the nearby meadow after live bait. "I don't s'pose he'll catch much," Orv grinned as the adults ambled back. "If he can see a trout, it can see him. Besides, those rainbows of mine are accomplished thieves."

Orv began the computer lesson by seating T.C. before his keyboard, a swoopy gadget shaped like a kidney by Mondrian. Obeying every instruction, she soon found how it felt to click a mouse and learned that Orv was not a man to keep his password secret from a friend. As he explained how icons work, she began to see how many pastimes old Orv had at his fingertips: a flight simulator, an encyclopedia, and something called Myst that he directed her away from after five minutes of fascination.

"It seems awfully complex for a child's game," she said of Myst, as he switched floppy disks.

"Child's game," he repeated wryly. "Hooked this ol' child like a trout. Now let's hit the Net, and you'll see what this rig is all about."

At Orv's direction she let icons draw her to the day's news, to movie reviews, to travel meccas, and to discussion groups in bewildering profusion. She had already discovered medical resources when Al Townsend padded in barefoot, wet to his knees and proudly displaying four pan-sized trout. She was amazed that lunchtime had sneaked up on them in such fashion.

Naturally they had trout for lunch, and Al, decorated to the waist with spears of weed seed, needed no urging to return for more succulent little fish. When he had trotted off, Orv asked the question T.C. had been asking herself: "Think you can find your way back on the Net?"

"I'm sure going to try," she said. And after a few errors, she found her way back to a screenful of data on the shortage of skin transplant tissue.

"Let me guess," said Orv as she sought more on that topic. "Ross has trouble he's not tellin' me about." Deep concern filled the old man's voice.

She turned a pleading gaze on him. "I don't know what he tells you, Orv. I just know he isn't sleeping well."

A relaxing of the gaunt shoulders, and a sigh of relief. "But he's not having some kind of physical tissue rejection, somethin' like that?"

Her answer was oblique. "You know it would bother him if he knew I was snooping around in this. You do know that?"

The old man nodded. "Thinks he's doin' us a favor by huggin' it close, keepin' his troubles to himself. Damn fool's been that way all his life. Just like his daddy."

And suddenly she blurted it out, hoping this wasn't a terrible mistake: "You knew he's been having terrible nightmares?" She felt tremendous relief when the old man nodded again.

"For a long time," he said. "He wake you up flailing around?"

She swiveled her head, gun-turret fashion, and regarded him with wry amusement. "Not through a solid wall," she said. "But the sounds carry."

"Oh. Me and my satchel mouth," said the old fellow. "Well shit, shoot, shucks, I can't seem to say anything right."

"*No hay problema,* you're not half as mouthy as I am. Does Ross say much about those nightmares to you?"

"About all I know is, sometimes they're not so bad, he says. Other times, I guess . . ." he trailed off with a headshake.

Choosing her words with care: "Orv, I think it has something to do with his visits for the transplants. I wonder how common that is to burn victims. He tells me so little about it, I'm tempted to ask some questions about it myself."

"Tempted? I'd say you're halfway to the Cal San Diego Burn Institute," said the old fellow, nodding at the screen. "But it seems like that's not a question he'd duck, if you asked."

She knew she was blushing and thanked her genes for giving her a natural tan. "That's only the first question. If he heard some of the others I have, he'd laugh at me, or get browned off."

"Well, lookee here," Orv murmured, gazing at her forearm. She saw the little hairs standing on end and quickly rubbed each forearm with the opposing hand. "Curiouser and curiouser, like Alice said. You feel like sharin' your wonderland with me?"

"Actually, I'd rather not. At least, not yet."

"If it gives you goose pimples it must be a codswalloper," he said.

"Let's just say I'd feel like an absolute idiot explaining it to anybody at this point."

"But it's what drove you to your first experiences with computers, T.C., so it can't be all bad. Okay, I won't nag. But maybe I can help you find what you're lookin' for. Anything you can find on the Net is fair game, I s'pose. Including us. This thing is really Big Brother, y'know."

With this agreement, he guided her through reference materials and provided a scratch pad. One thing she had not known until Orv mentioned it was that, while excellent burn centers existed in several states, much of Ross Downing's rehabilitation had been done in a quasimilitary hospital in San Antonio.

"Been doin' business there a long time. Brooke General in Santone was where they flew lots of us back in the big war," Orv offered. "GIs carried off the battlefield woke up in south Texas. I saw a few. Talk about your burn cases," he muttered with a headshake.

"And now they rehabilitate plain civilians there?"

Orv sat still, gazing at the screen yet seeming not to see it. "Some civilians," he said at last.

Their shoulders were companionably close, and now she cocked her head to give him a frank stare. "Orv, what are you trying not to tell me?"

"Uhh," he pulled back, favoring her with the grin of a truant child. "I'm tryin' not to tell you what I'm tryin' not to tell you, ma'am. It won't be on that screen, for sure. Young Ross, he'll always tell us what he wants us to know about his history when he wants us to know it. I don't feel right makin' those decisions for him. You ever do anything you'd just as soon not advertise? Me, too," he went on, not waiting for an answer. "Maybe him, too. Let it go, T.C."

"I know he worked for the State Department a long time ago."

"How'd you learn that?"

"He told me. He also said he grew to dislike it."

"Uh-huh," said Orv. "You know, I believe you can find a live discussion group of burn survivors by clicking down here." He extended a finger to the screen.

So that's not what this old sweetheart is keeping from me, she thought. *I'm warm, but not hot.* One thing she was now sure of, though: Ross Downing wasn't just any civilian.

Soon she was looking in on a lively discussion among burn victims. Some survivors swore by something called the Phoenix Society, which offered everything from burn survivor seminars to burn camps for child victims. Its peer-counseling service offered networking among survivors, and at this point T.C. asked Orv's help in joining the on-line discussion.

She identified herself honestly as a victim's close friend and was welcomed by two of the five others on-line. The moment she asked about unusual dreams, every last one of them confirmed it, yielding a burst of hope that soon began to fade. Chiefly those survivor dreams involved their accidents, or the subsequent damage and social outcomes.

Not all of these people cared to discuss it much. When she asked, "Are you always yourself in your dreams?" the replies were either affirmative or uncertain. She persisted, "Do you ever find yourself dreaming scenes from someone else's life?"

If any of these people knew what she was hinting at, they were ignoring it. The frequency of their dreams seemed to diminish as they recovered. To her specific question about dreams after tissue transplants, one replied that you could expect nightmares about restraint when you'd been restrained for delicate surgery.

She sensed that her questions were becoming an irritant without any special meaning to anyone else in the group. One person replied with a wish that he *could* dream another life; another dropped from the discussion. A third eventually made a plaintive request to get back to their previous topic: dealing with the general public.

At that point, T.C. thanked the group and asked Orv to help her move on to the San Antonio burn center staff roster.

"Get what you wanted?"

"I guess I just wanted some facts, and I got some," she said with a notable lack of enthusiasm.

His gaze was calculating. "But not the ones you wanted."

She gave him a shrug, intent on what was available to her on the screen now. The San Antonio burn center records apparently did not go as far as listing patients or appointment schedules. They did, however, list specialists: skin pigmentation, laser surgery, mandibular reconstruction, and mysterious procedures like conchal bowl grafts, which defeated T.C. from the outset.

But she was on firmer ground in the matter of allograft skin transplants, the grafting of human skin from one person to another. She considered broaching her topic with one of the doctors, then noticed that nurses were listed as well. Deep in her psyche lay the conviction that a woman, and one without the godlike image of a surgeon, would be most likely to talk to her as one human to another. *Okay, I'm an old-fashioned sexist; sue me.*

She jotted down all five names of female nurses on the special skin transplant roster and wondered aloud whether some program existed that would let her scan the telephone book of a distant city.

"Yep, but you can just ask the information operator and call whoever it is. Be my guest. It's practically a local call." Orv got up with a creak of knee joints. "I'd better check on the sprat. No telling what he's up to."

As her host shuffled outside, T.C. thought he might be deliberately separating himself from her prying, even though he knew she did it from the best of motives. She wondered if the old boy were kidding himself. Surely he knew that without him, she would not have known how to begin.

Only three of the names were listed in the San Antonio directory, and her first call reached an answering machine. She could try it again later. Her second was to a Horvath, Laura M., who sounded as though she'd been asleep. Yes, she was a registered nurse, and no, it was against regulations to discuss individual patients in this fashion. Still sounding groggy, the woman reacted to Ross's name with a pause and a slight rise in tone. "I'm afraid you'd have to go through channels if your friend is a junior G-man," she said, with a barely civil good-bye as she broke the connection.

Which left Quintana, Raquel T., and while dialing, T.C.'s mind kept repeating Horvath's phrase like a jingle. It had been spoken with a faintly dismissive tone but also as if it had some additional meaning. Maybe a wide-awake Laura Horvath wouldn't have used those words.

A small child answered on the third ring, but with the self-assurance of an adult, and T.C. asked for the nurse, Raquel Quintana. She heard a piping *"Mamacita"* and a clatter of a receiver.

A moment later, a softly modulated voice answered. T.C. gave her name as Teresa Contreras and said, "*Primero,* please tell your daughter she answers a telephone like a young lady. I'm a school-teacher, and I was impressed. She can't be more than five." With this, she hoped to make points in several ways, not the least being the fact that they shared an ethnic bond.

"Four, and she's my youngest granddaughter. *Y mil gracias,*" the woman went on. "How can I help you?"

T.C. told her up front how she had found the name and added, "I'm worried about my dearest friend who's had allografts in San Antonio, and I've just about exhausted the usual sources of help." It wasn't much of an exaggeration.

"I'm not sure I can help," said Quintana. "Is it a current patient? I'm retiring as of next week."

"His name is Ross Downing. I believe the phrase is junior G-man," she added with a forced chuckle.

The silence was deafening for a moment. "You must be very close," Quintana said. "That's not a term that's heard much. Well, let us say I'm familiar with Mr. Downing. Not as familiar as a ward nurse might be, as a surgical nurse I dropped in on him afterward, mostly in the OR over a space of a year or so. But he seemed to be an extraordinary man. I often wonder how these federal agencies recruit so many of our best and brightest, when you see how they operate. I looked in on Mr. Downing a few times in the recovery room. Is the problem something like despondency?"

"I'd call it anxiety. It's these dreams he has, after a graft from some donor. Ms. Quintana, is there any way you could trace the donors?"

"Talk to them? That was more common back in my student days, when railroadmen lined up to donate tissue for some scalded engineer or fireman. But we're getting into synthetically grown skin tissue, and a lot of natural skin allografts these days are from cadavers. You understand what I'm saying?"

T.C. swallowed hard. "I'd need a seance to talk to the person who donated skin for this last graft," she said.

"I'm afraid so. As it happens, I do recall, um, of course it's highly unprofessional to—but damn it, I've held my tongue to no purpose for forty years." A throaty laugh. "I've gotten awfully tired of other people telling me what professionalism means.

"In fact," she plunged ahead, her decision made, "this was very recent. I remember the donor was a young man, *guapo y fuerte,* such a shame. What stuck in my memory was his name: Alan Ladd, believe it or not. I wonder what parents think of when they saddle a child with an old film actor's name. At any rate, he had been flown from Ohio after some kind of industrial accident. A piece of metal had been blown into his throat, and they lost him. He became a major organ donor."

With a flood of ice down her spine, T.C. asked, "Did the donor have children?"

"There's no way I'd know," said Quintana. "Is it important?"

"I suppose not," T.C. lied. "Would the donor have been a junior G-man too?"

"I very much doubt it, Ms. Contreras. That isn't necessary for eligibility. Mr. Downing just happens to be a member of those agencies that send their casualties here if they're injured while on active duty. His Federal Institute for, um, Fiscal Means, wasn't it? One of those, anyway. It made him one of the juniors, not quite the FBI but we treated him equally well, never doubt it. I'm sorry about his dreams; burn trauma will do that."

And maybe borrowing skin will do it with a vengeance, T.C. replied silently. Aloud she said, "Has anyone ever suggested to you that the burn victim's dreams may somehow make him feel connected to the donor?"

"I wouldn't be surprised. A debt of gratitude, you mean."

"That too, but I meant . . . well, maybe a psychic connection."

"Surely you don't mean some kind of, of telepathic fantasy or something of the sort? That's nonsense," said Quintana, making it light but decisive. "I hope Mr. Downing isn't laboring under delusions of that kind. If he is, he could probably use professional counseling."

"No, no, just an idle thought of mine. Stranger things have happened," T.C. insisted.

"Not on my shift," said the nurse with a laugh.

T.C. could hear the soft rumble of Orv Ferguson outside and Al's excited patter in response. "Ms. Quintana, thanks for putting me at ease. I appreciate it. And for the record, I've already forgotten your name." Two lies in quick succession.

"I was about to suggest that, Ms. Contreras."

"Understood. Thanks again, and *vaya con Dios*." T.C. broke the connection as she saw Al bounce into the next room.

She sat staring at the computer, reviewing her suspicions, now beginning to wish she had never entertained them. Ross's dream had included an Ohio license plate and local flooding in that region. His subconscious might have dredged up the floods from recent news, but the allograft donor had died after an accident that tallied closely with the one in the nightmare. Was there any other way Ross might have heard about the donor's deadly accident? Maybe; the nurse had known.

If some telepathic connection of flesh was involved, it didn't seem likely that a man like Ross would be the only person it happened to. And Quintana, who was in a position to hear of such things, had dismissed the possibility out of hand. T.C. denied her burden of guilt for this snooping and put on a bright smile as she rose to greet the others.

CHAPTER □ 17

Even a resort town as small as Ruidoso could not be blanketed with Perrin's little group, especially when Anatol Kerman was not a full-fledged member. Tom Perrin chafed silently against the awareness that this time, his taskmasters hadn't given him the kind of front-burner mission a man could brag about. This was an el cheapo, not the kind of task backed by a heavy budget: the Malaysians, for example, or the Swiss, both of which had been known to pump in extra money from slush funds of their own, given a certain level of interest. The fucking Kurds, for Christ's sake, didn't even *have* a country. But they might, like the Palestinians, get one in time. From his years with the Company, Perrin knew that small-budget crap like this was usually authorized as a friendly gesture, for that distant and iffy future when the needy faction might become powerful enough, or simply troublesome enough for the wrong people, to return a favor. Among the enigmas Perrin didn't like to think about was the exact makeup of whatever committee it was that made those friendly gestures. Put bluntly, Thomas Perrin did not expect to know, *ever*, who signed the paychecks that let him spend half of his time on vacation.

Perrin was already wishing he were unwinding in Cancun after this can of worms was untangled. It had all sounded so simple at the outset: Locate the kid in Puerto Vallarta, rent one of the faction of highly rentable Mexican cops who could call on resources of his own, pull a snatch-and-grab, then arrange air transport to wherever Houston chose, most likely through Cuba.

More big airstrips were available south of the border for work like this than in the States. It would soon be time, he decided, to request a staging site from Houston Center. They would interpret that as a signal that he was close to his goal, and he had waited because he didn't want to send signals before he had good reason. It wasn't good to have to admit too many unforeseen complications.

The death of Gail Townsend had been a minor complication. The arrival of Anatol Kerman could have been minor, too; he might yet be a true asset. He wasn't a complainer, and he'd accepted the fact that, if he became a casualty, he might be on his own. The major Chinese fire drill had begun with this fierce little bimbette Rainey, so naive at first, so resourceful in the clutch.

Too bad Rainey had to go now. In other circumstances Perrin might actually have given her a recruitment pitch. Work undercover for top wages as a deniable for the United Nations, use her smouldering good looks and her astonishing resourcefulness in the service of mankind, blah blah, the usual bullshit that often drew in lonely people with the right qualifications. Rainey's dossier suggested a loner, and her appearance said it was almost certainly by her own choice. Exactly why she would make that choice, Perrin had no idea. From long experience he knew it was best not to think about those things too much when you knew someone was slated for the big putdown. Tom Perrin had enough troubles working with his limited assets.

There wouldn't be any more assets for this task under Perrin's direct supervision. The remaining big-ticket item would be when he called for one of the staging locations to stash the kid, once they grabbed him, and that's where Kerman might be of use if the boy did actually accept the Kurd, maybe even willingly go into an aircraft with him. At that point Perrin's task would be done—assuming the Rainey woman was put down. She'd seen too much, could raise too much hell to some reporter. It was a good thing she was running as a singleton herself with only Raymond Townsend, whom they were monitoring, as a potential asset of her own.

But Perrin knew better than to harden that assumption. She might find help somewhere, given time. It was up to Perrin's little band to make sure she didn't get that time.

Small expenditures weren't a problem. Because the Kurd lacked a driver's license, Perrin elected to have Kerman ride beside him, while Beale rented a gray Chevy sedan and McLeod took a sprightly little blue Neon. They tested the reception of their radios in this steep terrain while learning which of Ruidoso's twisting thoroughfares offered commercial lodging. Most major streets did, from big chain motels to bed-and-breakfasts.

Several small white sedans turned up, but none was the Datsun with the Arizona plates. By midmorning they were satisfied with their UHF communication channels, and Cody Beale had canvassed the area motels without success. It was pure chance that Perrin chose to drive north on Route 48 toward the airport as Ross Downing reached the same road driving south into town.

Kerman noted a road sign. "Alto Village. Are we outside of Ruidoso now?"

"I don't think so, but it doesn't matter. Could be more motels," said Perrin, noting that a hulking Winnebago, a hotel on wheels, was approaching them on the highway with its left-turn blinker activated. Perrin did not wait and turned right toward the Alto subdivision with his concentration on the road ahead. He saw the sparkle of Alto Lake. Had Perrin waited for the Winnebago to make its turn he would have found himself suddenly face-to-face with the driver of the small white car tailgating the van, a man wearing something that resembled a hockey mask. By the time Perrin glanced in his rearview again, the van filled his view, having completed its turn, and T.C.'s little Datsun passed into Ruidoso unremarked.

Route 48 becomes Mechem Drive near the center of town, and it was here that Beale spotted the Wal-Mart. He scanned its parking lot first, with a close glance at the rump of an older white Toyota nearby, and pocketed his transceiver on his way inside, seeking an outlet for the three cups of strong coffee he'd had earlier. On stakeouts they kept empty half-gallon milk cartons for in-car urinals, but he'd neglected it this time.

Moments after Beale entered the building, the little Datsun swung into the same lot, pulling into a slot that a white Toyota was just leaving. As Cody Beale relieved himself in one part of the store, Ross Downing made his way to Wal-Mart's array of computer software which, as he expected, proved less than exciting.

Beale had tuned his personal sensors for little boys and Latina women and saw nothing remarkable as he strode one aisle from Downing on his way back outside. Beale stood irresolute for a moment beside his Chevy, sucking a tooth and breathing heavily, wondering why fifty yards of brisk walking had made him dizzy. Then he got into the Chevy and backed from his parking slot. His rear bumper came within arm's reach of that Arizona license plate, but the car was small and white, and Cody Beale had seen a very similar car there minutes before and had trained himself to discard things he had already established as unimportant. Beale drove back to the street and headed south.

Ross Downing sighed and abandoned Wal-Mart as a source of the compact discs he sought, then got into the Datsun and decided that his luck in Roswell might not be much better. Las Cruces was only a half hour farther, though in a different direction, a college town and a dependable source for techies. Ross, too, drove south.

Beale turned right from Ruidoso's central traffic circle, noting the closely grouped lodges nearby. He was reporting to Perrin when his rearview revealed, almost obscured by the curve of the street, the familiar lines of a small white station wagon as it toured the traffic circle. "I may have a bingo at the traffic circle," he reported, giving the Chevy's wheel a vicious twist. He couldn't be certain yet because the little vehicle had been two blocks away in his rearview mirror. He could, however, step up his pace. The white station wagon hadn't been moving quickly.

The main drive, Sudderth, was becoming more congested between traffic signals in late morning, but Ross was in no particular hurry. The impatient bleats of someone's horn a few blocks back made no impression on him, or on the old pickup that had stalled while backing out as if for the express purpose of blocking Beale's way. By now, Beale had caught one more glimpse of the little white car, but one was enough: From its colors he made the plate as Arizona and confirmed it to Perrin.

Ross drove past the visitor center, then the Lincoln County Medical Center, and turned south again at the highway. Route 70 to Alamogordo and Las Cruces could be infernally hot but bearable with air-conditioning. Mindful that he drove a borrowed car, Ross Downing kept his pace moderate.

Cody Beale turned up the wick on the Chevy with its transmission selector in low range, chirping his tires as he powered around that damned old pickup. As a former cop he knew better than to call too much attention to his driving in this little hick burg, but the fucking Datsun had already bumbled out of sight. Cody Beale popped a sweat from the suspense. It might not be good for his heart, but this, closing in on his unsuspecting mark, was the fun part. The hell with his hypertension.

Beale snatched at the map on the seat beside him. A few blocks ahead, he recalled, this street and another ended in a V at Route 70. The Rainey woman almost certainly could not know she had a pursuer close on her heels, not the languid way she was driving. Since she seemed to be staying in Ruidoso, he would expect her to turn in some direction that kept her in town. And if she turned up Gavilan Canyon, Tom Perrin could tail her after an intercept from the north.

Beale said as much to Perrin, who agreed. McLeod announced his location only minutes away. "Proceeding east on Route Seventy," Beale told the little Scot, "toward the racetrack. You can take Seventy to the southwest, just in case."

At the last traffic light, Beale snapped his neck from side to side until it crackled like celery, searching the highway, cursing because while highway traffic was modest, he saw no sign of the Datsun. He judged that his Chevy was less than two minutes behind, and he figured to make up the difference quickly if, as he suspected, his quarry had driven northeast. Veering left, he sped toward Ruidoso Downs with a smile of firm expectation.

Ten miles farther east, well past Ruidoso Downs, Beale admitted defeat. The irritated Perrin had no joy in his search either, and, after a hurried look at his own map, concluded that the Rainey woman must have taken one of the turnoffs from Gavilan Canyon Road. McLeod's Neon, going like hell's hammers, was several miles down Highway 70 in the right direction and had come almost within sight of the Datsun when Perrin ordered him and Beale to help quarter the area around Gavilan Canyon. McLeod, obedient to a fault, made a swift turnaround and sped back.

And Ross Downing continued toward Alamogordo, wholly unaware of the excitement he had generated.

□   □   □

Meticulous quartering of the region around Gavilan Canyon took the men more than an hour. McLeod, always most comfortable in a group, suggested that they take lunch together.

"Use your noodle," was Perrin's reply. "We don't know one another, Dex. And if you so much as lift a pinkie at me again I will personally break it off." Dex McLeod had given a truncated two-finger salute to them like a goddamned amateur during one of their unavoidable passes that morning. Even Kerman had shaken his head at that.

But Dex, after all, had the virtue of obedience, and a man could do worse than have a dedicated moron backing him up. "I have twelve-oh-eight," Perrin said. "You break now, call in at fifteen 'til, and then Cody can take a half hour. Then me—us, that is." A few culs-de-sac still lay unchecked in the area.

By the time Beale broke for lunch, Perrin had mentally composed his telephone report for Houston. Kerman could monitor their radio link to McLeod while Tom Perrin concentrated on his report, and Perrin felt it was better if Kerman was not always privy to those conversations. Especially when Perrin had to shade the facts a little. So, using a telephone booth with the Pontiac in sight, Perrin made his call using the scrambler unit.

It was funny, he thought—funny like a tooth extraction—how some two-bit comm bitch in Houston could put a veteran facilitator on the defensive with a few simple questions. But it was just like the military: You saluted the uniform, not the bozette wearing it, and Tom Perrin kept his replies civil.

It took a five-minute wait before she confirmed a staging site, and at least Perrin could play the experienced hand when she did. "I know it well," he said, having accompanied an illegal to the place exactly once, years before. It was a way the hell and gone from southern New Mexico in open ranchland, a private airstrip using a dude ranch as deniable cover, but that suited Perrin just fine. As he broke the connection he was already seeing, in his imagination, a Lear or a Gulfstream wheels up and arcing toward the southeast with Anatol Kerman and that fucking little kid inside, headed to Cuba or Calcutta or hell, and out of his hair forever. And, as epilogue, troublesome Teresa Rainey furnishing lunch for coyotes somewhere in the New Mexico desert.

□   □   □

Las Cruces had prospered as host to New Mexico State U. ever since the school was a cow college under another name, and Ross benefited as a guest when he cruised the university bookstore. He picked up some compact discs for research and a few more from pure curiosity, then selected a couple of music CDs that he fancied. The music included a d'Ambrosio for its ballads and an hour of symphonic bossa nova with an endorsement from Jobim himself. On the surface of his mind, he thought his friend T.C. might find such stuff appealing at a time when she was already priming herself to grieve for the loss of little Al Townsend. He chose not to dig deeper into his own motives.

The fact was that Ross Downing had never known how to talk to a woman about affection, devotion, attraction. The more subtle fact was that in Teresa's company he suffered from all three and had long since accepted that they were bearable lashes against a man so profoundly damaged, inside and out.

Before that night of highway flame and horror with a dying child in his arms, he had taken his athletic good looks for granted, had found it unnecessary to court women because so many of them were easily won with his first quiet smile. And for Ross in those days, as for too many young men, anything easily won was lightly regarded. Now he wore a mask in public, and limped, and had met face-to-face with one of his old flames—the phrase now an abomination—exactly once before abandoning the idea. He felt certain that T.C. resisted the same impulse that sometimes caused other women to recoil from chance encounters. In resisting that impulse, she only increased his burden of affection, devotion, and attraction. It was a dilemma that became, in time, so familiar that it was almost a comfort to him.

He paid for his purchases, pretending not to notice the counter girl's avoidance of eye contact, and realized that it was past lunchtime. On his way out of town he stopped at a Mexican restaurant, ordering the meal to go. Both gazpacho and molcajete were messy arrangements through a Jobst, but Ross knew a verdant little city park where he could slurp and chew the spicy stuff without his mask, alone and, he hoped, unnoticed. High, thin clouds and a light breeze conspired against the midafternoon heat. Ross rolled both front windows partly down, finished the carton of formidable stew, and leaned his head back to enjoy the moment. The moment lasted almost two hours.

He woke to find three kids, aged ten or so, regarding him silently and platter-eyed from a few paces away. No telling how long they'd stood there as if rooted, gazing at this caricature of a face. He yawned. They fled squealing, one of them dropping a soccer ball as he raced off across park grass. Ross recalled the old jibe from . . . was it Groucho? "How much would you charge to haunt a house?" He sighed, rolled up the windows, and started the Datsun.

By the time he had crossed the Jornada del Muerto and climbed into the mountains, it was late afternoon, the sun transiting those clouds to pour down unabated. Ross refilled T.C.'s tank in Ruidoso, bought two flat circles of some awful peanut pattie concoction so Al would not feel left out—compact discs of his own!—and pointed the Datsun up Mechem Drive. The turnoff to Bonita Lake and the backside of Sierra Blanca lay only a few miles to the northwest.

He unwrapped one of those patties without thinking, then shrugged and took a bite. Dyed a near-psychedelic crimson and nubbly with peanuts, it compared to a real praline as a Ding Dong does to a Viennese torte, but Ross attacked it with gusto. He did not notice the blue Neon parked on the shoulder where Fort Stanton Road met the thoroughfare north of town.

□   □   □

When Dex McLeod's excited "Bingo, bingo, north on Route Forty-eight at Fort Stanton" crackled in Perrin's speaker, the Pontiac was far out of place for an immediate tail. To Perrin's question McLeod replied, "Could have made my car but I think not, and it's not our bird driving."

"You're sure of that?" Cody Beale's question. "I'm near the golf course, I can pick her up if you don't lose her."

"Not her, I said, but definitely our junker. Short hair, didn't get a good look. Tailing at two hundred yards."

"Stay back there," Perrin ordered. "Break off when Cody passes. And Cody, proceed with caution. I'm on my way." Meanwhile Perrin was ignoring his own advice, hauling the Pontiac's freight around at a pace that would have attracted any prowling police cruiser.

McLeod dutifully followed when the Datsun turned off, relayed the information, and fell far enough behind that he took the next turn toward the distant town of Carrizozo before realizing that the Datsun had taken a lesser road. He avoided a later tongue-lashing because he had already spotted Cody Beale's big gray Chevy growing large in his rearview before his mistaken turn. "Breaking off now. Straight on, Beale," he advised and watched the sedan rush past, Beale making not the least sign that he saw the Neon stopped at the turnoff.

Beale throttled back once he spied the white Datsun, giving it lots of room, confident that the driver would have to slow down before making any turnoffs from this increasingly twisted road. In this fashion he passed Bonito Lake, then paralleled Bonito Creek on what had by now become an unimproved mountain road. The Datsun's dust trail was Beale's friend, and he dropped back still more. Even if his quarry disappeared, it would leave a telltale for fifteen seconds. He passed a rutted double track to his left, an old mining road from the look of it, noting that it was blocked by a gate with a NO ACCESS sign. An older sign proclaimed GREAT WESTERN MINE. For the first time, Cody Beale entertained a doubt. Was it possible that the driver had made Dex McLeod and was now leading Beale into some sort of tactical mistake, maybe even an ambush?

Beale cursed as the Chevy's oilpan bottomed on a high center in the road. He reached toward his left armpit but decided to leave his side arm holstered. If he put it on the seat on a road like this, it might bounce to the floor. Then, abruptly, the Datsun appeared to his left, unmoving. Its snout was aimed at a metal gate with still another NO ACCESS sign, and a fellow in a long-sleeved shirt was bent over the securing chain. He did not seem to be hurrying and apparently was not interested in the big gray Chevy that grumbled past scant yards away. Beale continued several hundred yards farther, as far as this sorry excuse for a road permitted, and found himself at a trailhead well out of sight of the Datsun.

He reported what he had found to Perrin and learned that the Pontiac had passed the Carrizozo turnoff on its way toward him. "Suggest you pull off before the road becomes dirt," Beale said, "and wait. He could be trying to snooker me. If that's his game he could be scooting back past you any minute."

"A locked gate, you said?" Beale confirmed it. After a short pause Perrin added, "Sit tight 'til I'm positioned, you could be right. If not, he should be gone when you head back. Could be watching you, though. If he knows this area, he should know you've run out of road by now."

Beale acknowledged this, turned the Chevy around with much scraping, and sat back to await further instructions.

CHAPTER □ 18

Because Perrin's was the only car with two occupants, the task of reconnaissance fell to Anatol Kerman. Perrin felt better about that when Kerman said, "You must understand that I am acquainted with mountains," delivered with a smile that implied tremendous understatement.

Beale had already returned as far as the surfaced road with news that the Datsun was gone, the gate again locked. "I'll drive you up as far as that mine road, and you can hop the gate and work your way up to the property, see what's up there. Fences usually mark the property boundaries," Perrin told the Kurd, uncertain whether it was the same way in Kurdistan, or whether they marked a boundary there with a skull and crossbones—real skull, real crossbones. Beale and McLeod drove to the nearby South Fork Campground, effectively hidden from the road, and waited while Perrin delivered his passenger.

Kerman, agile enough to make the American envious, clambered past the Great Western's gate and set off at a casual pace, disappearing from view within moments while Perrin continued as far as the trailhead. The setup was just as Beale had described it, and Perrin shut off his engine. The silence was broken by snaps and gurgles of the Pontiac, as if it was chewing up some small, bony animal under the hood. He could hear the faint, repeated *thwack* of an axe somewhere in the distance.

By prearrangement, Perrin used his radio's clicker every few minutes. His single click brought an infuriating series of double clicks the first time because, of course, McLeod and Beale were also responding. "Cody, Dex, hands off. Your reception's okay." After that, he got only one response each time. Reception was still good. All the same, Perrin's nerves twanged like a harp; if this stateless foreigner managed to get himself nabbed despite his claims of competence, it would be Thomas Perrin whose ass was grass in Houston. One thing was sure: If the Kurd became a casualty, Perrin was under no stricture to recover him. In a way the man was an expendable pawn whose loss need not divert the team. Perrin, as field commander of this tiny battalion, sought to behave like a commander and met this thought of expending Kerman with a twinge of reluctance. He would do no such thing unless it was absolutely convenient.

The sun had dipped down among the trees before Kerman's first voice report. "No guard dogs or trip wires," he began, slowly and carefully. What the fuck did he expect, a company of dug-in Marines? Maybe he did, maybe he was used to that kind of welcoming committee. So much the better for caution, Perrin reflected as the Kurd went on. "Only one dwelling, with an outcrop of the mountain behind it, and a vehicle track leading to the southwest. Near the small dwelling are the white car we sought, a large black carryall, and a very old military Jeep, in a clearing about a kilometer from the road. Are you receiving?"

Perrin clicked him. The voice resumed: "No useful cover for a closer approach in daylight than a hundred meters. The dwelling is occupied, possibly by more than one person. Construction of stone and heavy timbers. It probably could be defended well, though its windows are large and I see movement inside from time to time.

"I must not risk close approach for a better view at this time. I can find nothing to show if Talal is here. A few trees within fifty meters, large enough for approach in darkness."

The son of a bitch is thinking about cover from firearms, Perrin thought. *Shit, he could be right if Rainey's found herself some competent assets.* They'd need to know more about that before making an assault. "Mr. K, do you see power or telephone lines to the place?"

"Both, and lines disappearing overland near that vehicle track." Kerman fell silent, maybe awaiting further orders or questions.

No wonder a political leader like Zagro had chosen to send this particular guy halfway across the world to grab his son for him. Kerman was a skilled military observer, and he could take a grunt's role when necessary. He'd sounded winded at first but no longer. He was probably in better condition than Perrin himself, posifuckingtively better than Beale, the Chicago eating machine. Perrin phrased it as a question: "Could you find cover to trace those phone lines back along the mountain?"

"That was my thought," Kerman replied. "Procceding in cover." Five minutes later he responded strongly to a click. Another five minutes after that, a faint response, then nothing for so long a time that Perrin's sphincter was chewing washers through his shorts.

Perrin heard an attempt at voice contact after a half hour, faint and choppy, still in the calm, accented tones of Kerman. He replied with, "Say again, say again, say again," but with no response. He broke his silence to Beale and McLeod only to tell them all was well, hoping it was true, knowing if it wasn't there was not a fucking thing any of them could do about it. You had to stay calm to command, or at least look and sound as if you were.

A goddamned knee-high kid and a pit-bull mean little cunt, he told himself, with a baleful glance at a blue jay that seemed to be cursing him. *What if they've given us the slip and traded cars with some fucking hippie out here?* He had begun to build on this scenario with increasing anger when Kerman's signal returned with poor fidelity.

"Broken country up," said Kerman, with a few lost words. Then, ". . . other dwellings but that one."

"Say again, say again, say again," Perrin advised.

"Returning. Will try again," said Kerman, evidently realizing that his transmissions were hash.

Now Perrin could feel his anxiety ebbing. The Kurd had done very well for them, and if there really weren't any dogs up there it should be a simple matter to surround the place after dark and establish that the kid was in place before taking any action. Houston's rules of engagement would put Perrin in the dumper if he cleaned the place out only to find the kid wasn't there.

Once he made the kid on the site, they could do what had to be done. If not for the damned kid, they could do a slop job, a nice vague term for taking out everything that moved—bystanders, pets, whatever. But young Master Talal Townsend-Zagro was the whole point of the mission, so a slop job was out of the question. A careless round from one of their MAC-10s could spell the end of Perrin's career.

The hermit, hippie, whoever the fuck it was up here driving Rainey's car, remained an unknown they could deal with as circumstance demanded. Perrin reminded himself that it was too easy to become infected with the Kurd's views, treating this little mountain hideaway as if it hid a paramilitary group. It was probably unnecessary to run anything like a classic assault, given the advantage of surprise. If you could hear axe blows all the way from the campgrounds, small arms fire would probably carry just as well and might result in a shitstorm of state police on a mountain road.

Well, that's what MAC-10 suppressors were for, but if Rainey had weapons she'd want them as loud as possible. The best tactic would be to throw down on them after dark, take Rainey and the kid without much noise, and let Beale put the woman away after separating the two. If the boy saw her go down, he might be a howling handful, and somehow Perrin doubted that the Kurd would approve quieting the kid down with a few good slaps and a faceful of duct tape. And maybe, if Kerman wanted kid-glove treatment for the boy, he could take responsibility for it.

As the shadows lengthened, Kerman's signal came in strong. "Can you pick me up where we parted? Five minutes away."

Perrin confirmed it and guided his Pontiac down the trail, their rendezvous so perfectly timed that he braked at the exact moment the Kurd reached for that gate railing. Maybe, thought Perrin, this was an omen of one of those no-sweat operations that, after too many pitfalls on the way, culminated in a magical whirr of coordination like a band of Chinese acrobats.

To look at Kerman as he climbed the gate you'd think he had taken a stroll on a city street—no twigs in his hair, nothing disheveled, not even beads of perspiration on his forehead. The only outward show of his exertions was a long, luxurious sigh as he settled into the front seat. Kerman said he could draw them a map, and soon the little caravan was retracing the route back to their rooms. It would be dark in two hours. By then, Perrin reckoned, he could have his team fed, packed, briefed, and moved into position.

□　　□　　□

Orv Ferguson was already at the cabin with T.C. and the boy when Ross arrived, and Orv showed off his first crop of the ferociously crimson, deliciously mild peppers he grew indoors. As Ross produced his booty, T.C. appropriated the candy. "Not 'til after supper," she told Al. "We're not whipping up a tuna-pepper salad so you can sit there and tell me you're not hungry."

Good feeling suffused the cabin as the bossa nova CD began to play. For Ross it was a fragment of fantasy, the old man filling the role of patriarch as he shelled pecans at the table while T.C. and Al completed, at least for the moment, a family ambience.

"You've got a sunburn, my lad," said Ross, moving in to dice pungent little peppers at T.C.'s elbow.

"Got a secret, too," said the boy. "I caught six trouts today."

"You didn't tell Orv?"

"That's not the secret." Al bobbed up at the side of T.C. "Can we tell him?"

"Sure," she said, distracted because the brush-tailed Montezuma crouched on the counter, face-deep in an opened can as he pursued stray morsels of tuna. "Ross, can you deal with this little thief?"

"Depends on which of our little thieves you refer to," he chuckled. "They both seem to lust for the fish up here." He proved that he knew which one she meant as he gently scooped up the coon cat and deposited Monte outside.

"Grampa's coming," Al piped.

"I knew that," said Ross.

"Tomorrow night," Al insisted.

Ross looked to T.C. for endorsement. She nodded. "Flying into El Paso and driving up. May be very late," she said, her smile a triumph of will.

Ross laid a hand on her arm, then removed it as their eyes met. "We'll think about that when the time comes," he promised, and she nodded again. Of course Al would be joyful, and T.C. would be depressed.

Yet Al would not be denied, and furnished details as the other worked. Ray Townsend had called a half hour before Ross returned, giving his schedule. He had even hinted that he was thinking of moving to the Southwest, ostensibly for his wife's health.

Ross mulled that over silently, realizing that a retired man with a grandson to hide might indeed consider dropping from sight with an abrupt move, especially if he knew the boy's father had a lot of clout and some legal grounds for a custody demand. Yet a covert relocation without Uncle Sugar's aid was a lot easier said than done and getting harder all the time. Ross himself could have done it, might even help Ray Townsend scrub away his tracks if the man was serious about it. Still, it sounded like the kind of thing a man might say before he took a hard look at all the difficulties, assuming he wanted to hide.

So, "I wouldn't take that too seriously," said Ross with a side-long glance at T.C.

"You bet he was serious," Al replied. "I heard him on the speakerphone ask T.C. if there was any body of water in Arizona. You know, for his boat."

"I told him no," T.C. put in tartly, "in Arizona we get all our water from grass, like ground squirrels."

"She did," Al said. "And he laughed, and then she named some lakes and stuff. He said maybe we could all take a few days, drive around and take a look."

T.C. pointed to the forks and tortilla chips with a nod to Al, who began to distribute them across the table.

"The drive sounds like fun, but I'd have to take a rain check," said Ross.

"Dunno why," said Orv Ferguson, carrying his shelled pecan fragments to T.C. "Seems like a good idea. Get away from here for a few days, travel with friends, exercise your social muscles for a change."

Ross did not intend his reply to seem as sharp as it did: "Then you go, Orv. Every time I go out in public someone gives me the Phantom of the Opera treatment. It gets tiresome, okay?"

"I'll say one more thing and then I'll shut up. You'd be among friends. That'd make a world of difference," Orv finished.

"You may be right, but even driving to San Antonio gives me more of society than I care to sample."

T.C. added the diced peppers and pecans to her tuna mix, stirring carefully. Without turning she said, "I thought you junior G-men had tougher hides than that," then cut her eyes to observe the effect of that phrase on him.

Ross folded his arms, the slick flesh around his eyes narrowing as he leaned back against the countertop, watching her. "I'd very much like to know whom you've been talking to," he said, his voice a virtual murmur.

"Nurses." she said. She hadn't meant to bring it up this way, but keeping it to herself seemed like sneaking around.

"Which nurses?"

"San Antonio burn center nurses. Horvath, for one." T.C. wondered why she invoked that name, the woman hadn't even been friendly. Maybe that was why.

Ross Downing had worked hard to learn how to smile again in a fashion that reflected real enjoyment, but there was no merriment in this one. "I don't believe you," he said. "You heard the name somewhere, but that's all you'd hear."

T.C. could never resist a dare, or a challenge. "Try Raquel Quintana. Grandmotherly, no-nonsense type. She was on duty for your last graft, I believe. The woman told me some disturbing things." When she turned to face him, she knew she'd made a mistake. Portions of his face were mottled, as if blood were pooling there. "She was only trying to help, Ross."

"I seem to be getting a lot of help I didn't ask for," he said, taking Orv Ferguson in with a sweeping glance. He put up his hands, patting the air with them. "Look, let's just . . . just change the subject for now. That stuff smells great, and I'm hungry." He raised his voice, made it lively. "How about you, Al?"

The boy hopped into a chair and made a lip-smacking parody of readiness. "They been starving me," he said.

Orv's chuckle was louder than necessary, and with these grounds for a temporary truce they were soon filling their bellies with dollops of dill-laced tuna salad scooped on tortilla chips.

They shared a wonderful moment when the bossa nova CD played a medley of "Brazil" and "Baia," all conversation put on hold by unspoken agreement, the lush arrangement and the pix-ilated samba beat conspiring like a drug to strike the diners mute. T.C. and Ross locked gazes and then shared a smile replete with conciliation and harmony.

The moment was shattered by a fitful scurry from the fireplace that startled both Al and T.C. Seconds later, Montezuma dropped from the stone flue onto the dead remnants of logs and squirted, like a melon seed squeezed between thumb and forefinger, to hide beneath Ross's tacky old easy chair.

"No problem," said Ross, with a grin. "But there's probably something out there that Monte is convinced shouldn't be there."

"Like what?" Al asked.

"Coyote, possibly a wolf. A few old lobos still around," Ross admitted. "I never heard of one attacking a human, but Monte would make a nice snack."

Orv Ferguson nodded. "Last year someone got pictures of a Mexican jaguar in these parts. Not to worry—unless you're the size of that little fella."

Ross stood, then moved to the big window and spent a half minute surveying his wooded surroundings. On his return he mused, "I wouldn't expect to see it anyway. Whatever it was, we don't have any livestock at risk. Live and let live," he added.

"I'll drink to that," said Orv, raising his can of Dr Pepper, and the others followed suit. Two hundred yards away among the brush a silent figure squatted with a handheld radio, describing the area, preparing to follow those telephone lines leading back up the mountain as Thomas Perrin had requested.

rv Ferguson noted the palpable tension that began to build between his friends again sometime after supper, and he used approaching dusk as an excuse to find less stressful quarters. "Besides, I have some notes on a new electrostatic gadget, and I wanta get my head scratching done before the jargon puts me to sleep," he said as he moved to the door with a wink to the boy. The mercurial Monte, sitting on Ross's shoulder like some tiny medieval demon, abandoned his perch and ran outside.

The old Jeep coughed to life instantly after rolling downhill a few yards for its inertial start, and soon the old fellow had it wheezing uphill, then out of sight. Ross stood in his clearing and listened to the vehicle, hearing the evening wind among the pines, feeling it on his scalp. Scar tissue had robbed him of the caress of a cool breeze on his face. Like many another small pleasure, that sensation was probably lost to him forever. And some well-meaning nurse might have taken more than that from him, he realized, because he would not lie to T.C. Perhaps if he put her on the defensive for her damned snooping, she would retreat without damage to their friendship. Reluctantly, he moved back into the cabin where she was clearing the table.

Ross resisted a temptation to sit before the TV where Al had begun channel surfing; that would only delay the inevitable. The TV, in any case, would mask low conversation from the boy.

With a flimsy towel in hand, he moved near the sink where T.C. stood. "I'll dry," he said.

Her smile was bright, transient, unconvincing. She said nothing.

"I think you owe me an explanation," he said after a moment. "You've been digging into, oh hell, even the phrase 'official secrets act' sticks in my throat, T.C. Look at it this way: If I hadn't had the job I had, my health insurance would've cut me loose long before this. Why have you been investigating me?"

"Because I care for you," she said, so softly he almost failed to hear it. More strongly now: "Partly, of course, I know I'm trying to repay you for what you tried to do for Littlebo, but it's not just that. I wouldn't let a goddamned dog suffer the way you do without trying to help. And you aren't the kind who'd help me follow the tracks I've been following. No, not you, logical positivist, tough-minded, hard-science Ross Downing! You piss me off, you know that?"

He felt caught between anger and amusement now, as though he had been trapped onstage with a mouthful of peanut butter, debating a brilliant improviser. "What tracks? Try and make sense, will you? Spell it out for me."

"Those damned nightmares, Ross. If they bother you enough to call a stupid answering machine long-distance in the middle of the night just to hear a joke you already know, let me tell you, mister, in my book that's suffering." She glanced toward Al, who seemed engrossed in some sitcom. "From what you tell me, it happens after a skin graft."

A pause as he pursed his lips in thought, a feat he could not have performed a year earlier. "So? That shouldn't surprise either of us. But I don't think it's the graft. I have to take medication, and the dreams don't occur without it."

"Huh." She gave that some thought. "Maybe that's part of it, too, a synergy?"

"A combination that's greater than its parts."

"Yes. But I wouldn't expect you to believe it without proof. Well, would you?"

"Probably not, but I'm listening."

"So listen to this and see how it fits with that nightmare of yours: The allograft they last gave you was from a guy in Ohio who died from an industrial accident when, and this is more or less a quote, a hunk of metal exploded into his throat." She let that sink in for two beats before adding, "You got more than a piece of skin from that poor guy, Ross."

He dried a mixing spoon and placed it in a drawer like a sleepwalker. "You're saying. . . ." He swallowed and tried again, "I'm having nightmares from a dead man's skin."

"*JesuChristo*," she muttered. "Don't let Al hear you."

"But it's preposterous, T.C. How can you expect me to take such a thing seriously?"

"I guess I don't. You mentioned four or five items in your dream that match the facts perfectly, maybe more that we don't know about. Maybe some of your other nightmares could be traced to tissue donors, too, I don't know." She made a throwaway gesture that flicked dishwater on them both. "Look, forget it. You wanted to know why I was investigating you. Now you know, and you're welcome, by the way."

He chuckled at that. "Okay, you had my best interests at heart, and thanks. I wouldn't have imagined your motive in my wildest dr—" He cut himself off.

"Say it: your wildest dreams," she urged him, enjoying the moment.

"It's way out there, T.C. It's so far out, I'll need time to get used to the idea."

"Consider the subject closed. I've said my piece, and as my ex used to say, you can wrap it around a prickly pear and stick it where it's always midnight."

Shaking his head with amusement: "The kids in your classes must come home with some pungent phrases."

"Only if they can read my mind," she said.

He could not resist it: "Don't give 'em any tissue samples."

"You're cruising for a mouthful of scrub sponge," she warned, the dripping sponge held up to view. They both laughed and resumed their chores.

Uncertain whether the ensuing silence was from her irritation: "An old steel penny for your thoughts," he said presently.

"Don't buy trouble that cheaply," she warned him, transferring a bowl from rinse water to the counter.

"Too late, T.C. I bought into it a long time ago. And God knows it wasn't cheap." That could sound like special pleading and he had sworn to himself he wouldn't indulge in it. This vexation, turned inward, chewed away at his qualms.

Still without looking toward him and speaking quietly, she said, "Institute for Fiscal Means. What the hell kind of G-man does that make you?"

All but whispering: "Shit. Orv, what have you done?"

"It wasn't Orv, it was a nurse. All Orv did was introduce me to the Internet without any idea what I was up to. And don't think I'll forget my question, and please don't make me ask it again."

"Fiscal Means is a small arm of the Treasury Department. I studied records, followed money tracks. They call it forensic accounting; I told you that before." He tried to put some finality in that: case closed, no mystery here.

She wasn't buying it. "And?"

"And it's one of those jobs that come with a badge," he said gruffly. "That junior G-man thing is a slur, really, as though we were cadets or something. The fact is, I did things that were once the province of the FBI until paper trails got so complex they demanded specialists. When it's a money trail, sometimes they dump the problem on the people who print it: Treasury. It's that simple." It wasn't even in the vicinity of simple, but perhaps it would suffice as an answer.

But she was on another tack, the one he'd never expected. "You were injured on duty. I've been thinking about that. Did you always investigate secret records while driving at night?"

"Don't be flippant. The fact is, sometimes we accompanied people who needed protection, or thought they did. When someone let us investigate original records that had to be returned with no one else the wiser, our informant could be in mortal danger. Don't ask me who it was the night of the accident. I can't tell you his name. You wouldn't recognize it anyway, and for your purposes it doesn't matter. He was just a guy with a family, trying to do the right thing, so scared out of his wits he insisted on driving alone in a car with more power than he could handle."

"And you were with him," she probed.

"I said he was alone. That was my mistake, I should've insisted that he let me drive." He drew a deep breath, released it like a marksman preparing to squeeze a trigger. "I was behind him in another car." He quit handling dishes now, placing both hands on the countertop. "T.C., it's done. We can't fix it by going over the details. If we could, I'd have had it fixed long before this."

"But you know all of it, and I don't. I think it's an explanation you owe me."

"It wouldn't help anything. It wouldn't make either of us feel any better. Quite the reverse, Teresa." He seldom used her real name, employing it only where a more eligible man—all right, then, a whole man—might say, "honey" or even "sweetheart." With luck, she might never realize that.

"Let me be the judge, okay?"

"T.C., will you stop?"

"No," in a furious whisper.

"All right, then. I let my man get too far ahead for a moment— it was dark, remember—and sped up, came up behind him on a curve. He said later he didn't recognize my car and thought he was in danger. He took off like a rocket in that damned Firebird. I figured I had no choice but to keep up, flashing my lights according to a scheme we'd agreed on. He wasn't thinking anymore, I guess. He . . . overtook a Dodge pickup towing a horse trailer. You know which one."

"Oh yes. Go on," she said, feeling a prickly heat sensation overtake her like an enervating fever.

"I know now that I should've backed off when he first started driving like a maniac. He'd be just as dead from an accident as from a bullet in his ear," Ross said dully. "He must've passed the pickup at a hundred or more. The pickup was doing eighty or so, and a mistake by either of them was bound to be a disaster."

As he continued, his voice grew dull with an old remembered anger. "So the Firebird swerved around the pickup. I think the fool's idea was to pull back ahead of the pickup tightly enough so that no one else could pass to squeeze in between them. In any case, I saw his brake lights go on as he swerved back into our lane."

A faint bleat of misery escaped T.C. as, with eyes closed, she envisioned the scene. When Ross fell silent, she whispered, "Finish it."

"I braked hard as soon as I saw that, because I knew the pickup would be in trouble. Then the trailer brake lights lit up, and the trailer started to sway, and suddenly that big Dodge pickup and the trailer were fishtailing, then slewing across the highway. I'll give credit to your husband . . ."

"Ex-husband. I don't feel so bad about blaming him, now that I know he was doing eighty," said T.C.

"But he did about as well as could be done at that point. It doesn't help to apportion blame. The trailer never came loose 'til the whole rig slid onto the shoulder. Then the trailer whipped around and sideswiped the pickup on the passenger side. I was aiming for the opposite shoulder, panic braking if you want the truth, and I remember it flashed into my head that I mustn't stop to help the guy in the pickup because my guy had disappeared down the highway. I couldn't see that your ex had been thrown from the driver's side. I was thinking the guy had lucked out, and I was home free.

"And then the whole sky lit upon my left, and I thought, Screw the informant, we've generated a casualty here. But by the time I got the car stopped I could see—" He paused, then resumed, the words coming out as if crushed from him. "I saw the little fellow inside, and I didn't see any choice. The driver's door was open, so I went in from that side. Another car stopped, I can't recall those details. There's a hell of a lot I don't remember after that." He leaned against the counter, head down, breath rasping.

"That's enough," T.C. said.

"You think so? I'm told our treasured informant turned up safe in a motel, complaining on an open phone line because his protective tail had disappeared. He claimed he didn't know about the accident, didn't realize he had helped it happen."

"Shut up," she hissed in a furious undertone. After a silent moment she added, "So my son was burned to death in a stupid pointless government fuckup that started because you couldn't keep another car in sight."

"That's about the size of it," he said.

"But nobody stepped in to pay Bo Rainey's bills."

"Not my idea. They said that, technically, I wasn't the proximal cause of the accident, and it was better to keep the high-speed chase aspect under wraps. It's a decision I disagreed with. Then and now," he added.

"You're right," she said. "Tell me something, Ross, if you hadn't felt partly responsible, would you have stopped?"

His reply was so long in coming, she thought he would refuse to answer until he said, very slowly, "To this day I don't know. You must underst—no excuses. I just don't know, T.C."

She looked at him with an unearthly calm, her gaze bereft of pity. "I see why you didn't want me apportioning blame. There was enough to go around, wouldn't you say?"

To this he had no answer.

□   □   □

When T.C. left Ross to finish their chores, she settled in an armchair before the TV set, inviting Al Townsend to squeeze in beside her. The boy sensed her mood, giving her hand a pat, snuggling close. They were both dozing when, for the second time that evening, Montezuma came skittering down the chimney to hide beneath the chair.

"That's it," said Ross with finality, glancing toward the windows. It was near enough to full darkness that there would be no point in peering from a window. "Some critter is out there again, and my guess is, it eats meat." With that, he stalked into the shadowed pantry and, without bothering with the cellar light, raised the trapdoor before moving down the stairs.

CHAPTER 20

"No, that's the strip at Conchas Dam," said Perrin, moving his finger upward and to the left an inch or so for Cody Beale. "Our airstrip isn't shown on these aeronautical charts. Trust me, it's there. On a pricey dude ranch that covers a lot of square miles, you can make a concrete runway look like a natural feature."

Kerman, no stranger to maps of broken country, saw that the team leader's fingertip lay over a small region of unmarked tan between higher, more darkly tinted ground to the west and a small river leading to the Conchas Reservoir in northeastern New Mexico. Noting the elevations of the area, he said, "I hope those numbers are not in meters. I would not want to risk Talal's life on a dangerous takeoff."

"Feet," said Perrin, elevating his regard for the Kurd still another notch. The savvy little bastard knew about air evac from high elevations; well, no doubt he would. "Around forty-five hundred feet. That's not as high as we are here, and it's a long strip. Houston tells me we won't be able to fly from here, somebody's got priority on the Lear. But we can drive there. Most likely you'll be taking off from there in early morning with nice dense air. Maybe tomorrow, maybe not. We've been told to wait for word from the Man that he's ready at the other end." He saw no point in adding that the other end lay somewhere near the Turkish border, and as usual he avoided the name Zagro.

"That readiness will probably be conveyed soon after I confirm our success from the airstrip at—whatever the place is called," Kerman said.

"Saddletramp Ranch," Perrin said. "It caters to foreigners who want a taste of the Old West and can afford to pay the tab. If you stay overnight they'll put you up with a staff member or two pulling sentry duty. They know what they're doing even though the guests don't. Got cabins out of earshot from any legitimate guests. Satisfied?"

The Kurd's shoulders relaxed a trifle. For a long moment he paused, eyes closed, as if communing with some voice the others could not hear. Then, "You tell me you have used this airstrip before. Salaam," he said, with a two-handed gesture and a rare smile for Perrin, who wasn't sure whether he was being treated to subtle Kurdish sarcasm.

"Getting dark now," said McLeod, with a glance toward the window of his room. "So Mr. K and I ferry the lad by Route Fifty-four, Carrizozo to Tucumcari, you two have your way with the little lady, and we rendezvous at the Tucumcari Greyhound stop in the wee hours."

Perrin made a gun of his thumb and forefinger, snapped the thumb down in McLeod's direction. "You got it. And we don't put Rainey down in front of the boy. We want him tractable." Kerman nodded at this. "Anybody need to go over any of this again?" He pointed toward Kerman's penciled map showing the cabin and a few important features near it. Headshakes met his glance. "Then let's do what they pay us for," he said, folding the chart.

Perrin saw to it that they left nothing in the rooms, not even the remnants of their hamburgers. Though the Rainey woman would probably not be missed immediately, the adult male might be. And if he turned out to be in that cabin, they'd have an extra package for disposal. In Perrin's highly specialized profession you tried to avoid unnecessary casualties, but you didn't leave loose ends, either. If a human package—collateral package, in trade jargon—was disposed of properly, there was no need to report it. This little understanding was, in the specialized world of controllers, a mutual accommodation. People sometimes disappeared in the vicinity of a team, and that was that. Plausible deniability might not be everything, but it backstopped a lot of sloppy operations.

They left Dex's little Neon in town after a thorough wipe down, Beale ferrying him behind the Pontiac. It was fully dark with no moon, and once past that high-country campground the potholes appeared in their headlights as hard shadowed as craters on a battlefield. They parked both cars at the trailhead and walked back carefully through the chill breeze, stumbling because Perrin had forbidden them to use their pocket Maglites, a stubby little Ingram automatic weapon bouncing from the shoulder sling inside Perrin's jacket. Perrin had seen the result of too much firepower in the dark; no one else carried anything more potent than a side arm. All four wore thin unlined leather gloves, Beale carrying their wire cutters, McLeod the inevitable duct tape.

It was Kerman who found the locked gate, and Beale, following previous instructions, who severed all four strands of barbed wire several fence posts away. It would have been impossible to drive a car up the embankment past the ditch and through that hole in any case, but Perrin had warned that, carrying at least two trussed packages out, the last thing they'd want to deal with in total darkness was a rusty barbed-wire fence.

Tom Perrin's voice made little more noise than the twang of wire: "Mr. K, take point—ah, the lead—since you know the terrain. There's no hurry, and neatness counts." They walked between the vehicle ruts without concern for the tracks they left. In another twenty-four hours all of their footgear would be discarded, as always at the end of a task. Perrin stopped the Kurd twice on their way up to the clearing, sensitive to the forced wheezes of Cody Beale. In the high, cold air his own breath toured his lungs like a million tiny fire ants, and when at last they saw the gleam of lighted windows, Perrin called for another rest. He felt like backhanding the Kurd because his breathing was far less labored than theirs.

Perrin's night vision was not going to get any better with those lighted windows in view. Presently, when everyone's breathing had steadied he said, "Move out," very softly, and dimly perceived the bulk of Beale as the big man moved into the clearing, McLeod a smaller dark mass in Perrin's wake. Kerman headed straight for the cabin as planned, Perrin matching him stride for cautious stride. Some small animal scurried out of their path, near enough that Perrin could hear it scrabble on aspen leaves. He smiled to himself. He didn't care about that, so long as whatever it was didn't bark or bite or spray something noxious.

They gave Beale time to circle behind the cabin to cut off any possible escape, avoiding the big window because it would have shed too much light on them. Over the murmur and mindless laugh track of a television set they heard some muffled movement inside, and a moment later Perrin grasped the Kurd's shoulder, pulling him near so that he could see what Perrin himself saw. They were peering beyond a kitchen that became a long room with two closed doors to other rooms. Teresa Rainey sat enveloped in an overstuffed chair near the center of that room, her arm draped over the shoulders of young Talal Zagro. The adult male was nowhere to be seen. It seemed that the two were alone, immersed in television.

Perrin retreated a few careful paces into darkness and nearer the steps to the screen porch, his night vision now worse than ever, Kerman at his side, McLeod a few steps behind. Softly into Kerman's ear: "I don't trust those steps, they might be noisy, and the man could be in one of the other rooms. Let me try to draw her out here. This should work," he said without explaining.

As they squatted on either side of the steps, Perrin unslung his stubby Ingram, a device that can use up its long clip in the space of a cough and looks almost as deadly as it truly is. Facing a man with such a weapon, many people simply freeze into speechless fright. That condition could be ensured by a blow to the midriff.

Then Perrin called out. It was a simple trick but one that most grown men never think of, let alone rehearse: a tiny, practiced falsetto. The Kurd was near enough that Perrin could see the astonishment in his sharp gaze. "I'm lost," the voice quavered, the adenoidal, tearful wail of a child. "Pleeeeease." And Tom Perrin scratched on the screen.

Inside, the boy said something, to which Rainey replied before raising her voice. "Just a minute," she called.

Perrin was the only one who could see her open the inside door to the porch. He steadied his internal rhythms, marinating himself in a professional calm as he repeated his pathetic, "Please."

Rainey took three quick steps, moving blindly across the dark porch saying, "Are you lost?" as she opened the screen door, and simultaneously Perrin came to his feet, clearing the steps in one fluid movement, jamming the nose of the Ingram's suppressor toward her solar plexus because the jab could fell her without a sound.

And he missed only because she was pivoting in darkness to swing the door wide, and the unexpected lack of contact made him stumble forward to one knee for an instant, causing her to yelp as she released the screen door, and then he tackled her legs so that they both fell onto the porch within a pace of the inner doorway, the woman screaming, "No!" Perrin letting the weapon go as he fought to cover her mouth with his hand, glad that he was wearing gloves and a windbreaker because her fingernails were sharp little rakes even through the nylon.

"Get the kid," Perrin said, wishing he could just blow away this little Latina wildcat right now, and Kerman stormed past them into the cabin. "Dex, the tape," he snarled, and McLeod was beside them in an instant, the woman's screaming snarls muffled by a big gloved hand in the meantime, and heavy footsteps resounded somewhere inside the cabin, and a voice was calling, "Talal, come to me," and Rainey uncorked a few more earsplitters while her arms were being pinioned, Dex securing her ankles with tape and then moving to her head which she was flailing side to side, bucking like a gaffed marlin, trying to bite, to butt, to damage them any way she could, heedless of the damage to herself.

A quick glance inside proved that Kerman hadn't found the kid and was now darting to the kitchen area toward that open inner doorway, but Rainey got one arm loose and raked it across Perrin's cheek so that he was forced to fight that arm down again, and as long as the damned kid wasn't there to see him do it, Perrin clipped her across the chin, twice. That was when she quit fighting, as if someone had switched her off, and Perrin took the tape from McLeod. "Check those rooms, Dex," he said, hearing a fast series of thumps somewhere and a wordless shout that could have been Kerman, and Dex scrambled up without a word, doing the job as he was told, and once the unconscious woman's wrists and mouth were taped, Perrin stood up, not seeing Kerman but satisfied when he saw Dex checking those other rooms, and he called out, "Cody, front and center!" It seemed obvious by now that Beale wouldn't be needed to cover the rear, but the sooner they found where the goddamned kid was hiding in here, the better.

And then Dex emerged into the big room again with his side arm in hand, Kerman still not in view, but a noise near the kitchen made Dex rush to that end of the cabin and then to that darkened doorway, and at the precise instant Perrin took a step into the big room toward the kitchen, a lightning bolt seemed to come out of the darkness, thunder and all, into the breast of poor little Dex McLeod who was only following orders, doing his duty like a good soldier and hadn't harmed anyone, at least not today. And the way he was flung backward like a Cabbage Patch Kid, arms wide, to land on the kitchen floor, it looked like he wasn't going to be following any more orders, ever.

What with the tremendous noise and mental shock, Perrin's first impression was that Kerman had squeezed off on McLeod from the darkness for reasons unknown. Before he could check that impression against a familiar metallic sound from Kerman's general direction, a doll-sized animal bolted from the curtainlike upholstery under that big overstuffed chair, probably spooked by the blast. It was followed almost instantly by a small figure, emerging from the same space under the easy chair, both of them spurting to the door not two paces from Tom Perrin, as if he were some piece of inert furniture, and Perrin recognized little Talal instantly and snagged him by the back of his shirt, one-handed. The boy saw Rainey's unmoving form and yelled like a steam calliope.

And because the kid's inertia jerked Perrin through the front door, he took only a couple of pellets from the second horrific blast behind him that splintered the door frame at shoulder level, sending fragments of wood into his hair.

Clarity came to Perrin in a silent thunderclap as he snatched up the struggling boy, stumbling over the inert Rainey, getting down the front steps somehow and setting off absolutely blind into darkness that, he knew, was without obstacles for fifty yards. That metallic sound from the kitchen area had been the cycling of a pump shotgun, and Kerman hadn't been carrying one, and whoever took Dex out must have first done the same to Kerman but in complete silence. Probably the WMA they'd seen in the Datsun. Well, too bad about Dex—and Kerman, too—even too badder about leaving Teresa fucking Rainey in condition to tell her story, but as he bawled aloud for Cody Beale to follow him, Perrin took heart at one main fact: He had the kid. This was the mission, with or without Anatol Kerman, and all that mattered now was getting this squirming little package to Saddletramp Ranch.

Okay, he'd lost an asset with an untraceable side arm, and an observer—oh, yes, and an Ingram still lying on the porch if Mr. Shotgun hadn't appropriated it. Tom Perrin was thinking that nobody would spray slugs into darkness toward him as long as he had the kid, and realizing that Cody Beale could make damned good time on foot beside him as long as it was downhill, when he collided with the trunk of a Ponderosa pine and cold cocked himself. It was Beale who carried the squalling kid from there down to the cars, carrying him by the back of his belt like a basket while he supported the stunned Perrin with his other arm. And bitched about it the whole way . . .

□   □   □

Ross had not intended to kill anything when he raised the cellar door and descended the steps, but he wasn't averse to scattering some birdshot from a twelve-gauge pump shotgun into a lurking predator just to remind it which species was the meaner of the two. In the high country, "live and let live" was only one side of the coin; its obverse was "trespass and get stung."

He knew his own basement too well to need the lights down there, and his dad's old short-barreled Remington Brushmaster lay wrapped in oilcloth near the stairs. He found it by rote and had turned back toward the rectangle of light from the stairs, taking his time because not even the boldest of the local little black bears would be rash enough to enter the cabin, when he heard T.C.'s footsteps on the porch and her plaintive, "Are you lost?"

And then he heard her yelp, followed by a body slam and screams, and he made his painful way up the stairs as fast as he could. A man's accented voice called out for "Talal," and in that moment Ross Downing knew that the worst was happening. The next moment was heartening, however, as an adult figure stepped into the darkened pantry and off into space above the stairs, caroming off the underside of the trapdoor without so much as a shout, plummeting headlong and walloping his head as he landed at the feet of Ross. The man was completely limp and did not move as Ross quickly patted him down, pocketing only a wicked clasp knife.

But upstairs, from the sound of it, T.C. wasn't faring so well. The rage of Ross Downing when his Teresa *stopped* screaming, and an unfamiliar male began shouting orders, was simply incomprehensible. Without conscious thought, he pumped the Brushmaster's slide, taking two steps upward, and brought the weapon to his shoulder as the doorway was filled with a sandy-haired stranger holding a side arm, backlit by the kitchen. His trigger pull was an emotional release, the stranger flying backward from the full force of a twelve-gauge charge into his upper torso at point-blank range.

A kind of inhuman calm possessed Ross as he juggled several perceptions at once, cycling the pump as he moved to the top of the stairwell. The man downstairs had no weapon of his own and couldn't find one in unfamiliar darkness, and his personal lights were bound to be dim if not completely out. Deal with him later. The man lying on the floor might lie there until the blast of Gabriel. Some unseen commander was still in the cabin, probably with a weapon, but so was Al, and a too-hasty shot from a scattergun could be a disaster for the boy. Ross knelt, peeked around the pantry doorway, and saw Al hurtle out the front door as a big, burr-headed blond reached for him. Ross snapped the shot high, taking out part of the door facing, but by the time he reached that door he could hear the man pelting off in darkness, Al venting squeals of terror. Ross did not think much about the boy, or about the vicious little Ingram burpgun lying on the porch. He saw only T.C., lying at his feet, and when he saw blood on her face he was certain they'd killed her for Al Townsend.

And even when she moaned as he removed the silvery tape from her mouth, his own tears splashing on her cheeks as he knelt above her, he was not thinking much in logical terms. He was thinking, *Whoever you are downstairs, you son of a bitch, you're going to wish you were dead.*

CHAPTER 21

T.C.'s first woozy thought, as she sat on the porch, was that it must be Al holding her close, but when she reached to hug him back she realized it was a man supporting her, and she writhed away with an oath. Then she saw that it was Ross, trying to wipe a trickle of blood from under her nose with a handkerchief. She took it from him and studied it dubiously. The light wasn't all that good but, "Couldn't find a clean one, Crispy?"

He vented a huge sigh. "No time. You'll make it," he grumped, getting up clumsily, taking the Ingram submachine gun as well as his shotgun as he made his way back toward the basement, ignoring the bloody wreck of a man on the floor. He deposited the Ingram on the kitchen counter, glanced thoughtfully out the window and switched off the light over the sink, reached for the pantry wall switch and snapped the basement lights on, risked a quick glance down the stairs. "If you're playing possum, mister," he told the motionless figure on the lower steps, "you're playing it against a twelve-gauge shotgun. I couldn't miss if I wanted to."

Then, without turning his head, he raised his voice. "T.C., can you get up? I need you in here."

The only light upstairs was now from the television. He heard her progress and her gasp as she saw the dead man lying spread-eagled on the kitchen floor. "Oh, my God. Who did this?"

"I did," Ross admitted quietly. "No choice, he was carrying."
It was not the phrasing of your ordinary paper chaser.

Initially the dead man's face did not seem familiar, but her
face hardened as she realized that within the open mouth and
glazed stare of the sandy-haired corpse lay the mortal remains of
someone who had, days before, blithely accepted a command to
kill her in cold blood while driving the streets of Tucson. "Don't
apologize. This is one of the bastards who grabbed me in Arizona." A two-beat pause as she considered the body, her nausea
virtually anesthetized by hatred and something else, something
akin to an impersonal regret. "He looks a lot smaller now."

"How about this one in the cellar?"

"What? In the—" she began, moving to his side, peering down
into the lighted cellar. The man lay on his back. "I'm not sure,"
she said and made a move as if to descend. "It all happened so
fast I recognized only the big tall one."

"No," he ordered, his elbow a barrier to her. "I didn't take
him out, he just did a header down the stairs all by himself. He
may be trying to sucker us, so let's do this right. I don't want him
grabbing you as a shield. You'll find packaging tape in my computer desk, lower left drawer. Bring it." She had never known him
like this, so cool and efficient, commanding without heat or urgency or doubt that she would comply. She hurried away to his
room.

He waited and watched the man below him, noting the man's
regular breathing and the blood that ran freely from a scalp
wound to pool on the bottom step. Well, scalp wounds bled a lot,
worse than a nosebleed, and all that blood might not mean much.
"Pity you didn't bash your brains out," Ross said to the man,
knowing it was a lie because they needed this man awake and
rational, aware also that he might be awake already, awake and
waiting.

T.C. returned in moments with a roll of clear tape two inches
wide, threads of opaque fiber running lengthwise along the tape
to resist stretching. "Wait 'til I tell you," he said and eased himself
down the stairwell until the mouth of his twelve-gauge pressed

against the man's abdomen. Then, in case the man was making a crucial decision, he said, "If this trigger is pulled, you won't bleed out for a few minutes. But there'll be nothing left of you below the navel. I'm told that hurts a bit. I'm sure you'll let us know."

And to T.C. he said, "Come down now. Take the shotgun. If he moves, can I depend on you to pull the trigger?"

She studied the man's face for a long moment before removing the pliable stuff on his nose. Then, "Just give me an excuse. This is one of them, too, behind that faggy little fake mustache, the foreign guy. I recognize that watch on his arm with all the gizmos, too. They took Al, didn't they?"

"I'm afraid so, but they've paid a heavy price."

"Whatever it is, it's not enough." She took the shotgun, offering the tape as Ross knelt on the stairs beside the unresisting Kurd. While Ross worked, using the man's own knife to sever the tape, T.C. sniffled at the blood in her nose, a fragment of tissue now stuffed into one nostril. "When do we call the cops? Those *chingones* must be on the road with Al by now."

"That depends on how we want to handle it." He stripped off the fake mustache with a *hmph* of mild surprise and turned the man over after some difficulty, stripping off the wristwatch, too. "Huh, a Tag Heuer," he said, squinting at the timepiece with its several dials and metal band. "You don't see many like this. The guy has money, and taste." Then he taped the man's wrists together, not failing to feel the sinew in those arms and shoulders. There had been a time when Ross would not have felt a pang of envy at another man's physical conditioning. He pulled the man to the bottom of the stairs and taped his shins together as well, a tactic that would let the man take tiny steps, though owing to the great power of leg muscles, this required many layers of tape.

The man stirred with a muted groan but did not open his eyes. Ross motioned T.C. toward him, then stood, fingering the clasp knife, his voice calm, conversational. "That knife of yours, buddy? Very sharp. Before you can get your hands or legs free I can have you gutted like a deer. Suit yourself." At his gesture, T.C. set the shotgun aside and helped drag the man to the center of the cellar flagstones. She helped Ross fold the man's legs, curious as Ross taped his feet using several long strands to circle his throat.

To T.C. he said, "If he fights the tape, it starts to strangle him. He'll learn that soon enough." The man was stirring more now, and blood smeared the flagstones as Ross turned him on his side.

T.C.'s stomach began to rebel now, as Ross inspected a flap of skin peeled from the Kurd's temple near the hairline. A repetitious throb at Ross's jaw hinted that he was continuing this work through a sheer effort of will. Then, abruptly, he stood and moved toward the stairwell. "Use this if you need to," he said, indicating the shotgun leaning against one wall, hurrying up the stairs.

She retrieved the weapon and then heard, from above, the unmistakable sounds of retching. She knew Ross had made it to the sink when she heard water running. She saw the man's eyelids flutter now, and for a moment he struggled weakly. To combat her own queasiness she strolled to their sturdy prisoner with the shotgun on him, her words masking noises from upstairs. "Couldn't let us alone, could you? I don't know how you found us, but you'd better pray that we get our boy back unhurt."

Astonishingly, the man spoke. "They succeeded, then," he said, and she saw some of the tension evaporate from his features.

"Not yet, they haven't. Al doesn't belong to them."

"Talal," he insisted faintly. "His name is Talal."

"And yours is gelding, if I have to pull this trigger. And there's a guy named Ray Townsend you're going to answer to. He's on his way now."

The Kurd blinked, considered this with stoic calm. "And what is that to me?"

"He's Al's—"

"Talal," said the Kurd stubbornly.

She kicked his shin. *"Callate,"* she spat, glad to have an object to vent her fury and to help settle her stomach. "Shut the hell up when I'm talking. I'm fresh out of patience. Ray Townsend is Al's grandfather, as you probably know. The smartest thing you can do now is tell us where your friends are taking him." The man only blinked. "Well?" She heard Ross come down the stairs but kept her attention focused on their prisoner.

"He is on his way to his true home. Your Mr. Townsend would tell you that much, if you managed to contact him," said the Kurd. "I would know if you had."

"Awfully smug talk from a guy hog-tied in a cellar. What you don't know is, Ray Townsend called us from—"

"Enough, T.C.," Ross said sharply. "The less he knows, the better." As she turned toward him, brimming with hot recriminations, Ross softened his order with a half smile, gesturing with a coil of monofilament cord in one hand, and his tone was droll. "The object of interrogation, they tell me, is to obtain information. Not give it. Agreed?"

She saw the Kurd's astonished gaze toward Ross and guessed that this was the first time the two had seen each other clearly. "Okay, I guess you're right. He says Al is on his way home. What do we do when he lies?"

"Various things," said Ross, trading hard stares with the man on the floor. "We'll talk about it upstairs, just you and I, after we improve the situation here."

They turned the man's pockets out, taking a new Western-style wallet, cash, and a small two-bladed knife. When T.C. took his new high-top Nikes, Ross found a single-edge razor blade hidden in a slit along the outside of the ankle padding. "That's the capper," he said with finality. "This gent is no first-time amateur. We take his clothes, right down to his skivvies. We don't have time for a microscopic search."

It took them another ten minutes to remove the initial bonds, strip the man down to his shorts, and truss him again, this time with fishing line as well as strapping tape. As an added indignity, Ross tied that blood-soaked handkerchief over the man's face as a blindfold. "You wanted the lady's blood. Well, now you have your wish," he said.

"Not my wish. Too much blood has been spilled here," said the man, who seemed ready to continue, then reconsidered.

It was evident from his accent that this man was, as T.C. had said, probably Kurdish. Ross said, "You mean here at the cabin, or here in the western hemisphere?"

"Everywhere," said the man.

"There's only one way you can keep more from being spilled, including yours. I'll explain it later," Ross told him. He might have added, *When I know what the hell to demand of you.*

"I will freeze," said the Kurd as they started to turn away. He lay virtually naked on the cold flagstones, still bleeding and wholly vulnerable but an enviable specimen for all that.

"I've been watching, and you're not showing the signs," said Ross. "I won't let you freeze, uh—" he flipped open the wallet and scanned a credit card, "Mr. Kerman. But your comfort isn't a priority here. And feel free to bleed all you like," he finished, his grin feral. With that he exited the basement.

He snapped off the lights below and lowered the trapdoor. His next words, as he stood with T.C. in the kitchen, seemed to come from a much older man, an exhausted man. "Would you make some coffee, T.C.? I'm afraid we'll need it. No, don't turn on that light," he said quickly as she reached for the switch.

She did as he asked, glancing from time to time at the notes he was making on his kitchen pad. "Why don't we just call the cops right now?"

"And say what? We don't know what kind of car they drive or which road they've chosen." He inspected the little stuttergun, a trophy from the enemy, then shook his head and hefted the shotgun again. "There's even a chance that they've left someone out there in the dark to dispose of us, so I'm going to have to shuffle around the clearing while you wait in here without lights. And believe me, the minute we bring police in on this, we lose all control of what's to be done about it. Maybe nothing useful, if someone decides Al's father is now his proper guardian."

He went on inexorably, building a case for utter impotence. "All the authorities will know for sure is that we've killed one man and are holding another, who could have diplomatic immunity on some level and who'll probably have a story that makes us out to be liars. Which means a nice slow process of police procedure, by the book. And they'll want our stories, separately and several times, which will take upwards of a day before they decide to do something. Or nothing.''

She was practically slinging the coffee carafe around now in her frustration. ''Meanwhile they're getting farther off with a friend of mine,'' she reminded him.

''And we've got one of theirs,'' said Ross with grim satisfaction. As T.C. turned from the coffee rig and folded her arms, glowering, he said, ''Look, Teresa, all you have to do is say the word and I'll make that call. I think—no, I'm virtually certain—it will result in so many official delays we can expect never to see Al again, but it lets me wash my hands of any charges that might be aimed in my direction. That's a very attractive alternative for me and you, too, thinking in our own self-interest.''

She locked gazes with him, nodding at what he had said, shifting her stance in a parody of indecision. Then, as if the *pock* of the percolator had told her something: ''Screw self-interest, screw the charges! I've got to do the right thing by Al.''

''That's my girl,'' Ross murmured. ''I have no idea why I bothered to mention it.'' He welcomed her careful embrace one-armed, perversely grateful for whatever had driven her back to him, inhaling the musk of her hair, knowing it might never happen again, his breast full with the moment. As she released him he said, ''This won't be . . . nice, you know, for him or for us. But we have to learn what he knows and hope he knows enough.''

''I think you've already given that some thought,'' she said.

''How'd you know?''

''You came upstairs to barf, so you were thinking ahead. Playing the pitiless son of a bitch doesn't come easy to you.''

''Well, in the present context that makes me look weak. So we're just going to have to pretend that it does come easily to me, or that guy downstairs won't tell us diddly.'' The unscarred flesh around his chin and throat became mottled with crimson. He pressed on with, ''So I take it we're agreed that we wring Kerman out, and we don't notify the police.''

''Damn right. Did you know you could still blush?''

"Until you came, I seldom had much to blush about, and don't change the subject," he said sheepishly.

She flashed a brief grin at that and said, "I love you, Crispy, and it's all the same subject," and kissed him quickly on the lips.

He found himself too electrified to respond.

□   □   □

After a brief discussion, Ross waited until T.C. had reported that Kerman still lay where they'd left him. Then she began to carry those aluminum cases upstairs to make sure that Kerman, if he somehow got free, could not find a weapon.

Ross took the Beretta from its foam-lined container and handed it to T.C., "Just in case," he said, nodding approval as she jacked a round into the chamber and flicked the safety catch. Then he pocketed a .45 Colt automatic that looked as though it had seen better days, picked up the shotgun, and left the cabin. With the TV switched off, little light remained to reveal the gradual progress of Ross as he slipped outside. Though he had no night-vision goggles, he knew it was possible that his opponents might be so equipped. He moved forward in a rhythm that was random, jerky, a series of movements that might deter a night-scoped marksman whose element of surprise would evaporate with his first muzzle flash.

As his eyes grew accustomed to the darkness, Ross slipped among the trees, pausing often to listen. At last, after circling the cabin at a distance of two hundred feet, he admitted to himself that his foray was, if not pointless, at best fruitless. Meanwhile he had left T.C. alone with a deadly enemy. He made his way back to the cabin, leg muscles tightening up from all this unaccustomed use, debating with himself whether to call on colleagues from his old outfit.

By the time he announced himself at the cabin and told T.C. they were probably alone on the mountainside, he had decided against trying the old-boy option. His erstwhile colleagues were men who still stood smartly to salute the System. They were good men, but they were not the sort who would leap from the bedsides of wives all over the Southwest to crisscross New Mexico in cars without communication units—the personal use of a government vehicle was only one step shy of treason—without so much as an ID workup.

Further, Ross had not only failed to work at maintaining those old ties since the accident but had actively discouraged friendly overtures from colleagues because he could not bear to see pity in eyes that had once held only admiration. The only ties he had kept were electronic, channels in which he could operate as an agent on extended leave.

And with his passwords, he might get more information by computer than he could with a dozen confederates.

"How's our ace doing down in the hole?" Ross asked as he spooned raw brown sugar into his coffee.

"Better than I am," said T.C. "I think he was actually asleep a few minutes ago. With you outside doing your thing, and Ray Townsend somewhere between here and Seattle, and Al on his way to God knows where, this waiting will drive me loco. I keep wanting to go downstairs and kick Kerman."

"Ease up on the caffeine, then," Ross said, heading toward the computer in his bedroom. "By the way, keep checking to see if he's rubbing the cord or anything. And keep waking him up every so often, but don't give him any idea of the time. We want him disoriented, uncomfortable, hungry, thirsty, and scared."

"Somehow I don't think that's going to give him the same kind of icicle suppository it did for me."

"Maybe not, but if we seem to know a lot about their operation already, he might develop a looser tongue. It's all I can think of to do right now," he admitted.

She followed him as far as the doorway. "And how do we do that?"

"Computer link to restricted files. Junior G-man stuff," he said wryly.

"Could you have done that before?"

"Who knew all this would happen? Christ, T.C., it's not as if I was digging into unrestricted Internet data! Everything I look up, sooner or later I'll probably have to justify.'' He booted up his computer. ''Don't you have a victim to abuse or something?''

''I thought I'd practice on you.''

''Think again,'' he chuckled, beginning to stroke the keyboard. ''And don't make the mistake of trying to scare Kerman with threats. If you do, we'll have to follow up, or he'll think we don't have the stomach for it.'' And with that, he gave her a wave that was more dismissal than sympathy.

□   □   □

Every half hour, T.C. made her tour of the basement, poking Kerman roughly with her foot, making no response beyond a smile when he asked for water. When he said, ''My neck is in pain,'' she only smiled again. And on her third visit, when he tried to engage her in a dialogue with, ''Talal will be well treated, you know; you need not worry for him,'' she did kick his backside.

''Worry about your neck,'' she said and checked his bonds again. He had not tried to wear them on the flagstones. Evidently, Kerman was content to lie there and let his neck hurt. That bothered her a lot. He knew that time was his friend.

T.C. had channel surfed nervously among several late talk shows, remembering nothing of what she saw or heard, before Ross appeared with copies from his printer. She snapped off the set and huddled with him at the dining table. ''What've we got?''

''Stuff you shouldn't see,'' he said. ''Don't forget, it's a good bet that you'll eventually get a grilling, and so will I, from authorities who are—let's just say, professionally unsympathetic. So, unless you're capable tomorrow of making yourself believe you haven't seen any of this tonight,'' as he rustled the pages suggestively, ''don't look.''

''Any of what?'' she said, making her eyes big, blinking with moronic innocence.

He gave her a nod and a grin that faded quickly. ''You didn't see a rundown on federal accommodations currently in effect with most-favored nations and what is quaintly known as quasi-nationals." He spread a half dozen sheets for her, stealing another lungful of woman scent as her hair brushed near his cheek.

She read silently for several minutes, then began to murmur. "Bangladesh, East Timor, Indonesia, Malaysia, Pakistan, Turkey, Democratic Yemen. If I'm reading this right, *all* these places are off-limits for our drug enforcement people?"

"Not exactly. We can snoop around there, we just can't do much there about what we learn. You'll notice that Kurdistan is not officially on that list," he said. "So you really can forget this one."

Outrage fed her scowl. "Why would there be such a list at all?"

"Long story. The short version is, they're all heavily Islamic, which means they aren't primarily concerned about what happens to idiots in the Christian West. And they all desperately need cash, and we want to help them become capitalists. And importing drugs into this country is the nearest to a sure thing anyone has ever found. The penalties here are relatively modest. In some countries it's an automatic death sentence. This," he tapped a page, "is our way of promising that only their clumsiest entrepreneurs will go down."

"My God," she husked. "Survival of the fittest cartels."

"And making drugs readily, cheaply available the way the Swiss do is the only way we'll ever end it," he said. "Galling, but that's the way it is. Anyway, Kerman may be involved in running arms, but he probably isn't part of some multinational drug cartel, and we can be damned glad of it."

"Why?"

"His people probably don't have ten million budgeted for this little peccadillo," he growled. "Among the cartels, the budget is dear, but life is cheap."

She scanned another page, then another. Then, "Croatian Revolutionary Confederacy, Shqiperia Tosk Relief, Provisional Kurdish Democratic Party. I'm guessing these are more bad guys."

"They can be, when they give up on diplomacy," Ross nodded, scanning the text above the list. "These are quasinational groups trying for recognition in the UN because they're fugitives on their own native soil. Some of their members come in through Canada.

And yes, often it's an illegal entry. But," he said, with a grimace that could have been a cynical smile, "you'll love this. To paraphrase Orwell, some illegals are more equal than others where our own national interests are involved. They call it a 'sensitive index.' Anyone on the index gets treated like a low-level diplomat even though he's potential trouble. For anything less than serial murder, the worst that'll happen to him if he's caught on U.S. soil is expulsion from this country.

"Which brings us to this final listing," he went on, pulling up a single sheet of paper, dropping it on the table as if it were particularly offensive garbage. "It's the specific rundown of Provisional Kurdish Democratic Party members on the index."

The list was brief. Her gaze ran past Ara, Bokhti, and Karjik. "Kerman, Anatol," she said softly. "You nailed him."

"In more ways than one," he said. "But this means someone thinks he's special. At a guess, it would be their top dog, Ravan Zagro, pulling the strings. Zagro himself isn't on the index, of course."

"Why of course, if he's a big shot?"

"Blowback. That was on a page I really can't show you, T.C." When she made no reply, he glanced at her, saw her lips compressed in vexation. "Sorry for the jargon. Blowback is what happens when you train someone to be a nasty customer and then, one fine day years later, you find he's gone over to the other side. Happened a lot in Afghanistan. The guys who hit the World Trade Center? Some of that was blowback. Seems that Ravan Zagro is involved in something big."

"And you can't tell me," she said.

"Not if I don't remember. It was in a briefing that wouldn't be available on-line. I recall it vaguely, but it wasn't important to me at the time." He drummed his fingers on the page, then shrugged. "Well, it may come to me. Right now, something should be coming to our friend Kerman, a little interrogation. What we have may be enough to shake him up."

"And if it doesn't?"

He turned to her with the look of a lost child. "We may have to use rougher methods."

CHAPTER 22

Exhausted from struggling, the boy had finally cried himself to sleep. He lay in the Pontiac's footwell now, literally covered by soft-sided luggage that would keep him from moving around. It had been Cody Beale's idea, after abandoning his own car in Ruidoso, to punch a small hole through the duct tape covering the boy's mouth. "Dribbling snot like that, kid's liable to suffocate," Beale said.

"Swell. I hereby elect you his nanny," Perrin replied.

"Hey, I got a nephew about half as hyper as this kid," Beale chuckled. "Kerman said they wanted him in good condition, right?"

"Probably doesn't matter anymore what Kerman said." Perrin guided the Pontiac from the highway to a road that would bypass the little city of Artesia. Under the circumstances, he hoped to avoid highway patrol vehicles by using secondary roads wherever possible. The beauty of an aeronautical chart was that it showed farm roads missing from road maps, and that option had suddenly become very attractive.

Beale said it in a jocular manner, but he meant it, "Hey, you didn't put that Ayrab down yourself, did you?"

"I don't burn my own assets, Cody. Besides, I counted on him to handle this kid. But the man was a royal pain in the ass from day one, and you never know how a raghead will react to questioning."

"You don't think he'd burn the mission to save his butt," Beale said, surprised.

"I think about all kinds of shit, and that's one possibility. But I have an idea Mr. K has flies on his eyes by now."

"You think? He was a tough little bastard, I give him that." To Cody Beale anyone who bulked less than two hundred pounds was little. "Why'n't you run that shitstorm by me again, Tom? I didn't see any of it." As if to himself: "Jeez, poor little Dex. Somebody'll pay for that."

"Cody, we have the kid. Chalk this one up as a win and forget about the rest. I ever hear one word that you've gone back there to even the score, I'll beach you like a whale. Somebody was waiting for us in there, man."

"How you figure?"

"Kerman, for one thing. He ducked into that pantry, and somebody took him out. I mean he disappeared like he was pole-axed. Not a word from him or a shot fired 'til somebody offed Dex from the same quarter. Had to be a shotgun, and whoever it was didn't waste time thinking it over like some clueless citizen." Perrin moved his shoulders, grimaced. "Same hitter who skimmed me on my way out with the kid. Hell's bells, you saw what my back looked like when I picked you up in town, *you* tell *me*."

"Birdshot," said Beale. "You got lucky, one graze and one lump just under the skin. How's it feel?"

"Like birdshot under my skin," Perrin said in tones that added, *You dumb shit.*

"Still bleeding?"

"How the fuck would I know? I don't think so."

"You better hope it was steel shot; lead poison's no picnic. I can tease it out if you wanta stop."

"And have me bleeding like a pig. No thanks. They used to have an Irish medic at Saddletramp, hiding out from the Brits. I could pop a couple of aspirin if you've got 'em handy." He touched the lump on his forehead, a lump still sticky with pine sap from the tree he'd collided with, wincing at the touch.

Beale unsnapped his seat belt and hefted some of the bags lying atop Al Townsend. The second bag proved to be his own, which he dragged onto his lap with much puffing and grunting, his pocket flashlight held in his teeth. Presently he located his shaving kit, then an array of pills in labeled plastic film containers.

"Douse that light," Perrin ordered.

"You want your fuckin' aspirin or don't you?"

"I don't want light in my eyes. Douse it," Perrin repeated, and the big man complied. "Is that a ground mist out there, or is it just me?"

"Here, these big buffered fuckers. Three enough?" Beale put his hand out, and Perrin took the pills with a grunt of assent.

When he heard the familiar metallic clink and hiss, Perrin said, "What the hell is that?"

"Bud Light," said Beale, wiping foam from a can. "You need somethin' to wash it down with, don't you?"

Despite himself, Perrin laughed as he took the lukewarm can. "Should've known you'd have a beer within arm's reach."

"Two, actually." A moment's pause as Beale put away his shaving kit and zipped the bag, dropping it into the backseat. The pill container went into his shirt pocket in case Perrin wanted more. Then, "Maybe you oughta slow down in case we run into another patch of mist."

"Patch, hell." Perrin was squinting now. With the beer can he gestured toward the windshield. "What do you call that?"

Another pause, this one very short, before Beale's answer, slow and distinct. "I call that a concussion, Tom, maybe a light one but . . . you seeing double?"

"No. Little fuzzy, maybe."

"Okay, pull over." No response. "*Pull over,* goddamnit, it's clear as a bell outside."

"I'm okay," Perrin insisted.

"Shit you are. You pass out on me while you're driving and whatever else happens, it goes on my report!" Tom Perrin's fetish for clean reports bordered on the religious.

"Asshole," Perrin grumbled, pulling over to the shoulder.

"Asshole yourself, asshole." But Cody Beale helped his mission leader in his groggy walk around to the passenger's side before getting in behind the wheel, adjusting the seat all the way back. "Now get some sleep, Tom. I can read a map and drive on shitty roads just like you can."

"Watch the speed limits," said Perrin, leaning back, eyes shut.

"I can do that, too."

Tom Perrin did not reply.

Beale bought fuel outside Roswell and, later, took the cutoff to Fort Sumner. Once they passed a New Mexico highway patrol vehicle without incident. The Pontiac's radio gave Beale something to do, but he heard no news bulletins about trouble in the Ruidoso area. All in all, it was settling into an uneventful night. Uneventful, that is, until Beale pulled over on a side road from Gordo Lake Reservoir, intending to empty his bladder outside because, once again, he had neglected to bring an empty milk carton.

□   □   □

Perrin didn't respond when Beale announced he was stopping for his piss call, so the big man shrugged and slid from the Pontiac. Then, because he hadn't seen another car for half an hour and it was the middle of the night, he extracted the boy from beneath those bags. It took a few moments to wake him up, and in the glow from the Pontiac's interior light Beale saw that the kid should be able to unzip without untaping his hands.

Beale inhaled, then grunted in satisfaction. It wasn't that he was growing soft on the kid. He knew little kids were notorious for their leaky plumbing, and he wasn't keen on driving any distance in a closed car that smelled of kiddypiss. He picked the kid up under one arm and nudged the back door shut, using his little flashlight to show him where the roadside ditch was. "Time to take a leak," he said, setting the kid down, steadying him by the shoulder because his ankles were taped.

And every move Beale made was closely observed by Ersell Barron, who had come instantly awake when the sedan pulled over on the opposite side of the road. Barron, who wore his running shoes and black jacket with the purple "Baron Bonkers" embroidery in olde English script even when he lay snugged into his fartsack, had guided his Honda bike off the road and into the scrub before crashing for the night. At first, Barron felt for his switchblade because run-ins with the law had taught him not to carry a firearm and it would be just his luck to be spotted by one of the fishing fools whose locked cars he had slim jimmed back at the lake. A quick hand with a slim jim could boost a saddlebag full of cameras and shit out in the boonies in no time at all, and nothing short of radio waves was going to catch you on a Honda 750. Not unless you flaked off and got caught sleeping. And Ersell Barron slept with hair-trigger awareness ever since his days as a guest of the state of Nevada in that garden spot of lockups, Carson City.

Now, Barron wouldn't tip the scales at over one-fifty with a sash weight under his arm, and the big porky dude's silhouette in the light from that sedan said he could be a handful. But unless Barron's eyes deceived him, the little bitty kid under the big guy's arm was duct-taped, and that caused a dozen scenarios to feed behind Barron's eyes, flickering past like images in a rock video.

For example, the little dude was mean as, as—well, as little Ersell had been twenty years back, and this was how his daddy always traveled with him. No, Bigfella had pulled the tyke off the street somewhere and intended to use him up, maybe right out here where Ersell could watch. Or the kid was some millionaire's heir worth a saddlebag full of cash, and Barron would just have to decide whether Bigdude was part of a syndicate, meaning you left him alone, or some desperate dipshit with expensive habits doing this on his own, in which case he might be willing to turn out his pockets as a donation to some honest passing biker who could quote his license plate. Or—

He slid from his sleeping bag and crept nearer to the ditch on his side, saw the flash beam wink on, saw Bigdude zipping up. And then he saw the beam playing at the crotch of the kid, a boy for sure, fiddling with his fly just before he made a sudden standing leap forward and down into the opposite ditch from Barron.

A gutteral curse and then nothing but starlight as the big fellow disappeared, followed by scuffling and faint bleats of pain and fear. Barron had no flashlight on him, but now he had a plan, figuring he could move around now without his own scuffing footsteps giving him away. Plan A if the keys were still in the ignition; but somebody had once told him, "Life is Plan B," and Barron duckwalked quickly to the driver's side and opened the door. The interior light came on.

Barron froze, seeing the guy slumped against the passenger-side door, and his heart started up again only when he realized the sleeper hadn't woken. Ten paces away, from the sound of it, Bigdude was whaling the bejeezus out of Littledude's butt, only instead of squalls Barron could hear only those muffled little hoots of terror. They affected Ersell Barron roughly as much as one cat's yowl from the outside world affects another cat curled up inside on a pillow. Barron had the keys in his hand in a second, duckwalking away again as the door swung nearly shut and the light went out.

Beale saw the interior light flick on, then off again, as he was grinding New Mexico rocks into his knee. "Little help here, Tom," he called, assuming that Perrin had woken. "Fucking kid did a brodie into the ditch."

No answer. "God *damnit*, this isn't funny," he shouted toward the car. And as Cody Beale stomped onto the road, he heard a stealthy motion somewhere in the near distance. He opened the rear door, flung the still-sobbing Al Townsend onto the luggage bags, and then saw Tom Perrin, jaw slack, totally out of it. He slammed the rear door and all but dived into the front seat, the interior light winking dutifully on again as he felt for a pulse.

The heart of Thomas Perrin beat strongly and regularly, and for a moment Beale felt awe in the presence of the incomprehensible. Then, with a sudden pang of dread, he reached into his shirt pocket and withdrew the translucent film container. "Ahhh, SHIT!" he bellowed into the night.

Fumbling in the dark, forbidden to use his flashlight, Cody Beale had given three white Percocet tablets to his mission leader. Beale had known cops who became addicted to the damned things as painkillers, not realizing that the oxycodone in Percocet was a flat-out narcotic.

Oh sure, Tom would ask for three aspirin, Beale told himself. And he recalled dimly that a single Percocet on top of a concussion could whack you like a mallet. Tom Perrin wouldn't be a very lively leader for a few hours. Beale straightened up and shut his door, drew a huge breath, resolved to make the best of it, and reached to turn on the ignition.

No keys. He hadn't taken them from the ignition, either, and Perrin certainly hadn't. "What the fuck?" he demanded of the night.

And the night replied, in a wheedling male voice from somewhere off across the road, "Missing something?" Beale's head jerked sideways. "No, don't get out," the voice went on, "not if you ever want to see your keys again."

After an endless few seconds of thought, Beale rejected bluster and pursuit on foot. "Okay," he said, sounding as resigned as possible, following it with a laugh. "That was a good one on me, buddy. You need a ride, hop in." Meanwhile he pulled the 9-mm Glock from the right-hand pocket of his jacket.

"Naw, I don't think so," said the voice. "Not much room in back, with that kid you got stashed."

No point denying it. Beale knew, now, why the interior light had flicked on while he and the boy were outside. And this asshole couldn't have failed to spot Perrin. "I'm taking him back to his mama," said Beale.

"Bullshit."

"Truth. His papa took him unlawfully, and I got him here, too, taking papa back to Santa Fe to face charges."

"You're not the law."

"In a way I am. You ever hear of a bounty hunter? Officer of the court," said Beale, hoping it sounded official.

"Now there's an idea. Santa Fe, huh? Maybe I'll just trade you the keys for the kid. You keep papa, and I'll get the reward for Junior there."

"That," said Beale, "is not gonna happen. I'd hitch a ride first."

Now the voice was moving, light scuffing footsteps coming up from behind. stopping maybe behind the car, or maybe not. "Lotsa luck, big fella. How'll you do that, with two prisoners?"

"I'd pay the guy. What'd you think?"

"I figure you'd just throw down on whoever stops."

Beale fashioned a cynical chuckle. "With what? They don't let us carry firearms anymore. You don't know much, pal."

"I know this: If you're gonna pay anybody, I'd just as soon it was me."

Here it was, negotiation time. "I got three twenties here for gas money," Beale said, lowering his voice as he twisted his head, hoping it would make this bottom feeder come close enough.

"Better if you just opened the door and stood outside and emptied your wallet where I could see," said the voice. "And maybe you ain't heeled, but I am. So be nice."

That last instruction had just the teeniest hint of pleading in it, so maybe this invisible entrepreneur was bluffing about having a piece in hand. Cody Beale moved the Glock onto his seat with a swipe of his hand as he opened the door and stood in dim light, his bulk hiding the weapon. He let his shoulders slump, hauling his cash from his wallet, making it into a roll. "I'll keep twenty for gas," Beale said, playing it to the hilt, stripping a bill from the roll. He sighed as he held out the wad, upwards of three hundred dollars but that might not be obvious from any distance. Jiggling the bait: "Man, I never knew those keys could be so expensive."

"Uh-uh. Put it in your jacket so I can see you do it, and toss the jacket as far as you can."

Beale hesitated when he had the jacket halfway off. "And when do I get the keys?"

"Get in and leave the door open. I'll toss 'em in."

Beale nodded, stuffing his roll of bills into the lightweight jacket. The rectangle of light from the Pontiac faded out at the road's opposite shoulder, so he must make his toss accurate. The big man hurled the jacket in a high arc and saw it flutter down at the macadam's edge. He shrugged to hide his satisfaction with the toss, then sat down, holding the door wide open with his left foot.

And now he saw a dark form ghosting from behind the Pontiac, crossing the road. "So how 'bout those keys, buddy," he said. No telling whether this slimeball had played it cute and left the keys behind the car or on a rock somewhere out in the darkness.

"Be cool," said the man, searching the jacket. "I seen many a flash roll in my time." After a moment an old windproof lighter sparked in the man's hand, sparked again, then began to throw fitful flickers of yellow light. A skinny specimen with the face of a ferret thumbed through Beale's cash, and his grin was a goad that made Beale tremble. Beale felt for the Glock, biding his time, listening for the clink of keys that would tell him he need wait no longer to erase that grin once and for all.

Ersell Barron exulted in the wad of twenties, tucking it into his pants as he snapped the lighter shut. A good night's work for a traveling man, he thought, reaching for the car keys in his other pocket. Then he paused. Once he got his car started, the bounty hunter might try to pick Ersell out with his headlights. Ditches or no ditches, Ersell wasn't too sure he could get back to his bike in darkness and fire it up before the big guy got his car moving. Besides, wouldn't it be funny as hell to just leave this self-described officer of the court stranded without his keys? In Ersell's considered opinion, any officer of any court would hump his own mother if he couldn't find a stray dog first.

Beale's first hint that he had waited too long came when the dim figure wheeled and vanished, a high-pitched giggle trailing him into limbo. Beale leaped from the car and slammed the door, stumbling across the road toward the sounds of footsteps and of laughter, both diminishing. The little flashlight might help, though now he wished it were one of the big multicell police head-bashers, and Beale made his way past the ditch feeling the onset of panic. The shrub he encountered felt like a barbed-wire sculpture against his thighs, and he went down on one knee, biting back a curse, and was instantly glad he kept silent because now he could swear he heard footsteps and panting, some distance off but coming nearer, then past him. Beale tried his flashlight, the beam raking across gray vegetation and something that could have been a metallic gleam as the beam began to fade. In seconds his beam dwindled to a feeble glow.

Cody Beale was glad of only one thing: Perrin wasn't beside him. Forgetting to install fresh batteries was a basic amateur's mistake, and Beale had finally made it at a time when absolutely *every*thing depended on properly functioning equipment.

Now Beale did something right, pocketing the flashlight, moving slowly in the direction where he thought he'd seen that gleam, holding the Glock in readiness.

Barron had almost laughed again when that little beam reflected off the chrome of the Honda after he'd flailed past the bike without seeing it. No time to grab his old torn fartsack. He could boost a new one or, hell, even buy a Hollofil bag with two hundred and sixty dollars and change in his pocket. He had maybe a hundred feet between him and the bounty hunter, and with any luck at all he could fire up the 750 in seconds. His headlight was all the advantage he needed. Baron Bonkers would have a great yarn to swap with other biker royalty in roadhouses of the great Southwest.

Beale heard the muffled whirring thump of a big bike starting up somewhere near. Then a soft exhaust flash in pink tinged with blue, and because Cody Beale knew, high-tech as it was, that even a 9-mm Glock was a short-range side arm, he ran forward, not noticing the remnant of an old sleeping bag until his feet were tangled in it, and as he fell full-length on his belly he fired once.

Barron snapped on his headlight and was looking ahead, so he didn't see the muzzle flash. But that hard, flat report across New Mexico hardpan was louder than the Honda by a bunch, and in one corner of his mind Ersell Barron felt vast betrayal by a man who claimed bounty hunters didn't go armed these days. *Sumbitch lied to me*, he thought, twisting this way and that around shrubs that could flake the paint off a rhino, and then he saw the contours of the ditch and went into it at a shallow angle, leaning forward against acceleration that would vault him three feet in the air before he hit macadam, heading for points north as he jazzed past the darkened sedan. Ersell Barron gave a rebel yell in pure elation.

And Beale knew the range was ridiculous as he stood up, taking a two-handed stance, but he had no choice and began squeezing them off, sending round after round in the bike's direction, each blast a flashbulb that lit up the arid landscape in sharp relief, aiming behind the source of that single moving highway beam. The Glock held seventeen rounds, and this piece of equipment was working perfectly, Beale pivoting as he kept the headlight ahead of his muzzle. He had lost count of his rounds as the big Honda roller-coastered down and up the ditch, then into the air, the bike ferret yodeling his triumph, and the bike's rear wheel slammed down onto the road first and catapulted the Honda forward, rocketing into the trunk of the parked Pontiac in a grinding shower of sparks. Until now, Cody Beale had never realized that a bike collision could sound so much like a train wreck.

Beale wasn't sure he was out of the woods until he dragged the biker's body off the roof of the Pontiac by its hair, checking its pockets, finding his money and keys. Ignoring the renewed sobs of the boy, he drove forward fifty feet to get away from the pool of gasoline and turned around so his headlights could play on the crash site. Feeling as if somebody had drained all the vinegar out of him, he dragged the remains of the bike down into the ditch. He kicked pieces of cast metal off the road, kicked the unprotesting body for good measure, turned it over so that the missing eye and cheek would show what a nine-millimeter exit wound could do to a man's head. Then he trudged back and retrieved Al Townsend, carrying him by the back of his belt, the boy's head and feet hanging down.

When he'd brought the kid close enough that he was practically nose to nose with the ruined face, its single eye lit by pitiless headlights, Beale shook him hard as if to drop him into the gory mess. "Look at that," he boomed, his words curiously without echoes in the desert stillness. "This guy saw you, and you see what it bought him!"

The boy crooned in misery and tried to arch his back. "If it wasn't for you the silly fucker would be alive now! You understand, kid? This is your fault 'cause you made us tape you up with all your yellin' and kickin' and raisin' hell." No longer shouting now: "Got it? You killed the guy."

The boy did not try to respond, and Beale continued to harp on his theme as he hauled the body down into the ditch with his free hand. How'd it feel to know he'd gotten a man's head blown off? he asked. Anybody who got curious about the kid would get popped the same way, he said. Cody Beale knew he was taking up valuable time, but he had an agenda beyond simply giving an outlet to his adrenaline. They would be passing through towns after dawn and Perrin might still be zonked out. Beale wanted to make certain that this little fart would keep still for the rest of the trip, and he felt sure this little demonstration would leave a lasting impression.

In this, he was wholly successful.

CHAPTER 23

For T.C. the brief summer night seemed to last a week. Accepting the strategy of Ross, she catnapped in the big armchair for an hour at a time, then replaced him in the cellar for a time while he sought more hints from his computer. And throughout the night, they inundated Kerman with endless questions, supplemented by an occasional prod with the shotgun barrel. At some point Ross had removed the blindfold from Kerman. Sleep deprivation, said Ross, could sap a zealot's will, given enough time.

But time was the enemy. Anatol Kerman seemed aware of it, patient in his answers, turning them into short recitals of injuries done to the Kurdish people. T.C. could not know how much truth lay in this litany of injustices, but, taken at only half of face value, it composed a sweeping indictment against several nations. During one of Kerman's recitations she realized that the pity she felt for these poor devils was, by extension, leaking over into her feelings toward Kerman as well. Exactly as Kerman must have intended.

Kerman, with a citation of Kurdish extended family relations that bewildered T.C., had already admitted distant kinship to little Al Townsend—Talal in Kerman's parlance no matter how many times she toed his ribs for it. Now she kicked him again, denying her guilt for it. "Some cousin you are," she raged. "Spend the night telling me why nobody with half a brain would want to live as Kurds do, while your buddies are taking that innocent little kid to this same living hell you're describing."

Kerman absorbed the light kick without complaint. "I do not expect you to understand the importance of inherited leadership and birth order among my people. This child is born to a responsibility, a tradition of leadership and of training. He has two younger brothers who are already learning these things you find beyond your grasp."

"Half-brothers, you mean."

"We do not count such things in quite the way you do, but let it pass."

T.C. felt goaded by the man's composure. "If this little kid is so goddamned important to his daddy, why didn't he come and get his own son instead of sending a bunch of murdering bastards like you to do it for him?"

The Kurd took his time responding. "Talal's father cannot simply abandon his people to reclaim his son. It would be seen as a basic failure of leadership."

"Then why not let his little brothers take Al's place? They'd probably love to, poor little guys."

"In years to come that will occur to them, I am certain. But the only way this role of leadership would fall to Kassi or Yarsan would be upon the death of Talal." He shifted his body in a vain attempt to find some less discomforting position.

"Great. You're teaching his brothers why they should kill him."

"That is not unknown here in the West," said Kerman darkly. "But we are not a race of murderers. And we protect our young leaders rather better than you do."

"Seems to me," said T.C., "his daddy would be smart to declare Al dead and get on with brainwashing the next kid in line."

"And suffer the consequences ten years later when Talal decides to make his claim public, for whatever reason. Ah, yes, that is the sort of short-term thinking we have come to expect in the West." The last phrase was nearly a whisper.

"Up yours. If it weren't for us short-term Western thinkers, there wouldn't be enough Kurds left to fill a phone booth."

He tried to answer, but nothing intelligible came out. She said, "What's your problem?"

"I thirst," he husked. Not a complaint, simply a statement.

She picked up her cold coffee cup and slurped noisily. "Sounds biblical. Won't help you. You already know how to get all the water you want." He said nothing. Prodding him with the gun barrel: "For the last time, where did they take Al?"

He swallowed, then managed, "For the last time, I do not know."

"That's a load of crap, buster. You'll get a whole lot thirstier, hungrier too, if you don't tell us."

"I accept that," he croaked.

Suddenly furious, she brought the barrel of the shotgun up and sighted down its length, into the unblinking gaze of the Kurd. "Accept this," she said, trembling with the urge, feeling the cold metal of the trigger.

"You have not the courage," he said.

"You don't know me very well," she told him, facing him down the shotgun barrel while inside her two voices quarreled. One snarled, *Show him; none of his bunch deserves any better,* while the other coolly replied, *And you will certainly never see Al again.*

"You cannot do it. I do know you," he insisted.

She nearly pulled the trigger in surprise when she heard the voice of Ross Downing from near the stairs. "Too easy for him, T.C. Put it down, please." He repeated "please" more softly before she lowered the weapon, still staring at the Kurd. The most chilling aspect of that moment was when Kerman flicked his glance from her to Ross.

He showed no sign of relief at Ross's interruption. If anything, she thought, Anatol Kerman's face registered only disappointment.

"You sure were quiet coming downstairs," she said, her voice shaking.

"No I wasn't. You were just, uh, let's say focused. Maybe a bit too focused," he added gently, taking the shotgun from her. Now he looked toward the Kurd. "If you think this woman is the standard issue, pal, you'll get your head blown off, you really will. I do know her, and she was about to do it."

"God help me, I was," she said and leaned her face into his shoulder.

"She was not," Kerman insisted. And smiled.

"Go back upstairs, get some winks," said Ross, patting her gently. "Seems I've run across some tidbits that might interest Mr. Kerman. Has he been cooperating at all? Before that little faceoff I interrupted, I mean," he smiled.

"Nothing helpful. Says he's thirsty. Keep him that way," she said and turned away.

She did not hear the next exchange between the men but, sitting down silently on the steps, let her curiosity have its way.

Apparently Ross had some small implement in one hand and kept clicking it idly, or not so idly. "No, don't look at those," he said to the Kurd, "look at me. I've run out of patience, now that I know who you are."

"And who is that?" Kerman asked.

"PKDP, to begin with," said Ross. "Provisional wing of your so-called democratic party."

"You have such a party yourselves," said the Kurd.

"Don't play games, Kerman. Your offshoot is a guerrilla party. Just so you'll know I know, several big players in the UN want to see those Caspian Sea pipelines—oil and natural gas—opened up across Iran to Turkey. That's big. Your PKDP snipers could delay the pipelines unless the UN bigwigs give you special treatment. In your particular case, like a facilitator team."

"I have no idea what you mean," Kerman replied huskily. Then, after a pause, the Kurd gave an abrupt moan.

It sounded to T.C. as if Ross were trying to talk through gritted teeth for a moment. "From here on out, that's what you get for a lie. I can snip you to pieces if you insist on lying. You're PKDP, and you've got a facilitator team with you."

"What makes you believe these things?" For the first time, the Kurd spoke with a lack of self-assurance.

"You mean, how do I know? You've got connections; *we've* got connections. Just bad luck on your part, Kerman."

"Ray Townsend," said the Kurd. "He has filled you with lies."

This time T.C. distinctly heard a soft scissoring click before Kerman grunted in pain. "I'm not certain you knew that was a false statement, but at this point I'll treat any wrong answer as a lie. And Townsend isn't my source. How would a retired engineer know about UN safe sites? You know the ones I mean," Ross said.

"Who does not know about the UN?"

"Careful," Ross said softly, and T.C. heard the repeated snick of some terrible instrument in his hand, a threat like the gnashing of metal teeth. "Facilitator safe sites. Coyote Canyon, Picacho, Saddletramp, San Angelo, Moab Wells. Not the sort of thing they tell Boeing people."

"You are government, then? Which one?"

"I'll ask the questions—and you see I already know some of the answers. You've heard of those sites?"

Silence. The teeth clashed again, suggestively. "Yes," said Kerman, as if disgusted with himself.

"Here, have a sip of coffee." A moment's quiet, then: "There you go, a small reward for a correct answer. Now, of those safe sites I mentioned, which one did I make up?"

"I swear, I do not know. How would I know?" Now the Kurd's tone was pleading.

"You know some are real, though." Pause. "Don't you?"

"I believe that is true."

Ross heaved a long sigh. "You're trying to be cute, to outthink me." His tone became more genial, almost conspiratorial. "Here's what I think of cute." And Kerman grunted in pain again. "This can go on as long as you like," Ross said, in tones so gentle it made T.C.'s own flesh crawl. "But let me tell you something about this nasty business. At first, losing little pieces of yourself will only get your notice, as I believe it already has. But gradually, it will push every other thing from your mind, until it fills every crevice of your attention."

Hearing this, T.C. sat in horrified silence, not daring to look back toward what was happening on the cellar floor, hating Kerman, despising Ross and herself in equal measure. But Ross would not quit, hammering gently at his captive with these intimations of horrors to come.

"You will have nothing left for anyone or anything else. For your God, nothing; for country, nothing; for the future, for your family, for your most cherished ideals, nothing.

"Now, there are a few people who learn how to retreat into those pain-filled crevices, simply to hide from the reality of what is happening a fraction of an inch beyond your eyelids. Some men never come back from there, Kerman. Because somehow they know, the way they would know from a far-off battlefield bulletin, what they'll find left if they ever do return.

"Are you one of those happy few escapees, Anatol Kerman? If you don't tell us where that little boy has been taken, for your sake, I almost hope you find that inner escape."

Then a flurry of impacts, sounding like the heel of a hand slapped hard against the flagstones. "No, damn you!" T.C. turned then, seeing Ross as he knelt beside the unconscious Kurd. As she hurried to them, Ross looked up with reddening eyes. "I—you shouldn't have been here. He started slamming his head against the floor as hard as he could. I think—let's go upstairs," he said, holding a small pair of pruning shears down against one leg as if to hide them from her. The shears glistened redly.

"Oh, Ross, Ross," she crooned.

"Don't say anything here. He may be awake." Ross nonetheless pulled up one of Kerman's eyelids, then the other, and shook his head. Kerman's wrists and hands were blood-slicked, but there was not as much of it as T.C. had imagined.

"Come on," she urged, and together they somehow made it up the steps without incident.

□   □   □

She had not seen Ross Downing this depressed in more than a year. With a wet hand towel draped around his neck, he sat at the dining table and supported himself with his forearms, staring down at nothing. "I think I could have done it, gone on with it, I mean," he said to T.C. as she spooned honey into his coffee. "But I don't think I can, now, even if he—"

Somewhere outside, a jay rebuked the dawn. T.C. glanced out a window at the glory of the new day and sat down across from Ross. "Do you think he'll die down there?"

"Not unless he manages to crack his skull. And why should he, when I've stopped . . . doing what I was doing." In a plea for absolution he said, "I didn't do him any serious damage, T.C. He'll have scars on one wrist, but I didn't . . . sever anything. The skin was already broken from where I bound him, and—never mind. What they say must be true: Given the circumstances, a human being is capable of almost anything he can imagine. I wanted him to think I was doing worse. Hell, he couldn't see what I was doing."

"Don't dwell on it, honey," she said. "Some torturers we turned out to be. Maybe Grandpa Townsend will have some ideas. He's due later today," she reminded him with false hope.

"Maybe." His tone said, Don't count on it. "I thought that guy was trying to master you there when you threw down on him, but I don't think so now." His gaze was mystified, awed. "T.C., he *wanted* you to blow him away."

"You'll get no argument from me. Maybe he didn't trust himself to keep his secrets."

"I wish there were something I could believe in with that kind of fervor." Ross exhaled heavily, stood up, looked around as though wondering where he was. "One thing I can do is look around the property for tracks, figure out where to bury that other body—something."

"You think Orv could help?"

"Good God, no!" Evidently even amateur torturers could be scandalized. "We're in this up to our scalps, T.C., but I'm not about to draw Orv into it." Montezuma, kinetic as a squirrel, rode his shoulder and searched his shirt pocket for peanuts as he moved to the porch. He turned back in the doorway. "Oh, it's going to take both of us to haul that body out to my wheelbarrow, but it's got to be done. I'll be back soon." With that he limped outside.

And two minutes later, she heard a hesitant half toot from the horn of Orv Ferguson's Land Rover just outside. Thinking furiously, T.C. tore her blouse off and grabbed a throw pillow from the floor next to the big chair. Proper as an archduke, the old man would never enter the cabin with her only half dressed. She hugged the pillow over her breast and thrust the screen door open with a bare shoulder, smiling brightly, waving with her free hand.

"Goin' into town," called Orv, leaning from the cab. "Wasn't sure you'd be up. Can I get you folks anything?"

She declined and thanked him, and with a parting wave he rolled across the meadow and out of sight. She shivered and thrust an arm into her blouse again, intending to hustle a breakfast for two until she saw the silent mass that still lay on the kitchen floor.

□   □   □

When Ross returned a half hour later, T.C. was on hands and knees, scrubbing the kitchen linoleum as if to erase her frustrations. He looked around him, perplexed. "You didn't put it downstairs," he hazarded.

"It was a him, Ross." She stood up, hands on hips. "I don't have any problem with that. A few days ago that guy tried to feel me up about a minute before he intended to kill me. No regrets," she insisted.

He spread his arms. "All right, David Copperfield, how'd you disappear him?"

"Dragged him out on a big plastic garbage bag. He's behind your toolshed in the wheelbarrow," she explained, and gestured at the floor. "Got this mess about cleaned up."

"How's our man downstairs?"

"I looked in on him once. Hasn't moved that I could see."

"He'll keep 'til what's his name gets here. Can't leave that body out there in the open." Ross pulled at what was left of his ear, a nervous habit of long standing.

"Don't do that. You know you aren't supposed—"

"Knock it off, teacher," he said shortly and turned back to the porch. "There's a low, unstable bluff near my property line where the overburden keeps falling in. If we can wheel him that far, I can dislodge a few feet of earth over him with the pickaxe. It'll have to do."

As they worked to avoid leaving a track with the wheelbarrow, Ross said he had seen Orville Ferguson's Range Rover parked at the gate, the old fellow inspecting a new gap in their perimeter fence. After Orv drove off toward Ruidoso, Ross had made his own cursory inspection, finding no suggestive tire tracks but several sets of prints. "I'm no great shakes as a tracker," he said, "but I could find only a few prints of one person leading back out. Big feet, deeper heel marks going out than the same feet made going in. At a guess, he was carrying Al. They may have had someone with a vehicle at the road."

By mutual consent, they focused on the facilitator team and not on the business at hand. To T.C.'s question about the size of such groups, Ross said he had no certain knowledge, though the teams were never large. It was known that such a team might include ex-lawmen, rogue retired agents, sometimes disbarred attorneys. "Professionals with flexible ethics and a taste for action who try to maintain a low profile, mercenaries at heart," he said.

"Ross, I'm sorry I brought all this on you. Now those people know where you live."

"You don't understand the way they work, T.C. Low-profile means, among other things, they probably won't show up again after they've got what they were after."

"Not like the Mafia, then?"

"Strictly business." He watched the body of Dex McLeod flop down a short, almost vertical declivity, as T.C. looked away. "It amazes me," he went on in tones that might have been comments on the weather, "how well that's beginning to characterize yours truly."

"That's not so," T.C. protested.

"I never thought so, but that was before my ethics got torqued around, the past twelve hours." He took a swing at the lip of the precipice with the pickaxe, nearly losing his grip on the handle. He smiled at T.C. "And the truth is, I feel more alive right now than I have for a long time. I've missed being active, more than I realized." He took another swing, this time to better effect.

"Give me that thing," she said and attacked the dry soil. "I won't argue about the low profile." *Thwock.* "For either of us, sweetie." *Thunk.* "Even if we were within our rights to shoot that bastard down there"—*thwufff,* as a half yard of overburden collapsed on the body—"couldn't we get hammered for this?"

"Oh, yeah, big-time," he agreed. "Judge, jury, and executioner they understand, under the right circumstances. But when you play undertaker, they can get pretty testy. The official term would be 'tampering with evidence.'"

"Or in this case," she said cheerfully, "tamping down the evidence."

"Your sense of humor can be downright frightening at times," he said with a headshake.

"I say, if you're going to do something, do it with a right goodwill," she retorted, panting with effort.

Five minutes later, Ross was distributing fresh dirt over the body as T.C. stood, breast heaving, and caught her breath. "I hate to say this, Ross, but, umm, are we going to have to do this again?"

He looked up, blinked. "Goddamn, I hope not. I know what you mean," he said, silencing her with a hand gesture, "but that doesn't have to be decided now. There's still a chance we might crack this Kerman lunatic, if he's as much a zealot about Islam as he is about Kurdistan." At his wave, she sent down more dirt and stones.

"You really think so?"

"Could be. You know the fried pork rinds we eat like chips?"

"You, maybe. I never cottoned to *chicharrónes* even in the barrio," she said.

"Pork is an absolute abomination to a Muslim. Sprinkling some powdered pork rinds over him would be, well, I don't know if there's a parallel in our terms."

"You're kidding."

"It may be unbelievable, but I'm not kidding. We'll just have to see." He finished, spreading more dirt mixed with stones. The body now lay under several feet of soil as Ross limped around the hillock to be met by T.C. and the wheelbarrow.

It was now midmorning. In another ten minutes Ross had guided the empty wheelbarrow to the toolshed and replaced the pickaxe. As they neared the cabin, he glowed with a bizarre sense of well-being because, whatever felonies they had just committed, or might soon commit, T.C. performed an act more salient to him as they walked to the front porch: She took his hand in hers.

Inside the cabin, T.C. began washing her hands in the sink, but Ross went straight to the cellar stairs. She heard his, "Oh, my Christ," from the cellar and then his shuffling return. Ross darted toward his bedroom. With a prickle of hairs at the base of her skull, she followed and asked the question she dreaded to ask. "Is he dead?"

"Don't know," he muttered, pulling out his weapon containers and opening each as fast as he could. "We should only be so lucky."

She stood perplexed, shaking her wet hands as he surveyed the weapons on his bed with a sigh of relief. "Can't you find out?"

"I can if I can find him. At least he didn't take any of our weapons. Don't you get it? The man is gone."

CHAPTER □ **24**

The turnoff to Saddletramp Ranch, though completely anonymous, is well positioned to be reached by badly surfaced roads from three directions, but only if the driver is well motivated. From the north the nearest hamlet is Sanchez; from the west, the key villages are Trujilo and then Trementina. Cody Beale came in from the east by way of Conchas State Park and Variadero in early morning, ignoring the uncompromising beauty that stretched beyond the Pontiac's hood. This semidesert land, steeped in sunlight for the past million years and deeply slashed by dry washes, lay half surrounded by low mountains with sparse vegetation. Occasional stands of cottonwood against the flesh-toned distance posted verdant notices of subsurface water to anyone who could read those leafy signs. Between Beale and those cottonwoods there seemed to be nothing alive, because Beale was not especially familiar with the local fauna: pronghorn antelope, pygmy owls, land terrapins, and horned lizards that would harm no one; gila monsters, scorpions, and rattlers that, if provoked, certainly would.

And bugs of all kinds, one of which now whacked his windshield with the effect of a tiny ripe avocado. "Goddamn it, Tom, where's the goddamn turnoff? There isn't any goddamn turnoff along here," Beale snarled, shaking Perrin's shoulder.

Perrin stirred, a good sign and none too soon. "Wuzza turnoff," he mumbled, then lurched upright, eyes wide and wild. "Where the fuck are we?"

"Welcome to the world. If this is still the world," Beale amended, gesturing toward the scene beyond his besplattered windshield.

Perrin carefully touched the lump on his forehead, then winced. Then he twisted to look behind him and sat back with a sigh. The kid sat erect in the backseat, pale and mute and watchful, without any visible sign of bindings. "Boy, I got walloped last night," Perrin said, checking his wristwatch.

"No sweat," said Beale, who was not about to volunteer anything about those pills, the *real* wallop his leader had taken. As for the scum biker, well, he hadn't decided whether to mention that anytime soon. One day it might be good for a laugh over a six-pack, but not yet, not on this particular day. "Tom, we've passed a wide spot in the road named Trementina, but as for turnoffs, well, just fuhgettaboutit."

"You mean we're lost."

"We're not, the turnoff is. I know exactly where we are on the map," Beale argued and whisked the air chart around to face Perrin.

Perrin squinted at the chart, then studied their surroundings. "You've passed it, Cody. Turn around and go back, and for Chrissake slow down. You expect a fucking stoplight at an intersection, you're going to be disappointed."

Grumbling, Beale did as he was directed. But Perrin had changed his mind and ordered a stop to change drivers, taking this opportunity "to drain the snake," as he put it.

Beale let the boy out to relieve himself, too, and Perrin nodded when he saw the hobbles of tape at the kid's ankles. "Every time you do something right, makes me want to cheer," he told Beale.

"You should'a been cheering all night instead of sleeping," Beale replied. Then he saw Perrin staring at the new scars on and above the Pontiac's rear bumper. "Crazy biker," he said quickly. "Rear-ended us bigger'n shit out in the boonies."

"And you didn't wake me?"

"If that didn't, what would? Hey, kid, how loud was it?"

"Awful. The gun was louder," said Al Townsend glumly.

Perrin looked down at his patch of damp sand and pondered this. "The gun," he said.

"Fuckin' right, the gun, my Glock. You think I was gonna stop and serve and protect that hophead 'til the smokeybears could get on the scene, like about day after tomorrow, and start askin' the kid here what he's doing all taped up? Well,—"

"Yeah, forget about it," said Perrin, as Beale shoved the boy back in the car. "We going to hear about it later?"

"Not from that biker," Beale snickered. "Could be days before anybody notices. We can rig a fender bender to explain those blems on the rental."

Underway again, they paralleled a barbed-wire fence for miles. After a few minutes Perrin saw the big man reach for his last can of Bud Light. "Not now," he cautioned. "Don't need beer on your breath when we reach Saddletramp. Those guys won't say it to me, but when they aren't running a dude ranch they're making reports."

"*If* we reach Saddle—what's wrong?"

Perrin had braked suddenly and now turned left and stopped. An old-fashioned gate, with a fence post insinuated under loops of wire, lay to the left of the road. Tire tracks suggested that the barbed wire blocked a trail used by many kinds of vehicle, though not every day. "Well, no wonder we passed it," Beale groused, getting out and trudging to wrestle the gate.

"You passed it. I didn't," Perrin called. He drove through the hole Beale had created, stopped, and waited for Beale to resecure the fence post. In a moment they were on the move again, Beale shaking his head at the wallowing ride, apparently to nowhere. "Talk about your high-class dude ranch," he said.

"Part of the mystique," Perrin said. "Time some visiting Swede gets driven through that fence, he thinks it's a hundred years ago and he bane t'ink he's Yon frigging Wayne-a."

"I love it," Beale grinned. No one spoke for several minutes, the trail free of obstacles and easy to follow.

Perrin located his little transceiver, selected a frequency, and was answered immediately by a prim female voice. "I figure we're expected," he told her.

"For some time now," said Ms. Prim. "Keep going beyond the ranch house, follow the signs to the staff quarters, please."

"Been there, done that; I know the drill," he said and switched off.

Beale said, "You know her?"

"Down, boy," Perrin said. "I've seen her. The couple of informed staff members there wouldn't interest you."

Beale said, "Right now, a three-legged circus freak would interest me." Then, "You think we'll wrap this up today?"

"You got a hot date?"

"In Reno? Never a problem. I really wanta put this one behind me, Tom."

A flag of cottonwood foliage flicked into view between rises of hardpan perhaps two miles ahead. "Me too," Perrin replied, "but that happens when we get a release from Houston. And the guy who could've unclogged that shitplug for us is a casualty."

"Dex?"

"Kerman! God, but you're slow," Perrin bitched.

"Maybe you're just closemouthed," said Beale.

"Okay, spelling it out for you. The kid is our package, to be kept in good condition, until Houston gets word from the Man on the other end. They bring in air support here to Saddletramp. Once they take the kid and clear the ground, we're out of the loop. Not until then."

"Another day, you figure?"

"Or another year. Shit, I don't know! We get paid, don't worry about it. Way I figure, Houston will forward my report on Kerman, someone in Ayrabistan will expect us to wait for Kerman to show up here—"

"Fuh*getta*boutit," Beale laughed.

"—And when he doesn't, in a few days they write him off and send somebody else to ID the kid and make the pickup." Perrin reset his rearview to observe the boy, who sat in one corner of the backseat, knees drawn up as if to make himself even smaller. "Hey,

Talal." When the boy only glanced warily toward him, he tried again. "Al, Talal, which is it?"

"Al." Pause. "You killed my mom. Not talking to you."

"Look, it was an accident," said Perrin, as if confessing a minor indiscretion. "She slipped. We were just helping your cousin, or uncle, some damn thing. You know, the guy who called for you back there in the cabin."

"Didn't see him."

"Jeez. You didn't see the guy who called you Talal? I heard him."

"I saw guys from where I was hiding. Not talking to you," the boy said stubbornly.

"You don't know the name Anatol Kerman?"

No answer, until Cody Beale turned in his seat with, "Answer him, kid."

"Long time ago," said the boy. "Yeah, I kinda remember. Some kinda cousin." Another pause. "I hate him if he sent you."

"He figured you'd remember him," said Perrin, nodding. When the boy only shrugged and looked out the window, hugging his knees, Perrin tried one more time. "How many cousins you have overseas, kid?"

This time Beale simply looked back. "Don't know. Lots, I think," said the boy.

Perrin said to Beale, "Seems you've thrown the fear of God into the kid."

"He was awake when I popped the biker back there. Gave him a good close-up, told him the facts of life. He got the point."

Perrin chuckled. "As in, the facts of life are death? Remind me to recommend you as a baby-sitter, Cody."

"Babe-sitter, maybe, if she's up for it. You don't suppose there's some stray poontang hanging around at Saddletramp? I mean, if we're gonna be just cooling our heels out here."

"If there is—no offense, Cody—but even if she knows English, chances are you won't speak her language. And the kind of jet-setters they cater to here probably don't sell it cheap. Besides, the staff likes to keep their functions nicely separated, so only a couple of 'em know about us. What happened when I was here before was, we got shunted off to a cabin and I only got a glimpse of the neat stuff.''

"The broads, you mean?''

"I didn't see any available strays," Perrin said patiently. "Tennis courts, corral, a pool, probably a bar—but no booze where I stayed—TV, plenty to read, decent food. It wasn't the real staff quarters. We'll still be on duty, what the fuck did you expect?''

"An end to this shit," Beale muttered and squinted past the Pontiac's hood.

□   □   □

They made the boy lie down in the backseat with tape over his eyes as Saddletramp Ranch headquarters came in view. Flanked by cottonwoods with trunks as thick as a man is high, the main building was made of logs brought from far off, with shallow arms connected by a roofed veranda, imported olive trees for shade, and, startling in this location, a lawn that might have been trimmed with cuticle scissors. Beale noted the word "Saddletramp" formed in a marquee with skeletal pieces of ocotillo cactus and got a glimpse of one of those jazzed-up swimming pools that are supposed to look natural with boulders that sparkle with semiprecious inclusions. It all worked so hard to look good, it reminded Cody Beale of an old whore in new shoes.

Perrin did not turn onto the macadam that kept proletarian dust from imperiling the composure of finicky dudes but dutifully followed signs that led them past the log headquarters with its gaggle of adobe apartments nearby. The signs carried such disparate labels as CHUCK SHACK, CORRAL, and JACUZZI, and in the near distance Beale thought he saw a couple of young stuff bouncing away from a barn more or less on horseback, headed for a bridle trail. It wasn't fair, he thought, that he was following the sign labeled STAFF QUARTERS ONLY.

Eventually the trail led them a mile beyond a prominence of land that completely hid the upscale buildings, and the staff quarters looked run-down enough to be genuine but seldom used. Squarish and wind-scoured, each small building had been hand-

crafted from adobe, large straw-and-earthen bricks of local materials. Cody Beale's tension lowered a trifle when he saw the wiring
and the water tank at the roof of each structure. It wouldn't quite
be camping out.

The leathery man who held the next gate open for them
looked like any ordinary ranch hand: checkered shirt, jeans, low-
heeled work boots, scruffy hat and all. He wore an old army-issue
.45 low on his right hip, resting his hand not on it but near
enough. He mimed rolling down a window. Perrin complied and
stopped.

The man's gaze flickered across their faces, then to the small
blindfolded figure lying full-length in the backseat. "Welcome to
Saddletramp, boys. You'll be?"

"Perrin and Beale with the package," said Perrin, showing his
ID. "I called in, but we should report to someone."

"To Clint. That's me."

"You're kidding," said Perrin, grinning.

Clint's smile and shrug said he was used to that. "Well, it says
all that needs sayin', even to most foreign guests. You won't see
'em except by accident. Been here before my time, I'm told."

"I have. Beale hasn't," Perrin supplied. "You still have that
mick medic here?"

Clint's accent and his lazy delivery suggested a lot of free-
range life sandwiched around some higher education. "No
medic. Otherwise, the same ol' s.o.p. Second 'dobe is for you,
and there's maybe a quarter-section inside this fence, and you
don't cross it. Anytime you're outside for a stroll you want to
wear what we've supplied, because dudes plinking at rabbits
sometimes get within sight of you. Looks primitive, but the beds,
the plumbing, and the grub are okay. You won't have any close
neighbors, and I'll need your thumbprints 'fore I head back.
Plenty of what you need in the fridge; if it's not in there, you
don't need it. And just in case it needs sayin', keep your package indoors at all times. Clear?"

"That's affirmative," said Perrin. "Hey, didn't there used to
be a hangar somewhere out here?"

A nod. "Mistake. Took it down after some city boy made himself an emergency landing, 'bout a year back. Created a bigger emergency than he thought. And don't ask,'' Clint said easily, again favoring them with that broad western smile.

"You wouldn't know when Houston's scheduling the package transfer, I suppose," Perrin said.

"Naw. I know you were rescheduled twice, which tells me you stepped in deep *caca,* and I know you took some casualties. And I don't want to know any more. What you've got might be catchin','' said Clint, waving them forward.

Clint did not leave until he had taken a pair of thumbprints, and he never spoke to the boy with the blindfold. He took the Pontiac's keys and wheeled a ridiculously tiny motorized scooter from the shadow of the adobe, lifting the scooter into the Pontiac's trunk without apparent effort. Perrin realized then that they were about to be left absolutely afoot, hull down on the horizon from civilization and limited to a quarter mile of rocky hardpan. No doubt Houston had ordered that as an implied slap on his wrist.

Clint's face took on a pensive look as Perrin explained the Pontiac's scars. "You couldn't wash the blood smears off?"

"We were rushed. You know how it is," said Beale.

"You guys," Clint sighed, not needing to explain further, and drove off without another word.

The adobe's outside walls were two feet thick, so the light from each window passed through an aperture like a tunnel. They found three single beds, two chairs, a desk with a telephone, adequate lamps, and an almost new Magnavox television. The refrigerator was well stocked, including a stack of frozen meals and the makings for sandwiches.

Al Townsend found the TV's remote control after they removed his blindfold. When Perrin took it from him to scan the news channels, the boy only glanced at the shelf of paperbacks before flinging himself on the only bed that did not have luggage on it. Having spent much of the night in speechless fear, he was asleep in minutes.

After pressing a tiny sphere of birdshot from beneath the skin of Perrin's shoulder with dirty fingernails and applying an adhesive patch, Cody Beale wasted little time in thawing a breakfast for himself in the microwave oven. When Perrin found no reference to the night's events on the news, he made himself a cup of instant coffee and lit one of his unfiltered Camels, curiously unwilling to meet Beale's gaze.

"And I thought stakeouts were dull," Beale said.

Perrin took a nervous pull on his cigarette. "Last time, I could shoot the shit with another transient team in that hangar," he said, firing twin gouts of smoke from his nostrils.

Beale forked more fettuccine Alfredo in, then said, "Maybe this is a slack season." Pause. "Or maybe they don't love you anymore."

Perrin's glance was quick, nervous, intense. He shook his head, then stood up and began a slow circuit of the room. His scrutiny seemed casual as he inspected a book, moved on to try a lamp, stepped into the toilet kiosk long enough to urinate.

When he emerged, Beale was clearing an empty plastic dish from the table. "I could use some fresh air," he said, taking a last puff from his Camel.

"After you've fogged up the room," Beale replied.

Perrin paused in the doorway, and Beale narrowed his gaze at the meaningful jerk of Perrin's head. "Shit, he's asleep," Beale said, but Perrin repeated the "come along" gesture. "And he's hobbled. Oh, well." And Beale followed the leader.

Perrin was turned away from the adobes as he lit another cigarette, cupping his hands to foil a light breeze, when Beale slouched up to him. "Just stand beside me," Perrin murmured. "We don't know who might be in one of those dirt bungalows with a shotgun mike."

"Whaddaya trying to do, Tom, make me nervous?"

"Cautious. This isn't like things were. It's like they don't trust me."

"Why not? We brought the kid in. Your casualties aren't their problem," Beale replied. "Course, there's that fuckin' ayrab who just might be thumbing rides by now, asking some farmer the way to Saddletramp."

"Rancher. And you know and I know that Kerman bought it

back there. That was a setup, Cody. In these parts they'd say we got dry-gulched.''

"You watch too many old movies.''

Now Perrin lit a fresh Camel from the butt of his last and flicked the butt away. "I watch *every*thing. Ol' Clint says he doesn't want to know more. Let me tell you why. He already knows everything Houston knows.''

"How you figure that?''

"They had three beds for us. Why not five?''

Beale considered this. "Not room enough. They'd have put Kerman and poor old Dex up next door.''

"Uh-huh,'' Perrin said, nodding. "But he already knew we had casualties. Plus, I can't see Clint riding that fucking stupid-looking scooter a couple of miles out here unless he knew he'd be riding back in our car.''

"He's got to get those blems fixed,'' Beale objected.

"How'd he know that in advance?''

"I guess he couldn't unless Houston told him,'' said Beale. "Okay, so he wanted the car out of sight. Perfectly natural.''

"He wanted us on ice, Cody.''

"He didn't ask for our pieces.''

"Not while we were two to his one and the car was still here. Give the man credit for a little smarts. Remember your basics, man. If your opponent could make lots of trouble, you shave his legs out from under him one little smile and one little sliver at a time. You don't make your move 'til he's on his knees.''

Beale grunted assent to this. "I still think you're just nervous in the service, Tom, but you're heeled, and I got more ammo in my little bag. Remind me to fill this clip. I squeezed off a bunch nailing that biker.'' After a moment he added, "So you were checking for bugs in there, huh. Find anything?''

"Nothing. Which doesn't mean there aren't any. It does mean we don't talk about our suspicions unless we're out here. But you know, it would be just plain good tactics to check around these other little places. We should do that anyhow,'' Perrin reasoned.

"Fine. you hang around here in case the kid wakes up, and I'll do a little recon.''

CHAPTER □ 25

Ross studied the shreds of Kerman's wrist bonds long enough to frustrate T.C. "What does it matter now?" she said at last, pacing the big room.

"A lot, if someone else set the man free while we were planting their colleague," said Ross. "If his friends are still around, I want to know about it."

"*Muy gachos,* that never occurred to me." She peered with fresh interest at the bloody mess that lay on the table.

"I don't think anyone did help, though," said Ross. "What I think is, I should've stripped his shorts off too. It's not unheard of for a man to keep more than one razor blade sewn in his clothes. Ever see a mustache razor?"

"Every time I trim mine," she said acidly, then admitted, "I never knew there were such things."

"Takes a little blade a half inch wide, thin as paper. Sew it into a seam and, if you ever need it, you let it cut its way out. I'm pretty sure this was sliced by a razor, or maybe a scalpel blade. Anyway, our man Kerman was strong enough to stretch the tape, and he didn't mind ripping some hide off. Quite a lot, in fact," he went on, pulling at an almost transparent curl of skin with tweezers. "And the blood made everything slippery. Must've helped him."

She shuddered and looked away from the objects of his scrutiny. She thought of Al again and rubbed her eyes lest they begin to betray her again with weeping. "Isn't there *something* I can do, Ross?"

"Not unless you can—whoa." He began to load the debris of Kerman's bondage into a zipper-lock plastic bag, then stuck it into the refrigerator. "Doesn't take long to booby-trap a car. Don't go near yours or my Cherokee either 'til I've checked them out."

For Ross to lie down and crawl beside each vehicle for his inspections was, both virtually and literally, a painstaking operation. After checking in the engine compartments he finally returned inside and pronounced their cars safe. "Something we might do," he said while washing up, "is visit the Lincoln County Medical Center, near the last traffic light on Carrizo Canyon. It's not likely he'd show up there, but you never know."

T.C. did better than that with a single telephone call and a dithery performance. A swarthy, wild-eyed gent with an accent had tried to bum a ride to the hospital, she said to the receptionist, but the man claimed he was from Roswell and he seemed to be bleeding. She had become frightened and drove off, she said, but her conscience would be clearer if she knew the man had received treatment.

The receptionist said she was sorry, but no such person had been admitted. After ringing off, T.C. passed on this information to an amused Ross Downing. "Why'd you say he was from Roswell," he asked.

" 'Cause I've noticed that people around here think half of Roswell is loco. I figured it'd cast doubt on anything he might say at the hospital."

"You have the makings of a federal agent," he said, chuckling.

"Yeah, but what I don't have is a trace on that Kurd," she countered. "Is there an emergency room anywhere else nearby?"

"Alamogordo. Artesia, maybe Carrizozo," he said, nodding to himself, "depending on which way he went. A long shot, but I might be able to get a hit off of police records through El Paso. I hope no one starts wondering why an agent on extended leave is checking on such things."

Ross was still reporting futility from his computer, and T.C. was feeding the ever-voracious Montezuma merely as a palliative for her frazzled nerves, when she heard the horn of Orv Ferguson's Range Rover.

The old fellow leaned from the cab when she stepped to the screen door. "Somebody snipped ever' last strand of our fence last night," he called over the engine's low thrum. "You folks have any trouble?"

She spread her hands and shrugged. "You might ask Ross, but he's been holed up with his computer all morning."

"You saying he doesn't know about the fence?"

It seemed the simplest way out of long explanations for her to say, "How would he? But I'll tell him."

The old man blinked, opened his mouth, shut it again as he glanced toward the big window. "I don't suppose you'd care to come around to the passenger side and get what I brung from town," he said, practically shouting.

"Sure." As she descended the front steps, Monte whisked between her feet and into the clearing where he stood on a moldering pine stump to survey his domain.

But when she opened the passenger door, Orv had his old six-shooter out of its holster where he displayed it on the passenger seat. He was smiling but staring toward the cabin, and now he spoke softly. "You need this?"

"I don't understand," she said, flustered.

"It just hit me, all of a sudden," Orv explained. "If there's somebody in the Downing cabin you don't want there, you might could use some help. But I reckon not, if you say so. And that fool miner's cat wouldn't be out here sunning himself." And now his smile became the familiar genuine article. "Sorry. Didn't mean to put your back hairs up, ma'am, but with that vandalism down at the road and all—"

"I understand, Orv. I appreciate it." She shut the door and backed away with a neighborly wave. "And I'll tell Ross about the fence, right away."

"You do that," Orv called and motored uphill.

Minutes later, after T.C. reported on her conversation, Ross emerged from his computer carrel shaking his head dejectedly, then rubbing his eyes. "I didn't really expect to find him this way. Umph, can't function without sleep the way I used to." He sank into the big easy chair.

The telephone rang at that moment, and gesturing for him to remain sitting, T.C. answered it with, "Mr. Townsend?"

But it was Orv Ferguson, and his mood was surly as he asked to speak to Ross.

The old man's news made Ross sit bolt upright. "What? Well, where is it?" A moment later Ross laughed shortly. "Not if my life depended on it. I've got an honest-to-God four-wheeler of my own, Orv. You sure it was taken after you left this morning? Sorry, stupid question. No, and it'd be pretty hard to sneak it past us, I think. Or maybe not, if they avoided the trail." He listened for a time, then said, "You know what I think about that thing anyhow. It wasn't grand theft auto; it was petty theft Tinkertoy. But it didn't just evaporate. Some kids on a joyride, I expect. It should turn up. Could've got through one of the old gaps along the property line. That's where we should look first."

After a few more uh-huhs, Ross broke the connection and turned to T.C. "So now we know how Kerman got out. Someone stole Orv's Jeep this morning after he left for town, and we've got only one candidate. I didn't say that to Orv, of course. There are some old fence gaps up on the mountain, not too hard to find."

"I can't believe that old junker could get past a county mountie on any public road," said T.C.

"But he could go cross-country for miles," Ross said. "Maybe I can pick up his tracks." As he spoke, he was wrestling his jacket on. "We can't be sure he isn't still hiding up here on the mountain somewhere, and if he is, we've still got a chance. But you should stay here to take Townsend's call. Will you feel comfortable here alone with the shotgun and the Beretta?"

She considered that, then nodded. "I'm not afraid now. It's Kerman who'll be smart to fear *me*. He won't get past me even if I have to chase him down with my Datsun," she said firmly.

"If you shoot the Jeep's tires first," Ross said, "maybe you won't have to put him away. We need him, Teresa."

"I know that." She hugged him quickly as he hefted the ugly little burp gun. "Take care of yourself, 'mano."

"Hey," he murmured, with a careless gesture, his eyes lit with an internal sparkle. Temporarily at least, the task seemed to have refreshed him, and at that moment she knew he was enjoying a flash of the casual machismo that had once marked the character of Ross Downing, junior G-man.

She watched him climb into the Cherokee, thinking how much his aggressive mode reminded her of Bo Rainey. "You know something, sweetie," she said to Ross, knowing only Montezuma could hear her. "I'd never tell you this, but I'm not sure I'd have liked you so well in the old days."

□   □   □

Ray Townsend called late in the morning from El Paso, his voice now familiar, belying his age with its vibrance. "I've rented a Ford, so tell Al I should be there in, um, two and a half hours. Check that," he said, and she heard papers rustling. "If the trails are as sinuous as they look on my map, make it two hours, forty-five minutes."

She did not want to shatter his composure by telling him Al was missing. "You'll need directions from Ruidoso," she began.

"I have a fairly close approximation from my CD-ROM library," he said. "If you're past Bonito Lake you'll be west of Forest Route One-oh-seven, off Forest Trail Thirty-seven. Correct?"

"That's right," she said, astonished at the notion that even unimproved county trails in New Mexico would be instantly available to a man in Seattle. A man who, moreover, seemed used to thinking in precise terms. "Turnoff's on your left, and it says no access but I'll unlock the gate for you." She gave him a few more details before he wished her a cheery good-bye. "I hope we have something better to tell you when you get here," she said after putting down the receiver.

That hope vanished when Ross returned two hours later, wolfing down the sandwich she had prepared. "Hasn't rained in a while, but I can't believe Kerman could've got through one of those old gaps without leaving some kind of tire tracks," he told her. "Maybe he just bashed a gap somewhere. He didn't go through that hole at the forest road, for sure."

She told him about Townsend's call, adding that she had trudged down and left the fence lock open during Ross's absence. "I dread the moment when we have to look that man in the eye and tell him the truth."

"Not just Townsend," Ross said. "We've got to tell Orv. I'm not sure how, but he knows something's going on here. May as well tell him the truth."

"Yeah? And what about—you know," she said, nodding in the general direction of that shallow grave.

"I think he'll just have to accept 'Don't ask' if it ever comes up. Not just from the legal standpoint, either. It's guilt he doesn't need. And that goes for Townsend, too," he added.

She moved nearer, standing behind him, and he leaned back so that his head touched her. After a moment of silent communion: "Try as I might, I can't make myself feel guilty for a damn thing," she said with a sense of wonder.

"Good, because you're not," he rejoined, reaching up to find her hand. "Sudden justice can be rough."

"Who said that?"

"I did. But if it's a quote you're after, an old Latin phrase from Cicero says, 'The more law, the less justice.' " After more quiet reflection, he sighed and stood up. "You've made me doubt a lot of old hardwired notions, Teresa. For that, you have my thanks. Right now I'm going to test one of those notions and try to get some rest. Wake me when Townsend shows, will you?"

She agreed and moved out to the sun-drenched porch, mourning the loss of the boy, wishing sunlight could thaw her frozen spirit.

□   □   □

The moment T.C. saw the maroon Ford Taurus nosing up the trail, she darted inside to wake Ross in his bedroom. "This must be Townsend coming now," she said. Ross lay propped up on pillows, fully clothed and awake, and levered himself from bed favoring his left arm. She knew that the morning's work would have exacerbated his old injuries, knew also that nothing she could say would persuade him to work more cautiously.

She went outside and waved the Taurus to a spot near her Datsun, her smile uncertain as the driver emerged. He was sturdily built and of average height, evidently in his late fifties. "So you're Teresa Contreras," he said, his manner hearty. "I'm Ray Townsend."

His handshake was firm, his grin wide in a long rectangular face below dark, neatly parted hair with graying temples. Those khaki trousers and hiking boots had seen a lot of wear, though the slight paunch suggested that Townsend was no fitness freak. Even as he greeted T.C., he was scanning the meadow. "Little booger is hiding, is he?"

"I wish it were that simple," she said.

Townsend looked at her in curiosity. Then he saw Ross Downing navigate the steps, and because his distance vision was good his gaze shifted into something more subdued. "Jesus," he muttered.

Ross met them halfway with that curious gait of his and pretended, as usual, not to notice Townsend's lack of eye contact. Their greetings complete with Townsend's insistence on first names, Ross invited him to the cabin.

Townsend stopped at the steps. "Don't tell me you've got Al napping like an ordinary human," he said. "I couldn't get him down in daylight without a boat anchor and a short chain."

"Mr. Townsend—" T.C. began, then faltered.

Ross interrupted. "The news isn't good, Ray. Al wasn't hurt when we last saw him, but that exfiltration team came for him with guns last night. And they took him from us. I'm—what can I say?"

Townsend shut his eyes. His expression was unreadable, but he seemed to lose inches in height. He opened his eyes again and said, very slowly, "The same people?"

"Identical," T.C. said. "Even that Kurd, Anatol Kerman, who claims he's kin to Al."

"Anatol? I knew the man once," Townsend said, surprised.

"That's him. We managed to isolate him from the others and tied him in the cellar. We intended to hold him until you arrived. Then early this morning he managed to free himself," Ross admitted.

They went inside then, Ray Townsend dropping into a chair as though robbed of all strength. He accepted coffee from T.C. while Ross filled in the essential details, his face pale, hands trembling.

When Ross had finished with the story of the missing Jeep, Townsend slumped back in his chair and stared silently out the big window for a long moment. "There's only one bright spot in all this," he said. "If any harm should come to Al, my goddamned ex-son-in-law would never rest until he had his full measure of vengeance. That's what Anatol is doing here. I'm as certain of that as I am of anything in this world." He said this not hopefully but with absolute conviction.

"If he was really sent as a protector, I almost hope Kerman catches up to the others," said T.C. "Those other scufflers would kill us in a second."

"So would Anatol, I think, if you got in his way. But he saved our lives once, at considerable risk, he and Ravan together with a few others," Townsend volunteered at last. "You know the name of Ravan Zagro, I suppose."

"Only vaguely, before T.C. showed up here with Al," Ross told him. "I should tell you that I have, um, special resources available. I could get dipped in thick yogurt for using them like this, but—" And in a few brief, sanitized sentences, Ross explained those special resources. He ended with, "Of course I haven't told you any of that. If you've been outside CONUS for Boeing as Al said, somebody thinks you can keep a secret."

"Depend on it; I had my clearances. But my work wasn't exactly cloak-and-dagger stuff. I was part of a contingent openly operating in Iran, developing facilities for KC-135 tankers the Iranians bought from Boeing, when the entire government of Reza Pahlevi—the shah—went down," Townsend said. "None of us expected what happened then. It all snowballed so quickly it took

American intelligence people by surprise. But suddenly I wasn't a valued technical expert but an arm of the Great Satan, and there I was running into the northern wilds of a hostile country full of Islamic zealots with my wife and our young daughter; Gail was about twelve then. And I didn't speak more than fifty words of Farsi, and the Kurds had their own dialects. Crazy times."

"Al never did tell us how they took your daughter," T.C. said.

A disgusted sound escaped Townsend. "They didn't, not then, anyway, and it was Gail's own idea. Not all Kurds are unlettered wild men. Some are very intelligent, cultured people, with the wildness kept just under the skin. Some of Ravan's clan got good educations under Pahlevi, and they understood that going back to the ayatollah's tenth-century ideas wouldn't be good for the Kurdish people.

"To Ravan and his family—God, but they have extended families!—Boeing's group had been symbolic of the future in those parts. There was also the fact that the whole irrepressible mob of Kurds are natural rebels. They got us across into Turkey, and from horseback to a flight home. I never expected to see any of them again.

"Until about 'eighty-six, that is. We'd put that whole part of our lives behind us years before the day I got that phone call from Ravan. When I heard Ravan Zagro saying he was an exchange student in the Boston area taking political studies, I couldn't have been happier. The man spoke half a dozen languages; he had saved our collective bacon. And then I made the worst mistake of my life: I told him where Gail was."

"Did I miss something?" T.C. asked.

"About seven years of life with a beautiful, spoiled teenager," said Townsend with a flash of humor, "something all fathers should miss. Gail more or less ran off at seventeen and contacted us after she got knocked around by some young fella I never met, and we compromised by paying her tuition, about as far from us as she could get. University of Vermont. Burlington." He fashioned a patently false smile for effect, "The skiing, you know. That's where she was when Ravan called me."

"Got it. She was majoring in winter sports, and you thought Ravan Zagro would be an improvement," said Ross.

"Sounds stupid, doesn't it? But he was a serious-minded young man, and Boston wasn't all that far from Burlington, and—well, he treated her like a princess, and I gather she was impressed by his mysterious meetings, and the upshot was, the following spring the two of them came to Seattle to ask our blessings."

He threw up his hands, then let them fall. "What could I say? Gail was of age, barely, and Ravan had been her hero since she was twelve years old! And the truth was, I thought he might be what she needed to settle down. You'd have had to see her to understand," he shrugged.

"I did," T.C. said quietly. "Al and I rode with her to a Mexican hospital. She was glorious, Ray. And for what it's worth, she wasn't in pain, not for a moment."

Townsend cleared his throat, nodded, sighed. "It's a comfort, and I haven't had many of those lately. Well, after they married, of course Ravan filled Gail with nonsense about how well she'd be treated as the wife of a Kurdish man of destiny, and she bought it, and a year later she flew off with the charismatic son of a bitch to Kurdistan."

"So Al really is Kurdish," Ross said. "Born there, I mean."

"If you want to get technical," said Townsend, then shook his head. "Listen to me, forty years of engineering and I try to weasel out like that! Yes, Al had dual citizenship, but when Gail sneaked them out of Kurdistan it was with a divorce that was legal there— or so I was told. Such things are still troublesome over there. As I understand it, the mother often takes custody of a son until he comes of age, eight or ten years old. At that point he's expected to return to his father."

"Damnedest split custody arrangement I ever heard of," said T.C.

"Yes, but it's ancient tradition. They're very big on tradition," Townsend nodded. "To give the devil his due, Ravan didn't try to interfere with Gail when she met up with a Brit journalist who helped her get out on a flight with Al, a few years ago. Just between us, I suspect Ravan knew about her plans, but it would have been politically damaging for him to give give her overt help in getting his own son out of there. Al was about four then. Gail never said it in so many words, but I also think she and Ravan agreed that she'd give Al up to him when the boy reached an appropriate age. The point was, Ravan wouldn't have let my grandson out of his sight any other way. She had to agree, or leave without her only son.''

"Agreement under duress isn't binding," Ross put in.

"Not over here, but try telling that to Ravan Zagro," Townsend retorted. "Those poor devils breathe duress every second of their lives, yet the Kurd keeps his bargains. And he's going to see that you keep yours.''

"Sounds as if you're making a case for that team he sent after the boy," said Ross.

"I'm trying to give you an honest account," said Townsend. "In the West we see things one way. In Kurdistan they view it differently.''

"He might have asked your daughter for custody before trying to kidnap Al," said T.C.

"Oh, he did," said Townsend. "You can imagine her response. She said she intended to keep Al, no matter what any court decreed. Elaine and I had no choice but to stand by her.''

"Um, yeah. The more law, the less justice," said T.C.

"That's very good," Townsend said with a keen glance at her. He saw her exchange looks with Ross and, when Ross smiled, added, "What was that about?''

"I stole that line from Cicero, I think," she said. "By the way, Al ran like a greased pig from Kerman and those others back in Tucson, but I doubt he ever saw Kerman up close. If he recognized the guy, do you think he'd go with him quietly?''

To this, Townsend gave no immediate answer. After some hesitation he said, "It's possible, but I doubt it. Hard to say. Al hasn't seen any of those people since he was four years old." He thought about it some more, then shook his head. "My guess is, it wouldn't have much effect, but I could be wrong.''

"Let's hope you're right," T.C. told him. "When they had me trussed up in Tucson, Kerman seemed pretty confident that Al would calm down once they got acquainted."

"And with Kerman off and running again," Ross put in, "they could link up at any time. I don't suppose you'd have any idea where they might be headed?"

Ray Townsend's answer was immediate. "I haven't a clue."

CHAPTER □ 26

When Beale returned to their adobe, Perrin was propped up on his bed reading a dog-eared paperback mystery. The boy still lay facing them, curled and motionless across the room. "Kid likes his beauty sleep," Beale commented.

"Or playing possum," said Perrin. "Could be planning to overpower me. So, find us a fourth for bridge?"

"Not a sign, but the doors are locked and you can't see much through the windows. Dust patterns are like little sand dunes around here. Judging from those, I figure nobody's been in any of these mud palaces since the last sandstorm. I guess this one's as good as any." Beale extracted the Glock from inside his belt to give his belly more room.

"If you say so," Perrin replied, getting up to stretch. "You hold down the fort while I walk the perimeter." Beale knew that Perrin was speaking for the benefit of audio pickups when he added, "Remember, we play this Clint's way. The package doesn't step outside, Cody."

"Oh, right." Beale grinned and gave him an eye roll, and, preparing to heat a cup of water for instant coffee, he lay the handgun atop the microwave oven.

"Never do that, not even for a second," Perrin ordered. "If that oven isn't shielded, it's popcorn time." Beale retrieved the Glock with a sullen glance and continued his chore as Perrin stepped out squinting in sunlight, the door hinges squealing.

A four-strand fence of barbed wire stretched off along the rolling, arid hardpan, a landscape dotted chiefly by vegetation extravagantly furnished with needle spines, and Tom Perrin knew he was leaving footprints a few feet shy of the fence line. Because Beale had left no prints here it was obvious that he hadn't done a perimeter check. After so many fuckups on this job, it might impress Clint to see evidence that Perrin, at least, took his work seriously. His head throbbed a bit with each step, a reminder of his headlong rush into last night's darkness. He recognized that extra wire, strung on insulators, for what it was: a painful jolt for any animal that so much as rubbed against it. He also realized what else it might be: a spit simple alarm sensor. A man could defeat it, but he could also get caught trying.

And why was he thinking like this? In the forenoon of a quiet summer day, his nervous imaginings seemed foolish. He turned right at the corner post and ambled slowly up a gradual slope to the next corner. From there he could see, toward the south, dusty green treetops back at Saddletramp headquarters and a rooftop that, unless memory lied, was the barn near Saddletramp's corral. He could make out a long subtle line that was the lip of a trail, probably the road to that nifty half mile of landing strip that, from the air, looked like a bleached dry lakebed. He saw no sign of the hangar he'd remembered and realized that it must have cost them more to make it vanish than to erect it. He saw no new structures. To his right lay the roofs of the adobes, toylike from this distance.

Off to the north lay the valley floor and, flanking it, wind-sculpted hills. A dust devil, a tornado in miniature, scrawled its ghostly finger across the valley as if it were in no hurry. The fitful breeze was becoming warmer, with a sting of grit in it, and Perrin hurried to complete his trek, having seen only one animal, a small scurrying lizard as broad as his palm with horns like some tiny dinosaur.

The door hinges announced him. He found the boy sipping a diet Snapple and silently watching Beale's soap opera while Cody Beale sat at the table, feeding fresh rounds into the Glock's clip. When Perrin elevated his brows, Beale said, "You don't want to take your eyes off him, Tom.'' Which meant that Beale had probably dozed off and caught the kid trying to leave. Sure enough, the kid's hobble tape was now reduced to a wad on his bed. Perrin wanted to ask what had happened until he remembered his own suspicion about audio bugs.

"If the kid gets cute," Perrin advised, "you know how to stop him." He mimed firing a pistol, turning so that Al-Talal could not see his wink toward the big man.

While rummaging in the refrigerator he told Beale of his uneventful perimeter check. "By the way, Cody, that fence is electrified. Touch a wire and you'll fry like a chicken." The boy's face told him that had registered, reason enough to say it. Such fences usually sent only jolting pulses down the wire a second or so apart, but under Clint's management the damned thing might actually be lethal. It would be a hell of an irony to get this snot-nosed little package all the way to the pickup point and then let him zap himself to death on a cattle fence.

□   □   □

Al had seen the rusty old fence ten minutes after the Tom guy went outside, when the Beale guy's head dropped onto his chest for about the third time and didn't jerk up again. Al had got the hobbles off right away and wriggled into that two-foot-deep window ledge, hoping the window wouldn't squall like the door did. But that window wouldn't open at all, and the big guy hadn't seemed to be sleeping very deeply, and Al had snuck back mouse-quiet, snooping around the room in search of something, anything, to help him get out of there.

Standing before the Beale guy who was slumped in a chair, he'd wondered if it would be possible to snatch that ugly squarish gun from its place right there in sight, up against Beale's paunch. But he knew it was really just a fantasy, something little kids did in movies while big guys snored, and in movies the kid always knew how to make the gun work, but all Al knew about it was that there was stuff like safety catches so you couldn't make the durn thing work even if you had it in your hand.

Just thinking about what might really happen if he tried it made Al need to pee, so he went back to the toilet and peed against the side of the bowl so it wouldn't make any noise. Flush it? He wasn't that dumb. He might as well shout or pop a paper bag, any of those things would wake the Beale guy. And so would trying to open that durn squealy door, which would just get a kid's head shot to a red pulp like the bike guy last night, a thing he didn't want to think about but would remember all of his life.

Instead, Al snooped around some more and found a big gun he didn't want to fool with in a piece of luggage, and it must've been the noise when he was pulling a zipper closed that made the Beale guy snort and jerk and by the time the guy looked around Al pretended like he was just coming back from taking his pee.

Here, what the hell are you doing, he roared and drew that little gun that shot about a million times, or twenty at least, and Al said he had just gone to pee, and the guy wanted to know why he was out of that tape stuff, and Al claimed he needed to for peeing, so the guy said why hadn't he heard it flush, and Al thought fast and said he hadn't wanted to wake him, and the guy blinked and looked around and then said real loud that he hadn't been asleep, which Al knew was total BS but it didn't seem like a time for arguing about it. And the Beale guy went and checked the toilet and flushed it himself, and then he didn't seem so mad anymore.

So the Beale guy put the gun down again, and Al said could he raid the fridge and the guy let him take only a Snapple, and after that they watched TV until the other guy, Tom, came back.

And now Al knew that, even if he somehow got outside, he'd have to avoid touching the fence. Unless the Tom guy was lying, and Al wasn't about to test that idea.

So while the bad guys were talking, this funny kind of cordless phone chirped, and the Tom guy answered it in a hurry, and anybody could see it wasn't a call he enjoyed a lot.

At first the guy sounded okay and all, but then he started saying "Kerman" a lot and telling all about how they'd been surprised at the cabin and saying he had faced a shotgun at close range to take the package but that was his job and he'd done it. Al didn't like to think of himself as a package, but nobody much cared what he liked. Of course Al remembered most of what had happened, though he'd been standing next to a great big chair as tall as Al with cloth over its legs that Monte always liked to get down under, and when T.C. yelled, Al had dived down to hide under the chair too scared even to yell for Ross. And then he'd heard somebody he might have heard before, years and years back, calling him Talal like everybody did then, footsteps pounding through the house, but he wasn't about to budge, not until that humongous bang, and Monte was pretty smart, so when he scooted, Al scooted too.

The big bang had probably been Ross, duking it out from the basement against those guys, but Al hadn't stopped to think of that at the time. And the Tom guy was right there in the room when Al tried to run for it, and it looked like T.C. was hurt, or worse, but Monte got outside and Al nearly made it too because the Tom guy was jerking his head around with his mouth open, but Al got hauled up into the air and that's when he started yelling his head off, and then he was being carried off toward the dark. Thinking back, Al was sure it had been Ross with the loud gun but he wasn't going to tell. If he could take back anything, it would be trying to run, not trying so much as getting caught. But running sure had worked before. . . .

Yeah, and that part about the Tom guy facing a shotgun, well, that was a load of BS too, he had his back turned to run when the second big bang came. Al decided if he ever got the chance he was going to tell on the guy. Not only that, but the part where the guy ran into something and not only dropped Al but fell on him, except the Beale guy was there too and picked them both up and kept going. And he fell once, too, but he had too good a grip on Al's pants.

But now the Tom guy was pretty mad, you couldn't hear it much in his voice, but the way his eyes went all squinty when he listened, anybody could tell, and he had to explain again how a guy got shot and how the Kerman guy had just disappeared without a sound, and he ended up saying that Kerman was down, and that he wasn't the kind of guy to go down if he could still kick.

It sounded like this Tom guy thought he was going to catch it good; Al sure hoped so. He kept asking when he could expect the flight, and he also said three times that the package was undamaged, which told Al that *some*body, *some*where didn't want these guys to hurt him too much. Maybe, if he figured out some way to pay them back for everything, they wouldn't really shoot him for it. The Beale guy might, though.

And Al had already figured out a couple of things that might make them sorry, only those things might make Al sorry, too. Like setting a fire, or stopping the toilet with a big wad of paper, or something worse. He wondered if T.C. had been hurt much. These guys had a lot to answer for. It seemed like the Tom guy thought somebody on that cordless phone thought so, too.

□   □   □

Perrin put down the little cellular unit with great care instead of hurling it across the room.

Beale asked, "They tell you when it's coming?"

Perrin seemed not to hear, staring hard at nothing. After a moment he went to the door and said, "I'm taking a smoke outside," and jerked his head to imply that Beale should follow. Beale stopped in the doorway and silently raised his forefinger toward the boy, who gave him a glum look and turned toward the television.

Thirty feet outside, the men faced each other. "This is starting to build a fire under me," Beale rumbled softly.

"Houston's feeling the heat, so they're putting heat on us," said Perrin. "And that means somebody up the line must be building fires under *them*." He lit another Camel and took a heavy hit from it. "Cody, I don't think they had a contingency for losing Kerman."

"For poor Dex, yeah, but not their fucking observer," Beale replied cynically.

"For any or all of us, I think, so long as Kerman could get that kid back to his papa. You saw that little asshole operate; he has to a be a valued man back home. More than that, he's a goddamn family member to the Man, and when he didn't show up here it really dumped a pile of shit in Houston's drawers.'' Another drag on the Camel. ''They want Kerman as bad as they want the damn kid.''

Beale sighed and glanced toward the adobe. ''They tell you that?''

Perrin shook his head. ''But that's how it's working. Shit, if I'd known that I'd have handled it differently, kept him stashed at the car instead of—'' He waved a hand listlessly.

''Instead of letting him take his chances like the rest of us,'' Beale finished for him. ''Tom, that was Kerman's own idea. Wanted to play hero for the Man, get some of the glory.''

''Well, I'm willing for him to take it all, but I don't think he's going to show. One good thing about it, we know he isn't in some rinky-dink jail, 'cause if he was, Houston would know it and I wouldn't be getting the third degree.''

''On the other hand,'' Beale said slowly, ''we could grow long beards waiting for Kerman to show—even if he's loose.''

''No, we wouldn't. I happen to know he could've contacted his people. Say he can't find his way here. If he gets to a phone, someone can bring him here.''

''Somebody like us,'' Beale said.

''Maybe. I can't think of any other reason why we're still here.''

''Sure you can, two reasons, at least. One, they're using us for cock-walloping baby-sitters for as long as it takes them to locate Kerman, or to give up on him,'' Beale said. He hawked and spat and hooked his thumb under the butt of the Glock snugged against his gut. ''Or two, they need somebody to take a fall for losing this Kurd when nobody told us he was made of solid gold. So they don't intend for us to leave Saddletramp. Not now, and maybe not ever.''

Perrin flipped the Camel's butt away and essayed a half smile. ''Well, that might be a little far-fetched,'' he said.

''You want far-fetched? Try a motherfuckin' dude ranch that

doubles as an unofficial, deniable UN port of entry! That's why it works. And I was thinking, while you were jerking those guys off on the phone, I don't know about you, but in case they mention it, nobody takes my Glock, so fuhgettaboutit. I came in with it. I'm going out with it. One way or another. Just thought you'd like to know," he said, then wheeled and went back inside.

CHAPTER □ 27

Any notion they may have had of keeping Al's abduction from Orv Ferguson was dashed when the old miner's Range Rover pulled up with a friendly horn toot in early afternoon. He had intended to "borrow the sprat" for an afternoon of fishing, he said, and was clearly pleased to meet Al's grandfather, even more so to learn that Ray was an engineer. But Orv could see that they were depressed, and he said so. The crevasses of his face became angry parentheses around his mouth when T.C. told him the news.

"I knew you folks had a problem," he said, "when you claimed Ross didn't know the fence had been cut. Shoot, I can tell that draggy footprint of his a mile off. He knew about the fence before I did."

Ross, who had been rechecking his network sources in the vain hope that Anatol Kerman might have surfaced somewhere, emerged from his room in time to hear this. His abject apology to the old man was accepted without hesitation. "Figured you had a good reason," Orv said. "But why aren't we out beating bushes and talking to the state police?"

"It's a long story," said Ray Townsend.

"Got nothin' but time, and maybe I could help," said Orv. "But don't feel obliged. I have things to do up at my place anyhow."

"No, no," Ray protested, "I'll tell you about it, perhaps we can brainstorm. The young lady and I have been knocking our heads together without striking any sparks. Unless Ross has come up with something,'' he amended, tossing the younger man a hopeful glance.

"Nothing useful,'' Ross said, gently rubbing his eyes. "I probably should rest my eyes awhile.''

As Ray beckoned for his fellow engineer to visit the coffee-maker, T.C. plucked at the sleeve of Ross's checked shirt, which was buttoned at the wrist. Ross jerked slightly but said nothing. "You've been bleeding,'' she said, pulling at his wrist with gentle insistence.

"Don't,'' he said very quickly, and she released her grip. *"No problemo.''*

"That's *'no hay problema,'''* she corrected, "only I don't believe you.'' Her eyes searched his face, concerned and questioning.

"I checked it, and it's nothing serious,'' he said, nonetheless inspecting the stain on the sleeve with obvious irritation. "I don't need mothering, T.C. I need a little shut-eye after fighting that screen so hard. But only for an hour, okay? Don't let me sleep longer than that.''

She gave him an ill-tempered shrug and turned toward the older men, as Ray Townsend began to murmur an abbreviated account of Al's history. She watched Ross close the bedroom door and decided that he must have scratched himself at some point in their despised work that morning.

Nerve endings in scarred flesh, she knew, often failed to send pain signals. In normal chores Ross had poked small holes in himself more than once without being aware of it until later. But this time, he had bled on the inside of his forearm where he had not been burned so seriously.

He had not been burned badly there because the inside surfaces of his forearms had been pressed against Littlebo as the flames raged over them. And he had stepped into that inferno because he felt responsible for the whole chain of events that—

She thrust away the internal monologue. She had scripted it already, had followed it to the end, and had been unable to apportion blame because, finally, blame had been disinfected by a salve of forgiveness. Ross Downing had not been the one who drove erratically; had done more than his duty without pausing to think of himself. Could she, Littlebo's own mother, swear that she would have hurled herself into the volcano that was the cab of Bo Rainey's pickup?

In the bathroom, with few wasted motions, Ross doused his father's old safety razor in rubbing alcohol before scrubbing a patch of pristine skin above his wrist. Ranked near the razor atop his toilet tank lay squares of gauze, strips of adhesive tape, several cotton-tipped swabs, and a milky tube of fluid known to many as Superglue and to a few as cyanoacrylate.

His medication never took immediate effect, so his first irrevocable step was to swallow a dose, washing it down with water, letting the tap run. He knew his hand would shake if he paused, and he brought the razor to contact the soft flesh of his forearm a bit too quickly. Because no amount of observation can bring real expertise, he failed in both the proper angle of contact and his pressure on the razor. His second try only forced a shallow slice into the skin. Two more tries and he found his hand shaking, more from tension than pain, but this time a translucent, inch-wide sheet of his skin began to extrude through the underside of the razor. He persisted, the pain now equally stubborn, until he had denuded a rectangle of skin roughly the size of a large postage stamp.

By now a thin upwelling of clear serum fluid atop this wound had become pink, then crimson, and Ross blotted it with a square of gauze, which he left in place for only a moment. The crucial operation now lay in one-handedly persuading the largest curl of Kerman's skin to lie flat on Ross's own raw flesh. Chiefly by good luck he managed to use a cotton swab to apply tiny smears of cyanoacrylate to both ends of that vellumlike curl without inundating the entire patch. The most remarkable property of cyano-acrylate is its ability instantly to cement skin to skin. It also stung like the very devil, and Ross saw that he had probably removed his own dermal skin layer more deeply than necessary. A competent physician would have spread the graft broadly as a mesh of skin, but even such a pitiful measure of success as this had Ross feeling giddy with relief as he pressed more gauze over his handiwork.

Gauze and tightly stretched adhesive strips formed the best pressure dressing Ross could manage. When he eased himself down on his bed, he was trembling.

It was a half hour later, as Ray sat with his new friends on the porch listening to T.C. describe her decoy effort in Albuquerque, when she suddenly glanced up and paused. Ross stood in the bedroom doorway, staring toward the big window, holding on to the door frame as if he might fall. He seemed to have shrunk in every dimension as she stood up and moved toward him. "You okay?"

His nod was abstracted. His jaw sagged open slightly as he blinked and steadied himself. Then, "I may have found something," he husked, too quietly to be heard beyond her.

She clasped her hands at her breast. "Something on the computer?"

He swallowed with an effort, began a headshake, then met her gaze. "That'll be my story," he muttered. But the look in his eyes was haunted. It reminded T.C. of his expression after those nightmares of his—not fear, exactly, but certainly disorientation mixed with awe. Even as she stood before him, he straightened, seeming to regain his bulk, voice stronger now. "I've got to get back on-screen for a location. Tell them—whatever," he said, nodding toward the porch, and hurried back to his computer. The screen was dead, none of the familiar lights aglow.

T.C. announced that Ross suspected he had a lead and would join them shortly. Distracted as she was, she managed to continue her tale as far as the small piping voice that had suckered her to the porch the night before. She broke it off with, "And it was those men, and Ross was downstairs and couldn't get back up in time when they burst in here." She turned toward Ross as he approached, a folded printout in hand, and she had never seen him infused with more determination. "I'm afraid to ask," she told him.

"And I'm a little afraid to tell, because I could be dead wrong," said Ross, with a smile that asked forbearance. "Still, it's the only lead I've got. A spa called Saddletramp, available to the dips— uh," he caught himself using the jargon of his trade, "the diplomatic cadre who like to play jet-setter. The place is a few hours north of here, somewhere west of Tucumcari." He offered her the printed sheet.

She frowned in uncertainty. "I can't read this. It's in French," she said, as if insulted.

The older men scooted their wicker chairs near to read over her shoulder. "Not surprising. French has been the international language of diplomats for centuries," said Ray. "I can stumble along with it." She handed the page to him. Ross's printer had duly downloaded a full page ornamented with small full-color pictures along the margins. T.C. noted, next to a tiny figure swinging a racket, that "tennis" was the same word in French. But "*équitation*" would have been a puzzler without the squiggle of a mounted rider. Since prices weren't quoted she knew that when they used the phrase "*spa exclusif*" they meant it.

"Huh, direct flights," mused Ray, lips moving steadily as he translated for himself. "This place isn't for your ordinary mortal, I can tell you that much. It talks about an authentic Old West flavor, but it gives exact modern coordinates. How very like the French. Where did you find this, Ross?"

"Well, I knew the name from one list I had, yet it isn't on any roster of guest ranches, spas, or whatnot in English. But trust the Internet to be linked with special offerings in Europe. It was in the exclusive lifestyle category. Luckily, American diplomats have access to some of the passwords. And I know a few of those."

"And they're holding my grandson? That's a little too exclusive for my taste," Ray Townsend grated. "How can you be sure?"

"I can't yet." Ross paused before continuing. "Look, Saddletramp is a known haven, one of several, for people who get special diplomatic waivers against things like customs and immigration checks. Other countries have them, too. I mentioned the name of the place to Anatol Kerman. He, well, I got a reaction I can't explain. The implications just hit me."

Here his gaze slid to T.C. for the briefest moment, and she felt an inexplicable rush of goose flesh down her arms as he went on more slowly. "But Kerman wanted Saddletramp. Wanted it a lot. It was his goal," he finished.

Orv Ferguson unfolded his arms and gnawed at his lip, placing a stubby finger on the page Ray held. "I've been reading coordinates for fifty years. That's San Miguel County, or thereabouts, and it's got miles and miles of nothin' but miles and miles. You think this Kerman fella managed to get there?"

"I think he'll try," Ross nodded. "Whether Al will be there I don't know, but—yeah, I'm sure Kerman thinks so. It says there's direct air service on that scrap of elitism?"

"You read my mind," said Ray, handing the page back to Ross. "That's what it says. I wonder what would happen if I rented a plane and damn well flew in and faced them with the facts."

"I think you'd have a better chance wearing a ninja suit on a midnight stroll through Beverly Hills," Ross said quickly. "We might be met by private security people empowered to do whatever they have to, to keep the world's pampered dips from the least hint of discomfort."

Orv: "You mean they wouldn't even care about a kidnapping?"

Ross: "They probably would, if it didn't involve one of their own guests. But Kerman apparently has carte blanche to retrieve Al for his father, and I doubt the boy's maternal grandfather would carry more weight at that place than the dictates of Al's father. I'm not an attorney, and I've never run across any case that's at all like this."

"I've talked to some attorneys about it," Ray Townsend said.

"Then you know more than I do. Ray, let's imagine we got some county mounties to raid Saddletramp and found Al. Would the law be on our side?"

"I wish I thought so. You know lawyers. Members of a big firm made a lot of confident noises, but they talked about protracted delaying tactics based on the presumption that Al was with us in a familiar environment. The third fellow was one I know. What he told me was a lot clearer, and he wasn't so optimistic. He did repeat the old bromide about possession being nine-tenths of the law.''

"If we cut to the chase," T.C. broke in, "it sounds like we can't be sure the cops would help."

"Depending on what they heard from the opposition," said Ross with another meaningful glance at her, "they might even be persuaded to come to this cabin and take it apart, right down to the flooring. If forensics people get into this, there's no telling what they might claim."

T.C. knew that he was speaking volumes to her in those few words. She had scrubbed the kitchen floor, but she could have missed some errant spatter of blood. She'd heard of DNA matching, and its exotic nature was beyond her.

Orv stood up and beckoned to Ross, moving off toward the distant fireplace. " 'Scuse us for a minute. Sorry, but I have to do this," he said.

When the two of them stood together across the room, Orv Ferguson said, "I'm gonna chew the whole enchilada, boy, but you owe me this much: Is that fella Kerman here on the premises?"

Ross released a pent-up breath and smiled. "Bless you, Orv. No, and I really think he's heading for Saddletramp. I see what you were thinking; I'd better set Ray's mind at rest on it, too."

Seating himself again, Ross said, "Orv had the idea that I might have done something with Kerman. I almost wish I had, but the bastard took off on his own, almost certainly with Orv's old Jeep. That's not to say he could drive it halfway across New Mexico, but he could have linked up somehow with his friends."

Frustrated more with each passing minute, T.C. blurted, "Aren't we wasting time? There's this place you say we can find. I say let's find it."

"I'm with the lady," said Orv.

Ross gave a single nod of finality. "That makes it unanimous. We have some tactics to plan, depending on what each of us can do. T.C., I know you can scribble notes faster than I can. Would you mind?"

Ray Townsend looked around the table, his eyes brimming. "I

can't tell you," he began, then cleared his throat. "Al is all I have of posterity, so you must know the gratitude I feel. Just bear in mind that if we can't depend on the law, what we must do could brand us as outlaws."

"The thought has crossed my mind," said T.C., getting up to collect notepads and pencils, and Ross grinned at her gift for understatement.

□   □   □

Ray Townsend's aviation license gave them an extra dimension of operations, but a few telephone calls proved that they could find no suitable aircraft rental in Ruidoso. "I'm not rated for a twin," he explained between calls, "so I need a single that'll take us all, with a little cargo. And there are mountains lurking around here, and mountain flying can be deadly even if you know the airplane. I'm not comfortable flying anytime but daylight, and it should be in something I'm familiar with. That limits us a lot. I'm not exactly Tex Johnston, you know."

Ross: "Who's that?"

Ray, with a comic grimace: "Spoken like a Lockheed man. Tex was from really from Kansas, could fly anything Boeing had. Barrel-rolled a prototype seven-oh-seven on a test flight in view of half the population of Seattle. The point is, I'm not a patch on him, so I need all the advantages I can get."

He continued his calls while Orv Ferguson enumerated all the hardware he owned that might be used as weaponry. Ray eventually put down the phone with a satisfied grunt. "The closest place I can locate anything I can fly is in Alamogordo. How far's that by car?"

"Hour and a half," Ross replied. "What kind of plane?"

"Cessna one-eighty," said the older man. "Tail dragger, a tailwheel instead of a nosewheel." He glanced at his wristwatch and stood up. "I'll drive the Taurus there and fly back before dark, if someone can pick me up at the Ruidoso airport."

Orv said he could and indicated he was thinking ahead, with, "Will that plane seat five?"

"If a couple of them are small," Ray nodded. "And I could land a tail dragger and get it off again from anything like flat ground. Cruises at a hundred and fifty, six-hundred-mile range if the winds aren't against it, and it'll fly higher than I care to go unless I have oxygen."

T.C., who knew little about aircraft, said, "I thought you'd want to fly low."

"Not for surveillance," Ray said, pausing at the door. "Oh, it'll get down low and slow if we need to, nap of the earth in fact, but first we need to eyeball this Saddletramp place from high enough that we won't be noticed. Aerial surveillance can tell us a lot. Thank God I brought the Hasselblad along." He made a wry, lopsided smile. "Thought I'd be taking pictures for recreation, but those big negatives will be perfect for extreme enlargements on fine-grain film." And with a quick wave, he hurried outside.

Orv Ferguson left minutes later. "I'll be back 'fore long," he called, heading for his vehicle. "I'm not sure just how much ordnance I've got up at my place."

T.C. waved from the porch, then turned to face Ross. "You've got some explaining to do," she told him.

His glance combined guilt with a hint of triumph, and then he began to roll up his sleeve. The bandage on his forearm was an awful botch, the sort of thing a man might do one-handed. It had bled too much.

T.C. pointed toward the bathroom. "I can do better than that."

"For bandages, yes. For chills down my back? I doubt it." As he sat obediently on the toilet while she worked, his forearm over the stained old sink, he clarified the point. "T.C., what's under the gauze is a little of what I collected after Kerman got away. Yeah," he said, meeting her gaze, "I did it when I went in to take my nap. It's not much, maybe half a square inch of Kerman's skin. I had to uncurl it for the half-assed allograft, and no doctor would applaud the job I did, I just wasn't up to stapling the tissue, sorry about that. But I've watched 'em do it too many times."

She paused, her face pale, and shook her head. "You took a skin graft. By yourself. Just because I had that weird idea."

"It was my only hope, and don't knock it when it works," he said. "Hell, it wasn't brain surgery, those dermal and epidermal layers aren't deep. In fact, the toughest part was getting my safety razor to lift off a section of my own hide, size of a postage stamp, only a hundredth of an inch deep. I've had worse falling off a motorbike. It didn't take long."

She shuddered, gulped, and watched hydrogen peroxide foam as she poured it over the wound Ross had created. "You are absofuckinglutely nuts, Crispy. You don't know what diseases that man might have."

"I'll mend. I always do. Guys who've been badly burned have antibodies that pump iron. But I was hurting, so I took my medication and lay down for a while." And now his voice lowered. "Not a very long while, I guess."

She tore a fresh sterile gauze pad from its paper, applied ointment, lay the gauze carefully in place, grateful that she had a task to occupy her. "I don't want to hear any nightmares right now, Ross," she pleaded. "And now I'm starting to wonder whether this is a wild-goose chase."

In answer, he shut his eyes and breathed deeply. "I'm hurting all over," he muttered, all but whispering. "I can't use my legs below the knees, but I'm going to make it. I must."

"What are you—" She stopped, realizing that he was reliving it, surrogating another man, another place.

"Rocks and trees, spinning, or I am. Dizzy. But I've seen a chart, and the American said Saddletramp, and that's all I can think about now because that's where I'm going. Because that's where Talal will be."

She knelt beside him and cupped his face in her hands. "Stop it, Ross," she begged softly. His use of the name Talal bore a validity that vibrated like some vast bell. "I believe you. I believe— him. We're both loco, you and I. You say any of this to the others, and they'll back out. Any sane person would. You know that, I hope."

He nodded, watching as she carefully rolled his sleeve down and buttoned it. "You know what really bothers me, Teresa? It makes hash out of everything I know."

"Or thought you knew," she said, her smile coming unbidden.

"That's it exactly. You spend your life depending on logical principles, and now this."

"It's probably logical on some level we don't understand," she pointed out. "So it doesn't hit me that hard, because I never thought I knew all the angles."

"Ouch," he said, standing up.

"Bandage too close?"

"No, your insight is. You just told me you aren't as arrogant as I am."

"Always thought you knew it," she said, and hugged him.

CHAPTER □ **28**

The wrangling did not begin until that evening after Orv returned with Ray Townsend and current aviation charts from Sierra Blanca Regional, the airport serving Ruidoso. They sat at the table, huddled around an aeronautical sectional chart, as one or another of them made occasional notes. As always, Montezuma remained shy of newcomers but watched Ray Townsend from the haven of the big chair.

With years of experience in his oddball hobby of naval bombardment in miniature, Ray wanted to rely on air surveillance followed by quick snatch-and-grab tactics. "With an air cannon like the ones we use to shoot potatoes, I could lob fused dynamite bombs a quarter of a mile," he said at one point. "Or drop 'em from the plane, even."

"You're kidding," said Ross. "You could blow up your own grandson by sheer accident."

"Assuming he's at that dude ranch," Orv added. "It's not an absolute certainty."

Ray's ideas died hard. "No, I don't mean we should try to destroy property. We drop a few rounds near the place! It'd look like a mortar attack, and in the confusion I could just go in and find him. You wouldn't have to go in with me, I'd chance it."

"You know, I believe you," said Ross, with a strained glance at Orv. Having only his old family friend as his engineering para-

digm, Ross had always thought of engineers as men of stolid caution. That naïveté was crumbling now as he recognized in Ray
Townsend a middle-aged man with the enthusiasms of an adoles-
cent.

"And how long to build your spud gun?" asked Orv, who
hoped to make a point.

"They're mostly plastic pipe, a motorcycle battery, some
switches and valving—couple of days. A bungee catapult could be
even quicker," Ray added, realizing that they might not have two
days to prepare.

"Give those people an excuse like that and they could have us
rounded up by sheriff's deputies," Ross objected. "By that time,
nobody would believe anything we said. We might as well go to
the authorities to start with, Ray. We need a more subtle approach." He said it as if he were trying to avoid saying "a more
sane approach."

"Seems to me," said Orv to his fellow engineer, "you favor an
engineering solution before we know the parameters."

"I admit it. When all I have is a hammer, the whole world is a
nail," said Ray. "I guess I'm grasping at straws. What other kind
of solution do we have?"

"Espionage," said Ross. "Deception, subterfuge, whatever. A
political solution."

"Which still means our first step is a high overflight to set a
few parameters," Ray insisted. "Any argument on that point?"

There was no dissent there. It was Orv's suggestion that they
move their operations closer to Saddletramp—much closer—
camping out with sleeping bags rather than taking motel rooms.

"In this summer weather, camping out is a breeze," the old
fellow explained. "And we can move around the terrain as we like
without being obvious. My Range Rover's just the ticket."

"I can take the Cherokee, too," said Ross.

"They know the Datsun too well," T.C. injected.

"You could drive my rental, but we don't want a convoy. Why
not fly with me," Ray offered. "I'll need an extra set of hands
tomorrow morning when I'm here," he placed a manicured finger

near the blue worm of New Mexico's nascent little Canadian River, "with the camera."

She did not care much for flying in little airplanes that carried fewer than fifty people, but at least she would be doing something useful, and T.C. agreed. "But we'll all need radios—I mean, won't we?" She put her hand on Ross's, deferring to him.

"Cell phones are fine," said Ray. "I brought mine, so everyone bring his own."

"Whoa," Orv said. "Not so fine."

"I don't have one," said T.C. as though admitting an oversight.

"I don't either," Ross shrugged.

"Me neither," said Orv.

"Well, buy some early tomorrow," said Ray.

"That's not the problem," Orv explained. "Why d'you suppose we don't have them? For one reason: The reception is goofy in parts of New Mexico and plain old nonexistent in others."

Ray sighed. "Too long the city boy, these past years. Sorry, I guess it's hard for me to get used to the idea that people would still live where you can't get good reception."

"Ray," the mining engineer said patiently, "that's *why* some people live out here. Count me among 'em. That's the other reason I don't have one. You're right, though, we do need radios."

"Maybe I could pick up some handheld two-ways at the airport," Ray said.

"Or cheap at Radio Shack," Ross said. "There's one on Whitlock right here in Ruidoso, but it won't be open when we leave. I've seen another one in Roswell, which is on the way."

T.C. studied the lists growing around the table, leaning virtually against Ross to do it, and hoped no one would suggest tallying the dollar amount. Her personal list included an extra sleeping bag for Al—not *if* they recovered him, but *when*. The difference to her peace of mind was vital.

"Extra gas, and avgas for the plane, check. Sticks of eighty percent, fuse and caps, spotting scope, check all. Shoot, I'm forgetting something," Orv muttered, toying with his pencil, then getting up to pace the room.

More telephone calls by Ray proved that the simple little air-strip near Conchas Dam was in operation, though without any amenities beyond tie-downs and solar-powered runway lights for the occasional vacationing pilot. The Conchas State Park official confirmed that cellular phones were usually next to useless in the entire vicinity.

"New rope," Orv exclaimed at last, hurrying back to the table. "Stupid, stupid." He scribbled the notation.

"Why new," T.C. asked. "My ex always got his worn in, to remove that scratchy stuff."

"I know why," Ross said. "My father swore by it but I'm not sure it works. Orv, does it really stop the varmints?"

"Never had a rattler cross it yet," said the old man.

"Omigod," said T.C., with a pleading glance toward Ross.

"You need traditional manila, T.C.," Orv told her. "It's the little whiskers on a new rope that get between a snake's belly plates. They won't cross it, that's a fact. Not often, anyway."

"So there are rattlesnakes out there," said Ray.

"And here, and yonder," Orv nodded. "All over. They like warmth, so they've been known to get right chummy on a nippy night. Where we're headed is about fifty miles west of Tucumcari, and the town has its annual rattler reunion in August. They aren't kidding, folks. Lay the rope around your fartsack—wups," he said, making a grimace for T.C. "Sleeping bag," he amended.

T.C., dryly: "Any more oh-by-the-way-we're-screwed hints of a similar nature?"

"Well, I'll bring mosquito nets. Shake out your boots every morning. Tarantulas aren't that poisonous, but a scorpion will zing you just for fun," said Orv.

"If you're trying to scare me into staying here, forget it," said T.C., nevertheless looking a bit uneasy.

"Tryin' to make you ready for a little ol' New Mexico camp-out is all," said Orv. He glanced at his list and began to fold it. "I'll bring a propane stove and plenty of grub. It'll not likely rain, but if it does those drops come three to the dozen, so don't spend much time in dry washes. They fill up with runoff faster'n scat."

"We won't have a car at the Conchas strip, so we'll meet you there with your four-wheelers about noon," Ray reminded the older man.

"With our radios and your film ready to develop," Ross said hopefully, as Orv stood up and stretched.

Taking this as his signal, Ray also stood up, refolding his air chart. "If you were serious about that invitation, Orville, I'll stay with you."

"Wouldn't've said it otherwise," said Orv. "Anyway, I've always wondered whether another engineer would think my place makes sense. This I promise: It's different."

"But you could use Al's cot," Ross said.

"Orv's spare bed is probably more comfortable," T.C. said, smiling at the older men.

"But," was as far as Ross got.

"Let the techies bond, Ross," T.C. said, and he subsided.

□　　□　　□

When the Range Rover's headlight beams had flickered away through a nearby aspen grove, T.C. passed her arm around Ross's waist. "Let's go to bed," she said.

Ross sighed, disengaged innocently. "Going to be a long day, that's for sure, but you go ahead. I'll wash the cups and stuff and see you in the morning."

And five minutes later, when he stepped into his bedroom, he stopped dead, astonished to find T.C. in his bed, her head propped on one arm. She was smiling. "But I thought," he said.

"I said, *let's* go to bed, you fool." The smile did not change. Or maybe just a little.

"You meant together," he said, disbelieving.

"What a doofus," she said, marveling, as he began to remove his shirt. "Ray knew. Orv knew. I'll bet Monty knew. Here, let me get that sleeve. We don't have to do anything but snuggle if you want," she continued, easing the sleeve off. "But this is sort of like going off to a war or something, Ross. We could be in separate cells this time tomorrow. I haven't been with a man since—well, the truth is, not since the crash." She still found it hard to mention Littlebo's death directly.

He removed his trousers, then his shorts, preternaturally aware of her gaze on him, hurrying to snap off the lamp that shed such pitiless light on his burned body. "Neither have I," he said, lifting the covers to slide in beside her.

"Well, it's your own fault. I'm just traditional enough to wait for you to ask, and—wow," she said, as he pressed toward her in darkness, stroking her hair. "I didn't know 'til now whether you were burned there," she finished.

"Thank God for small favors," he said, his erection endorsing his words.

"Mmm, as large a favor as I'll ever need," she giggled, naked beneath the covers, welcoming a thrill of goose flesh as he cupped one breast in his hand.

"That's my line, and unless I miscounted, ohh, yes, I thought you might have two of 'em," he said. She thought he murmured, "Glorious," then, but was not sure. A difficult word to pronounce while teasing a nipple between his lips.

She parted her legs, eased an arm beneath his neck, found his lips with her own and, having surrounded him, surrendered to him.

Very soon, too soon, he finished, their faces slick with tears of mutual joy. After a brief silence: "We're a pair, aren't we," she chortled. "Reminds me of an old joke, you know the one? 'Oh, we fucked and cried all the way to San Francisco.'"

"Remind me to take you to San Francisco sometime," he replied and moved against her.

She gyrated her hips experimentally. "Hey, *amado mio,* you're still there," she murmured in sweet surprise.

"Just because I got off, doesn't mean I have to get off," he said with false impudence. "With luck, dear heart, there may be lots more disembarking down there."

She giggled again, loving the byplay, undeterred by her failure to climax, wise in her patience. And presently they began again, Ross moving this time as if he might continue forever, obedient to the commands of her body and not to her little yips of what could have been pain—but were not. And when pleasure erupted in her, Teresa welcomed it with a joyous squeal, crooning little moans of delight for him.

And not long after, she told him she had faked it and that he would be obliged to do it for teacher until he got it right, and Ross played the student's part wonderfully well.

Snuggling innocently with her at last, he said, "I'm afraid that part of me won't be so crispy again for a while."

"You know, I've always hated that," she said, massaging his scalp.

"My hair?"

"Idiot. No, that nickname. Crispy, for God's sake!"

"Then why did you—"

"Because it was your idea. But I never likcd it. As if you wanted to trumpet the very thing that sent you up here to sulk for the rest of your life like a, a . . ." Analogy failed her.

"Hermit," he supplied. "I know. I couldn't stand how people saw me, Teresa."

"Ponypoop, my love. You couldn't stand how *you* saw you. Get over it. I did, a long time ago."

A long sigh as he relaxed against her more fully. "Might've given me a signal or something."

"I've been sending dit-dahs for two years, Ross. Somehow it didn't seem quite right to simply grab you by the crotch."

"In the future, give it serious consideration," he murmured and kissed her ear. And eventually, mumbling endearments, they drifted into sleep.

□　　□　　□

They had nearly finished loading Ross's Cherokee when the two engineers drove down from Orv's place, dawn flushing the meadow with light. The glow on the meadow, the hustle and bustle, their clipped conversation in hushed tones—all had a dreamlike quality for T.C. Perhaps, she decided, it all seemed unreal because they were setting out on this attempt with only the vaguest, half-assed idea exactly what they were going to do.

Orv turned off alone toward the Interstate. At the airport, Ross kissed T.C. good-bye with unrestrained pleasure. "I ought to watch you take off," he said. "I'll catch up to Orv at the Roswell mall. He's going to spring for the radios."

Ray had his reasons for not filing a flight plan. He was singing, "We'll take the high road, and you take the low road, and we'll be at Conchas befooooore ye," in a surprisingly sweet, youthful baritone, as he removed the tie-downs from the white Cessna. He broke it off, cheerful as a chipmunk, when T.C. peered into the upholstered cabin. "Might be chilly up there for you, T.C.," he called. "Bring a warm jacket. Too bad you don't have a flight suit." He didn't have one either but looked quite the professional as he made a walkaround inspection in his tan whipcords, aviator sunglasses, and well-worn brown leather jacket. "Ross, if you see baseball caps on the way, grab us a couple," he said.

Ross sent him a snappy salute, passed his own down-filled jacket to T.C., and drove the Cherokee to the perimeter road where he parked to await their takeoff. T.C. sat beside Ray, accepting his advice on her harness, trying not to think about the way she felt about this dinky little aluminum flivver. It seemed as if she could've punched her way through it at any place she chose. She adopted a mantra, *This is not your father's Oldsmobile*, she thought as the propeller swung fitfully.

A moment later the Boeing man was checking controls, watching his instruments, speaking in a monotone over the soft, sizzling drone of the engine. She thought he seemed a bit tentative at the controls but, craning his neck, Ray taxied to the end of the runway before stopping for a moment. Then he turned onto the runway, nothing soft about the engine's roar now, and as the tail came up T.C. was too impressed by the initial acceleration to pay attention to the fluttery sensation in her midriff. The flutter became a fishing weight as the airstrip dropped away.

She waved toward the toylike Cherokee as they climbed out with a mile of runway left, seeing Ross waving, wondering if he could see her arm or was just waving on general principles. He had a bucketful of those, principles enough for both of them, which was all to the good because she felt the need of an ethical rudder, worrying that she might be a little light in the principles department. It bothered her that it *hadn't* bothered her much to pile dirt on that *hijo de puta* who'd copped a feel back in Tucson, moments before he intended to kill her. It bothered her that she didn't give a damn how many more of those guys went into shallow graves. Kerman? Well, he nagged at her a little. She couldn't figure out why. Maybe it was just that he seemed genuinely concerned for Al, his distant kin whom he hadn't seen for years. But if that Kurd turned up at Saddletramp to get between her and Al again, she'd tear up that qualm like tissue paper. Everybody thought Anatol Kerman was such a tough customer. What had Jack Nicholson said as the Joker in that movie? Well, if Kerman got in the way, *wait'll he gets a load of me,* she promised.

Still climbing, Ray laughed and pointed forward to their right. T.C. saw the squarish speck of a vehicle crawling along the ribbon of Route 70. "But we left him behind," she said over the engine's steady beat.

"My buddy Orv," said Ray happily, "I think. Those four-wheelers look a lot alike from aloft. Relax and I'll wing-wave him." He dipped the Cessna's right wing, then the left, continuing in a bank toward the north. "Can you get my sectional chart? Behind you in my little bag with the Hasselblad."

She located the chart, partially unfolded it, and soon began to get the rudiments of air charts, matching symbols on paper to features that she could see below, the early sun imparting long, hard shadows to the arroyos and tabletop buttes of this largely untenanted land.

She identified Fort Sumner far away to their right after a half hour, and then Santa Rosa, near enough that she could see its little airstrip, to the left of irregular promontories. Ray seemed content to talk on the plane's radio, which pleased T.C. who was occupied with her own thoughts. Chiefly, she stayed mired in her quandary over whether to call in the authorities—not that it was really her decision, that was properly Ray's. Whatever happened now, within a few days, bright, grinning, hell-raising little Al Townsend would be gone from her life again. *He's not mine,* she kept telling herself.

The sun had risen above the Cessna's high wing, and they could see without squinting when Ray, having chosen a compass heading for most of the flight, asked for the chart. She was feeling the chill by then, knowing they were a mile above the broken landscape, which put them at eleven or twelve thousand feet above sea level. He added power again, handing back the chart, running a finger along a dusty rose line on paper, then pointing downward.

She could not identify their location until she saw the molten steel glint of sun bouncing up from water far to their right and read "Conchas Dam" on the chart. Then the curve of that rosy line and the tiny groupings of structures just ahead became Variadero and Trementina. Not many miles from there lay the soft-penciled X matching the coordinates from Ross's printout: Saddletramp.

She would have hated the place for its name if nothing else. She'd divorced one saddle tramp and now—But that wasn't true. Beau hadn't become a drifter until after, when they split up. She hadn't been fair to him, might at least have remained on friendly terms. Maybe after this she could trace him somehow, not to take up with him again but just to assuage her guilt, smooth over old scars, old recriminations. It occurred to her to wonder why now, after all this time, she was ready to forgive Beau. And of course she knew that the answer was a hundred miles away, driving his Cherokee into Roswell, and she smiled at her own transparency.

She could feel in the sympathetic vibration through her rump that the engine was working harder. When she asked, Ray said they were at thirteen-five, close to his self-imposed ceiling without breathing from an oxygen bottle. And at last, still following the thin scrawl of road, he jerked a thumb to their right. She saw it, nearer than she expected, between the rise of mountains near the road and a broad ravine that fed Conchas Reservoir. Saddletramp didn't look like much from here, she thought. You could put your foot down and stomp it.

"Get the camera," Ray told her, nervously watching as she did because that was the way people were with those boxy little gadgets. He throttled back a bit and checked settings on the nubbly black camera, then showed her how to aim and trip the shutter.

"Get a couple from here," he said. "We'll take more coming back over the river canyon."

Though that river wasn't much as watercourses went, the ravine contours influenced the winds a lot. For the first time, T.C. had to swallow hard. Ray noticed. "If you're going to fill your pockets, don't do it on the camera," he said cheerily. *Well unfuck you and your old box Brownie*, she replied silently, her irritation chasing away the queasiness. And she got more photos, and then Ray veered away southward, expertly winding the film like a coffee grinder, throttling so far back that the engine's drone became a whispery whirr.

"I'll try to sneak over, they might not notice us," he explained with a wink. They were still very high but now virtually gliding, the altimeter dial lazily moving backward like a clock that had changed its tiny mind.

Ray managed to maintain his course, the minuscule dude ranch now on their left as he took more photos. She noticed a group of dirt-colored dwellings a mile from the dude ranch and what looked like a dry lakebed with rusty vehicles—a junked car, a horse trailer, several smaller cargo trailers—strewn just beyond the lake's edge.

A jade green swimming pool of irregular shape lay near the central building, with several tanned figures sunning themselves on towels. Not far away in a corral, a slim mite perched on the top fence rail and gestured as a colorful long-haired, two-legged creature bounced atop a larger four-footed one, circling inside the corral, going nowhere. T.C. grinned. She had sat a saddle horse the same way when trying to impress her fiancé. Beau had been impressed, all right, said she rode a trotting horse like a monkey humping a football.

Ray banked again as they flanked a trail that wound back toward the state road, finishing the roll of film before he handed her the camera. They were only two thousand feet above the reddish hardpan before he swept past the road and throttled up, turning toward the south with a surge of acceleration.

Ray turned to her again. "You notice their airstrip?"

"Uh-uh. Not on the chart, either. I looked."

"Good girl. But I think it's there. Maybe we'll see it better in Santa Rosa."

"I don't get it," she admitted.

"They've got avgas at the municipal strip right on the edge of town, and a courtesy car. And they tell me there's a quick photo shop in town."

"Won't Ross worry about us?"

"Look at the time; most shops are just opening," he said. "With a decent tip to somebody we should have big blowups in a couple of hours. Don't let me forget to buy a loupe, eight-power should be enough, then back to Conchas by noon."

In the end, it wasn't a decent tip, it was a walloping bribe. But because he spent the last few minutes talking with a sunburnt young man who had topped off his fuel supply, Ray Townsend had a look of smarmy satisfaction to go with the manila envelope full of eight-by-tens when they took off from Santa Rosa Municipal a half hour before noon. T.C. studied the photos until they circled the Conchas strip. Once she saw what Ray had seen, a couple of those blowups were very, very interesting.

CHAPTER □ 29

Ray had their Cessna anchored to tie-downs beside the Conchas airstrip and was studying his photos with the magnifying loupe when the Range Rover came in sight, followed closely by Ross in his Cherokee.

T.C. selected the Cherokee while Ray joined Orv Ferguson, who led them a short distance to a vantage point near the state park's golf course. There they pulled their vehicles close together, windows rolled down, while they attacked the egg salad sandwiches Orv had brought for lunch. The pilot and the mining engineer huddled over their new handheld radios, serious toys despite their small size—fourteen channels, range up to a few miles.

Sitting in his Cherokee with T.C., Ross showed off the baseball caps with logos of the University of New Mexico, New Mexico State, and Texas Tech. "Something to offend everybody," he said, passing two of the caps across to Ray, appropriating the UNM cap for himself. The fourth cap was in another bag, plain olive drab made festive with silver embroidery across the bill, as elaborate as an admiral's, and he plopped it onto T.C.'s head with a flourish. "And now the big surprise," he finished, grinning as he shook two larger garments from the bag. He checked the tag on one, unfolded it. "I didn't forget you, Ray," he said, holding up another garment. "Hope you take a large."

"*Caramba la bamba,*" T.C. chirped, hopping from the vehicle and holding the coverall up to her shoulders. She saw the adjustment tabs, the many zippers, the pockets along both trouser legs. "I think it'll fit. Where'd you get it?"

"Roswell," he said, "while Orv was doing Radio Shack. And it's not supposed to fit. They're not actual military flight suits, but a lot of folks don't care, very popular with UFOlogists. I suppose when the mother ship comes down, they want to be dressed for the trip."

Ray, amused by their new togs, said, "Go ahead, T.C., try it on. People wear 'em over their clothes sometimes. See whether I get an unexpected urge to stand at attention." She had to wriggle and tug because the coverall was a snug fit over her jeans. But when she snapped her waist tabs, the effect suddenly became both military and, tightly formfitting, a shape to catch a man's eye.

Ray Townsend brought his hand up in a slow salute, nodding judiciously. "By God, if it isn't almost the Civil Air Patrol," he smiled. After a thoughtful pause he added, "A name tag and a winged pin would help. Stuff a sectional chart in that right shin pocket and you'd pass. Maybe not to real CAP, but—"

Ross bit another crescent from his sandwich and squinted into the man's gaze. "Do I detect an agenda here?"

"I'm not sure—you might think it's a little wild and woolly. But I talked with a senior mechanic in Santa Rosa this morning and got some tidbits about search sweeps."

"But the CAP is an Air Force outfit," Ross said, puzzled.

"Right, but it seems that search and rescue operations in New Mexico don't work quite like anyone else's. The state police coordinate things, ask for ground search teams, bring in the CAP for air search as necessary," said Ray. "And I'll give you a load of guesses what kind of aircraft they use." He was jabbing a forefinger toward the little plane he had rented.

Ross quit chewing. So did Orv. "I be *damn*," said the old man.

"You mean little prop jobs," Ross prompted.

"I mean Cessna one Eighty-twos. White, to reflect the sun, a lot like this one. Not quite the same model but close enough for most people.

"Another thing. Remember you can't depend on cell phones in these parts? The CAP can orbit a plane over a search area as a comm relay for ground search teams," Ray went on and waggled his brow. "Give you ideas?"

"Too many," said Ross, finishing his sandwich. "And I haven't seen those photos of yours."

"All of a sudden I'm not hungry," said Orv, rewrapping the uneaten portion of his sandwich.

Only a mild breeze kept the summer sun from baking them in their automotive ovens as Ross and T.C. crowded into the Range Rover, T.C. making notes, she and Orv Ferguson letting the younger men do most of the brainstorming because, clearly, those two understood more about officialdom.

Then, passing the photos around, Ray turned to T.C. "There's supposed to be an airstrip at Saddletramp. What d'you say?"

"No sign of one," said T.C. "Or on the chart. Maybe they land on the ground."

"I probably could do it with the Cessna, in a pinch, though that's not my point. These charts are regularly updated. Cartographers don't always make a big deal out of a changed feature, they just reflect the facts. And the fact is—here, look at that little alkali dry lake," he said, pointing toward the photo that Ross held. A mile or more from the main structures, paler than the brush-dotted terrain nearby, a fat sinuous worm of white spanned more than a half mile of flat ground. "No brush on the lake bed," Ray prompted.

"Alkali's not much as potting soil," said Orv, who had been cussing his containers of veggies for a generation.

"Neither is concrete," Ray countered, "and I think that's what we're seeing. Now take the loupe and look near the ends of the lake." He handed Ross his little eight-power magnifying loupe.

"Well my, my, would you look at that," Ross muttered after a moment, still peering closely. He looked up at Ray. "Skid marks?"

The Boeing engineer nodded. "Made by aircraft landing pretty hot, I'd guess. Maybe executive jets. From a distance it looks like any other little dry alkali sink with irregular curves, but you can draw a straight line fifty feet wide down the entire length of it. We're looking at an airstrip, hidden in plain sight. Wouldn't surprise me if those vehicles provide runway lights. And if you look closely near those trailers and junk, you'll see vehicle wheel tracks.''

Ross had noticed several trails leading to and from the corral, probably bridle trails, Orv said. In one photo they could see three mounted riders on a trail that circled a stand of cottonwoods.

Yet it was the short vehicle tracks leading from the dry lake that commanded most of Ross's attention. "Every one of those tracks leads straight from the dry lake, like they were towed off by the shortest path,'' he said. "With all the wind currents around here, those tracks won't last long. I'm guessing the tow job was done very recently, maybe in the past day or so.''

Orv tugged at the photo until Ross relinquished it. After thirty seconds of close study, he said, "I get it. They park all those junkers on the concrete so nobody would think of landing there.''

"And tow 'em all off again when they expect one of their own flights,'' Ray said.

"So they expect one now,'' T.C. blurted, eyes wide.

"Yeah,'' said Ross and Ray together. Their shared glance said they hadn't thought it through that far.

T.C.: "Wouldn't that be illegal, putting barriers on an airstrip?''

Ray: "Possibly, but I doubt it. It's private property. Very damn private. You were thinking of turning them in for that?''

"Whatever,'' she shrugged. "Anything to stop them from landing a plane there now.''

"That would be tipping our hand, and we don't know that it has anything to do with Al,'' said Ross.

"We don't know that it doesn't, either,'' Ray replied instantly. "I'd like to just shut the whole bloody place down awhile.'' He retrieved his photos, the top one showing the central building with its corral and outbuildings. "But if we came barging in with a search and rescue story, all those people would have to do is make one little phone call to the state police.''

"Ohh, boy," Ross said in a near whisper. More loudly he said, "So this is where you ask for volunteers."

"You're being cryptic," said Ray.

"Well, state cops are part of the Department of Public Safety. As it happens, in my work I've, um, interacted with law enforcement all over New Mexico and west Texas."

"Spit it out, Ross. You know somebody," Orv said.

"Yeah, here and there. One in the state police office in Tucumcari. Or was." His glance toward T.C. was cautious.

"But that's great," Ray crowed, buoyant as a teenager. "Fifty miles from here. What does he do? Who is he?"

Ross avoided T.C.'s gaze. "Worked up from dispatcher in administrative services. Name's Louisa Larkin. Probably married by now," he said, as elaborately casual as a Marc Antony remarking, "Cleopatra? The name's vaguely familiar."

"Louisa Larkin," Orv smirked. "Real nice how it rolls off the tongue."

T.C., very softly, unheard across the space between the vehicles: "And did she, sweetie pie?"

"Huh?"

"Roll off the tongue. You heard me." She tried to keep her gaze innocent, but he saw that, in some perverse way, she was enjoying his discomfort.

"Not for a long time," he muttered, the back of his neck growing rosy. He saved his dirty look for his neighbor. "Thanks, Orv. Last time I dropped in there—let's just say she'll know me on sight. Can't swear she'll be happy about it, but she might feel like she owes me a favor."

T.C. understood instantly, patting his knee. "I take it she preferred the old Ross," she said.

His nod was dismissive. He said, "If I were working a case on active duty, I might be able to promote a telephone extension in the office for a day. Or maybe not. I could try."

"Guys," said T.C.

"If you can, we're cooking," said Ray. "I take it we're on the same page: You're the state cop who validates us as part of a search and rescue group. But while you're there you'll be way out of range of our radios."

T.C. coughed for attention. "Guys," she tried again.

"You can't patch in from the Cessna?"

Ray's face fell. "To the state police? Oh hell, of course. Someone please wipe the egg off my face."

T.C. put two fingers to her lips and blew a piercing blast. All conversation ceased. "Thank you. I'd just like to remind everybody how fast this scam will have us wading into *mierda profunda* if any of those guys are hanging out at this dude ranch and they see me."

Orv frowned and thought it over. "They've seen you that close?"

Before she thought about it she had replied, "Close enough that one of the bastards tried to feel me up." Something feral moved in the old man's eyes, but he said nothing.

Ross knew which bastard she meant. "I doubt he'll do it again," he said evenly.

"You know," she said, turning a brazen grin on him, "I feel the same way. But say they recognize me. What then?"

"Druther say they don't," Orv put in. "Can't you, oh shoot, you know—strap your boozum tighter, put your hair up, somethin' like that?"

"It'll take more than that," she predicted.

"Sunglasses," said Ray. "Bleach your hair."

"Christ, it'd take a makeover," she said. "Blonde to brunette is easy. The other way around isn't. Do we have the time for that?" She was answered by shrugs.

"They don't know me," said Ray, "or Orville, so we might just have to wing it, I mean literally, while you two do your things in Tucumcari, see how it goes there."

"Wing it with what story? Who exactly are we supposed to be looking for out there?" Orv's question centered them again.

They framed their approach step by step. If Saddletramp had no guests, and always assuming Al was there, then every soul on the site might be alert and dangerous if Ray announced a missing boy.

T.C. knew better than that. "This morning, some dudette was learning to ride in the corral. She bounced like, uh, like the saddle was a hot skillet. Would staff members ride that badly? Possible, but there were people at the pool, too. Buffing their tans like George Hamilton. Ranch hands I've known don't go in for that, not an Arizona *vaquero*, anyhow. They're brown on their wrists and faces with a tan V in front, and pale as a tortilla everyplace else," she assured them.

"The same in New Mexico," said Orv. "So maybe these fellas will be on their best behavior in front of the paying guests."

With these educated guesses, they decided that a forthright description of the boy would be as good as any story. Impersonating officials was another matter, but they could think of no better tactic after a half hour.

"I've got a bad feeling about this," Ross admitted. "While we're sitting here, someone could be landing on that airstrip."

Ray checked his wristwatch. "Look, we all know the odds are pretty long. We can shorten 'em if I go up again, right now, and watch the area while Orv finds us a place to camp. You two head into town, see what you can do. Is there any reason I can't try to have you paged at the state police offices?"

"They're not that large, but it shouldn't be a problem if you ask for Agent Downing. Not a state cop, but Agent Downing. Don't call before, say, two-thirty. I should be there by that time."

"Oh, and Ross? Maybe you can bring me some jerry cans of avgas from Tucumcari."

Ross nodded, then studied the Boeing engineer for a count of five. "I can see problems with whatever we decide, but since Al's your grandson you have more at stake than any of us, Ray. Just promise me you won't try to swoop down on those guys by yourself and become a dead hero or some damn thing. Wait for backup, okay?"

A slow, tilted smile creased the face of Ray Townsend. "Should never have told you about my hobby," he said.

"You worry me a little," Ross acknowledged, returning the smile, then stepped from the vehicle with T.C. following.

"Takes all kinds, boy," said Orv, starting his engine. "And since we've only got four kinds, we'll have to dance with who brung us. See you here around seven, or I'll wait."

□   □   □

Tucumcari is an old town, comfortably larger than Ruidoso though still no metropolis, and it is served by a good interstate built on the bones of fabled Route 66. Ross stopped at the first pay telephone he saw on Second Street and let T.C. call some of Tucumcari's half dozen beauty salons. She kept watching him, numbering the times he looked at his watch, and turned away when she had counted to eleven.

Presently she hopped back into the Cherokee and repeated the directions the woman gave her. "Takes some negotiation for this much effort on short notice, sweetie," she said as he drove away. "It's not the money, it's the block of time."

"How much time?"

"Could be close to three hours. I'll bet she'll try to be done by five. Here's the number." She handed him a scrap of paper.

"Look for me around five," he said, as they crossed over the railroad tracks.

□   □   □

Though Ross had been through several bouts of cosmetic surgery since his last visit, they knew him on sight at the Department of Public Safety. *Maybe we all look alike to them,* he thought ruefully as he approached Louisa Larkin, one of two women he had ever considered as a mate.

Larkin glanced up, let her eyes slide off as people often did, then looked sharply at him. From the sudden reddening on her cheeks he knew she recognized him before she said, "Ross," in a breathless small voice and stood up quickly to offer her hand. She hadn't changed all that much since their last date, when he had spent most of an evening telling himself that his newly scarred features made no difference to Larkin, that he'd told her by phone what to expect, that nine months of enforced separation would enhance his welcome to her apartment, her arms, her body, that—blah, blah, all of the brave bullshit he had wanted so much to make true.

And he had known with the night's first kiss, with her involuntary tremor of revulsion, that the relationship was forever changed. And he had made the big good-bye easy for her, inventing a change of duty station, but she almost certainly saw the subterfuge and, when she cried, he knew they were tears of relief. After that he had called her once from San Antonio. Neither of them needed to say it was over.

Now he took her hand, squeezed gently, let go, and indicated the upgrading of her work area with a gesture. "Coming up in the world," he said in compliment. "Any other developments of note?"

Her smile and nod were distracted. "I'm seeing a nice guy. You'd like him." Translation: Don't even try. "I'm stuck here or I'd take you out for a doughnut," she said, stammering a bit. "You should've called."

"Actually, it's business," he said, noting that her fine lank frame was still erect, her honey-tinted hair still lustrous, her face still unlined. And finding joy in his lack of desire. He simply could not prevent himself from an instant's comparison of the willowy Larkin with a bumptious little Latina who was, at that moment, trying to disguise her own sultry appearance. *God, but I can be tacky*, he told himself, pleased beyond measure with his good fortune.

This was not the first time he had asked to use an office extension, and Louisa Larkin was almost pathetically eager to comply. *If she does me enough favors professionally,* he thought, *Larkin can erase some personal feelings of guilt.*

Something for everybody.

The job, he said offhandedly, giving Larkin just enough of the truth, involved a failed marriage. His lies were chiefly lies of omission: "We can't expect the woman to testify if she thinks her son is at risk. We're not about to call out search and rescue, you know how the press covers SAR like a blanket. It'd be on the AP wire in an hour."

And then, implying that the boy had slipped away on a back-packing trip, he asked her about habitations of interest between Trementina and Sanchez. Larkin quickly located the only site that might qualify: a secluded spa called Saddletramp.

He sat in a straight-backed oak chair beside her as Larkin's flickering fingers brought up the Saddletramp data on file. "Two numbers, both unlisted unpub," she said, invoking verbal short-hand.

"May as well have 'em," he said and laboriously wrote them down. He felt a glow of excitement when he saw that state police records revealed nothing of the place's dual nature. "They have a liquor license," she murmured, "and all their special taxes are current. No captive-breeding permits or any of that exotic crap, pardon my French." She grinned at him, trying for some of the old camaraderie. "If the youngster wanders that far, at least he won't be chased by a cheetah."

After more scrolling of data, she sat back. "They don't submit guest registers. I've had to call for it a couple of times at that inn at Conchas, but never there. Any reason I should?"

"Not yet, if at all. We've got our own bear in the air, so to speak, a Cessna. He'll report now and then, and I expect he'll get patched in to your lines. If he does, I'll take it. Oh," he went on smoothly while skimming his notes, "if the Saddletramp people do query, I'm overt on this. You can acknowledge me and the air surveillance."

Then, because he did not want Larkin to go into the dumper if this imposture all came crashing down: "It's not a CAP unit, just an adjunct air patrol." And to forestall any questions from Larkin, he got an outside line and called the beauty salon, asking for one T.C. Rainey.

Larkin was more than content to return to her work station. Ross was finishing his call—T.C. said that she might be a bit late and asked him to pick up some wraparound sunglasses—when Larkin called over to him. "Just like old times, Ross." It was a call patched in from an aerial radio frequency.

Ross punched the flashing button. "Downing," he said, knowing it could be only one person. "Any activity you can report on an open channel?" If Ray couldn't take that hint, this drill was going to be hopeless.

A hiss and buzz in the background, coming and going with Ray's transmissions. "Negative, open or otherwise, sir." *Good man.* "Just checking our comm lines on station. Ah, I'm going to need fuel."

Ross confirmed that and rang off, then spent another ten minutes doodling on his notepad. Assuming the placement of those vehicles meant an impending flight into Saddletramp, either master Al Townsend hadn't been picked up yet, or he had already been taken away by car. Lurking in every *if, either,* and *or* was the fear that, however vivid his dreams, this one was a fantasy conjured entirely by hope and medication. He had, after all, mentioned Saddletramp and other sites to Kerman.

But if the dream was valid, Anatol Kerman had been a man in some trouble. If he managed to reach Saddletramp, he probably wouldn't be found sunning himself by the pool or cantering around on a bridle trail.

Ross made another call, to Tucumcari Municipal, and learned they had Phillips avgas before he strolled past the work station of Louisa Larkin. "I may be back tomorrow. It's nice to be working with you again, Larkin. Really," he said in all honesty.

"I'm just glad to see you back at a hundred percent," she smiled, exaggerating for him. "I hope your young man has that backpack full of drinking water."

Ross paused on his way out long enough to say, "I imagine he does. He's a pretty resourceful youngster."

CHAPTER □ 30

Al thought about his resources as he toyed with his dinner of microwaved pasta. He knew how to make Beale, the big guy, mad: Jiggle the toilet lever just right and water would keep peeing down from the roof tank indefinitely, gurgling like crazy. When told to fix it, Al just let his jaw hang down and shrugged like a dumb five-year-old, so Beale had to fix it himself, the little alcove echoing with humdrum curses Al heard every day on the playground though most grown-ups didn't know it.

He knew how to get the other one's goat, too: complain about the impenetrable smog of his cigarette smoke until Beale chimed in on his side. Then the Tom one would stalk outside and suck fiercely on his Camel.

Al's other resource was the pair of short little bullets, as many as he dared swipe from a cardboard box in a bag between the beds while both guys were outside. While Grampa and another old guy were laughing and yarning in the garage workshop one afternoon, he'd heard Grampa's story about dropping a shotgun shell into a campfire once upon a time. So you didn't have to put a bullet in a gun to shoot it, but then, there wasn't any open fire here.

Other than those resources, Al didn't have much in the line of weapons, or distractions. The books didn't have pictures. He folded paper airplanes from some remaining pages of half a book by Louis L'Somethingorother, but the big guys wouldn't let him out to toss them. He watched TV a lot, the Beale guy seeming to enjoy the cartoons, too. He folded a little bitty water bomb out of paper once, but the durn paper leaked and they took it away before he could decide what he wanted to do with it. By the time Al finished that cruddy pasta at suppertime, he was almost wishing for the plane the big guys were waiting for.

The light from outside had grown dim, and the three of them had been watching TV through one stupid sitcom and part of another, when the Tom guy heard his phone, though he called it something else, chirping. He scrambled up and fumbled it from his jacket, which had fallen between the beds, and the Beale guy lowered the volume on the TV, turning his head a little, sucking a tooth as he tried to listen in.

As he talked, asking whether a Mister Kay had reported in, the Tom guy seemed to relax little by little, shaking a cigarette out, then glancing at the Beale guy and putting it back, crossing the room to make some instant coffee, crossing again to warm his cup in the microwave. He used a piece of cardboard from a frozen dinner as a coaster because neither one of these trolls had cleaned the microwave yet, a chore Al often had to do at home, so the glass insert that rode around in the microwave was so yuckified with spilled-over food it looked like somebody had left a pizza in there. And that gave Al an idea.

And because the Tom guy was starting to smile as he listened, so did the Beale guy, and Al slipped out of his corner and went to the toilet just to hear it flush and gurgle. Pretty soon the call was over, and try as he might Al hadn't been able to follow the conversation, so he hit the lever just on general principles.

The Tom guy was saying, "Something something Kerman, so it looks like we'll be flying out something morning."

The water was gurgling worse than usual as the Beale guy clapped his hands. "Hot damn, no more something in this pissant something, I can hardly," he paused and raised his voice. "Kid, jiggle the got-damn handle!" And more softly again, "If I get to kick his little ass just once it'll all be something."

And Al jiggled, but deliberately not enough, and came out doing his downcast dumb act, shrugging as the Beale guy rushed past him to fix the toilet. Al had done all he could at the moment, but it wasn't much, and he was starting to worry again. If this missing bad guy was coming in on a plane, and these two guys were so happy, it couldn't be good news for Al.

□   □   □

All the way back to Conchas, Ross kept stealing glances at T.C. as he drove. At last she said, "Just let me know before you go off the road, sweetie. All that aviation gasoline in back."

"Sorry. I can't get used to the new you."

She was carefully trimming the embroidered cloth wings from round shoulder patches he'd picked up in the secondhand shop inevitable in Tucumcari. "You have a weakness for chippies? This is the same me, even if I do look like a bimbo." But she fluffed at her now unfluffable hair anyway.

"You don't," he protested, not very convincingly. "But you do look—different," he acknowledged. And after another moment: "Take the glasses off." He had picked up her wraparounds and tarnished old lieutenant's silvery bars at the same secondhand store.

The late sun was in her eyes, but she did it, turning sideways to face him. Her hair was now a shade, actually different shades, between yellow and brown, no longer straight and lustrous but coiled like a thousand little soiled yellow springs. It had taken a lot of makeup to lighten her face and throat; the bright add-on fingernails had been the simplest of the changes. Trimming her lush brows had been hardest to accept. Now she waggled them all, fingers and brows too, at him while she batted her eyes. "Like it?"

He gazed briefly at the transformation, the grin spreading across his face. "I suspect there's no right answer to that, my love. First let me say the sooner you change back to the way you looked last night, the better I'll like it."

"Uh-huh, sure. Meanwhile, you've got a letch to jump the bones of a total stranger."

"Maybe a little. Jesus, T.C., you bring me back from the dead and then complain because I'm twitching."

"Who said I complained?" She donned the sunglasses again and stuck her tongue out at him. "Just making sure we're on the same page. The truth is, this makeover makes me feel, uh, kind of sexy."

"Wanton," he supplied.

"Wantin' is right." She patted his knee, turned, faced forward again, and resumed trimming the patch to separate those stylized wings. "But I can wait. If it was that old girlfriend of yours that's turned you on, I can wait a loooong time," she warned.

Long moments passed before he said, "Amazing. She looks the same, friendly enough, but there's nothing there anymore. From either of us." Another brief smile but quietly reflective. "You tend to have that effect." When she did not respond, he prodded, "Penny for your thoughts."

"Al, of course," she said, as they passed a CONCHAS DAM road sign. "I don't know if you can fully appreciate how I feel about that little guy."

"I knew the first time I laid eyes on him, but I wasn't sure you did. He's a surrogate, isn't he?"

She nodded, then looked away toward the Conchas airstrip on their left. "I don't see the plane."

"That means Ray's still on-station." At that moment his shirt pocket beeped for attention. Ross palmed his little radio and said, "Cherokee."

"Huh? Oh." It was Orv. "Thought that might be you on the highway. This is Rover, at the strip. Come join me. Tex drifts close once an hour and we talk. You got his liquids?"

Ross had chuckled at the code word, "Tex," an obvious reference to Boeing's Tex Johnston. Now he replied, "That and more. You'll see. Does Tex have anything to report?" He was turning off the highway now and nodded as T.C. pointed toward the Range Rover, now visible in the distance.

"No action, he says. Claims that's the best sign. I liked him better before he took that moniker," Orv grumped.

Now Ross laughed outright. Orv was no fan of things Texan. "Well, remember Tex was really from Kansas," he said.

Another voice, staticky with a buzz in it: "I heard that, Rover." Though the Cessna was not near enough to see, it evidently came within marginal range for the handheld radios during the southernmost part of its patrol pattern.

"You must be running on empty, Tex," said Ross.

"Topside tanks, not far from it. My personal tank, just the opposite," said Ray, who had been flying for hours without relief for his bladder. "I'll be with you shortly. Tex out." The static and the buzz abruptly ceased.

Orv Ferguson had his windows down to welcome the breeze, and soon the three of them were exchanging news face-to-face. "My gawd, T.C., you're a painted hussy," said the old man. "If I didn't know you, I wouldn't know you."

"And I'm not quite finished," she said. "You wouldn't have a needle and black thread, would you?"

"In my ol' Dopp kit, I think." Orv rummaged behind him for his shaving kit, a cracked leather survivor from several wars ago.

A half hour later the sun was poised atop low peaks on a technicolor horizon when Ray Townsend ghosted his white Cessna onto the airstrip. They helped him link its tie-downs as he described his patrol. He had seen absolutely no sign of activity near the dry lake, other than multilegged dots that were couples on horseback, and still tinier dots that emerged now and then from one of the adobe huts far removed from the central buildings. For the most part, he said, he had flown high and wide of the ranch, keeping that false lake in view where any aircraft would have shown up as plainly as a fly settling in a bathtub.

"I seriously doubt they have equipment for a night landing, especially on such a short strip," Ray added, testing a tie-down. "So I'm not going up again now." He tossed a mock salute, which T.C. returned. He marveled at the silver bars on the shoulders of her flight suit and the wings she had carefully sewn high on its left breast. "I don't know what air force you fly for, lady, but I'd like to enlist," he joked.

"Ross got you stuff just like this today and I've sewn your wings on, so we'll be in the same outfit," she replied, then rushed to help Ross who was struggling with a jerry can of aviation fuel.

It was dusk before they had lugged those cans to the Cessna and emptied them into the wing tanks. "Now can I go somewhere and collapse?" T.C. asked plaintively. "I stink and I'm pooped."

Ray seconded the motion. They ate at an inn not far from the golf course, watching shadows creep across their vista, Orv assuring them that he had found a good camping spot literally beneath the landing pattern of any aircraft headed for the ranch.

"It'd probably be a twin, maybe even a small jet, if it lands hot enough to make long skid marks," Ray mused, "so it'll have to make a final approach that's a few miles long. Easy to spot, too. Just in case, maybe we should maintain two-hour sentry duty through the night."

"Let's say an airplane comes down at midnight. What would we do about it?" asked Orv.

"Been thinking about that all afternoon," said Ray. "I jump in the Range Rover, bounce like a basketball to the highway, and drive like hell to the Cessna," said Ray. "Half hour or less to the plane, another eight, maybe ten minutes' flight time. Without the weight of a passenger I can land that puddle jumper in a quarter of the runway so nobody who needs the whole strip could take off with me blocking them. Meanwhile, you three cut the fence, I suppose it's barbed wire, and drive there overland. No point in driving to their access road, it's a long way around and we'd alert them when we drove past the central buildings. If I can't land as a barrier on the strip in time, maybe you can do it yourselves. Oh, yes," he said to Orv's concerned glance, "I saw where you were cruising around out there near the streambed, so I dropped down later and checked the terrain. No ravines I could see in your way. But don't overdrive your lights, just in case I missed one," he said earnestly.

"Betcher life," said Ray. "And we oughta be heading out in

that direction about now. It'll take a little time to set up camp without lighting up the area.''

T.C. kept time surreptitiously as they followed Orv's taillights. It took them just over forty minutes, the last ten jouncing overland with parking lights near the eroded slash that was the home of a small river course. She said a good Protestant prayer in hopes that Ray Townsend would not have to reverse that path in the middle of the night while they rode toward a concealed airstrip by dead reckoning.

Though they could not see the lights of Saddletramp from their campsite, Orv swore that landing lights would be visible from there. He had driven a pair of tent stakes ten feet apart into unforgiving hardpan that afternoon and found them again without difficulty. "Our gunsights," he explained. "Line up on them and look for landing lights. And hope we don't see any.''

The traditional campfire was impractical here for two reasons, one of which Orv had known for half a century: It could have been seen from the ranch, and suitable hunks of wood for an Anglo fire had always been hard to come by among these sparse and spiky, unpromising shrubs. T.C. brewed coffee on Orv's camp stove, feeling the paradoxical night chill of a country that broiled at noon, while the men arranged their sleeping bags. The vehicles on their flanks loomed twenty feet apart at moonrise, angular as packing crates; new manila rope pinned by tent stakes defined the area.

Ray had a special problem: the jerry cans had only half filled his tanks. "Assuming the night is uneventful, I'll be doing a long patrol tomorrow. Tucumcari's close, but I'll need to launch at dawn so I can be back soonest. That means I'll take the last sentry duty of the night and drive off at first light. And that means," he sighed, "I should turn in now." With that, he moved away from his friends toward his sleeping bag.

During dinner they had already worked out much of their ruse for the next day, and it was obvious to all of them that they would have some improvising to do. T.C. was impressed to see that, while she and Orv were tentative in this approach to imposture, Ross

Downing seemed unperturbed, almost offhand, by it all. He had played many a role during his career and, when reminded how risky this one was, quoted the old bromide, "In for a penny, in for a pound." The only one of them who could flash an impressive ID if necessary, Ross knew enough about overlapping jurisdictions to be glib—unless someone probed too far.

Presently Orv decided to turn in, having chosen the third watch. T.C. and Ross flipped a coin for first watch. "No more coffee for me now," said Ross when he saw T.C. would take first watch.

She slurped, smiling at him in the pale reflection of a big quarter moon. Softly, "You think I'm going to let you sleep?"

"I've noticed you tend to, uh, squeal," he said.

She did not bother to tell him that her ex, in brash cowboy whimsy, had once dubbed her "Old Yeller." She wouldn't have objected so much to "Young Squealer." "I don't care if they hear me," she said.

"Well I do."

"Chicken."

"Hussy," he chuckled. And then, holding her close with his good arm, "I may not have a chance to get around to this tomorrow, Teresa, but it goes without saying that I love you."

"Big mistake. Nothing like that should go without saying, Ross." She turned toward him, drew her palm across the ruined desert planes of his face. "I should've said it to you a long time ago, but I thought you'd misread it."

"As pity," he guessed.

"Or gratitude. Whatever. You're too touchy about people's reactions, you know. If we continue to make love in the dark forever, it'll be your choice, not mine."

"Hmph." He considered this for a moment. "Easy for you to say, you don't see the looks in people's eyes."

"What do you care? You won't be in bed with them," she replied.

"Awfully sure of yourself," he teased, kissing her forehead.

"I know what I'm good at, sweetie."

And soon afterward, as Ross snugged into his sleeping bag, T.C. dry-washed their cups and took up her two-hour vigil.

□   □   □

And when she woke Ross later, she sweetened the experience for him without so much as a warble.

CHAPTER 31

The little radio beeper alerted Al right away because thanks to the durn snoring he was already awake, thinking about stuff, and not being a total brainless dweeb he stayed curled up and listened while the Tom guy talked on his radio and shuffled around in the gloomy relic of a room, making instant coffee noises. The guy's initial gruffness gradually turned to something like cheer before he finally said, "Don't worry about us, we'll be ready."

Because these bad guys didn't give him credit for good sense, after trying to be crafty for a while they had talked pretty freely around Al. They expected an airplane here, right here in the middle of noplace, and they were supposed to take good care of Al in the meantime. So whatever the Beale guy said, no matter what terrible things he had done to other grown-ups, he probably wouldn't kill Al, just break him in a few places.

And they expected that airplane pretty soon, probably before lunch. Al loved flying, but one thing he didn't want was to fly anywhere with these two. The previous afternoon he had heard the rasp of an airplane engine somewhere in the distance, not once but twice. Maybe it was the same plane that would land today. It was Al's fondest hope that, when the plane came, he could mess up their plans somehow. Somehow. They might spank the tar out of him for it. But they'd have to catch him first.

Pretty soon, Al heard the sounds of the Beale guy being woke roughly and the Tom guy telling him not so loud, asshole, why wake that kid before we have to. Just for that, Al was tempted to jump from his cot and start whining for a big breakfast. On the other hand, he learned more when they imagined he was still asleep. So he let them imagine.

By the time his captors had made themselves a breakfast that smelled and sounded like burnt bacon and eggs, Al knew they didn't expect the airplane right away. From the way the sunlight hit his eyelids when the Tom guy went outside for a smoke, Al decided it was a long way past dawn. They even turned on the TV, keeping the sound down, to watch CNN. He found out it was half past nine from the little numbers on the TV screen after the Beale guy hauled the blanket off of Al and made him get up. They weren't even going to fix him any eggs until he worked up a good serviceable snivel and threatened to tell. And it worked. Just whom he was supposed to tell, Al wished to Jesus he knew.

The Tom guy tried not to show it, but he was nervous as a kid in the principal's office. He spent almost as much time sucking on Camels outside as he did inside, while the Beale guy diddled with the TV. He diddled, anyway, until Al heard the plane.

It was just a thin whine like yesterday, far off, and maybe the big guy hadn't heard it because he didn't move. The other guy, outside, must be waving to it by now. But in a flash of awareness something told Al, *Do it now,* and just as if he'd planned this in detail, Al left the remnants of those runny eggs and scurried to the toilet. He didn't spend enough time there but it evidently didn't matter so long as he got the water to draining noisily.

"Goddamn it, for the last time, learn to—" the Beale guy thundered as Al started back across the big room.

Al cut him off with a nasal, wheedling, "I'm eating," which made the guy jump up and head for the toilet, pantomiming a backhand swipe in Al's direction, endorsing it with a string of curses as he attacked the toilet lever for the umptieth time.

Al passed by the plateful of eggs while digging into his pocket. The two little bullets rattled dully in his hand like beads and Al lifted the glass plate in the microwave and dropped them beneath it. He'd intended to leave them there obscured by hardened glop until someone heated more instant coffee, but that airplane was nearly overhead, louder than the times before, and Al couldn't wait. He shut the microwave door and twisted the timer knob and punched the button and, because running out that open door would have sent him straight into the arms of the smoker, he went back to his eggs as the microwave began to whirr. For an eternity of seconds nothing happened, the Beale guy glancing from the microwave to Al to the TV, Al's hands shaking so hard he couldn't hardly pick up his spoon, but as the big man lowered himself into his chair a muffled explosion cracked the microwave's door, and then another louder one blew the door completely open.

The Beale guy shouted and flung an arm up as glass showered outward, Al halfway under the table by that time, and Al saw a shadow fill the door and then both guys were standing in the middle of the room shouting at each other and that's when Al took off through the open door.

The only places to hide were behind those other little buildings, and Al knew he was leaving prints in the new dust, so he broke for the most distant part of the fence, hoping he could find a higher gap there between the bottom strands of wire and the ground because he believed that the electrified fence would kill him at a touch. He heard a "There he goes" shout as he reached the fence and flopped down, whimpering because now he could see that there wasn't room to pass under, and he was still scrabbling with both hands like a dog burying a bone, trying to make the space deeper, when he was gripped hard and jerked backward by both ankles and flipped over on his back.

The Beale guy's upper lip was peeled back over his big yellow teeth, and he would have really walloped Al this time except that the other guy was hollering, "We've got him, don't damage the package," grasping the Beale guy by the shoulder and pointing up at the airplane that Al figured had to be the one they were waiting for.

So when both guys looked up at the plane, Al did too, unable to run with both of his ankles still held despite his efforts to kick, and it wasn't even a small Boeing but a little single-engined prop job like his grampa flew sometimes, only his grampa was a jillion miles away, maybe back at the cabin with T.C. by now. Al knew a plane like that could carry several people, and this one was dipping so near, one wing low, he could actually see that there was only one head visible in the cockpit as the plane curved away.

"Shit, that's not ours, is it?" asked the Beale guy, his voice heavy with scorn and disappointment.

"Wouldn't put it past 'em, but Clint said Lear," was the reply as Al was whisked up like a toy, and what made Al maddest was that he couldn't help blubbering like a little bitty kid. Well, he couldn't stop it, he was so durn, so *damn,* so *god-damn* mad at these big bullies.

The Beale guy glared as the plane went on, still turning a few hundred feet up. "Got half a mind to blow the sumbitch out of the sky," he said. "Who the hell is it, then?"

"Hold his legs, Cody, and come on back inside. I'll call Clint and we'll find out." With the big man's arms hugging Al as he galloped, hugging him so tight it hurt, the more Al fought, the more it hurt, and the more it hurt, the louder he cried. They were almost back to the first of the little adobe houses when the Beale guy stopped, because the Tom guy had stopped ahead of him.

Through the pounding of blood in his head, Al heard a whistling rush somewhere in the distance, coming nearer and then past them overhead, now a familiar sound like all the vacuum cleaners in Seattle. And all three of them looked up and saw the sleek, long-finned arrow that was a Gates Learjet, turning for a landing.

□   □   □

Ross had intended to come down on Saddletramp Ranch like Sennacherib hit Babylon, not with weapons drawn but with crisply worded requests delivered in tones of strained politeness that suggested he didn't have to be polite, all of it backed up with a three-second display of ID in its expensive leather holder. It worked well enough that the woman who met them just inside the double front doors didn't ask how the pair of vehicles had arrived, well enough that she was nervously fingering the tight coil of hair high on the back of her head as she said they currently had seven guests, none of them—in the parlance of the man with the badge—an underaged white male.

But that's when the whipcord gent in low-heeled boots ambled out from an interior office room with an empty holster on his hip, introducing himself as ranch manager Clint Logan, and after his startled double take at Ross's face he offered a handshake of confidence and old calluses. He spoke and moved as if he were in no hurry, his self-assurance apparently unshaken at the news that elements of an adjunct air patrol, under cognizance of the state police, were seeking an underaged white male believed to be lost or deliberately hiding in the vicinity of Saddletramp.

Ross identified the older man as Mr. Orval, a geologist and expert tracker, and the flight-suited woman as Lieutenant Cory.

"That wouldn't've been you buzzing around spooking our saddle mounts yesterday, would it?" Clint said to T.C. "Some of our guests are real dudes who don't even speak much English, and a nervous mare doesn't help."

"Sorry," she replied, no contrition showing. "I'll ask the other search elements to give you a little more altitude today, if they can."

"Today?"

As if to endorse its immediacy, the urgent drone of a small propeller reverberated through the big room. "That may be one of ours," said Ross.

"I'll give them your message," said T.C., who turned on her heel and went outside.

Ross assayed the steel in Clint's eye, produced his ID again, and invited Clint to call the New Mexico Department of Public Safety in Tucumcari for confirmation.

"I believe I'll do that," said Clint, with a smile, but before he could reach his office a telephone rang and he hurried to answer it. He held the gaze of the terribly burned man for a moment, then turned away as his brow furrowed at something he heard on the phone.

Ross Downing held his ground but turned to mutter, "You two take a look through that big barn," to his old friend. "Ask around, can't hurt. Let's see who gets antsy."

As Orv left, Ross heard the manager's softly gutteral, "You're sooner than I expected. I'd rather you didn't just yet." Then, after a few seconds, "I have priorities, too. Either right now, and I mean now, or abort. Yep, you'll recognize two regulars on foot. Expedite on the spot. My authorization."

It was Ross's intention to keep the ranch manager inside until T.C. and Orv were out of sight and to occupy the man briefly with a yarn about a delinquent youth with a backpack. The story might play whether or not Clint had guilty knowledge of Al Townsend. Still, Ross identified anxiety's ally, an old enemy of his, in his sudden urge to urinate.

But Ross had no time for delaying tactics as Clint strode quickly past him, hurrying outside to the long covered porch. "Never enough power for some folks," he said mildly, leaving Ross behind. The man moved to the corner of the structure, then reached to pull a lever on a small electrical switch panel separate from the main circuit breaker enclosure. Then he hurried back past Ross and inside, toward his office. "You might want to check the stables for that young fella of yours. Be with you d'rectly," he called, marking himself a true southwesterner with his final phrase. He was moving a lot faster now.

Ross waved, limped past the main building toward the barn, not seeing Orv or T.C., and as he walked he let his gaze sweep past the little switch panel. The raised letters ON were above, as with any respectable switch panel; the legend OFF was below. The lever had been pulled down, not up. Clint Logan had casually implied that he was supplying power, but he was removing it.

Electrical circuits do not lie, and some are transparently straightforward. The insulated wires from that switch box visibly led to a distant transformer attached to an electrified fence. At that instant, Ross knew. He did not know the details, but Clint Logan had lied when he didn't have to.

Logan was guilty. With that conclusion, Ross became acutely curious why the man had gone back to his office.

□   □   □

Orv Ferguson wasted no time as he disappeared with T.C. through a sturdy door into that towering clapboard barnful of honest, fondly recalled odors that tickled the nostrils: hay, sweat, old leather, horse manure. He called Al's name twice, ignoring the curious glances of a stablehand in earnest conversation with a pale young man whose every stitch of western garb was still creased from its factory folds, silently screaming, "Tenderfoot." No answer to his call but echoes, a shrug from the stablehand, and an equine snort from somewhere. T.C. advanced on the two men with a perfunctory nod and began to speak. Orv turned back as he heard a faint beep on his radio. Reception could be chancy inside.

Abruptly, outside, the radio spoke louder: ". . . Believe it's Al. Two men are chasing him."

Orv could not see or hear the Cessna. "Where?"

"Mile north of you. Group of adobes near the landing strip, ahh, *damn*," said Ray, "they caught him trying to go under a fence. If they hurt that boy, I'll shoot their—wup, they're looking in my direction. I could use some help here," he finished.

"Wilco," said Orv, his ancient military jargon suddenly fresh as spring water in his mouth. Except that T.C. was not to be seen and neither was Ross. An old principle flitted into place: *Don't split your forces.* But that's exactly what they had done.

Remembering their roles, Orv bawled for the lieutenant, then set off at a septuagenarian's trot toward the ranch headquarters. He was still making dust puffs, calling for Ross, when the bladelike angularity of a Learjet speared the sky, banking around the ranch. In an aerial confrontation, Ray Townsend would be absurdly outclassed.

□   □   □

Al thought maybe the Beale guy had forgotten him when both men reached the little house, the Tom guy pouncing on his radio, which was already beeping. So Al started to fight again, yelling, filling the durn place with noise, and found himself whisked outside, a big hand covering not just his mouth but practically all his face. So Al did what came naturally.

The Beale guy yelled, jerked his hand away.

From inside: "What?"

Beale guy: "Fuhgettaboutit." Now he held Al from the back of his pants so that he hung like a dummy, cutting off some of his breath, and he could hear swooshes and clanks from inside, and then the Tom guy popped into the sunlight fully loaded down with those two huge cloth sacks.

"Where the fuck you going?" said the Beale guy.

"All of us," was the reply. "Follow me. Clint's cutting power to the fence. Here, you've got a free arm." And he handed one of the big bags over.

By craning his neck, Al could see they were not moving toward the gate but out across the landscape again, and when he remembered to listen he picked up more news than he could handle, both good and bad. The killer fence was dead now, so these guys were going over it. They were headed toward those old trailers and stuff, and that *Star Wars*–looking little jet would land there any minute now, and as soon as the three of them could pile in they'd be off again. And according to the Tom guy, they weren't to stop for anything, especially not people in a couple of strange vehicles. Covering fire, whatever that might be, was authorized.

"I'm sure in a mood to do exactly that," said the Beale guy. "Shame I can't use this little turd for target practice." And, his chest heaving, he stopped at the barbed-wire fence as the other guy dumped his bag over it and then cautiously touched it.

Al hoped the guy would stiffen with sparks frying his hair like Wile E. Coyote, but sure enough, the fence was already dead. The Beale guy lowered his bag over too and waited with Al hanging from his arm and then called out, "By God, that looks good!" And in the distance Al saw that little white jet settling down, engines whistling, into the desert a half mile off, aimed more or less toward them.

□ □ □

Ross eased inside the big room, noting that the woman seemed to be trying to make herself small off in a corner, and he approached the office where he saw the manager closing a desk drawer with a booted toe as he spoke rapidly to a whopping big handheld radio.

The belt holster was now full of side arm that looked like a .45 auto. Clint Logan was saying, ". . . already cut power to the fence so you can climb over and head straight for the end of the strip. The Lear could get there before you do. Don't stop for anything, especially not this fucking SAR team here in four-by-fours. All right, I'll authorize covering fire, but only if absolutely necessary. Bet your ass it'll be on my report. If I ever see either of you again," he paused as his gaze darted toward Ross who stood silent near the doorway, "never mind." He replaced the receiver as he saw the burned man wheel and limp back outside.

□ □ □

Ray Townsend heard Orv say he was coming in the Range Rover, but Ray was too busy to respond, now that he'd seen the little executive jet flash past. He needed both hands for the Cessna as he saw the Learjet banking for its final approach, straightening as it settled, its landing gear now extended as it approached the end of that disguised airstrip.

Ten minutes previous, Ray would have scoffed at the notion of deliberately imperiling a million-dollar jet, and his own FAA license, based on the off chance that his grandson might possibly be a potential passenger. But that was before he'd seen the small, dark-haired figure chased down by grown men and plucked squirming from the desert floor. Now those men were struggling back toward the runway, pausing to cross a fence, and one of their burdens was almost certainly his own Al, and whatever Ray Townsend had to do to keep that Lear from swallowing his grandson, Ray would do.

Its pilot had to be good because he was about to make fresh skid marks along the first hundred feet of runway, and Ray would have to be better if he hoped to get this puddle jumper hauled around to land at the other end of the strip, absolutely head-on at two-thirds of the Lear's speed.

If Ray made his move too soon, the Lear could spool up those turbines again and abort the landing. If he made it too late, he and the Lear would meet about halfway down the runway in a fireball that Ray didn't want to think about. If he made it juuust right, the Lear would have bled off too much speed to porpoise up again, but Ray, in a more gossamer craft, could still pour the coal to the Cessna and—

The time for analysis behind him now, Ray set his flaps and lined up with the Cessna's nose pointing down the runway, throttling back but not too much, not flaring out for a gentle squeaker landing but sizzling right along, his tail feathers still up as he literally flew his little plane down onto the airstrip surface. One wheel touched down, then the other, without slowing much, the white Lear growing from a distant toy to an onrushing winged artillery shell, its nose bobbing downward as its pilot saw the imminence of a suicidal collision and began panic braking, and as Ray went to full throttle a puff of smoke burst from beneath the Lear as one of its main gear wheels blew, and it began to slide gradually to Ray's right as the Cessna swept upward for a crucial twenty feet of altitude, the Lear's tailfin knifing between the little Cessna's wheels as Ray felt a buffet of wind and then, magically, he was rising untouched to fifty feet above the desert, and a pall of dust was erupting in his rearview.

CHAPTER 32

When the Beale guy swung Al up and over the fence, the Tom guy was reaching to grab him, unprepared for the scary snarl that roared past them a hundred feet away. Twisting around like he was, Al kept his eyes fixed on those guys, and his legs were still four feet in the air when the Beale guy let out a scream like a woman, staring past Al, his eyes wide with disbelief. The other guy twisted around to see behind him, and Al, now focused on his nearest target, caught the Tom guy smack under the chin with the hardest kick he could deliver, and the guy stumbled over one of those bags and fell sideways into the fence, and suddenly Al was free, dropping onto the Tom guy's back, then up and running on the opposite side of the fence.

As he looked back, Al could see that the Tom guy was caught by his clothes at several places on two different strands of barbed wire, fighting it like an animal, and the Beale guy, instead of rushing to help him, was backing up, stumbling, then breaking into a run roughly in Al's direction but still inside the fence, looking back, shouting something.

And when Al looked past them and saw all the gleaming white and the tan dust that was heading their way, it was like some kind of video game with the sound nearly off. No wonder the Beale guy had screamed. It was that swoopy jet plane sliding along at an angle toward the fence, coming like a rocket sled with stuff trailing it in a huge cloud of dust, one wing angled kind of up, the other wing level and taking out fence posts *whick whick whick* though now it wasn't coming so fast, and the Tom guy was fighting the fence and then turning, still caught on the wire, his mouth open as he turned toward Al and the wing caught him at belly button height like the biggest sword in all creation, and then Al gave all his attention to the stickery shrub he sideswiped because he wasn't looking.

Fifty yards behind, that damn Beale guy had reached the corner of the fence and was yelling in a hoarse falsetto as he climbed over the top strand and caught his jacket and tore a hunk from it when he jerked loose. Then Al heard the first of a lot of bangs, and some gutteral little whines went past Al, and if those weren't bullets then Al had never watched a western. Maybe the guy was a total nutcase or maybe not, but with the help of that fence Al had now opened more of a lead, and if he didn't maintain it, the guy was going to blow Al's head clean off. Or, if he got close enough, pluck it off.

The Beale guy had made a lot of hollow threats before, and this could be more of the same, but Al decided against trying for a king's X to ask him about it. In Al's opinion, when a big fat bad guy is pounding along behind you, shooting a gun and screaming dirty stuff, you don't slow down to ask whether he's made new plans or how the rules have changed.

After getting used to the altitude at Ruidoso, Al ran even better out here. The third time he looked back, he saw the Beale guy throw his gun away in a rage, staggering like a drunk when he did it and no nearer to Al than before, and that's when Al slowed to a walk, making sure he didn't run into any more stickery junk, just keeping the same distance. By now he could see he was halfway to that big barn they had passed in the car, and he had ridden horses before so he thought sneaking in there might be a good idea.

Far off, a little airplane circled past the big dust cloud, looking like it was going to land, and Al's only regret was that the dust wasn't on fire. He saw that the Beale guy had broken into a run again, stripping off his jacket as he shambled forward, one sleeve caught on his wrist and dragging the jacket on the ground, and Al hightailed it for about fifty yards and then stopped, satisfied now that he could outrun the creep, and looked him in the eye.

The guy's face was already sagging, not its usual shade of dirty pink but a weird color of fish belly gray, when Al thrust his thumbs in his ears and waggled his fingers, sticking his tongue out at the same time. Then the Beale guy's face worked some more and his arms dropped and he went down on his knees, showing those big teeth again as he stared big-eyed at Al but not saying anything, and Al did something he'd never done before and would never admit to doing now. He gave the guy the finger, jabbing it upward a few times for good measure, and the guy went forward on his face with his arms still down at his sides, and Al heard him fart a big one.

That was the last sound the guy made, and that little plane was sinking down behind the dust cloud and Al figured he had better things to do than get chased by somebody else, so he hunkered down and snuck off among the stickery brush, and when he came to a lot of old tire tracks, he followed them.

□   □   □

The burned man was faster getting to his Cherokee than Clint Logan figured, and the old gent in the Range Rover was already kicking up dust ahead of him. Luckily for this situation, they took the wrong trail. It would peter out in minutes behind a little rise that obscured the landing strip, and they'd either have to come back or cut across the hardpan, but that gave Clint the tiny narrow slice of time he needed because, once those two facilitators whisked the boy aloft, there would be nothing to admit or explain.

Clint spotted the Lear dropping toward the strip only because he knew exactly where to look, and he figured two minutes, three at most, before the little jet would be rushing off again. He flicked through his mental file searching for help here and now, discarding Cookie, the wrangler, and the other hands with an angry shake of his head.

This, he realized, was partly his own fault, based on the expectation of one small boy with four facilitators and no pursuit, an error to be faced manfully during the debriefing that was sure to follow. With so few paying guests this week, Clint had let himself get caught shorthanded. The only staff member on the ranch who knew anything about facilitator teams was the tight-assed book-keeper, Lindholm, and as good a linguist as she was for glad-handing guests, she'd be no help in a tight spot. He was trotting toward the barn before he became fully aware that he and he alone must get the Ford pickup and buy more time, cutting those trespassers off somehow while watching for air surveillance. His hole card was that Clint knew every wheel rut and declivity on the ranch.

At the rear of the barn, near the tarp-covered Pontiac, stood Saddletramp's pickup with the long, dude-friendly cab. Clint floored it dead cold and coughing from beneath the eaves, circling behind the outbuildings, and he didn't see the dust cloud in the distance until he had the pickup's nose aimed toward where he expected to see those other vehicles emerge from the gentle rise of land.

The other vehicles were nowhere in sight, but he knew instantly that the Lear had botched a landing, maybe big-time, though he saw no flames. His first, most prudent impulse was simply to turn around and drive off, hit the highway, and never look back. But Clint Logan maintained a pretty nice offshore savings account pre-cisely because his intelligence did not respond to impulses of that sort.

He couldn't see the airplane itself yet; maybe it had just gone off the runway without serious damage. Even if it was seriously damaged, that couldn't be Clint's fault. His own mistakes might be forgotten in the shadow of a greater mishap. He saw the upslant of a swept wing and the small boy afoot at virtually the same in-stant, and he sighed with a surge of hope.

□   □   □

The big pickup came slewing along so fast, that Al didn't have time to get out of sight, didn't even know if he should. Instead, he froze, scanning around him for some place to hide if he needed to. The guy saw him and waved and stopped the pickup, and if he'd started for Al, it would have begun another serious game of tag.

But the guy looked kind of like a cowboy, and he pointed toward the long smudge of dust that hung in the air where the airplane had slid, and he called in a friendly way, "Son, anybody hurt back there?"

"Don't know," said Al, though he knew, all right. He felt a little bad about what had happened, but when he flashed again on the image of the Tom guy standing over his mom back in Mexico, he felt a lot more good.

The cowboy tried again, squinting in the sunlight toward the plane. "Came to see if I could help. I guess they're okay. You need a ride somewhere?"

Al hesitated, because he didn't know whether he could trust this guy, but just about all of somewhere was somewhere else than this, and that was good enough for Al. He started toward the pickup, nodding. "If you're going to town," he said. He had no idea what town, but towns had telephones and stuff.

"Hop in back, then," said the guy, who hadn't asked any questions about those two other guys and made no move to help Al over the tailgate, so Al still felt in charge of himself. As the pickup turned around, Al could see that the second airplane had landed safely some distance from the first, and a teeniest kind of two-legged dot was moving around the crashed plane while a new snake of dust was rising from off to the right, moving toward the crash. After that, Al was too busy hanging on to see any more, and when the pickup slid around behind that big old barn, Al was sitting between a pair of hay bales, feeling better every second.

The cowboy didn't seem to be paying attention to Al, leaping from the pickup, running over to a great big canvas tarp, so Al hopped down and said, "Aren't we going to town?"

"You bet," said the cowboy, rolling the tarp up to reveal a long hood, then a pair of car doors. "Pickup's for the ranch, car's for town. Hop in."

And when Al saw what car it was, the cowboy grabbed him.

□   □   □

T.C. decided it must be all that corrugated metal roofing on the barn that kept her from getting a clear signal on her radio, so she settled down and took the barn's rooms one at a time, calling Al, alarming one of the ranch hands in the tack shed so much that, after one look at what she held in her hand, he dropped the bridle he was holding and backed against the wall without a word. She kept going, and moments later the young fellow sprinted for daylight.

While touring the hayloft she had heard an engine start up behind the stables but couldn't see what kind of car it was or which way it went. She knew Al well enough to know that, if he heard her calls, he would raise hell in some fashion. From the pervasive silence in the place it was beginning to seem that the barn wasn't the place to look. She thrust her side arm into one zippered breast pocket, swung down the two-by-four rungs of a wooden ladder, hearing the snuffle of a restive horse nearby, and paused as the sound of a laboring engine drew nearer outside. It was a big engine, perhaps the Cherokee's. T.C. strode outside and brought her radio from a thigh pocket.

It was horrifying to hear Ray Townsend's distracted, ". . . over by the wreck, you can't miss it. Oh God, oh God, he was right here with this one that's spread all over the place, there's one in the cockpit too, and he's not moving."

Now Ross: "Take it easy, we see you. Al's probably okay, we'll spread out and—"

By sheer happenstance T.C. stood immobile in shadow as the big pickup hustled to a stop fifty feet from her, and her olive drab flight suit blended with the weathered boards. She recognized the ranch manager who seemed tightly focused on pulling a big tarp from the hood of a Pontiac, and something internal thumped her under the ribs as she saw the small form vault from between hay bales behind the pickup's cab. "Al's here at the barn," she muttered into her radio. "Come on." She snapped off the radio, sidling toward the man who tugged furiously at that tarp.

Al hadn't seen her either, so she couldn't wave him away. Now fully in the open, she took more steps as Al, his back to her, asked, "Aren't we going to town?"

"You bet," said the man, buying seconds with more meaningless nonstop banter while he flung the car door open, and then Al's gaze flashed across the car, and the man snatched him up in a bear hug as Al tried to run.

"I won't hurt you," the man said, and then he saw T.C.'s stealthy approach as he fought to restrain Al's legs. He turned to face her, expressionless, a double armspan from the pistol she carried.

"Right." She hated that her voice shook as she continued. "You weasels are through hurting this little boy." Holding the weapon with both hands, sighting along it into the man's face, she said, "Hi, Calvin. Get down from there."

Al burst into smiling tears, struggling to comply.

"I don't think so," the manager said slowly. For a man staring into a gun barrel he showed a lot of composure. "Those things shoot every which way, lieutenant, if that's what you really are. You know you're as likely to hit him as me."

"Not this one," she replied, her aim unwavering. "Put him down, *cabron.*"

The man flung Al toward her without warning, and she tried to catch the boy one-handed, redirecting her aim as the man bounded away. She squeezed off two rounds in quick succession, the man's right leg snapping forward as if electrically galvanized, and he fell on his side with a grunt.

Patting Al, then shoving him behind her, T.C. advanced a pace on the man and aimed at his geometric center. "You don't listen."

"You—took off my boot heel," he said with a grimace, flexing the leg, rubbing his knee.

"Told you this one shoots straight." A lie—she had aimed for his legs. "The next one takes off your *cojones,* so stay down." She fumbled the radio out and repeated her call, adding that Al was unhurt.

Despite the need to keep blinking, T.C. didn't realize that tears coursed down her cheeks until the man lying before her gave her a half smile. "Just between us, ma'am, I could use a good cry myself," he said.

□   □   □

In another five minutes, Ray Townsend held his grandson in his arms while T.C. and Orv stood by, exchanging details of the past quarter hour. Ross Downing leaned against the Cherokee's fender and spoke of other things with Logan, who now stood with his hands crammed into his back pockets. In response to Logan's question, Ross shrugged. "He stole an off-road vehicle and we haven't seen him since. He's your problem, but he could still turn up. If he does, for your own good, make sure Kerman knows it's over. The boy belongs here, and here he stays. We've got too many credible witnesses if we have to blow this to the media." He paused, searching Logan's face for thorough understanding. "And if we do, no more Saddletramp, maybe no more facilitator teams. Certainly no more career for you."

Logan thought it over. "I'll pass it on. This Kerman fella wasn't even part of the team until the wheels came off the operation, down in Old Mexico. You think maybe that bunch of idiots offed him for some reason? They claim you took out one, maybe two."

"Wish I had. They lied," Ross said easily, "and we can't face them with it now. We found one smeared under that Learjet's wing and another one facedown with dust in his eyes. I didn't stop long enough to establish the big one's cause of death, and frankly, Logan, it's not my problem."

"Sounds like you're dumping them with me as the dumpee," said Logan glumly.

"That's what you do, isn't it? So go and do it, and in my report Saddletramp is off the hook. Believe me, you don't want us to have any more problems. You people have a rep for accommodation, and all I want now is to let that little boy grow up an American. That's where you can help, and that's why I'm so accommodating. So, do we have a mutual accommodation here, or don't we?"

A slow nod, resigned and weary. "That's a weird team you got there, pardner," said Logan, aiming his chin toward the little group. "Just for my peace of mind, would she really have shot my balls off?"

Ross gazed at T.C. for a moment and smiled as she reached to tousle the boy's hair. Then, "She would've scrambled your eggs. That woman," he added, "is the wolverine in your petting zoo of relationships."

"Tell her I really wouldn't have hurt the boy," said Logan.

"Tell her yourself," said Ross.

Logan shook his head and turned away. "I think I'll just leave well enough alone," he sighed.

CHAPTER □ **33**

Everyone but Al thought it would be best if the boy became the only passenger in Ray's flight back to Ruidoso. Al outvoted them. Leaving Ross and Orv to drive their vehicles back, the trio spent a lazy three hours cruising above the achingly romantic desolation of central New Mexico. Every so often, Ray would skim lower over the flattest portion of the desert and peer out his side window. And when he did that, he would nod and cackle softly to himself.

They took a taxi into town. Shortly after six in the evening, as they strolled down Ruidoso's Sudderth Drive exchanging licks from their frozen yogurt cones, T.C. heard her radio's beep. They made rendezvous with their vehicles at the visitor center, and by sundown the adults were all arrayed in stocking feet, sharing beer on Ross's screened porch. Al, barefoot, continued to leaf through the Calvin & Hobbes book T.C. had bought him that afternoon when they failed to find him a replacement machete as promised, and he interrupted with questions now and then. He liked the dinosaurs and snow goons better than the words, he said.

It was no surprise to them that Ray proposed to fly Al back to Seattle. The shocker came when Ray made his further intentions known. "I like Ruidoso," he said and swigged at his beer. "I like it a lot. I think my wife will like it too. Clean air, less rain, good place to raise a boy."

"I hear you," Orv drawled. "Giving it serious thought?"

T.C. held her breath as the Boeing man settled farther into the porch swing. "I did that during our flight today, watching my passengers. Good thing I'm not the jealous type. Then again, Seattle's got its points, but now it'll have a lot of memories my wife and I shouldn't dwell on. And I need a project of some kind to keep me occupied. I'm tired of getting rousted by fish and game people every time I unlimber the number one turret on my battleship."

Orv chuckled at that. "I doubt anybody here in Lincoln County would give a rip as long as your shells weren't explosive. But there's no place you could sail your ships in these parts. Unless you put wheels on the things," he added.

"Great minds, similar thoughts," said Ray. "Lots of empty real estate in New Mexico, begging for a *Graf Spee* or a USS *Iowa* powered by a VW drive train and turrets with spud guns, sailing across the desert at flank speed. I'd just need an opponent."

"You really are bonkers," Orv said. "Count me in. I'm a passable welder."

The two touched bottles together, and Ross smiled as he saw the surmise in T.C.'s gaze. "Cut to the chase, Ray. Does this mean we'll be seeing more of that one?" His nod was toward Al.

"More than you want, probably."

"Oh, suuure," said T.C. "I won't complain 'til he's a six-footer."

"I doubt he ever will," Ray said. "Gail was nearly as tall as Ravan, so we won't see Al in the NBA."

Ross said, "I had the idea Zagro was a big, fierce type."

"Politically, yes. Physically he's about average height. You have to remember that your source," and now Ray pointed his beer bottle toward his grandson, "wasn't much bigger than a woodchuck when they were last together." Here he smiled at the boy, who was focused on his book but now turned toward the adults.

Holding his place in the book, Al asked, "What's nil?"

"Nothing," said T.C.

"But I wanta know," Al frowned.

"I told you, nil means nothing. Zero, zip. It's Latin, okay?"

"I guess," said Al, pawing back to a previous page. "Well, what's gender?"

T.C. blinked. "You want to take that one, Ray?"

"Told you he was too young for philosophy," Ray muttered, then raised his voice. "Gender is, uh, sex."

"Huh," said Al. "A funny book, a schoolbook and a sex book. Cool. I bet I can make all the faces Calvin does," he said and tried to prove it.

"See what you've done," T.C. said to Ray.

"You're the schoolteacher. Part of my hidden agenda is that I intend to pawn this lad off on you a lot," Ray grinned.

"Breaks my heart," she replied. "Even if I do live in Tucson."

"My God, I forgot," Ray said, genuinely flustered.

"But she doesn't have to stay there," said Ross lazily. "Teachers fluent in Spanish aren't unheard of in New Mexico."

"This is all going a bit fast for me," said T.C., putting her hands up in surrender. "Al, it's getting too dark to read out here. Don't strain your eyes," she added in aside.

"That's what I mean," said Ray. "We'll have to work something out, T.C. Really, I'd help you relocate. I'm not rich, but I'm not poor, either."

"You can't have her," Ross said quickly. "I saw her first."

Ray winked at her. "Decisions, decisions."

"You know," she said, getting up to stretch, "that's the truth. But I intend to sleep on this one."

□   □   □

By the following morning, T.C. found herself pleasantly bewildered by the options Ross had offered, including marriage, occasional visits, or anything in between. While she felt that her best option would inevitably bring her to Ruidoso, she pleaded for more time, perhaps a few weeks in Tucson to think it over.

Preparing breakfast with Al and his grandfather in attendance to feed Monte, Ross tried to invite the old miner down to share the meal. Orv did not answer. They were polishing off the last of the sausage patties when the phone rang, and Ross excused himself to answer it.

"You see anything in the sky this morning?" were Orv's first words.

Ross peered out the picture window. "Haven't been out. Weather headed our way?"

"Nope. Bunch of turkey buzzards doin' their thing over the ravine, so I went to take a look. You can just barely see the Jeep's radiator pokin' out past the rocks about forty feet down."

"Oh, Christ," Ross breathed, the implications flooding in. "And buzzards don't eat Jeeps."

Again, "Nope. But they're sure interested in what else is down there about twenty feet from my poor ol' velocipede. Facedown." A pause. "I could'a told him it pops outa gear. Now that I know what to look for, I can see where he slid off."

Ross recalled his hallucination and the dizzying sensation of crawling upward while in dreadful pain, and he was forced to put his hand on the wall to steady himself. "Ray and Al will be leaving before noon. I'll try and help you give him a decent burial after that. Okay?"

"Yep. Durn fool. In a way, I'm glad to see him there. Tells me you weren't feeding me a line about him. Don't get me wrong, I wouldn't have blamed you."

"I understand, Orv. See you later."

Ross caught the engineer's eye and motioned for him as he went to his bedroom. He shut the door behind Ray and told him of the morning's discovery.

"I really should help. In spite of everything, I still owe Ravan's family a kindness or two," Ray said unhappily.

Shaking his head, Ross said, "Al needn't know about this. We'll give Kerman a proper burial. Oh, I took Kerman's wristwatch the other night, and I'm not comfortable keeping it under the circumstances."

"I wouldn't want it," said Ray.

"It's a good one. A Tag Heuer," Ross insisted. "When Al's old enough, you might want to—"

"Let me see it," Ray Townsend interrupted suddenly, his voice unaccountably husky.

Ross took the timepiece from his top desk drawer and handed it over. The engineer snapped on the desk lamp, turned the watch over, and grunted as if struck in the solar plexus. After a long pause he muttered, "I never thought it would last this long. Or Ravan either." And when he looked up, his gaze was haunted. "The inscription, *'Azadi,'* is all I knew of the Kurdish motto, so it's what I had put here. This was a wedding present."

"From you?"

A nod. Now Ray fished out his wallet, a grotesquely fat and disreputable handful like a Dagwood sandwich of leather and plastic, turning over the faded plastic pages full of photographs. At last he teased out one snapshot hidden between two others and passed it to Ross. It was a snow scene, two young people laughing toward the camera in expensive togs, skis slung over their shoulders. The girl was blonde, slender, big breasted, gorgeous, the man handsome and swarthy, with a handlebar mustache that would have been stylish a century ago.

Ross studied the photo for ten seconds, then handed it back. "I recognize Kerman, of course, but who's the beauty?" He knew the answer before it came.

"Gail, before they married. But it's not Kerman with her. It's Ravan Zagro."

"They look that much alike?"

"No! Ross, Ravan didn't send his cousin here to reclaim his son; that never seemed like the man I knew. But I suppose he couldn't let his people know he had left them, even for a week or so." Softly, a benediction of sorts: "He did what he felt he had to do. The man lying dead in that ravine is Ravan Zagro."

□   □   □

Despite the smiles and waves in parting, Ray Townsend's eyes were hooded with sadness. T.C. sighed as the rental dropped below the meadow contours, then said, "*Now* will you tell me why the hell you've been so antsy all morning?"

Ross told her as simply as possible, nodding as her expression began to crumble. "Apparently he didn't leave Kurdistan until he heard what happened in Puerto Vallarta. I feel for him, too, and I won't try to tell you his troubles were over in a second. It probably happened soon after Orv left his place."

"But in your—dream, he was still alive for a while?"

He nodded. "I'm sure he thought he could make it. If he hadn't been thinking of Saddletramp, I wouldn't have had a clue. But the strangest part was that I didn't, ah, get any of that until later."

"After he had died," T.C. supplied and then clasped him to her. "Oh, Ross, Ross, there must be some way you can avoid this happening in the future."

"It never happens without the medication. I'll just have to get a different prescription, complain about side effects or something."

They turned together and strolled back toward the cabin. "One word about the main effect," she warned, "and they'd mark you as plain crazy. And if you told them, you would be."

"So stipulated," he said. "I don't propose to tell anyone that I located Al Townsend wearing the skin of a dead man."